LIBRARY-NEWARK, OHIO 43055
W9-CET-067

HAWKS

also by Ray Rosenbaum

FALCONS

HAWKS

a novel by

Ray Rosenbaum

LYFORD
Books

The characters in this novel are fictitious. Any characters (except historical figures) resembling actual persons, living or dead, are purely coincidental. The dialogue and specific incidents described in the novel are products of the author's imagination and creativity. They should not be construed as real.

LYFORD Books
Published by Presidio Press
505 B San Marin Dr., Suite 300
Novato, CA 94945-1340

Library of Congress Cataloging-in-Publication Data

Rosenbaum, Ray, 1923-
Hawks : a novel / by Ray Rosenbaum.
p. cm.
ISBN 0-89141-477-0
1. World War, 1939—1945—Fiction. I. Title.
PS3568.0777H38 1994
813'.54—dc20 93-34197
CIP

Typography by ProImage
Printed in the United States of America

For my children and
their precocious offspring.

Chapter One

14 November 1943
Mountain Home Army Airfield, Idaho

Captain Ross Colyer dropped from the B-24's bomb-bay catwalk to the concrete parking ramp. He immediately turned up the collar of his chocolate-colored sheepskin flight jacket against the chill wind sweeping off distant, snow-covered peaks. A half-dozen men emerged from olive drab U.S. Army staff cars where they had sought shelter from the swirling snow flurries. Three of the men were in army uniforms with bulky olive drab overcoats; one of the three displayed the eagles of a full colonel on his shoulders. The other trio wore identical civilian garb—heavy blue melton overcoats and fur-lined caps with earflaps.

Despite the greeting party's grim expressions, Ross felt his sun-browned features crinkle into a spontaneous grin as he saluted the approaching officers. It had all started here, he mused. Less than a year before, the *Happy Hooker,* B-24 tail number 402117, gleaming new from the factory, and her crew of exuberant young airmen had gone off to war. His smile slipped. It wasn't the same crew he'd departed with. Only six of the original nine were aboard for the return trip.

The three missing crew members were not the only casualties of German Me 109s and 88mm flak guns. The *Happy Hooker,* her dark green and cream camouflage coat dulled by sun and desert sand, bore a collage of bright aluminum patches. One of her twin vertical stabilizers, its shining, unpainted oval a sharp contrast to its twin, gave her a faintly rakish appearance. A sheet-metal crew had worked for a full week at Benghazi to repair the battle damage she'd suffered on that last nightmarish mission.

With gun positions stripped of their menacing .50-caliber machine guns, the *Happy Hooker* reminded Ross of a once proud queen, now aging and vulnerable. Only the painting of a saucy, scantily clad woman, which covered almost all of the left side of the nose compartment, remained unscathed.

Ross dropped his salute to shake the colonel's outstretched hand. "Burton, base commander," the grizzled officer announced briefly. "Welcome home."

"Thank you, sir," Ross responded. "It's good to be here."

The colonel grunted, emitting a plume of frosty breath. "I understand you have a war correspondent aboard."

"Yes, sir. Clayton Henderson with the *New York Times.* He's doing a feature article on the airplane's return trip."

"So I hear," the colonel remarked dryly. "And your copilot—a man returning on normal rotation, I believe."

"Yes, sir. Lieutenant Bridges."

"Very well. Lieutenant Dixon"—the colonel waved a hand toward a pink-cheeked youngster—"is our PIO. He'll take your reporter to the public information office and brief him. Bridges has leave orders waiting and is free to go. You and your crew will be taken directly to your quarters.

"You will remain in quarantine until these gentlemen behind me—they're from the State Department—finish debriefing you. After that, you'll be given orders for thirty-days' rotation leave. Until then, you're not to communicate with anyone outside this base. Is that understood?"

"Yes, sir. General Flynt, back at Benghazi, made absolute secrecy a condition of his permission for us to bring the *Happy Hooker* back here unescorted."

"I'm sure he did." The colonel's glacial expression cracked briefly. "Captain, what you did back there caused some red faces in high places. I don't say that I condone your violating most of the rule book, but I suspect that most of us in the flying end would have probably done the same thing. We'll take good care of your airplane. After all the fuss over it, I wouldn't dare let anything happen."

Burton turned to leave, then paused. "Uh, before you go on leave, Colyer, how about coming over to my quarters for dinner? I'd like to hear, privately and off the record, just exactly how you pulled off that crazy stunt, and also what you can tell me about that Ploesti raid."

"Thank you, sir. I'll call your office when we're released from quarantine." Ross saluted the base commander, then turned to where TSgt. Ham Phillips was loading the crew's B-4 bags and flying gear into the canvas-covered bed of a waiting six-by-six.

The Tennessee-born flight engineer wore a grin equaling Ross's own. "We did it, Cap'n," he chortled. "We brought her right back where she belongs. Class twenty-six her, my ass. This ol' girl'll be flyin' ten years from now. That is if some green crew doesn't do what the friggin' Jerries couldn't."

"Right you are, Ham. Look, get the rest of the crew out here before we load up. I want to impress upon them that we're confined to the base until debriefed—no outside calls or visitors. This will probably be the last time we'll all be together with the *Hooker*. I just have a few words to say, that's all."

"Aw, shit, Cap'n. Don't be sayin' things like that." Phillips lowered his gaze to watch his boot scuff the thin layer of snow. He sounded close to tears. "They aren't goin' to break up the crew . . . take away our airplane. Tell me they won't. They say we're all headed for the Pacific. Why not as a crew and with the same airplane?"

"I wish we could, Ham. I sincerely wish we could. But we have to face facts. The *Happy Hooker* has had her day. Saving her from salvage to use as a trainer was the best we could hope for."

As he waited for Ham to assemble the others, Ross walked to the edge of the ramp and stood, hands thrust deep into his pockets, taking in the activity normal to a wartime training base. Fatigue lines etched into his handsome, well-formed features made the young pilot appear older than his twenty-six years. Crow's-feet marked the corners of deep blue eyes that had once twinkled but were somber now. Together with a certain gauntness of face, they were the trademark of a man who had faced the ultimate test—violent death.

Ross counted two dozen or so four-engine B-24 bombers squatting in a double row. Ground crews, hunched against the cold, carried out seemingly endless grooming of their charges. He cocked his head, listening to the bellow of four straining Pratt & Whitney engines from a plane on takeoff roll. Home again, he told himself. In the next breath, he admitted: It isn't home after all. It's like I've never been here before.

He heard the crew chattering behind him and turned, prepared to make the most difficult speech of his life.

The interrogation room, situated at the far end of the rambling frame ground-school building, carried lingering odors of chalk dust and floor wax. Ross heard the pounding of booted feet and the ribald conversation of a just-dismissed class passing through the corridor on the other side of a thin beaverboard wall.

A civilian named Travis, wearing a single-breasted brown suit and highly polished tan shoes, lounged in the sparsely furnished room's single comfortable chair. Travis, who appeared to be in his early thirties, tapped the open file folder in his lap with a yellow number-two lead pencil as he studied the folder's contents. He looked up and turned a penetrating gaze toward Ross.

"This shouldn't take long," Travis said. "I have only a few final questions. You have no objection to our taking notes of this meeting, I assume?" He gestured toward a second man seated at a battered table, pencil poised over a steno pad.

"None whatever," Ross responded.

"Very well." Travis's pallid, aquiline features tightened. "The report filed by our ambassador in Ankara states that your escape from Turkish control created a sizable diplomatic incident. Would you care to comment on his statement?"

"I was—as we all were—under orders never to surrender as long as we had means to resist. Fighting men have an obligation to attempt escape if captured. We were asked to give our parole, and we refused. It was our duty to escape if at all possible."

"I see you've been doing your homework." Travis allowed himself a frosty smile. "There's a small flaw in your reasoning, however. You speak of rules governing prisoners of war. You were interned in a neutral country."

Ross shifted his lanky, athletic frame in the uncomfortable student desk-chair. "I don't see the difference," he said. "The Turks forcibly prevented us from returning to U.S. jurisdiction."

His interrogator shrugged. "That's for someone else to decide. I'm just here to record your statement. Now, the ambassador speaks of an investigation, still underway, to determine if your actions were responsible for the death of your copilot, Captain Templeton." His eyebrows arched in an unspoken question.

"Once we landed, Captain Templeton was no longer a crew member under my control. He was aide to Brigadier General Sprague and replaced my regular copilot for the Ploesti mission only—the general's orders. Templeton chose to devise his own escape and was killed in the attempt."

Ross hesitated, then continued. "I fail to see how the ambassador can link Templeton's death to my crew's efforts to restore the airplane to flyable condition for the purpose of escaping."

Travis nodded but didn't comment. He made a quick, penciled notation before continuing. "What about fuel for your flight to Syria? You landed at Ankara with nearly dry tanks. The Turkish government is curious: Where did you obtain several hundred gallons of scarce gasoline?"

Ross couldn't restrain a broad grin. "We bought it," he replied.

"Bought it? From whom and with what?"

Ross's grin widened. "Why, from Lufthansa, the German civilian airline. We used money collected from the crew."

Travis's aplomb dissolved. "You what?" he gasped.

"We departed Turkey courtesy of the German government," Ross responded brightly. "Didn't the others tell you?"

Travis shook his head and closed the file folder. "I found your crew to be singularly uncommunicative, Captain." He pursed his lips in disapproval. "I assume you gathered that the ambassador is highly displeased by your actions—"

"You can tell the ambassador that I'm not all that overjoyed with *his* actions," Ross snapped, cutting Travis off. "Ask General Sprague. The ambassador's wishy-washy refusal to help almost scuttled our attempt to return a combat plane and crew to action against the enemy."

Travis got up from his chair. "I'll forget you said that, Captain." He made a slashing motion to the stenographer. "This war is being fought in different ways on different fronts. Don't look down your nose at the role diplomacy plays.

"Unless you have something to add, this wraps up our debriefing. But a word of advice: Be careful what you tell that *Times* correspondent. Both the State Department and the War Department are watching him. Having to bring back a junk airplane because of the public pressure his articles generated didn't set well, I'll tell you."

Ross felt a surge of anger. He'd grown to like the tall, skinny reporter—his chronically wrinkled khaki uniform unadorned by insignia other than his correspondent's patch. Henderson's myopic gray eyes and thick horn-rimmed glasses concealed a razor-sharp mind. Stories he'd filed from Benghazi describing the crew that had rebuilt its airplane and escaped, only to have the army prevent them from returning the plane to the States, had produced a storm of protest. The army made a reluctant exception. That the *Happy Hooker* now sat on the Mountain Home flight line was due entirely to the reporter's efforts.

Ross stood and faced Travis. "Have you ever had your ass shot at?" he asked harshly.

"No, the department disapproved my application for military service. My occupation is considered essential." The civilian's tone was cold.

Ross took a deep breath. "You should try it. It changes the way you see things—believe me."

Ross sat abruptly as his interrogators stormed out without responding. He rubbed his faintly aching head and grinned ruefully. Maybe his hangover made him snappish. The other crew members had finished their interviews the previous day and departed on leave that morning. The navigator, 1st Lt. Kevin Hanson, had put together the previous night's going-away party. "Ross, I'm forecasting a big whiskey front to move through tonight," he'd announced. Watching the men depart as individuals—no longer part of a close-knit crew—left a void. Feeling very much alone, Ross headed for his BOQ room.

Ross's B-4 bag, packed early that morning, sat on the unmade bed. He'd call the base commander's office and accept the colonel's dinner invitation, not that he looked forward to the evening. It seemed that the entire crew had done nothing but talk these past few weeks. Everyone wanted clear, black-and-white answers to questions—answers he didn't have. Some questions were best left unanswered—Capt. Broderick Templeton III's, "BT's," perfidy being one.

Ross picked up the square light blue envelope—held at the orderly room pending his arrival—with its distinctive, back-sloped handwriting and reread its contents.

Dear Ross,

I appreciate the letter telling me of BT's death. You must have had a difficult time as well. I'm living with my parents in D.C. If your travels bring you this direction, please call me.

Love,
Janet

She would want to know of the exact circumstances surrounding her husband's death, Ross realized. Well, she was the last person to whom he would divulge BT's disgraceful, cowardly conduct. Hiding behind the protection afforded by his father, Senator Templeton, the arrogant young officer had thought to build an army career through devious political maneuvering.

There'd been a time during their brief romance at Hickam Field when it looked as if Ross and Janet had a future together. That ended when she married his adversary. Now, he had no intention of rekindling the spark.

He turned his attention to the eight-by-ten-inch buff envelope containing his orders. He brightened. Following thirty-days' leave he would report to the training base at Topeka, Kansas, for B-29 flight training. The Superfortress! It was Boeing's vastly improved big sister to the B-17. He'd yet to see one, but the bomber fraternity was filled with stories of the B-29's superior characteristics. It would be the Far East this time, he knew—pounding Japan's home islands from distant dots of coral sand in the vast Pacific Ocean.

About to leave the spartan surroundings of his BOQ room, he noticed another envelope at the foot of his bed. The mail orderly must have left it during his interview with Travis. It bore a military return address and an Official Use Only postmark. Inside was a single sheet of paper—a form letter with his name typed after the mimeographed Dear . . .

Ross read the trite phrasing quickly. He was being welcomed to the 27th Bombardment Wing (Heavy), Far East Air Forces. His current orders would be amended to include an end assignment (to remain classified) following transition training. After skimming the remainder of the letter, he sank to a sitting position on the bed, his face a picture of dismay. The letter bore a stamped signature block. It read:

Elliott Sprague
Brig. Gen., U.S. Army Air Forces
Commanding

Ross placed a stack of quarters on the shelf beneath the officers' club pay phone and set his third Scotch and water of the evening alongside. It probably wasn't a wise thing to do, tossing back three drinks before going to the base commander's house for dinner, but he was boiling mad. He fished a slim address book from his pocket and dialed the long-distance operator.

"What number are you calling?"

"Alexandria, Virginia, operator," he told the bored-sounding woman. "Exeter six-five-five-three-eight."

He drummed his fingers impatiently while she made the necessary connections. A woman's voice answered on the third ring: "Lieutenant Colonel Wilson's quarters."

Ross raised his eyebrows and grinned. So it was no longer Maj. Ted Wilson. "Doris?" he inquired. "This is Ross Colyer. Don't tell me that old fraud got himself promoted."

"Ross!" came the pleased response. "It's so good to hear your voice. Where are you calling from?"

"Mountain Home, Idaho. Just got here yesterday. Tell me, is your lord and master in?"

"Unfortunately, yes. He's here in the kitchen getting in my way. Talk to him, please. Get him from underfoot."

Ross waited for Wilson to come on the line, then greeted his previous commanding officer: "I hope you're not trying to make some of that god-awful chili."

"Nope," Wilson replied. "Fire laws here in the East are too strict."

Ross laughed, then sobered. "The reason I called you at home, Colonel—are you still in personnel?"

"Afraid so. The closest I get to an airplane these days is to meet some visiting VIP."

"Colonel, I swore I'd never be guilty of trying to manipulate an assignment, but I'm desperate."

"How so?"

Ross gave him the essence of his orders, paused to insert more quarters, then continued. "I'd give my left nut to fly the B-29. But under Sprague? That son of a bitch almost got me killed in Europe. He hates my guts. My entire tour will be sheer hell. The Japs will be my best friends by comparison."

Wilson chuckled. "I'll see what I can do. Listen, can you come to D.C. while you're on leave? Stay with Doris and me for a few days. I'm sure we can work out something a bit more to your liking."

"I don't see why not," Ross responded. "I'll spend some time with my father in Justin Falls, but there's nothing to keep me there a full thirty days. I'll see you in a couple of weeks—okay?"

Ross hung up with the sense of having had a hundred-pound weight removed from his shoulders. Shit! he thought. I didn't even ask him about his health. Oh well, he must be doing all right if he got promoted.

27 November 1943
Alexandria, Virginia

Lieutenant Colonel Ted Wilson poured Ross a generous measure of brandy and slouched in a well-used armchair beside the fireplace. Raising his coffee cup—he'd avoided alcohol all evening, Ross noticed—Wilson toasted, "To better days."

Ross raised his glass, then sipped the velvet-smooth Drambuie. Gazing at the dancing flames, he hated to break the warm, relaxed mood. Finally, he said, "You look great, Colonel. Is the—uh . . . ?"

"Old pump acting up?" Wilson completed Ross's question. "Not as long as I avoid any food that's fit to eat, stay off the booze, and don't lose my temper. After you pulled me out of that Stearman back at Thunderbird, I was ready to chuck the whole damn business. Life without flying . . . well. Anyway, after Doris and the flight surgeon finished chewing my ass, I decided to stay on active duty—I waived a medical discharge—and fly a desk." He shrugged. "They tell me there's no reason I can't stay around until retirement.

"Now, what the hell went on over there in Turkey? Wait, let me put that another way: How much can you tell me?"

Ross's features contorted in a grimace of embarrassed discomfort. "Colonel, you've put me on the spot. I know your security clearance is higher than mine. It's the damn State Department that has a gag on me. All I can add to what you read in the papers is that the main brouhaha is over BT's death. I wasn't responsible, but I'm not real popular with the ambassador over there.

"I have a letter from Janet, BT's wife—widow. She wants to see me. She's right here in D.C., as a matter of fact. She and I were close friends at Hickam, but I can't give her the facts, and I won't lie to her. I feel like a dog, but I'm going to duck a meeting."

"Maybe she needs to know some facts, Ross."

"Not from me, she doesn't."

"Oh?"

"No. Damnit, Colonel, she knows that BT hated my guts, and she must assume I hated his. Anything derogatory I tell her . . . well, it'd just come across as—well, you know."

"Jealousy?"

"No! Well—okay, maybe that's what she might think."

"And she has no basis for thinking that?" Wilson's voice was tinged with amusement. "Look, I know I'm coming across like the neighborhood gossip, but I seem to recall the other pilots laughing about a monumental drunk you threw at Thunderbird. It was very close to the date that Doris received BT and Janet's wedding announcement. As a wise sage once said—I think it was Bob Hope—'Methinks thou protest overmuch.'

"Ross, listen to someone who has been there. If you have feelings for the girl, go after her. Tell her the truth. If she rejects you for it . . . well, she probably isn't worth the effort. Do you follow me?"

Ross glared. "BT didn't deserve her. He treated her like dirt. But, by God, someone else can tell her that. Like her father. He's a full bull; he has access. Colonel Richards knew that BT was an asshole, but he also knew that his daddy was a U.S. senator, chairman of the military affairs committee. He spoiled her rotten; now let him tell her some unpleasant facts of life."

Ross sat back in his chair, looking shaken by his outburst. Then, with a rueful grin, he added, "And that was Shakespeare you were butchering, as you damn well know.

"Look, sir, I didn't come here to talk about Janet Templeton and me. I know I was way out of line asking you to change my assignment, but when I called, I'd already had a bad day. Then I opened that letter signed by Sprague. If it causes any problems, just forget it."

"Ordinarily, I'd say it was a simple matter," Wilson said slowly. "The guy in charge of rated assignments is a friend, and I've already talked with him. He'll bend over backwards to accommodate anyone with your record and decorations. But . . ." He paused and sipped his coffee. "I got a peek at your master two-oh-one file, Ross. There's a flag on it—one that means 'Political Interest.' Now, just what the hell is that all about?" He shot Ross a quizzical look.

"Oh, shit!" Ross threw up his hands. "That goddamn Templeton—BT's old man. He thinks I'm responsible for his son's death in Turkey. I also detect General Sprague's fine hand in this, as well. BT was his aide, you may recall. Sprague would have the senator's ear. The old bastard wants to keep me around as a whipping boy. He'll never forgive me for calling his bluff on the Ploesti mission. He wanted to take over my airplane. Well, anyway, thanks for trying."

"Just a minute, now. I didn't say it was impossible. But my guy says it means taking you out of bombers. How do you feel about flying single-engine stuff?"

"Fighters?" Ross blinked. "Uh—I've never given them a thought. I was really looking forward to getting my hands on the B-29. I'm strictly a bomber man. It'd mean going to fighter transition, learning tactics and gunnery—the whole bit." He sipped his drink and grinned. "But why not? Hell, I always thought those guys had it easy—running around outside the flak, short missions, no crew to worry about. Yeah, that might be fun."

"Fun, I doubt," Wilson responded dryly. "But fighter manning has priority just now. Seems that the Zeroes are giving Far East Air Force a hard time."

"Hmmmm," Ross muttered. "What plane would I be flying?"

"Mustangs—the P-51. It's a hot new fighter being rushed to both theaters as fast as they can build them," Wilson replied. "It's the only thing besides the P-38 with enough range to be effective in the Pacific, and the Lightning can't maneuver with a Zero. It's just too big and too heavy for dogfighting with the Japs."

"All right!" Ross exclaimed. "So how do I get out from under Sprague's thumb?"

Wilson's face crinkled with a cunning leer. "Be sneaky. I've acquired a degree in sneaky, working here in Washington. Look, I'll amend your orders from B-29 transition to the multiengine instructors' course at Kelly. With your combat record and duty as an instructor pilot at Thunderbird, it's a logical assignment. Do you remember old General Smithers, commander of Western Flight Training Command? He's the one I talked into springing you from Thunderbird."

"Sure I do."

"Well, he's also the one who talked me into staying on active duty, and we keep in touch. Sprague pissed him off when that pompous bastard was putting his B-24 wing together, so he'll go along with the scheme.

"As soon as you report in at Kelly, apply for fighters." Wilson leaned forward and tapped the palm of his left hand with his right index finger. "You see, instructors are a prime source of combat pilots. If you go to Topeka for B-29 transition, you're in the pipeline to a combat outfit, and there's no changing your mind. But instructors are up for grabs for any combat assignment. Even if General Smithers wasn't primed to approve it, Training Command couldn't refuse the request."

Ross laughed. "Colonel, you do display talent I never suspected. I like it."

"Okay," Wilson continued. "It will all take a few weeks to go through. Meanwhile, you'll have to finish the six-week instructor pilot course, but when Sprague starts collecting his bomber crews, you'll be out of reach. Senator Templeton isn't going to get involved in a minor amendment of orders, and by the time Sprague goes screaming to him, we can stonewall it. Okay?

"If you want to cut your leave short, I can have you report in here, get your orders amended, and have you on your way before Templeton and company know what's happened."

"Done." Ross crossed the room to shake Wilson's hand. "I don't know how to thank you."

The colonel sobered. "Wait until you're out there on some jungle strip, where the heat, the flies, and malaria are a bigger menace than the Japs. Then write and tell me about the fun you're having."

"Just put Templeton and Sprague on the next island, and I'll do it," Ross said, as he tossed back the last of his drink.

Chapter Two

6 December 1943
Alexandria

Janet Templeton accepted a cup of coffee from Doris Wilson with murmured thanks. She regarded Ted Wilson over the rim of the cup. "I feel bad about intruding on your Saturday morning, Colonel. I apologize." Her evenly chiseled features formed a warm smile.

"Please, no apologies," Ted rumbled. Janet's willowy build and delicate, heart-shaped face beneath a cap of rich, auburn hair, combined with her throaty manner of speaking, worked its usual magic. Blushing, the colonel continued, "I'm just happy to meet you at long last. Ross has told us so much about you. My condolences on the loss of your husband, Mrs. Templeton. I know this must be a trying time for you. Doris was a distant cousin of BT's, you know."

Janet's penciled eyebrows rose fractionally. "Why—why no, I'm sorry, I didn't know. I imagine that BT mentioned you, but scatter-brained me didn't remember." She paused and seemed less sure of herself when she continued. "It was BT, and Ross, I wanted to talk to you about. Do you mind?"

"Not at all," Doris interjected. Her tone attracted Ted's attention. He glanced at his wife; she was contemplating their visitor with narrowed eyes and an unnaturally sharp expression. Ted knew there was no close tie between Doris and the Templetons. Why all this interest?

"Thank you." Janet held her coffee cup in both hands, as if seeking to draw warmth from it. "This is difficult," she said hesitantly. "I don't know what happened over there in Ankara . . . to BT, I mean. The War Department letter said that terrorists threw a bomb into a cafe where he happened to be eating. General Sprague also wrote me a nice letter, praising BT's heroism during the Ploesti mission and calling his death a 'tragic accident.'"

"I take it that you don't accept the official explanation," Ted said cautiously.

"My father-in-law, Senator Templeton, doesn't," Janet stated flatly. "But he won't tell me why. Nor will anyone else. The senator evades me; I haven't even talked with him since BT's funeral. I asked General Sprague to meet with me while he was here in Washington, but he sent his regrets. I wrote Ross and asked him to call me. I received a letter from him postmarked Kelly Field. He said his leave was cut short, and he didn't have a chance to get in touch."

"I see," Ted said, his voice thoughtful. "These things can be frustrating for families. I'm sure that Ross intended no slight. His leave *was* cut short."

"Ross and I were close friends at Hickam, Colonel—"

Ted held up a hand. "Ted, please—Janet."

"Very well." She flashed a dimpled smile. "He and BT didn't get along. It was over something that happened that day the Japanese attacked Pearl Harbor. But Ross's letter was very formal, almost distant—not like him at all. I wanted very much to see him—well, because he and I always talked out our problems together. And right now, I need that kind of a friend. Did he mention planning to call me?" Her voice had a forlorn, pleading note.

"You poor dear," Doris said briskly. "I'm a weak substitute for Ross, but please, drop in anytime and have coffee—and girl talk." She threw Ted a pointed look.

"Thank you, Doris." Janet had regained her composure. "I'd really like that. I'll try to do just that before I leave. You see, I've decided to take a job in a defense plant. I'm about to drive my mother up the wall, I know. A friend in Seattle wrote and asked me to come live with her and work in the Boeing factory. I feel so . . . useless these days, so I decided to do something for our country—and get out of mother's hair."

"I applaud both your patriotism and your good sense," Ted responded. "A demanding job doing something worthwhile is the best antidote for grief there is. And write Ross again. I'm sure he was having an off day when he wrote. He's a great guy, really."

Janet stood and retrieved her purse. "I know that. I was probably just having a down day myself. I feel so much better after talking with you two. Oh, and Doris, I *will* drop by again before I leave."

Ted returned from seeing Janet to her car and poured more coffee. "Now just what the hell was that all about?" Doris asked, her square, olive-hued features set in a frown.

Wilson sipped coffee and grinned. Janet Templeton was a looker, all right. But he wouldn't trade his wife's ripe figure and outgoing personality for the redhead. True, Doris presented a tough, irritating exterior, but inside, she had a heart made of mush. "What was all *what* about?" he countered.

"The Widow Templeton did not drive all the way out here to seek solace and companionship," Doris replied. "That girl is a smooth number. She's about as distraught as a mortician. She reeks of money and influence: That casual skirt and sweater set was from Julians. And she *drove* out here—no bus for her. Where does she get tires and gasoline? So what if her papa is a bird colonel? You're a light colonel and *I* don't see any extra ration stamps.

"No, Broderick Templeton the Third was a little shit—and you know it. She wants more details about how he died, all right, but she isn't driven by grief. And she thinks *you* know. Do you? What did Ross tell you?"

Ted threw his hands in front of his face in mock defense. "Lady, lady, spare me your cruel inquisition. I plead ignorance—to everything."

"Answer my question." Doris was relentless. "What did Ross tell you about BT's death? And don't give me a bunch of crap about it being 'classified.'"

"Contrary to your apparent belief, Ross is not a blabbermouth," Ted responded. "He and his crew were debriefed after they landed at Mountain Home, I do know that. I would assume that they were ordered not to discuss their escape from Turkey. That's normal.

"I agree that Janet probably came here on a fishing trip. I'm also confident that we'll see more of her. But I simply have no information to give her—or you," he added with a grin.

Doris's sniff and, "Your little nose is getting long and pointy, Theodore," hit closer to the mark than was comfortable. True, Ross hadn't divulged details of the crew's escape, but, like any good War

Department staff officer, Ted had unofficial resources. Broderick Templeton III, in collusion with his father, had tried to buy his way out of internment and died in the process.

Janet nursed the aging Mercury convertible through light traffic. The flashy vehicle had been BT's pride and joy at Hickam, but wartime shortages hadn't been kind to it. The powerful V-8 engine gulped rationed gasoline and oil at an alarming rate. Janet glanced at the mismatched cigaret lighter and grinned wryly. BT had raised holy hell when someone stole the original. He'd called the provost marshal and demanded a full investigation.

He wouldn't appreciate the way she'd let the car run down. Cold-weather starts produced ominous noises. Did she dare start a cross-country drive with it? She would have Oscar, down at the Standard station, give it a good going-over. Oscar had a heart murmur and was classified 4-F, but that didn't keep him from being susceptible to fluttering eyelashes. He would give her a good price on any work needed . . . *if* he could find the necessary parts.

She had nibbled her lower lip free of lipstick by the time she parked in the driveway of her parents' quarters at Bolling Field. The future stretched before her like a vast desert. Damn BT! Their marriage hadn't been all that great, but being a homemaker at least gave her life a semblance of purpose. She knew he was seeing other women even before they left Hickam. But, like so many other servicemen's wives, she'd shrugged it off. It's the war, she'd told herself. He'll settle down once it's over.

Only BT could survive combat, then get himself killed doing something stupid, she reflected. I'll probably never know how or why, but the fact remains that I'm single, on my own, and don't have the vaguest idea how to earn a living. BT's insurance was a surprisingly large sum, but it won't keep me forever.

The impulsive trip to visit the Wilsons. Why had she gone? Just to get out of the house, probably. They were nice people, and she would return to gossip with Doris—maybe even confide some of the concerns and doubts she couldn't discuss with her mother. A smile twisted her lips as she inserted her key into the front door. That colonel—Ted—knew more about BT than she would ever learn from him. Well, to hell with it. She couldn't bring BT back. It was time to get on with her life. What would a job building airplanes be like? she wondered. What kind of clothes should she buy?

7 December 1943
Kelly Army Airfield, Texas

Ross moved to where sunshine warmed a portion of the cavernous hangar and shrugged deeper into his sheepskin-lined bomber jacket. The morning was clear and, for Texas, calm. But a breeze swirling off the ten-acre concrete parking ramp belied Chamber of Commerce claims that south Texas enjoyed balmy weather the year-round.

Ross gazed around the sprawl of buildings, hangars, real estate, and airplanes. Temporary frame structures clustered around the staid, brick structures of the training base's prewar portion like poor, unwanted, slightly scruffy relatives.

He recognized nothing from his cadet days here. The Stearman biplanes were long gone, replaced by sleek, all-metal AT-6 Texans—their performance almost equal to some first-line pursuit planes in use when the war started. But he missed the brightly painted blue and yellow fabric-covered trainers, with their jaunty open cockpits.

The Multiengine Instrument Instructor's School, as befitting its elite status, occupied a remote hangar with parking space for its dozen stripped-down B-25 medium bombers. A Jeep wheeled into a parking slot marked MAJOR ABERCROMBIE. A flying suit–clad man, with gold leaves on the shoulders of his A-2 leather jacket and the usual floppy-brimmed, grommetless service cap, leaped lightly to the ground. He approached the similarly dressed group of pilots with a wide, almost shy smile on his craggy, uneven features.

"Mornin' fellows," he drawled, returning twelve snappy salutes with a casual, gnat-brushing motion. "Sorry I'm late, but I'll make up for it—keep you an extra half hour this evenin'." He waited until the polite laughter died down and added, "Come inside, and we'll get this so-called show airborne."

After drawing cups of steaming coffee from a waiting urn, the men seated themselves in student desk-chairs. Major Abercrombie tossed aside his jacket and took up his position in front of a blackboard covering the entire wall.

"What single factor kills more aircrews than any other?" he asked without preamble. Without waiting for an answer, he continued. "Aircraft accidents, that's what. Not enemy action—that's well down the list. Accidents on takeoff, landin', midair collisions, flyin' into mountains while lost. Pilots seem to find new ways to break airplanes every day.

"Is there a common denominator to these accidents? Sure." Again, the major answered his own question. "By far and away, most happen durin' the hours of darkness and in bad weather. Why? Well, mostly because the pilots got some rather indifferent trainin'. There's a war on. Get crews into combat. Don't let 'em get into situations they can't handle and lose one durin' checkout."

Ross found himself nodding in agreement. His own B-24 checkout was a perfect example.

"Okay," Abercrombie said, warming to his presentation. "How are instructor pilots selected? I'll tell you. Just like a lot of you, I was made an IP and ended up in the right seat because I was considered an above-average pilot. Ergo, I could teach others to be just as good. Most IPs are unhappy with the job, and a lot of these just go through the motions.

"That's why we're reversin' the process. First we teach pilots to be professional teachers, then we teach 'em to fly a particular airplane. That's why you're here, gettin' ready to work your ass off for the next six weeks.

"I've seen your Form-fives and Dash sixty-sixes. You're all experienced pilots; most of you have combat time. Here, among other things, you're gonna learn to fly instruments like you've never learned before. Holdin' altitude within plus-or-minus fifty feet, an airspeed tolerance of five miles per hour, and a headin' within five degrees will seem sloppy by the time you finish.

"We have some new toys to show you as well. A new Instrument Landing System that makes landin' with a hundred-foot ceilin' and a quarter-mile visibility a real ho-hum affair. Take a good look at the runway when you leave here. You're not gonna see much of it in the future. You go under the hood before takeoff and come out after your instructor calls minimums for landin'. In between, you'll be strictly on the gauges."

Ross glanced at the man sitting to his right; Alex Taylor, the name tag on his flight suit read. They exchanged understanding nods. Taylor's suntanned, lantern-jawed features wore a chronically sad expression, but something told Ross that they would end up friends. Probably the students would be assigned on the traditional buddy system; he'd approach Taylor during the first break. He returned his attention to their instructor's next words.

"We'll be flyin' the B-25, gentlemen. Why this plane? you ask. It's simple. I was given the job of puttin' this school together, and I happen to like the B-25. That good enough for you?" More chuckles. Ross sensed the wary reserve shown earlier start to relax.

"It's a good, solid airplane with a stable instrument platform, and it's forgivin' of mistakes—as much so as any gravity-defyin' machine can be, at least. Your checkout will be short and sweet—no emergency procedures or written tests. You'll have an IP on board at all times, so you can concentrate on learnin'. A typical mission will have one pilot in the right seat providin' practice instruction to the one in the left. You'll find that, quite by accident, you'll learn more about the airplane that way than we could ever teach you." He paused and looked at the back of the room.

"Okay, you're 'A' Flight—and Lieutenant Benton, who just walked in, is your flight instructor. You'll meet your ground-school instructors at the various classes. If there are no questions, I'll see you 'round the airpatch."

Ross climbed unpainted wooden stairs leading to his second-floor room in the transient officers' quarters. He entered the twelve-by-twelve-foot cubicle and wearily flung the manuals issued to him that morning on the OD blanket covering a folding steel cot's four-inch-thick mattress. He sourly surveyed the room's early austere decor: chair, wood, w/o arms; table, wood, utility, 28x50 inches; and dresser, wood, w/drawers.

A single window, uncurtained and with an opaque green roller blind, provided a view of the adjacent BOQ building, identical to his in every respect. Is this to be my future? he asked himself. An endless series of drab BOQ rooms, with paper-thin walls letting you hear your neighbors snore, groan, and fart in their sleep? Unimaginative meals in mess halls smelling of sweat and rancid mop water? A regimented schedule for turning in laundry and dry cleaning, for drawing items of personal equipment, for medical and dental checkups?

Would he ever get married? Until the war ended, he would still have the same living conditions to endure; family housing was unheard of. All he'd gain would be the heartache of being separated. Few of the married officers he knew could afford to have their spouses join them. Even then, off-base housing was usually little better than a room in the "Q." He shrugged resignedly, changed into Class A uniform, and headed for the club. First Lieutenant Alex Taylor, assigned as his buddy, would meet him for a drink and dinner.

"Whatta you think of this setup?" Taylor asked over heaping plates of spaghetti and meat sauce.

"I'm impressed with what I've seen so far," Ross replied. He drank from his glass of Chianti and continued. "I went through a half-assed checkout in the B-24. Thank God I had a good instructor in '17s. And he's right about instrument flying. We lost a lot of crews, new ones especially, in that crappy English weather."

Alex finished chewing on a mouthful of spaghetti. "Yeah, I went through primary, basic, advanced, and C-47 transition in the desert. I had damn near four hundred hours—so help me God—before I ever flew through a cloud. Where did they send us? India. Clouds with mountains in them; rain so damn heavy you couldn't breathe out in it. But this business about landing out of a hundred and a quarter, saying it's ho-hum, that's bullshit."

A waiter removed their empty plates and slid apple pie and coffee in front of them. Ross glimpsed a figure approaching their table. He looked up and recognized Major Abercrombie.

"Evenin', gentlemen," the major said affably. "I think I recognize you two from the group I talked with this mornin'."

"That's right, Major," Ross said as he and Taylor stood.

"Sit down, sit down," Abercrombie insisted.

"Join us for dessert? Coffee? After-dinner drink?" Ross asked.

"Don't mind if I do, Captain. I've had dinner, but I will have a cup of coffee . . . and maybe just a spot of that vile Mexican brandy the bartender serves with a straight face."

The major seated himself, and their talk turned to flying, with the somewhat strained camaraderie that exists between field grade and junior officers. Abercrombie lit a cigar and asked pleasantly, "Colyer, lookin' over your records, I see you applied for transfer to fighters the day you reported in."

"Yes, sir, I did."

"That's kind of unusual, Cap'n. You sayin' you don't think much of our school here? You applied for it, didn't you?"

"Well, sir . . ." Ross fumbled for words. "You see, Major, I had orders for B-29 school. I've had a tour in bombers, and I think I'd rather fly fighters. I just put in that application so it'd be on top when we graduate."

"I saw that about the B-29 orders bein' amended. It was done at army headquarters—in Washington." His eyes narrowed. "You have somethin' against back-to-back combat tours?" he asked shrewdly.

"No, sir, most certainly not. I fully expect to do another combat tour."

"I see. From the amount of fruit salad you wear, Colyer, that must have been a right interestin' tour you flew."

Ross shifted uncomfortably. "It had some interesting moments, I guess," he muttered.

"I'm sure it did, I'm sure it did. We'll have to get together some evenin' and swap war stories." Abercrombie stood. "Well, I'll be moseyin' on. Thanks for the drink. You'll be seein' me from time to time. I might even fly with you. Hope you two aren't disappointed with our little show here." The major strolled toward the bar next door.

Ross put his head in his hands and groaned. "Oh, shit! Why is it I always get crossways with instructors? It happened in cadet training and again in B-24 school. That major seems like a good guy, and he thinks I dodged a second combat tour by rigging this assignment in Washington."

Alex smiled. "So let him. Hell, if I could pull strings in Washington, I don't think I'd care what the hell he thinks."

Ross shook his head and laughed. "It isn't the way it looks at all. Come on, I'll roll you for drinks."

"Deal," Alex replied. "By the way, I wouldn't get too involved swapping war stories with that guy."

"No?"

"Nope. I can see you got two rows of ribbons, but . . . Aren't you a bit curious as to why we're *really* flying B-25s?"

"Well, like he said, he just likes them."

"Naw, there's more to it than that. A guy in the room next to mine told me that Major Elrod Abercrombie flew the Tokyo raid with Jimmy Doolittle."

"The hell you say," Ross exclaimed. "Took a B-25 off a carrier deck?" He whistled. "You're right, I wouldn't want to try and top that one."

Two slim-hipped youngsters, both wearing pilot's wings, moved to make room for Ross and Alex at the bar. As Ross reached for the dice cup, he overheard the one to his left say, "So I screwed up. The old man had a levy to send someone to this stupid instructors' course, and I got nailed. Sending a P-47 flight commander to multiengine training, for Christ's sake. Now I'm down here for six weeks with a bunch of old, gray-headed bomber fucks learning how to fly straight and level. Sure as hell, the squadron will ship out to Europe while I'm here."

Ross shrugged and grinned at Alex. His companion's face had turned deep crimson. Ross was about to laugh off the slur when Alex asked, "Hey, Ross. You know why they make them P-47 cockpits so small?" His voice carried up and down the bar.

Ross sighed. Oh, well . . . "No, Alex, I don't know. Why?"

Alex cackled shrilly. "It's the only way them Jug pilots can find their ass without using both hands."

The dark-haired lieutenant, his already swarthy complexion deepening, turned to face Ross and Alex. "I don't have to ask which one of you said that. I can tell by his looks. It was the dago."

"That's enough, both of you," Ross ordered. "There're ladies at the tables behind you. If you want to use gutter language, do it outdoors."

"Yes, *sir,* Captain *sir,*" the angry lieutenant responded. He spun on his heel and stalked to the door.

"You didn't have to stop things," Alex snapped. "I can take care of myself. Jews won't fight, anyway."

"Jews?"

"Sure, couldn't you tell? Hell, I can spot one a mile away. I'll bet *he*'s the one who weaseled out of an ETO tour. Everyone knows they're afraid of getting shot down over Germany."

"No, I didn't know that," Ross answered slowly, recalling a number of names such as Swartz, Goldstein, and others in his old outfit in the Eighth Air Force. He rattled the dice cup and shot a quizzical look at his companion. "What'll it be: California rules or liar's poker?"

15 December 1943
Washington, D.C.

Brigadier General Elliott Sprague's beetling black eyebrows tended to move together when he became angry. They were touching just now. His jaw was thrust forward, and his pale green eyes resembled chips of ice from a million-year-old glacier. His mind remained crystal clear, however. Too much was at stake to start venting his wrath.

"Damnit, General, I was promised that wing," he rasped.

"I know you were, Elliott. I endorsed the recommendation myself." The two-star general, seated behind a nonregulation desk of imported rosewood, made no effort to be conciliatory. His weathered, pockmarked features resembled a disgruntled mastiff; soothing hurt feelings was not his forte.

"Nevertheless," he rumbled, "you managed, in your own inestimable way, to piss off our ambassador in Turkey. He screamed to his undersecretary. The secretary of state screamed to Marshall. Need I go on with this sordid little recitation?"

"How about someone in the War Department standing up on his hind legs and yelling right back at those striped-pants civilians at Foggy Bottom—huh? That weasel they have for an ambassador in Ankara was ready to let us rot there. And all the time he was in bed with Senator Templeton scheming to buy BT's way home. I want your okay to request a meeting with General Arnold, by God."

"You won't get it." The grumpy two-star bent a glare in Sprague's direction that would have cowed a charging bear. "Now come to the fucking party. You know better than to go running around flailing your arms and screaming 'no fair' in this town. Just take your medicine and shut up. You're lucky you didn't get an official reprimand in the process."

Sprague, his bluff called, slumped in feigned dejection. "Okay, so what's my punishment? One of the training commands?"

"You're dreaming, Elliott. Get any idea of a quick second star out of your mind. Now, personally, I'm not unsympathetic to what you did over there. If the Ploesti raid had been a spectacular success, why, you'd probably be getting the Medal of Honor. But it wasn't, and the smart money boys are putting distance between themselves and anyone who had an active part in the mission.

"So get your head down, stay out of the newspapers, and let things cool down. You're a combat man, and I'm putting you in a position to do what you do best—kick ass and drop bombs."

"Another B-24 wing? Back to England?" Sprague's voice and expression were glum. "After I've been through a B-29 checkout?"

The glowering two-star let out a moan. "Elliott, Eaker wouldn't let you set foot in England, and you know it. No, I can get you in a Superfort outfit, but as a *deputy* commander. And don't bitch. I had to put my neck on the block to do even that much."

Sprague's expression acquired a suspicious squint. "Deputy commander of what, sir—and under whom?"

"Okay. Here's the thinking. Hitler is on the ropes. The B-29s won't be needed in Europe—by the time a runway-lengthening project can be finished, at any rate. Chiang Kai-shek has promised to provide bases in China. We'll hit the Japanese home islands from there."

"The China-Burma-India operation? You're giving 'Vinegar Joe'

Stilwell the Superfort?" Sprague scowled. "Hell, he's a ground-pounder. He'll have us bombing outhouses."

"Uh—that's been discussed. The alternative is to give them to Chennault. Claire has already made his pitch—directly to the president, no less."

"That crazy Indian? Don't tell me you're thinking of making me deputy to that grandstander? Besides, he's a reservist, and I outrank him."

"Elliott, your gratitude for my saving your ass—keeping you in '29s—overwhelms me. Get it through your head that you are not in a strong bargaining position. Now, you'll be working for K. B. Wolfe. He's putting together a plan for a new, numbered air force, the Twentieth, for CBI very heavy bomber operations. Until we get the command-and-control aspects ironed out, the VHBs will be under direct control of the Joint Chiefs."

Sprague brightened. "Now that I like," he said with a measure of his old enthusiasm. "When do I start?"

"The orders are cut and effective today. See K.B. in the morning. And, Elliott . . ."

"Yes, sir?"

"Don't do something dumb. That CBI operation is touchy, and a diplomat you ain't."

Sprague settled back in the staff car's rear seat and stripped cellophane from a fresh cigar. He turned to the nattily uniformed captain beside him. "Walter, my boy, are you still sleeping with that secretary over in personnel?"

"Wh-a-a-a?" the startled aide stammered.

"Don't act surprised, Walt. I know all about it. So her husband *is* overseas. Now, by Monday, I want to know all there is to know about one-each Brigadier General Kenneth B. Wolfe. How he parts his hair, what his favorite booze is, what he reads in the crapper—the works, understand?"

"Uh—yes, sir. I believe so."

"Good. And try hard, hear? He's the only guy standing between me and a second star. Those railroad tracks on your shoulder aren't going to become gold leaves until I get promoted."

Wearing a wolfish grin, the general leaned back and puffed happily on his freshly lit cigar.

Chapter Three

26 December 1943
Alexandria

Doris Wilson opened the door and greeted Janet with a warm smile. "Come in. You don't know how glad I am that you called. Ted, the bastard, pleaded urgent work at the office and left me with this after-Christmas mess to deal with. Well, to hell with it. Wade through the scene of the crime. I'll pour us some sherry, and we'll kick off our shoes, put our feet up, and have a good, old-fashioned gossip."

"Oh, thank you, Doris," Janet replied with a shy smile. "I feel terrible imposing on you just now—the day after Christmas. But I'm packed and ready to leave for Seattle. I just *had* to say good-bye. You were so nice when I was here before. Ross is very lucky to have friends like you two."

Doris handed Janet a glass of tawny sherry and sank to the sofa alongside the fashionably attired redhead. She crossed her ankles on the coffee table and raised her glass. "Here's to all the best in your new life, Janet. I know you'll enjoy Seattle. As for Ross being a lucky guy to know us, it's the other way around. He saved Ted's life, you know."

"No!" Janet's eyes grew round. "I didn't know."

"'Sa fact." Doris sipped her drink. "Ted had a heart attack flying a trainer with a new student aboard. Ross talked the kid down with messages he wrote on a blackboard. Those open-cockpit Stearmans didn't have radios, you know."

"We didn't keep in touch after Hickam," Janet murmured. "But that sounds so like him."

Doris lit a cigaret and squinted at her guest through the smoke. "You two have something going at Hickam, by any chance?"

Janet blushed. "Not really. The three of us—BT, Ross, and I—saw each other a lot; there wasn't much social life other than on the base. Ross was always the shy one."

"And BT wasn't," Doris observed dryly.

"No, it could never be said that BT was shy," Janet said with a ghost of a smile. "He sort of swept me off my feet. I was young, we had just entered the war—it all happened so suddenly. Then Ross was wounded and shipped back to the States. . . ." Her voice trailed off. "Something happened the day the Japs attacked. BT never said what, but the two of them were bitter enemies from then on."

Doris raised her eyebrows. "BT didn't tell you? Well, he was my cousin, so I don't feel bad about giving you the unvarnished truth. Ross had to point a gun at the little shit to get him in the cockpit of that B-17 he tried to save."

"*Ross?* Pointed a *gun* at *BT?*"

"You got it right, kiddo."

"So that was it," Janet breathed. "That explains a great deal." Her voice turned brisk. "Doris, do *you* know how BT died?"

The full-figured brunette stood and crossed to the rec room bar. She returned with the bottle of sherry and replenished both glasses. "Are you sure you want to know?"

"I have to know. Doris, I've never mentioned this to anyone—even mother. But after the funeral, I discovered I had no sense of . . . call it loss. I cried—I felt sorry for what happened to my husband—but I didn't feel devastated, the way a wife should feel. Then I thought: He may have died bravely, defending his country. I'd feel terribly guilty if that were the case."

"Don't—feel guilty, that is." Doris frowned, then continued. "I know what happened, at least I think I do. Ted doesn't know that I know. Men can be such smug bastards. But you see, Ross was aircraft commander of the plane that General Sprague and BT were on over Ploesti."

"I knew that."

"Very well. They had to land in Turkey and were interned. Turkey is neutral, you know."

"Yes."

"Well, Ross devised a plan to repair the plane and fly it out. Once they had the plane ready, they had no gasoline. They could buy it, but they didn't have any money." Doris paused while she portioned the last of the sherry. "BT conned the ambassador into transferring money to a bank in Ankara—not to buy gasoline, but to bribe his way aboard a ship. Something went wrong, and he was killed."

Janet drained her glass. "I see," she said dully—except the words came out, "I shee."

"Okay, I've spilled my guts," Doris said. "Do you feel better? Or worse?"

"I—I don't know." Janet seemed close to tears. "Just sort of empty. BT wasn't a *bad* person. His damn father . . ." She straightened. "I feel better. I suspected—knew—something like that had happened. Now, I've taken enough of your time. I must finish a few things yet before I go."

"Sit down, Janet," Doris ordered, then her brusque manner softened. "Have some more sherry." She waved Janet's protest aside and retrieved a fresh bottle. "If I ever knew someone who deserved to get sloshed in the middle of the afternoon, you're that someone."

Doris returned to her former position—ankles crossed on the coffee table. "Now, what do you intend to do with your life?"

"Well, go to Seattle and get a job. I really hadn't thought much beyond that."

"Then now is the time to give it some thought." Doris's voice was firm. "Are you sleeping with anyone?"

"*What?*"

"I asked, 'Are you sleeping with anyone?' A man, to be specific."

"Heavens, no. What kind of person do you think I am, Doris?"

"A normal, warm-blooded person," Doris replied serenely. "Look, can't you see what's going on in this country since the war started? It's no longer a world dominated by men. Who are building the planes, tanks, and ships? Who do you see driving buses and trains? Women have suddenly realized that they can do all sorts of things they never dreamed of. They can earn their own living, make their own decisions as to where to live, what work to do, and yes, damnit, who they want to sleep with."

"*Doris!* Why—why . . ."

"Don't sound so shocked, honey. You're young, you're single, you're intelligent—and sinfully good-looking. Why not do what *you* want to do for a change? You've been smothered. Go on out there to Seattle and make your own life. Do what you like; to *hell* with what other people think."

Doris was humming to herself as she stored seldom-used good china and silver she'd gotten out for Christmas dinner, when Ted let himself in through the back door. "Hi, I'm home," he called. "Is that Janet Templeton's car in the driveway?"

"Yes, she stopped by for a visit," his wife replied cheerfully.

"Oh? Where is she?"

"In the guest room, asleep." Doris joined Ted in the living room; she was only slightly unsteady. "That girl would have never made an officer's wife," she stated owlishly. "Can't hold her booze. Now, how do you want your turkey leftovers: on a plate or in your lap?"

29 December 1943
Nanking, China

Officer candidate Nakano Yusaki's five-foot-four-inch body stood at rigid attention. The chill wind swirling about his shorts-clad legs went unnoticed as he listened to Sergeant Shigeo's screamed imprecations, which would have blistered paint. "You're stupid! You do everything backwards. You goof off. Enlisted soldiers goof off; you men are training to be officers! Now, one more time around the obstacle course. And I will deal sternly with anyone I see avoiding the high wall. Go."

Yusaki raged inwardly as he led the other eleven members of Blue Squad at a brisk trot. The fools: Didn't they know that physical fitness was an inflexible standard for officers? True, his days of kendo training with a bamboo sword had toughened his muscles until his stamina exceeded that of his peers, but one slacker caused unwarranted hardship on others of the squad. He attacked the high wall with savage determination.

Perhaps he should have been content with being a private, he told himself—muscles screaming in protest as he danced through a grid of knee-high crosspieces. The enlisted garrison soldiers he'd seen in Hankow, lounging about the food stalls and dance halls, appeared to have a carefree life. But one look at his brother Tadao in his flashy lieutenant's uniform had fired Yusaki with hitherto unknown ambition.

The orders for him to report for active duty had come as a surprise; the war news was of nothing but overwhelming victory on all fronts.

The fighting in far-off places seemed remote, and life in occupied Hankow was good. He earned more money with Ozaki Pharmaceutical than he believed possible. Letters from his mother told of shortages and long hours of work for everyone. Even his father, an aging, half-crippled retired admiral, served as a neighborhood leader.

Yusaki felt faintly guilty, but the girls at the dance halls were lush and willing. He owned not one but two suits of luxurious, gray wool. It had been his dream to return home wealthy and successful, to make his father proud.

At the training center, however, he heard rumors—whispered scraps of information forbidden as topics of conversation—that told of reversals in the heady progress of Japanese conquest. Navy task forces, sailing forth with banners proudly flying, limped back to home ports with sobering damage and noticeably fewer numbers. Places with names such as Midway, Wake Island, and Guadalcanal disappeared from bulletins from the front. Closer to home, an advance through eastern China to link Peking with Indochina had bogged down.

Yusaki pounded down the last stretch of the obstacle course well in advance of his mates. Making a determined effort to breathe without gasping, he came to attention before a scowling Sergeant Shigeo.

"A creditable performance, Candidate Nakano," the NCO conceded ungraciously. "May you reflect credit on the staff here at your next station."

Yusaki knew better than to speak unbidden, so he held his breath. Next station? He expelled his breath, and even allowed a smile to form, as Shigeo continued. "Your scores on the examination for aviator training are satisfactory. You leave tomorrow morning for flight school in Peking."

2 January 1944
Kelly Army Airfield

Lieutenant Benton slouched in the B-25's right seat and raised his voice above the engines' staccato exhaust. Even at idle while taxiing, the individual stacks protruding through the cowling set up an uneven barking. "Okay," he told Ross, "yesterday's landing stage was your last day of fun. Put on your hood."

Ross, satisfied with the engine run-up, reached for the blind-flying hood and adjusted its straps behind his head. The device, resembling a long-billed cap, allowed the pilot to see the instrument panel but blocked any visual reference outside the cockpit.

"I'll line you up on the runway heading," Benton said. "Set your gyrocompass directly on two hundred ten degrees and don't let her get so much as a hair off. Just one degree will have you off the runway before you get airborne."

Ross nodded and settled himself in the seat. He'd made low-visibility takeoffs before, but completely blind was something else.

"Okay," Benton continued. "Now, adjust your gyrohorizon so the little airplane is exactly on the artificial horizon. That will be your primary reference after lift-off. At eighty miles an hour, raise the nose one dot above the line. Hold that until you see a positive increase in altitude on the altimeter. Ignore the rate-of-climb indicator; increasing airspeed will give you a false reading at lift-off."

Ross applied half power and released the brakes. The bomber quivered and accelerated as he fed in more throttle, using asymmetrical power to keep the gyrocompass exactly on 210 degrees. He felt the rudders take effect at 50 MPH airspeed and crammed on full power. Nose up at 80, he told himself; there, she lifted off at 90. Hold climb attitude. "Gear up," he called at 110 MPH. Setting the manifold pressure at thirty-five inches and the props at 2,350 RPM, he felt the lightly loaded craft surge upward. He couldn't resist turning to face his instructor and flashing a satisfied grin.

Members of "A" Flight had quickly settled into a routine: four hours in the cockpit, two in the left seat and two in the right giving instruction to your buddy, followed by four more hours in ground school, interspersed with trips to the "idiot box"—a flight simulator invented by a sadistic group of engineers at the Link Corporation.

Days of grueling, exacting effort followed. Ross learned to his chagrin that he wasn't nearly as good a pilot as he'd thought. "Learn instrument flying until it's second nature," Benton drilled into him. "Only then can you concentrate on flying low-visibility approaches, coping with rapidly changing clearances, in-flight emergencies, and the like. Most accidents happen when the pilot loses control while doing something else."

Benton unveiled the new instrument-landing system during their fourth week. "Here's how it works," he told the seated class. He produced a three-by-five-foot chart as he continued. "Here, at the end of the runway, we place a radio transmitter that aims a very narrow beam of signals aligned with the runway and sloping up at a three-degree angle.

This is an extremely narrow beam—no wider than an airplane fuselage when you get close to the runway threshold.

"The signal is picked up by the airplane. The cross hairs on that instrument you've noticed on the lower left-hand panel move toward the signal. There's a slight difference in the longitudinal signals. One activates the blue side of your instrument, and the other gives an indication you're on the yellow side. That's to tell you which side of the beam you're on. Now, the vertical beam, the 'glide slope,' intersects a low-frequency beacon called the outer marker, one mile off the runway at exactly a thousand feet.

"For landing, you fly outbound until you cross the low-frequency beacon. Make a procedure turn and intersect the longitudinal beam; the vertical cross hair will center. As you pass inbound over the outer marker, the horizontal cross hair will center. From there on, you just keep the cross hairs centered and, bingo, you can fly her right down the runway centerline and touch down on the numbers."

Scattered laughter and derisive hoots followed Benton's explanation. Subsequent practice flights—one of Ross's was on a foggy morning well below the three-hundred-foot ceiling and one-mile visibility minimums prescribed for an automatic-direction-finder approach—made dedicated believers of the now enthusiastic pilots, however.

Ross, armpits soaked with sweat, walked away from his last checkride, weary but triumphant. Benton had pulled out all the stops. Following a simulated engine fire on lift-off, he'd placed cards over the artificial horizon and gyrocompass, reducing the flight instruments to the basic turn needle, airspeed indicator, and the highly erratic magnetic compass. Under simulated weather conditions of a hundred and one, Ross commenced an emergency return to the field and wrestled the laboring ship into approach position before Benton announced the loss of the ADF radio. With the ILS as his only navigational aid, there was no way to locate the outer marker.

When Ross had accused the cheerful instructor of being a miserable, sadistic bastard, Benton replied, "Okay, I just got shot. I can't help you lower flaps, gear, read airspeed. . . . You're on your own, hotshot."

Ross had grinned and devoted himself to putting everything he'd learned to use. The grin slipped as, after positioning himself on the glide slope, gear and flaps down, runway coming up, Benton said, "Oh, shucks. Tower just called and says there's a construction vehicle stalled on the runway. You'll have to go around, climb back to the outer marker, and hold."

Ross had located the now dead outer marker by using the intersection of the lateral and vertical ILS beams, only to learn that the engine fire had flared up again; he'd have to lower the gear to keep the landing gear tire from catching fire.

Ross stood, drink in hand, and watched Lieutenant Benton laughing and slapping his leg as he related some hilarious event to Major Abercrombie. The graduation party was in full swing. The officers' club ballroom reverberated with shouts, laughter, and a jukebox rendition of Glenn Miller's "String of Pearls." Bastard, Ross thought goodhumoredly. I know what you're telling the major, and I'll get my revenge. He felt a certain pride, however. No other student had been subjected to the same wringing out, and he'd passed with flying colors.

Benton saw Ross across the room and waved his hand with a beckoning motion. Feigning anger, Ross joined the group, who were still enjoying Benton's description of the checkride. The instructor turned to Ross and said, "You don't deserve it, after the profane language you heaped on me, but I'm going to introduce you to the classiest gal at Kelly. Ross, meet Ruth Lasher—Captain Ruth Lasher, I should say. She's a nurse over at the base hospital. Ruth, this is Ross Colyer."

Ross looked into the woman's smoky gray eyes, crinkled at the corners by her smile. Her oval face wasn't pretty, he thought. The nose was a bit large, a prominent jawline emphasized her chin, and her black hair, cut short and without curls, didn't give her a movie star look. She shook hands with a cool, impersonal grasp.

"Tally deserved any foul name you called him, I'm sure," she said to Ross. "I just hope you used some new ones I haven't thought up. He concedes that you showed him an impressive bit of flying, however."

"Sheer survival instinct," Ross replied. "Dance?"

"I'd love to," Ruth answered, moving into the circle of his right arm. She was a good dancer, Ross discovered immediately—pliant, dancing close, but following gracefully.

"Are you Benton's girlfriend?" he asked.

"Heavens, no," she replied with a tinkling laugh. "Tally is married to that long-suffering blond standing at the punch bowl. She's also a nurse, and I value her and Tally's friendship above all else. I'm here tonight with one of Tally's friends."

"I see." Ross led his partner to a relatively uncongested area. "No steady boyfriend?"

Ruth leaned back to see Ross's face better. "No applicants," she replied.

Before Ross could respond, the music stopped. He escorted her back to where Benton and Abercrombie were chatting. "We must discuss this applicant situation in some depth, I believe. May I call you?"

"I'm in the book, as they say."

Major Abercrombie interrupted. "Captain Colyer, would you join me for a drink in the bar?"

"Certainly, Major." Ross turned to Ruth and pressed her hand. "Thanks for the dance. And I know where to find a phone book." He glimpsed her fleeting smile as he followed Abercrombie into the adjacent room.

"I won't keep you away from the party more than a few minutes, Ross," the school commandant said, "but we have a little graduation ceremony laid on for tomorrow. The cadets have a pass-in-review parade each Sunday, and we sort of use it for background color. We award a certificate to each class's outstanding graduate. I just wanted to tell you that you were selected. If you'll meet me on the reviewing stand a few minutes before thirteen hundred, we'll conduct a brief rehearsal."

Ross set his untouched drink back on the bar. "An—an award?" he stammered. "I had no idea. I—well, I'm overwhelmed. Thank you."

"You're a good pilot, Colyer—and a better instructor. So much so, I've requested that you be kept here at the school."

Ross gaped. Before he could voice his protest, Abercrombie held up his hand to cut him off. "What I'm asking is: Are you going to use your Washington contact to buck the assignment?"

"Major, uh," Ross said, fumbling for words. "Look, sir, here's what happened. . . ." He explained how he'd asked his former CO to help keep him out of General Sprague's B-29 wing, and that had been accomplished. "I was looking forward to getting into the Superfort," he concluded. "But after thinking it over, I've decided I really would like a crack at fighters."

"I see," the sober-faced major said thoughtfully. "But you still haven't answered my question. Are you going to ask your friend to help you avoid instructor duty here?"

"No, sir," Ross replied after a slight hesitation. "I wasn't proud of the way I handled the other situation. I won't pretend I'm overjoyed at the idea, but I'll do a good job, I promise you that. Still, I'm not going to withdraw my request for fighters," he added stubbornly.

Abercrombie chuckled and slapped Ross on the shoulder. "Fair enough. I'll see you at the reviewing stand tomorrow. Now, let's get back to the party."

Ross, unable to hide his dismay, downed his drink in one swallow. The major stopped short of leaving. "By the way, don't get involved with Captain Lasher unless you're serious. Ruth's husband was killed at Salerno. She's something special, and we all sort of look after her."

Chapter Four

26 January 1944
Eagle Pass Army Airfield, Texas

Lieutenant Colonel "Tommy" Thompson closed Ross's 201 file, centered it neatly on the desk before him, and leaned back. His square face, bulldog jaw, and thick black eyebrows formed a picture of displeasure. Pinning Ross with a withering glare, he barked, "Frankly, Captain, I would rather not have you here. I protested your assignment after we received your records and was told, not too politely, to fucking well forget it.

"Now, I run a replacement training unit. The 341st will never see combat. We take fighter pilots with experience in older airplanes, upgrade them to the P-51, then send them overseas. That's all we know how to do, and we do a damn good job of it. We aren't prepared to take a bomber pilot and turn him into a fighter jock. Besides, you don't have the background to fly the hottest fighter in the inventory. Get the picture?"

Ross swallowed his rising anger. "May I say something, sir?"

"Yeah, go ahead."

"I'm a good pilot; I've proven it. I'm determined, and I want to fly fighters. The airplane hasn't been built that I can't fly as well as, or better than, ninety percent of the pilots in the entire Air Corps. The day I can't keep up with your other students is the day you can send me packing."

Thompson snorted. "I've heard that kind of bullshit before. I've had the unpleasant job of scraping most of your kind off the runway with a shovel and shipping them home to mama in a rubber bag."

The irate group commander threw both pudgy hands in the air. "I don't know why I'm bothering to tell you all this. I'm stuck with you. I wanted to send you right back to Kelly on TDY to go through fighter tactics and gunnery in an AT-6, but they don't have a slot.

"Instead, I'm sending you down to the 787th Squadron. Major Cipolla is the closest thing to a mother hen I have. Cappy flew P-40s with Chennault and became an ace killing Jap Zeroes, a plane that had him outclassed in every category. Listen to him, for Christ's sake. Forget that noble crap about keeping up. If I see you can't hack it, I'll bounce your ass outta here so fast it'll make your head spin. Dismissed."

Ross stalked out the door of the raw pine and tarpaper-covered building that housed Thompson's office. His ears still flaming, he crossed the graveled parking lot to where Ruth waited in her red '41 Ford convertible. The top was down, and he threw the bulky briefcase containing his records into the space behind the front seat with unnecessary vigor.

The nurse roused from a languorous sprawl in the unseasonably warm winter sunshine and cocked an eyebrow. "My, my," she murmured. "Were any blows exchanged? What went on in there?"

Ross slammed the door, causing Ruth to wince. "That pompous ass. That arrogant sonofabitch! You'd think I had leprosy. 'We don't want you,'" Ross mimicked in a shrill falsetto. "'You aren't qualified to be a fighter pilot.' Well, I'll show that overbearing bastard. He'll eat those words, I guarantee it."

"Oh, Ross. What a rotten way to start. I know how much this assignment means to you. What will you do?"

"I'll fly rings around every stupid fighter jock in this flea-bitten outfit," Ross replied through clenched jaws.

Ruth gave a resigned shrug. "Okay. Where do we go next?"

"I don't have to report to my squadron until tomorrow morning." His expression softened. "A motel in town?" he asked.

Ruth gave a throaty chuckle. "Now, how did I guess that you might suggest that? While you were in there doing battle, I persuaded a nice sergeant to let me use a phone. It seems that the Eagle Pass Motel—cabins with kitchenettes by day, week, or month—doesn't have room for so much as a stray cat. They can't even remember when they had a vacancy. The woman laughed at me, in fact. I can stay in the nurses' quarters tonight. I assume they have BOQ rooms for student pilots?"

"Oh," Ross's face fell. "I'd sort of hoped—you know. You'll have to go back to Kelly tomorrow."

"How well I know." Ruth placed a warm hand atop one of Ross's and grinned mischievously. "The always-prepared army nurse put her bivouac gear in the trunk. I suspected this might happen. I suggest we check into our separate quarters, visit the commissary to buy steaks, and camp out beneath the stars tonight."

Ross poked the dwindling mesquite-wood fire. Amid a shower of sparks, flames painted his somber features with a rosy glow. Ruth curled inside the circle of his left arm, a GI blanket around her shoulders. "Beautiful, unbelievably beautiful," she said softly. "I never knew the sky could hold so many stars."

"I suppose I should come up with something profound—something witty—something Clark Gable might say about now," Ross replied. "All I can think of is tomorrow. Where do we go from here, Ruth?"

"You go on to be chief of staff, Ross Colyer. I'll go on to invent a cure for cancer or something—save thousands of starving children in Africa or India." Her voice tinged with sadness, she added, "Don't you dare make me bawl. I don't want to remember anything about tonight that isn't beautiful."

"There'll be other nights," said Ross.

"Don't count on it."

"What do you mean?" Ross leaned closer and peered into her face. "Hell, Kelly isn't all that far away. We'll both have days off."

"I have overseas orders, Ross. I ship out next week."

"What?" Ross jerked upright, almost letting Ruth fall to the packed sand. "When did you find out?"

"Two weeks ago. I didn't tell you because I knew what you'd say."

"I don't understand."

"The marriage business. You would insist on a quick ceremony before we parted ways. My mind is made up. No wartime marriage. Robby's death almost put me into the psych ward. I vowed never again to go through those days and nights of waiting for that Western Union messenger to park his bicycle in front of my door.

"I'm fond of you, Ross—almost too fond. These last few days have been wonderful. You helped me through a bad time. But I just can't face going through with you what I went through with Robby. I simply can't. What I'm saying may hurt you terribly, but losing a lover and losing a husband are different. I'd be heartbroken if anything happened to you, but broken hearts heal; broken lives don't. Can you possibly understand?"

Ross stood and paced between the pup tent—sleeping bag already unrolled inside—and the fire, where Ruth huddled beneath her blanket. "Taking life one day at a time—taking pleasure, love, as you find it—letting the future take care of itself. You don't really believe in that," he said flatly, looking down at her upturned face.

"I know. I try to convince myself that it's the only practical outlook, but I can't," sighed Ruth.

Ross knelt, gathered her into his arms, and lifted her seemingly without effort. "Major Abercrombie told me you were something special. He just didn't say *how* special. You haven't seen the last of me, Ruth Lasher. This war can't last forever. Now, ma'am, come with me. Your canvas boudoir awaits."

27 January 1944
Garden City, Kansas

Janet watched the leather-faced mechanic wipe his hands on a rag already saturated with more grease than he was removing, and stroll toward her. She returned the empty Nehi bottle to its rack and stubbed out her tenth cigaret of the morning. The man's doleful expression wasn't cause for optimism. "Well?" she asked as he stopped in front of her.

"'Fraid your water pump is shot, ma'am. I kin maybe repack it an' get you as far as Denver, but I'd hate to see you start out with a gimpy engine. They's a couple of stretches ahead of you where there ain't nothin' but empty highway for fifty miles or more, an' it's all uphill from here."

"Can you install a new one?"

"Lordy, ma'am, not a new one. I got a connection in Topeka, a junkyard, that can maybe send me a used one, but I ain't been able to get new parts for more'n a year."

"How long will that take?"

"Well, if he's got one, he could maybe get it on the afternoon bus. Get here sometime tomorrow. I could maybe work late tomorrow night and have you on your way Sunday. I'd have to charge you for the phone call whether he's got one or not," the man cautioned.

Janet waved her hand in irritated dismissal. "Don't worry about that." She lit another cigaret and paced the tiny, cluttered office, returning to the island of warmth surrounding a cherry-red space heater. The Mercury had been a source of trouble during the entire journey. Overnight in Columbus, Ohio—leaky radiator. Two days in St. Louis while a sharp-faced station attendant searched for a black-market tire to replace a blowout—the recap Oscar had proudly produced. That night spent in a crummy motel room, listening to a rowdy party next door. Now this.

She wheeled to face the abject-looking mechanic. "I have a job waiting for me in Seattle," she snapped. "I'm supposed to be there Monday, but I'll never make it by then. Go ahead and make the call."

The stooped, elderly man's face twisted as if in pain. "Ma'am, I hope you won't get riled, but do you mind if I give you some advice?"

"Go ahead."

"Well, I got a daughter—'spect she's 'bout the same age as you. I'd sorely hate to see her set out for Seattle, all by herself, in any kind of car. 'Tain't safe for a young woman to be travelin' alone. Anyways, you're gonna have more trouble with this one afore you get through them mountains. They's snow in some of them passes, an' a blizzard can blow up afore you can blink an eye. You know how to put on tire chains—iffen you got any? People've died in their cars in them mountains."

"Just how, then, do you suggest I get there?" Janet asked, her voice dripping with sarcasm.

"You take the bus from here to Denver an' get on an airplane. You could be in Seattle Sunday night, maybe."

Janet uttered an unladylike snort. "Really. And what do you suggest I say when some snotty airline clerk asks"—her voice raised to a nasal falsetto—"'And what is your priority, ma'am? Our flights are all booked solid for the next six weeks.' Believe me, I went through all that before I decided to make this drive."

"Well, I wouldn't know 'bout none of that, but you're sure as thunderation facin' a lot of grief tryin' to get there in *this* car. You got a clutch that slips; you need a valve job. . . ." The man shook his head.

"All right, say I do take the bus from here. What am I supposed to do with the car? And all my things in it?"

"Well, there's Ronnie Suggs. He runs a used car business over on Fourth Street. I reckon he'd buy it."

"Sell my car? What am I supposed to use for transportation when I get to Seattle?"

The stooped shoulders shrugged. "I 'spect most people ride the bus to work there. 'Course you can always buy another one, iffen you can afford it."

"Oh, my God, what a mess," Janet sighed in exasperation. "How much do you think your Mister Suggs will give me for it?"

The mechanic returned to the inoperative Mercury and walked around it with a speculative scowl. "Well, you got fair rubber, and no big dents and such. I reckon you might get about five hundred for it."

"*Five* hundred? I was offered nine before I left D.C."

"Yeah, I hear tell cars fetch good prices back East. But you ain't back East," he added sagely.

Janet slumped into the soiled, rickety chair she'd occupied most of the morning and propped her chin in her left palm. Finally, she asked, "Where can I find a pay phone?"

Janet uttered a sigh of relief when she saw the travel-stained Greyhound bus rock to a stop with a shrill hiss of its air brakes. "It might be late," the buxom waitress acting as ticket agent had cautioned. It was—two hours late. Through the steam-fogged cafe window, Janet watched an assortment of rumpled arrivals gather to reclaim their luggage.

Smartly attired in a tan whipcord suit, one of the new outfits she'd selected as appropriate for a working woman, Janet donned her wool coat with its sensibly warm fur collar. Next, she gathered up her purse and a shopping bag containing a variety of items she anticipated would ease the long ride. A paperback copy of *Forever Amber* rested on top. She'd heard it was racy; hopefully it would provide some diversion. Actually, she rather looked forward to a restful trip, curled up in a secluded rear seat, with the worry of that balky Mercury behind her.

Finally, Janet left the warmth of the cafe and took her place in line behind a dozen or so weary passengers waiting to board the Greyhound. The uniformed driver stood just inside the bus's open door and took a count. "I can take ten," he announced. "Servicemen first." Two youngsters wearing peacoats over their navy blues wormed their way forward.

Janet watched in dismay. She counted more than ten GIs and sailors, faces slack from having traveled two days or more, waiting ahead of her. Hurrying to the front of the line, she called, "Sir, it's important that I get to Seattle. I'm supposed to report for work there Monday."

The driver favored her with a bored look. "They put on an extra bus today, I hear. He should be through here before midnight."

Janet stood wordlessly, her mouth working silently with stunned disbelief. A middle-aged woman waiting to get back on the bus turned and asked, "You going to work in one of the defense plants, dear?"

"Yes—yes," Janet stammered. "Boeing—I'll be building airplanes."

"Very well," the woman beamed. "Take my place. I'm only going as far as Golden to visit my grandchildren. I guess I can do that much for the war effort. My son is somewhere in the Pacific; he's a marine, you know."

Janet went limp with gratitude. Mumbling inane expressions of thanks, she struggled up the metal steps and stopped, confronting a press of hostile-faced individuals who choked the aisle. She realized that all the seats were filled, and that these people were destined to stand. My God, she thought, it's an eight-hour ride to Denver.

The driver slid into his seat and closed the door. After starting the engine, he said, "You'll have to stand behind the white line, ma'am. Government regulations say I got to have a clear view to the right."

Janet elbowed into a narrow strip of floor space and gasped, "Is—is the bus always this full?"

"Mostly, ma'am." The driver pointed to an overhead sign that read PLEASE DO NOT TALK TO DRIVER WHEN COACH IS IN MOTION, and eased into the late afternoon traffic.

Janet crammed her coat and shopping bag into an already filled overhead rack. She clutched her purse to her chest with one hand and steadied herself with the other. The five hundred dollars she'd realized from selling the Mercury seemed to shout its presence. She gave fleeting thought to her two big suitcases. An effusive Ronnie Suggs had assured her that he would place them on Railway Express; they would maybe even be waiting for her in Seattle. That offer followed her reluctant agreement to include her remaining store of gasoline ration stamps, which Oscar the mechanic had mysteriously produced for her in D.C., as part of the deal.

Darkness finally obscured the dreary, wind-scoured landscape. Janet regretted her selection of shoes for the trip—beige kid pumps that matched her traveling suit. Now, after less than an hour, her leg muscles screamed from the strain of keeping her balance. She kicked off the offending footgear and winced at the feel of the dirty, gritty floor beneath her bare feet. She inched closer to where the bus's whining heater blew a blast of hot air across the ice-cold floor. Feeling better, she glanced at her legs. The painted dye, advertised to be indistinguishable from real silk stockings, was streaked and blotched. I look like a damn Appaloosa, she thought.

Laughter amid raised voices from the rear of the bus attracted her attention. The two sailors were entertaining a pair of giggling, not-so-young females. The pungent odor of raw liquor wafted forward in the stagnant atmosphere. I could stand a jolt of that myself, she thought grimly. She realized that she hadn't eaten since noon, when she'd forced down a greasy cheeseburger and a Coke. She defied the admonition against talking to the driver and, moving forward, asked, "Do you stop for dinner?"

"Twenty-minute stop in Golden, ma'am. You'll have time to maybe grab a hotdog and coffee," came the laconic reply. Janet regretted, for the tenth time, turning down the offer of a seat. A youngish man, a rancher by his looks, had touched the brim of his ten-gallon Stetson and said, "You're welcome to my seat, miss. I don't mind standin'."

That had been shortly after leaving Garden City. Janet had given one look at the slovenly woman seated alongside who was trying to quiet a squalling infant with a grimy-looking bottle, and politely refused. Now, she considered asking him if he would mind if she took him up on his offer. As she rehearsed her plea, she felt a firm but gentle pressure on her right hip. She shifted her position, but the pressure remained.

Janet's lips set in a firm line. Okay, she was on familiar ground now—an arena where she understood the rules. She turned her head and regarded a pair of eyes, barely visible in the dim glow of the instrument panel. She recognized a middle-aged man she'd noticed earlier standing several feet behind her. He'd worked his way forward and now stood directly behind her, his free hand cupping her ungirdled buttock.

She realized that an icy glare would be wasted in the darkness. Her voice was low but dripped with controlled fury: "Remove your hand, you worm, or I'll scream for help."

"Aw, c'mon, Red. It's a long ways to Denver. You getting off there?" an oily voice asked.

Janet turned and faced her fellow traveler. She reached up, removed his tweed cap, and patted his balding head. "My, but you're a nice old man," she murmured. "Give my regards to your unfortunate wife and children."

Turning back to the front, she thought, Stopover in Golden, eh? I'll have a seat when we leave there, by God, if I have to sit on that slimy bastard's lap.

30 January 1944
Eagle Pass Army Airfield

Major Anthony "Cappy" Cipolla faced Ross across the open P-51 cockpit. The major's drooping, billed service cap was pulled low against the early morning chill, and his eyes were concealed by dark aviator glasses. Only a sharp, aquiline nose and full mouth were visible above the leather flying jacket's zipped-up collar.

"Pretty much the standard cockpit layout," he said. "This is the B model. They're working on a D model that'll have a bubble canopy and a few other improvements—a better gunsight, for example.

"First thing I want you to do is sit inside for a while. Take your Dash-one and get to know the location of every switch and control, and what they do. Things happen pretty fast in the air; you won't have time to look things up in a book. Take your time now. I'll see you in ops after noon chow. This afternoon you can shoot three or four landings. Have fun." Cipolla leaped from the wing and trotted toward the ops building.

Ross dumped his seat-pack chute into the bucket seat, lowered himself into the cockpit, and closed the canopy against the biting wind swirling off the barren Texas landscape. Immediately, the roar of in-line aircraft engines and rumbling fuel trucks and the shrill cries of ground crews ceased. He took stock of his surroundings. Damn, it's cramped in here, he mumbled to himself. His shoulders and head cleared the sides and overhead canopy by just about the same scarce inches that his knees cleared the instrument panel. He visualized strapping in with a Mae West life preserver, bail-out bottle clipped to his chute harness, helmet and oxygen mask in place. Would he ever feel comfortable?

They said that the Mustang, with drop tanks, had an endurance of nine goddamn hours. He fumbled for the relief tube clipped beneath the seat and imagined using it while wearing full flying gear. Now that presented a challenge. Oh, well. He turned to examine the clutter of switches and controls.

Ross took his place in a line of airplanes taxiing toward the take-off point. The plane's three-point attitude, with ten feet of raised nose obscuring forward visibility, required making sweeping S turns. He'd forgotten what a nuisance it was, after flying airplanes with tricycle gear. At the oversized run-up pad, he swung the fighter's nose into the wind, set the brakes, and shoved the throttle forward, letting the tachometer stabilize at 1,700 RPM. Right mag: No drop. Left mag: Nothing more than a quiver. The big, twelve-cylinder, Packard-built Rolls-Royce engine purred evenly.

He watched the two ships in front of him line up on the runway and execute a formation takeoff. Then he was number one. He switched to the student frequency. "Cactus Mobile, this is Cottontail Three, ready for takeoff. Over." He was surprised that his voice didn't reflect his sudden tension.

"Roger, Cottontail Three. You're cleared into position and hold. Over." He recognized Cipolla's clipped accent—could look across the runway and see him, in fact. An orange and white trailer housed the mobile control tower to allow instructors closer contact with students. Ross eased onto the runway, lined up with the white centerline, and stopped in the midst of a mass of black tire marks.

Following the major's instructions, he keyed his mike and read off critical instrument readings. "Cottontail Three. Oil and coolant temperatures in the green; fuel selector on fullest tank; cooler doors open; ready to roll."

"You're cleared for takeoff, Cottontail Three."

Ross advanced the throttle about halfway and released the brakes. Watch for torque, he thought, mentally repeating Cipolla's warning. The spinning, four-bladed prop tried to force the nose to the right. Add power gradually and hold the plane straight with left rudder; don't force the tail up now. He glanced at the airspeed. Good Christ, he was doing a hundred and hadn't even reached full throttle. He crammed the lever all the way forward and eased back on the stick. The airplane leaped into the air like a flushed quail. Back pressure, set up your climb; check your airspeed—my God, a hundred and eighty. He remembered Cipolla's words: Get your gear up as soon as you're airborne; you'll rip the wheel-well covers off at two hundred. He fumbled at his left for the gear lever and heard the wheels retract with a muted *thump*.

By the time Ross thought to reduce power, he was at five thousand feet and indicating 300 MPH. He leveled off and took up a westerly heading. "Go west of the field and get the feel of her before you try to land," Cipolla had advised. "Do some steep turns; try different power settings and such. No stalls today—intentional ones anyway."

Ross cleared himself on the left, applied stick and rudder, and immediately found himself in a screaming forty-five-degree bank. G forces crammed his butt into the seat cushion. A light touch brought the plane straight and level, and an awed grin split his face—what a flying machine. Before he knew it, he'd been racing around the sky for twenty minutes. He pressed the mike switch. "Cactus Mobile, Cottontail Three requesting landing instructions. Over."

"Roger, Cottontail Three." Cipolla's voice was tinged with amusement. "I was beginning to wonder if you were ever going to come down. You're cleared to enter a base leg for Runway Zero-one-five. Call turning final. Over."

Ross acknowledged and set up a descent. It would be a conventional pattern; three-sixty overheads would have to wait. Four landings later, he parked the sleek fighter and reluctantly shut it down. Damn, this was flying. He crossed to ops and slung his chute on the counter.

Cipolla was waiting, his darkly handsome features spread in a wide grin. "Not a bad show," he said. "How do you like her?"

"What an airplane," Ross replied in an awed tone. "I was behind the damn thing from the time I started rolling." He closed his mouth with a snap. "That won't happen again," he added. "I'm ready to go back up right now."

22 February 1944
Peking, China

Despite aching muscles and a mind fuzzy from intense concentration on the principles of air navigation, Yusaki penned his weekly letter home with swift brush strokes. Lights-out was only fifteen minutes away. He finished with just enough time to scan the letter quickly:

> Honorable parents,
>
> With pleasure I advise that my fourth week here is finished with passing grades. The work is difficult and demanding. Inferior marks or attitude result in immediate expulsion. Less than one half of our original number will graduate, they tell us. The school at Nanking was a pleasant interlude by comparison.
>
> Physical training is intense. A fighter pilot must be aggressive and tenacious, and we learn by doing difficult feats. Today our wrestling instructor opened the course by selecting two students at random. The winner was allowed to return to ranks. The loser was required to wrestle the next man. If defeated, he remained there until he bested a challenger.

There are seventy cadets in the class. To be defeated by all is grounds for expulsion.

The obstacle course includes a tall iron pole. We are required to climb the pole and suspend ourselves by one hand for ten minutes. Those unable to do so are booted to the top for another attempt. Again, cadets unable to master this feat are expelled.

We hone our reaction time by catching flies. It is known that fighter pilots must have lightning reflex movements. I am proud to say that no fly has escaped my grasp for more than a week now.

Tomorrow we meet our flight instructors and make our very first flight in an airplane. I pray that my hand may be steady and my eye sure. To bring the shame of failure to the house of Nakano is unthinkable.

Yusaki

21 March 1944
Eagle Pass Army Airfield

Ross looked to his right where the brooding mass of the Sacramento Mountains formed a sawtoothed horizon. The Mustang seemed to savor the subzero, rarified air at twenty-five thousand feet. He grinned inwardly. After weeks of grueling effort, today he faced the fighter pilot's ultimate challenge—one-on-one engagement. He was invincible—hurtling above the gray- and dun-colored Rio Grande valley at more than 300 MPH, with four wing-mounted .50-caliber machine guns awaiting his command. This being a practice aerial combat mission, the guns' ammo cans were empty today. Instead, a gun camera would record his attempt to down a mock enemy.

He returned to reality with a jolt. Get with the program, Colyer. Get your neck on a swivel. That pair of black-painted fighters you're looking for will nail your ass while you're daydreaming. He swept the blinding, cloudless sky in all directions, pausing to check that his wingman was in position. Gus Swenson, an intense youngster just out of P-40 school, trailed along, two hundred yards off his left wing. Ross checked his reflective gunsight for the tenth time. The illuminated circle of green light, clocklike pointers around its circumference, was ready.

Where the hell were they? Ross asked himself irritably. They should have made contact long ago. He searched the sky overhead once more.

For that matter where was Major Cipolla? The squadron commander was someplace where he could observe the exercise. Ross tried to place himself in his adversary's role. How would he attempt to pull a surprise attack?

Out of the sun, naturally. Gain altitude, get off to one side, then roll down and in toward the target, reversing the roll at the last minute to fire ahead of the enemy. It was the classic fighter pass. Ross had studied diagrams, watched gun camera film, and listened to his instructors until he was sure he could do it perfectly. Okay, the other pilots would know that, so they'd try to surprise him. How? If it were me, Ross told himself, I'd dive out of the sun, pass well behind, then zoom up and shoot from beneath. His earphones came to life. "Six o'clock high, Red Leader."

Ross snapped his gaze to the rear. Sure enough, two black specks quickly became crosses against the sun's searing brightness. An involuntary chill coursed down his spine. Christ, they looked just like Me 109s. Well, let them come. This time he wasn't in a cumbersome formation of B-24s, unable to maneuver. He checked again. The rapidly closing aggressor was attempting a tail attack on Gus's ship. "Break now, Red Two," Ross called.

Gus rolled into a diving turn to the left. Ross's heart leaped. The pursuer was following. It must look to him as if he could easily turn inside Gus and have a perfect deflection shot. Ross hesitated fractionally, wondering where the hell number two was, then entered a level turn to the left. As planned, the attacker's speed took him ahead of Ross's ship. The black Mustang, having rolled into a steep turn in front of Ross's slower-turning ship, was caught dead to rights. Now, he had no escape but to break down and away—where Gus, who had performed a split S, was waiting for him.

Ross gave only fleeting attention to the successful coup. Where the hell was the second black ship? Anytime you have the chance, gain altitude, he recalled hearing Cipolla lecture. He shoved the throttle forward, letting the gang-bar carry fuel mixture and prop RPM to the war-emergency setting. The big V-12 engine uttered a bellowing response. The altimeter started spinning clockwise.

He glimpsed the diving attacker behind him; moments later, he would have been caught unaware. He rolled level. Let the bastard get just a little closer but not within range, he told himself. Now! A jinking turn to the left. He saw the black shape turn to cut him off. Retarding the throttle, Ross flipped into a sloppy barrel roll to the right. Recovering, he grinned with unholy glee. The dumb shit flying the black ship was now beneath and ahead of him, and turning.

Shoving the throttle full forward again, Ross tightened his turn. The plane ahead filled the circular gunsight. His finger poised, he paused. Then, in a flash, just as he pressed the trigger, the gunsight was empty. Damn! The guy had made a diving, twisting turn and was now far out of reach. Ross took off in angry pursuit.

Colonel Thompson half sat, half leaned on the bar stool and swirled the ice in his drink. "Well, I suppose you're going to engage in some more crowing about your protégé," he growled.

Major Cipolla waited until he'd sampled his own drink, then responded, "I'm already tasting that forty-pounder of Red Label, Colonel."

"He hasn't graduated yet," the group CO said smugly. "He'll fuck up; I have every confidence. You're good, I concede that. But even with your personal attention, Colyer is not fighter pilot material. I got instincts about things like that."

"Highest air-to-ground gunnery scores in the squadron at Matagorda Island," Cipolla mused aloud. "Hasn't made less than ninety-two percent on any written test. He's given tips on instrument flying to half the other pilots."

"Keep going, Cappy. I'm listening."

"What do you mean?"

"Air-to-air gunnery. Tell me about his simulated combat record."

"Someday I'm gonna catch one of your spies at work and beat the shit out of him," Cipolla said mildly.

Thompson snorted and regarded his prize squadron commander with a wicked leer. "Can't hit the air with his fist, can he? Want to double your bet, Major?"

Cipolla scowled and ordered a refill. "Course completion is still two weeks away," he muttered without conviction.

Chapter Five

24 March 1944
Eagle Pass Army Airfield

Major Cipolla sat on the edge of his desk. Jerky movement by highly polished, nonregulation chukka boots revealed his agitation. "Damnit, Ross. You do everything perfectly, right up to the time to shoot. I've looked at every foot of your gun camera film. You have some slick moves and haven't had a half-dozen solid hits from your opponents. You get into position, but you miss. Do you realize you have yet to score a clean kill?"

Ross, elbows on knees, slumped in a chair and glared at the floor. "I've looked at that same film, Major—a half-dozen times. I just can't figure it out. It seems like I—I just go blank."

"Or freeze?" Cipolla asked softly. "You know what buck fever is, I assume."

"Sure, but this is different. Hell, I flew combat. Our crew shot down our share of Me 109s and Fw 190s."

Cipolla gave the dejected pilot a long, thoughtful look. "You know, that may be a clue. Your *crew* shot them down. You, personally, didn't pull the trigger!"

"Aw, come on, Major. These damn guns aren't even loaded."

Major Cipolla stared into space, seemingly talking to himself instead of Ross. "I remember my first kill. A fabric-covered Jap patrol job. I just flew up behind him in my P-40 and let fly. He caught fire. Neither of the two crew members got out. Everybody bought me drinks that night. Called me 'Ace.' I'd killed two Japs on just my third mission. I never told anyone I'd puked up my guts after I landed. Nor did I tell anyone that I got the clanks and missed my chance to get another kill three days later."

Ross's eyes narrowed. "Did you ever have that feeling again?"

"Nope. I had a long talk with myself. You see, I thought I hated the Japs when I went overseas—couldn't wait to kill as many as I could. Well, hate is the wrong emotion. It's one that will get you killed. A cop doesn't hate the bank robber or the killer he's trying to arrest. But if necessary, he'll shoot to keep the guy from escaping to kill someone else. If he hates anything, it's what the criminal stands for.

"This business isn't much different. We're the nation's cops. Look at it this way: We're the hawks of the people world. Left unchecked, mice and rats would overrun the earth. So hawks help keep things in balance by killing them. They don't know this, of course. They kill to eat; it's an instinct.

"And that, Ross, is the trademark of a fighter pilot—the instinct to destroy the enemy, as efficiently and dispassionately as possible. From that day on, I considered myself a hawk. Japs were mice, threatening to overrun the world."

"And it worked."

"Yep. Now, I'll lay it on the line for you. I can hold you over for additional training for technical deficiencies—needs more flying time, gunnery practice, and the like. But I can't, and won't, hold anyone over because they aren't psychologically prepared for combat."

"You're calling me a coward," Ross snapped, his eyes blazing.

"No way. You've flown a combat tour in bombers—looked death and destruction straight in the eye and didn't blink. Given time to apply logic in a dogfight, you'd come up with the right answer. But right answers have to come instantaneously—a reflex. In other words, instinctively. No discredit. You're a brave officer and a great pilot, but with your attitude, you won't last five missions in a fighter."

Ross leaped to his feet. "That's bullshit, Major! Put me up against the best damn pilot you have in the squadron—the group. I'll prove you're wrong."

Cipolla studied Ross's white-lipped expression for a moment. "That pilot is me, Colyer. Get into your flying gear. Takeoff in thirty minutes. I'll whip your ass."

* * *

Ross threw his Mustang into the air with harsh, punishing movements. Within minutes, his throbbing rage turned to icy, detached composure. The stick and rudder became extensions of taut motor nerves. Without conscious effort he transmitted his every thought to the control surfaces.

A coin toss had designated Cipolla the aggressor. Where, when, and from what quarter would the attack come? Ross's first reaction was to climb. Take up a position at about thirty-five thousand feet, close to the '51's operational ceiling, and eliminate the major's high attack out of the sun. No, Ross knew that he was no match for the experienced combat ace upstairs. Smiling grimly he decided to do just the opposite. He nosed over and, leveling off at a hundred feet, took up a heading for sector five—the area reserved for simulated air-to-air combat.

Okay, he muttered under his breath as he streaked across the desolate terrain, come on down and mix it up. I can see you coming. By halving the sphere of the aggressor's attack, he could concentrate on the intensely blue sky, with only a few puffy cumulus to provide scanty, inadequate concealment. He reached the sector's northern boundary and reversed course. What was the cunning veteran up to?

Tight lipped, Ross systematically scanned the pristine dome of desert sky. There, almost on the horizon—a flash of sunlight reflecting off glass or metal. He lost it. Then suddenly he was staring a spinning, eleven-foot prop directly in the face. Jesus Christ! The racing airplane was coming head on. Not only head on, but slightly lower than Ross's own jackrabbit-scattering altitude.

About to haul the stick into his gut and break straight up, he hesitated. No, that's exactly what the sonofabitch wanted him to do. Cipolla would use his superior speed—he must have his ship past the redline—to loop above Ross and dive from behind for a shot a child couldn't miss.

At the last split second, Ross stood the Mustang on one wing without climbing. With its wingtip brushing cactus, he crammed on war-emergency power, then pulled the protesting craft into a gut-wrenching, climbing turn. Clawing for altitude, he searched ahead for his attacker. There! By God, he was above the other fighter. Hold the altitude advantage, all the way to forty thousand if necessary, he told himself. He felt the oxygen auto-mix regulator start feeding its dry, biting gas.

The powerful engine screamed at max-continuous-rated power, its supercharger at high boost. He watched the altimeter wind steadily upward. Cipolla's ship was still below the horizon. Ross's altitude advantage had dwindled, however, to a thousand, perhaps two thousand feet—not much. The altimeter's short hand, the one measuring tens of thousands of feet, crept close to four. Up here, the rarified atmosphere dictated a change in breathing. Instead of inhaling, he let the regulator feed his lungs with pressurized oxygen, then he forcibly expelled it. He was far above the student altitude limit. To hell with it. He was in a sudden-death struggle; there'd be no second chance.

Then Ross saw his adversary level off and turn away. All right! He turned to give chase. At last he could use that slim altitude advantage. The distance between the two ships narrowed. Ross frowned. Watch that sneaky bastard, he told himself. Not even the greenest novice would turn tail and flee in straight and level flight. What did his elusive quarry have in mind? It came to him in a flash—a long-ago description of a maneuver the Russians used with their slower P-39s against the superior Messerschmitts.

He focused his attention on the dark plume of exhaust pouring from Cipolla's engine. Suddenly it disappeared. Now. He hauled his own throttle to full idle and raised the nose. There he was. The ship ahead flipped into a snap roll. Had Ross remained straight and level at full power, he would have gone screaming past, unable to set up a firing pass. Cipolla would have neatly reversed their roles.

Calmly, coldly, Ross took up position for a classic firing pass from above and to one side. He started the gun camera running before the squadron commander's ship entered his sight picture. Then he held the target centered for a full three seconds. Ross swooped away in a victory roll and pressed the mike button. "Tallyho, Red Aggressor," he called cheerfully.

25 March 1944
New Delhi, India

Elliott Sprague assumed one of his more pugnacious poses and growled, "Gentlemen, I am dismayed at the negative reaction I detect regarding my B-29s. This airplane is capable of destroying the Japs' home islands in a matter of days—not weeks, not months, but *days*. I don't believe you appreciate the sophistication of this machine. Its central-fire-control system does what the B-17 boys thought the Forts could do—

penetrate deep without fighter cover. It can deliver a bomb load equal to a whole squadron of your B-25s and B-24s. Its radar bombsight gives it deadly accuracy either at night or during adverse weather conditions.

"Now, General Wolfe sent me over here with instructions to put airplanes over Japan not later than the third week of May. And that's a Joint Chiefs' mandate, by the way. I plan to do just that, gentlemen, if my boys have to service the damn planes all by themselves—load the bombs, pump the gas, and pick a target. There sure as hell isn't a shortage of command in my outfit; *I'm* ready to give the go order and lead the formation myself."

"You seem to be reading from a different directive than we have here in New Delhi, Elliott." The gaunt-faced speaker, Brig. Gen. Wesley Overholt, favored Sprague with a deceptively soft smile. With the exception of Major General Chennault, commander of the Fourteenth Air Force in China, Overholt and Sprague ranked the other eight members seated at the long teakwood table. "Unless you have something that supercedes General Order Ten-oh-four, then General Stilwell, as commander of all U.S. forces in the China-Burma-India theater of operations, will issue any ops orders designating targets, times, and the like."

"Twenty Bomber Command is a unique animal, Wes." Sprague adopted a patronizing tone. "The Joint Chiefs feel that so little is known in the field about the Superfort's performance envelope that the very heavy bombers will operate without regard for local priorities. Naturally, they had to provide a chain of command for administrative matters."

"Then why didn't they say that, Elliott?" Overholt asked mildly.

Sprague scowled and pounded the table. "Damnit, while we sit here squabbling, those Jap factories are enjoying one more day of turning out guns and airplanes. When you tell me that this base in China—Chengtu, is it?—has fuel and spare parts, we'll get this show on the road. We can argue the piddle-ass details afterward."

Chennault, although senior officer present, had remained silent throughout Overholt's and Sprague's sparring. With a faintly sardonic smile on his lean brown features, he asked, "How much runway do you need for a fully loaded takeoff, General Sprague?"

"Seven thousand feet, General."

"I see. And what will you require in the way of fuel, ammo, bombs, and the like at Chengtu?"

"These things are in the Matterhorn ops plan, General Chennault. By basing out of fields here in India, we can land at Chengtu fully armed, top up to six thousand gallons, and launch for the mission. Twelve aircraft at twenty-three tons per plane comes to roughly two hundred eighty tons of fuel per sortie."

"And you'll need another few tons for the return trip to India, I assume."

"Yes, sir. But that figure might be high. We'll land back at Chengtu with some fuel on board and return to our bases at Kharagpur with empty bomb bays."

"Of course." Chennault radiated sincere interest. "Now we need to know about your plans for turnaround. How many planes per week are we planning to put over Japan?"

Sprague swelled with importance. This was more like it, he told himself. "Another squadron of fifteen aircraft and crews are en route, sir. A buildup to one hundred combat-ready planes is set for the end of May."

It was Overholt's turn to smirk. He saw where Chennault was leading the unwary Sprague.

"Very well, Elliott," the Fourteenth Air Force commander said, "since I'm in charge of all air bases in China, I'm very much interested in your needs. To begin with, we don't have a field in all of China with a seven-thousand-foot runway."

"*What?*" Sprague erupted. "I have the report right here. Twentieth Air Force Headquarters was assured in February that the runway work at Chengtu would be completed by fifteen March."

"That was a good plan," the two-star added cheerfully. "I was most pleased when I read it. Unfortunately, the Chinese workers building the fields are not very familiar with deadlines. However, work was progressing quite satisfactorily when I was there last week. I'd say the runway extension will support limited operations by the end of April."

Chennault ignored Sprague's spluttered retort and continued. "The supply situation is even more sticky. As of today we have twelve hundred tons stockpiled for Matterhorn at Kunming, the China end of the Hump run. We can move it the six hundred miles to Chengtu at a rate of about twenty tons per day. No trucks, you know, just small boats and carts.

"We had a good month for Hump tonnage in February—ten thousand tons. Sixteen hundred tons of that are earmarked for Matterhorn, of course. But if we are to support your plan of a hundred sorties per week, well, we wouldn't have that much materiel stockpiled at Chengtu until . . . oh, let's say sometime in 1946."

Sprague flushed angrily. Realizing that he was being mocked, he snarled, "This is ridiculous. I am offering you the means to leapfrog this bogged-down ground war. When facing an octopus, kill the head, then use the tentacles for soup. When can I see General Stilwell? A reevaluation of priorities is obviously called for. Allocate all Hump tonnage to Matterhorn for ninety days, and the Japs will fold. In the meantime, I'll fly missions directly from Kharagpur with reduced bomb loads."

"General Stilwell is with the task force in Burma trying to recover Myitkyina. I doubt you want to make the trip," Overholt observed. "Look, Elliott, we're not being obstructionists. Placing the VHBs over Tokyo is uppermost in everyone's mind. But, as you can see, there are some very real obstacles. You can add to the list that the runway extensions at Kharagpur and Chakulia aren't scheduled to be finished until early May. That's the very earliest that you can take off at max gross weight.

"Now, I suggest that we meet after lunch, Elliott, and I'll brief you on the situation here in the CBI. It's a bit complicated and requires some explanation."

Chennault lit a fresh cigar and regarded General Overholt with a wintry smile. "Since I'm apparently not invited to your briefing, Wes, let me make sure you understand my position—the reason I'm here, in fact. My crews in China are living off the land, buying rice and cigarets from the Chinese. There's only enough fuel for two sorties per week, which is probably just as well since there aren't spare parts to support more. If you consider fiddling with supply allocations, bear in mind that the Fourteenth is the only thing keeping the Japs from marching, unmolested, all the way from Peking south to their army in Indochina. That route passes through the bases protecting Chengtu, by the way."

"Since General Chennault has expressed his concerns, I'd best get those of SEAC on the record, don't you know." This from a ruddy-complected liaison officer wearing the uniform of a British army brigadier. "Lord Mountbatten is most concerned that we won't be able to honor our commitments regarding the invasion of Burma. It wouldn't do to go mucking about with allocation priorities, don't you see."

Only the swishing whispers of overhead fans stirring the humid air disturbed the ensuing silence. There was no formal statement of adjournment. The conferees just rose and wandered outside exchanging desultory pleasantries, leaving Sprague sitting in tight-lipped silence.

* * *

"I decided to postpone a formal briefing, Elliott," Overholt said. He and Sprague were the only occupants of the headquarters' war room. As if to emphasize the informal nature of the meeting, the nattily uniformed officer seated himself on a tabletop. "I thought an off-the-record chat might be more productive, just now. I don't blame you for being upset and frustrated over the inability to get on with your mission. The CBI won't compare with operations in Europe, however."

"Wes, you people have a ground-army mentality," Sprague snapped. "You're pouring resources into a futile effort to beat the Jap in his own environment. I was briefed before I left Washington, for Christ's sake. I know all about Stilwell's obsession with driving the Japs out of Burma so he can build a road to China. And Chiang Kai-shek's inept Chinese armies led by corrupt warlords. Everyone around here has his own little empire. You're all running around in circles, chasing your tails. Well, I'm not going to get sucked into that game. I'm here for one purpose, by God—to drop enough bombs on the stinking Jap islands to sink them."

Overholt sighed. "Elliott, like it or not, you were sucked in, as you put it, the minute you stepped off your airplane yesterday. Let me put you in the picture. Otherwise you're just going to be butting your head against the wall."

Crossing to the organizational chart, he tapped the first of two boxes along the top row. "Let's start with Lord Mountbatten, commander in chief of the Southeast Asia Command. He's a Royal Navy admiral and a good officer, but the British are more concerned about holding India than attacking Japan. Since we Yanks supply most of the arms involved, Mountbatten made Stilwell his deputy commander. But SEAC is basically a strategic planning organization; Mountbatten doesn't actually *command* anything.

"Next we have Generalissimo Chiang Kai-shek, Supreme Allied Commander in China." Overholt pointed to the other top box. "Stilwell is his chief of staff, but since there are no Allied ground troops in China, the position is virtually meaningless. Chiang rules all of China that the Japanese or the Communists don't, and he has a direct pipeline to President Roosevelt. He also controls a hundred divisions of Chinese troops, but he's more interested in bottling up the Communists in north China than in driving out the Japs. It appears he's leaving that job for us. Yet he continually presses Roosevelt for more arms and supplies, arguing that he's not sure how much longer he can hold out. We walk a fine line, providing him with just enough material to protect Chennault's bases in China.

"So we now come to Lieutenant General Joseph Stilwell. Among the many hats he wears is that of the commander of all the U.S. troops over here. Now, General Stilwell is one of the most brilliant military strategists we have, but he's a ground officer. He figures we won't defeat the Japs until we march into Tokyo. He mostly wants us to airlift supplies and to give close ground support to the Chinese troops that Chiang lent him to retake Burma.

"That's my boss's job. General Stratemeyer"—Overholt pointed to a box farther down the chart—"is Stilwell's air adviser. He uses the Tenth Air Force to defend our bases here in India, to support General Stilwell in Burma, and to keep the Japs from shooting our transports out of the sky."

Overholt eyed Sprague's dazed expression and smiled. "Finally we come to the wild card in the deck," he continued. "General Chennault. He is a legend, of course. What he did as civilian commander of the American Volunteer Group is astonishing. In the process he became Chiang's favorite son and still has his ear, a situation that Stilwell finds troublesome. Stilwell and Chennault differ on basic strategy. Claire thinks he can defeat the entire Japanese empire with his Fourteenth Air Force, *if* he gets enough supplies. 'Vinegar Joe' says it'll take the infantry to get the job done, and since he controls the distribution of all supplies in the theater, you'd think that would be the end of the argument. But it's uncanny how often Roosevelt sides with Chennault.

"So, welcome to our happy little family, Elliott. Now, here's the master plan—one that has the general support of all parties, at least for now, anyway. We retake Myitkyina in northern Burma and reopen the shorter, lower altitude air route to China. We build a truck route from Ledo, India, through Myitkyina and hook up with the old Burma Road to China. Next we lay a POL pipeline from Budge-Budge to Kunming. This logistics thing must be whipped before we can even begin to consider a full-scale move into east China."

Sprague's battle signs—bushy black eyebrows touching, his lantern jaw thrust forward—signaled his anger. "General Wolfe and the Joint Chiefs think otherwise, Wes. Those bases around Chengtu must be finished and supplied . . . and defended."

Overholt's friendly demeanor grew chilly. "Elliott, don't flaunt JCS policy, please. You're a member of an elite outfit, but your B-29s can't perform feats of magic. First of all, it will take thirty Chinese divisions to provide protection for VHBs inside China. The Japs can't afford to let us set up shop that close to Tokyo. They'll probably throw everything they have into an effort to destroy the threat."

"What the hell are Chennault's fighters supposed to be doing?" Sprague rasped.

"The Fourteenth is on the ropes as it is, trying to help the Chinese armies keep the Japs north of the Yellow River and protecting their own bases. It always comes back to logistics, Elliott. Every spare part, every drop of av-gas, every bomb and round of ammo arrives at either the docks in Karachi or Calcutta. From there it must be moved up the Brahmaputra River valley to India's Assam Province. Five hundred miles by barge, broken-down truck, and a narrow-gauge railroad. And during the monsoon season, which lasts from June until October, travel slows to a crawl.

"Next, it crosses another five hundred miles by air across the Hump to Kunming, and you're still six hundred miles across primitive country from Chengtu. They use pack animals, small riverboats, and alcohol-burning trucks to move it the rest of the way. I even saw coolies rolling single drums of av-gas along the road.

"I heard an apt comparison the other day. Assume that during the War of 1812, you wanted to fly B-29s out of San Francisco. After a twelve-thousand-mile sea voyage, your supplies reached Boston—that's Karachi. Using the transportation system existing at that time, you moved it overland thirteen hundred miles to Kansas City—that's Calcutta. There you hauled it five hundred miles up a narrow, twisting river valley to Denver—that's Chabua, India. Next, you had airplanes with a service ceiling of twelve thousand feet fly it through twenty-thousand-foot mountains to Salt Lake City—that's Kunming, China. From there you took it overland to San Francisco—Chengtu. Get the picture?"

Sprague considered Overholt's words in silence, his lower lip outthrust, his face an impassive mask. Finally, he stood and strolled to where situation maps covered one entire wall. Hands thrust in his hip pockets, he examined the maze of lines and symbols while he talked.

"Unbelievable, Wes. Un-goddamn-believable. General Wolfe is going to throw a foaming-at-the-mouth fit when he gets the true picture. If you can arrange a Blue Streak priority, I'm going to send my group CO back on the first ATC plane available to give K.B. a firsthand briefing. This isn't a situation report I want to put in writing.

"I can't let those high-priced airplanes just sit there on the ramp, Wes. I can fill up some time with training missions, but after I set up headquarters, I believe I'll go to Kunming and see Chennault's bombing operation close up. Could be there are some targets we could take out from Kharagpur. We can operate out of five thousand feet, if we keep takeoff weight below a hundred and twenty thousand pounds."

Overholt eyed the suddenly subdued bomber commander with wary suspicion. "You wouldn't be thinking of taking sides, would you Elliott?"

Sprague turned and regarded the deputy air commander with a look of injured innocence. "Wes, look, I speak my mind—call the shots as I see them. But I'm a team player. Once I have my marching orders, I don't question them. I'm convinced the VHBs can shorten this war by a year or more. But I've had my say. That will be the last you'll hear of it. Okay?"

25 March 1944
Calcutta, India

Sprague watched a white-turbanned room-service waiter replace empty plates with coffee and brandy. His guest, Col. Morton Sims, observed, "So we're all dressed up with no place to go. I can't believe they would let us rush over here before the goddamn runways were even finished."

A bemused smile softened Sprague's features as he regarded the strident Calcutta street scene beneath the balcony outside his suite. "Events do take unusual turns in this business, Mort. No, sir, a man never knows what to expect next." His manner became brisk and businesslike. "Now, when you get home, tell General Wolfe that I sent you personally because the matter is too sensitive to trust to official channels. Tell him I haven't seen Stilwell; he's in Burma right now. His staff is doing everything they can, but Wolfe had best warn General Arnold that it will be the end of May before we can launch a mission. Conditions here are unbelievably adverse.

"Next, call General Wolfenbarger. Tell him I asked you to meet with him privately—take him to dinner or something. Tell *him* that placing Twenty Bomber Command under Stilwell will be a disaster. The man is almost never at his headquarters and can't be reached. The three-star platoon leader is in the jungle leading a futile attempt to take back some outpost he lost in '42. His staff has done nothing but put roadblocks in my path.

"Tell him also that Chennault isn't the answer. The man has delusions of grandeur and is more interested in helping his old pal, the generalissimo, fight the Chinese Communists than he is in defeating Japan. Come hell or high water, I am going to launch a mission by the first of May. He can avoid the flak by going ahead with the plan we discussed before I left—rescind General Order Ten-oh-four and place the Twentieth Air Force under direct control of the Joint Chiefs of Staff."

Colonel Sims stirred his coffee and avoided meeting Sprague's fiercely intent gaze. "You have a problem of some kind, Mort?" Sprague snapped.

"Sir, I'd feel a whole lot better if maybe you could give me something in writing about all this."

"Mort, what did I promise you if this operation was an unqualified success?"

Sims gulped. "A—ah—wing and a star."

"You seemed pleased at the time. Has something changed?"

"But, sir. What if—"

Sprague waved his hand, shutting off the discomfited Sims's protest. "Mort, we're both going to retire in our present grade if we don't put the Twentieth Air Force on every front page in the States. We're in a backwater theater taking orders from a worn-out infantry three-star. Do you see him letting that happen?"

"Probably not."

Sprague snorted. "Probably, hell. The war will be over before we get our first mission off the ground. Now, get on the fucking team, Mort. And when you get to Washington, be convincing. Do you hear me?"

Chapter Six

10 April 1944
Miami, Florida

Ross winced as he tossed his bulging B-4 and canvas duffel bags into the base cab's trunk. Where the hell was he headed that required so many shots? Dengue fever, for Christ's sake—he'd never heard of it. His arm felt as though someone had hit it with a meat ax. He settled into the sagging rear seat and told the bored-looking cabby, "The ATC terminal."

The grizzled driver, a mournful expression on his gaunt features, flicked a glance in the rearview mirror. "Shippin' out?"

"Looks that way," Ross responded.

"With them two rows of ribbons, I'd say this ain't your first trip."

"You'd be right."

Unabashed by Ross's cryptic answers, the man continued. "Got two boys of my own in. The oldest—he's a flyer, too—he's been missin' in action goin' on a month now. War Department telegram said he was on a mission—Germany, I reckon. He's a gunner on one of them big bombers."

Ross regretted his brusque manner with the loquacious oldster. He opened his mouth to offer commiseration and discovered he didn't know what to say. Memories of missions past flashed through his mind—savage fighter attacks, relentless flak barrages, planes tumbling from the protective womb of their box formation, his crew members counting chutes. It had all seemed so impersonal then. You didn't know the victims—didn't want to.

The man was groping for reassurance, Ross realized. He'd noticed the man's use of the present tense: He *is* a gunner. It would be so easy to say: Oh, I expect you'll be getting a letter from him any day now. A lot of them walk out, you know. Or, he may be tucked away in some POW camp. The Jerries aren't noted for putting flyers on POW lists right off. It would be a lie. He felt faintly irritated at the man's placing the war on such an intimate basis. It stirred up feelings in Ross he'd rather not dwell on.

Cryhowski and Reed were his men, killed while under his command. Why hadn't he made the effort to visit their families? He'd made a vow that he would, that day in Ankara as he marched behind the cart carrying their coffins to the air terminal. Okay, he'd written long letters. He told himself that he would have made the trips if his leave hadn't been cut short.

Be honest, Colyer, he admonished himself. You didn't know what the hell to tell a grieving family. Something like: They were brave men who gave their all for their country, so you and I can be free? That's bullshit. They were just ordinary guys, trying to stay alive while they did what had to be done. They were unlucky. They would have hooted with laughter if anyone had tried to tie lofty, patriotic motives to their actions. But you didn't talk that way to civilians, he'd discovered. Even Janet, the ultimate pragmatist, had given him a quizzical look when he'd tried to explain his feelings to her after the Pearl Harbor debacle. Oh, he knew guys in uniform who mouthed words like that—about duty, honor, and country. He didn't trust them.

The cab drew to a halt in front of a rambling frame building. A sign proclaimed it to be the 7344th Air Transport Wing's passenger terminal. He huddled in the chilly drizzle and waited while the driver extracted his baggage. Pressing a dollar bill in the driver's gnarled hand, he grasped a bony shoulder and mumbled, "Keep hoping for the best. Don't ever give up hope."

Ross made his way through milling bodies to a chest-high counter, dropped his baggage to the floor, and handed his papers to a sharp-faced corporal standing behind the counter. After carefully checking Ross's War Department AGO identification card and shot record, he spread the orders on the plywood countertop.

Ross scanned the littered waiting room. Through a fog of cigaret smoke hanging in the humid, overheated atmosphere, he spotted the pair of lieutenants he'd met in the transient officers' quarters the day before. Slumped on a wooden bench in a far corner, both looked badly hung over. He grinned. Rostock, the tall, blond one, had left for "town" early last night, announcing his determination to "get his ashes hauled" one more time before shipping out. Gantry, the shorter, dark-haired one, appeared to be suffering from a similar night of debauchery.

Ross turned as the corporal bundled up his documents. "You're Blue Streak all the way, sir. Nobody except maybe a four-star general is going to bump you. Somebody over there is sure anxious to get his hands on you."

For the first time Ross realized that he and the two nonrated lieutenants were the only company-grade officers among the waiting group of passengers. Eagles, stars, and braid adorned all but a warrant officer with an attaché case fixed to his wrist by a thin chain, and four civilians wearing tan military-style raincoats and dark homburg hats. The C-54 was a VIP flight, it appeared. How, then, did he and the two lieutenants rate? Rostock and Gantry had divulged that they were intelligence officers—no details. Okay, so where did that leave him?

He grinned at the clerk. "You say I'm Blue Streak all the way. Where, may I ask, does 'all the way' take me?"

Ross received a chilly look in response. "Plane lands in Bermuda for fuel. After that, I dunno." The corporal turned his head and made a point of looking at a wall poster behind the counter. It read: LOOSE LIPS SINK SHIPS. Properly chastised, Ross wormed his way to where Rostock and Gantry dozed. "Okay, everybody, fall in outside for calisthenics. Hup, hup, hup," he called cheerfully.

Rostock regarded his tormentor through one bloodshot eye. "As a stand-up comic, you face a short career with a gruesome ending, Captain. Show some respect for the terminally ill."

Ross chuckled and crowded onto the bench alongside the suffering pair. "You can sleep on the plane," he said without sympathy. "Right now I'd like some dope on where your orders say you're headed."

"Oh?"

"Yeah. Look around. This is a VIP flight. My orders give me a Blue Streak priority. Do yours?"

"That's what the man said—whatever it means."

"It means we'll still be on that plane after all this brass is bumped," Ross said. "Now, that makes me wonder. I'm just a run-of-the-mill throttle bender. What makes you two so valuable?"

"Intelligence—photo interpretation."

"I'll be damned." Ross shook his head. "Do your orders give a destination?"

"Yep. APO New York, Station Seventy-eight. I'd guess since we're going the southern route, that's a headquarters in Italy."

"I don't think so," Ross said slowly. "That's my destination as well, and I don't believe I'll be flying P-51s in Italy."

Both lieutenants now showed signs of interest. Gantry favored Ross with a scornful look. "The flight crew is wearing suntans. They're going someplace where it's warm."

"You're right about that," Ross muttered. "Gents, I think I know where we're headed."

"Yeah?"

"Yeah. Only place outside of England with Mustangs is the China-Burma-India show. Put any thought of chasing dark-eyed beauties through Rome out of your mind, lads. The only thing you're apt to find out there to chase is a water buffalo."

12 April 1944
Cairo, Egypt

Ross and the pair of dejected intelligence officers sat on their duffel bags and smoked while they waited to board the battered-looking C-46. Cairo represented the end of their first-class travel. From there, transportation would be via the weekly shuttle to Calcutta. Ross's surmise was confirmed by one of the C-46 pilots. Station 78 was one of three hastily constructed airfields around Calcutta.

Lieutenant Rostock fieldstripped his cigaret butt and observed, "That has to be the ugliest fucking airplane I've ever seen." His expression was morose, his voice edged with disgust. Both young officers regarded their future with bitter dismay.

Ross removed his cap and wiped away a trickle of sweat before it reached the corner of his eye. The flies here, he remembered, fought determined battles for every drop of precious moisture. "She's a workhorse, though," he said. "I was talking to the pilots at breakfast. They haul eight thousand pounds of freight over twenty-thousand-foot mountains in that beast. That's all a B-24 can carry with *four* engines."

No one commented. They just regarded the dirty, oil-streaked Curtiss Commando with unspoken dislike. Its bulging shape—some compared it to a pregnant whale—its twin engines set close to the fuselage, and a disproportionately thin wing were all designed for utility, not beauty. Ross needed no explanation for the three evenly spaced patches of new aluminum on the horizontal stabilizer. The ship had been in a brush with the enemy.

A quick look inside verified his suspicion that they faced an uncomfortable ride. An aluminum bench along one side was shaped to receive six human bottoms. An assortment of crates and sacks lashed to the floor with a cargo net took up the remaining space.

A Jeep arrived in a swirl of dust and halted in front of them. Three men dismounted; two had tanned and wrinkled skin and the third wore a rumpled set of OD fatigues. Ross recognized the two pilots he'd met at breakfast. "Well, we have a crew," he observed. "Guess we're about to get this show on the road."

Gantry slid to the sandy verge alongside the parking ramp, propped his back against his duffel bag and muttered, "I'll believe it when I see it. Wake me when we're ready to go; I couldn't bear to be left behind."

The fatigue-clad crew chief strolled to the airplane and started a preflight check. The fliers hunkered beside Ross. The pilot, a soft-spoken Texan, said, "Be a few more minutes. Got one more piece of cargo. Soon's it's on board, we'll get under way."

"I just hope it isn't a big piece," Rostock responded. "That cargo compartment looks pretty full to me."

"Nope. Just a mailbag—and movies. Christ, I wouldn't dare go back without mail and movies. That's about the only reason we make this trip. Well," the pilot stood, "that looks like our deliveryman. Time to get the gear in the wells. Look, Captain, if you want to come forward after we get to cruise altitude, the engineer's jump seat is a better ride than those bucket seats."

Ross squeezed into the little folding seat behind the C-46's throttle quadrant and watched Arabia's vast, empty landscape slide by below. Dun-colored sand dunes stretched in all directions as far as the eye could see. "Christ, I thought the country around Benghazi was bad. That stuff down there is scary."

"Bet your ass," the pilot—Kendrick, he'd introduced himself—agreed. "It's still early and only about a hundred degrees. By summer it'll hit a hundred and twenty. Wind blows day and night. It's clear today, but a sandstorm can kick up in less than half an hour—visibility at eight thousand feet goes to zero. I've seen Aden—that's our first stop—go below minimums after you have the field in sight from twenty to thirty miles out."

Ross sat silently, letting the monotonous drone of the twin Pratt & Whitney engines and the warmth from a brassy sun streaming through the windows lull him into lazy contentment. Rousing, he asked, "You fly the Hump?"

"At least one trip a week. Guys line up for the Cairo shuttle run; it's like a vacation. But anyone who's C-46 qualified flies the Hump."

"A rough ride, huh?"

"It can be. The friggin' weather in those mountains is fierce—turbulence, ice, hundred-mile-an-hour winds. You lose an engine and you're hurtin'. One of our guys had an engine fire about a month ago and had to jump. He walked out—some tribesmen helped him hide from the Japs. His story will flat curl your hair. There are natives in there who still use blowguns and poison darts."

"I saw some patches on the tail surfaces," Ross said. "Flak or fighters?"

"Jap fighters. The only antiaircraft guns they have are twenty- and thirty-seven-millimeter stuff. We stay above it."

"What kind of fighters?"

"Early-model Zeroes, mostly; a few Oscars. But they haul ass anytime they see our fighters, so we've only lost a few transports to them. They're rotten pilots, really. I reckon they send their green pilots here for seasoning before they go to the Pacific. Their bombers are something else, though. They're good.

"But then, you may not be flying out of a Calcutta base. You know which outfit you're gonna be assigned to?"

"Don't have the slightest clue. In fact, I'm curious as hell why they were in such a big rush to get me over here. Are P-51 pilots that scarce?"

"I wouldn't know about that." Kendrick made a minute course correction with the autopilot, then added, "I'd guess that you're going to one of the fighter outfits earmarked for eastern China."

"China? *East* China?"

"Yeah. All I know is o-club gossip, you understand, but things are getting hot. Our Hump tonnage to Kunming on the China end has about doubled. With the Burma Road closed, everything, including av-gas, has to be airlifted. The word is that they're stockpiling supplies to support B-29 strikes on Japan from a base in China. I suppose they plan to use the '51s for escort."

"Basing B-29s in China has to be the craziest damn thing I ever heard. Good God, it takes a small army to keep a '29 in the air.

They have engine problems, radar problems, electrical glitches. . . . A guy from Smoky Hill Air Base in Kansas told me they're lucky to have a forty percent in-commission rate. And that's next door to the damn factory."

The sad-faced transport pilot gave an unconcerned shrug. "I don't doubt you, but this operation doesn't make a lot of sense anyway. Divide command between a limey admiral, a U.S. Army ground-pounder, and a hotshot fighter pilot like Chennault, and you got a screwed-up situation even before you start engines. Thank God the Air Transport Command is a separate service.

"But the B-29 business is no rumor. God only knows what they're going to do when they get here, but they're on the way. And there's a mountain of fifty-five-gallon drums of av-gas waiting for them at Kunming. I know that for damn sure. I think I must have hauled most of it myself."

Ross, bewildered, could only shake his head. "Okay," he asked, "what about China? Are any '51s stationed there now?"

"Not that I know of. Fourteenth Air Force has some P-47s, P-40s—left over from Chennault's American Volunteer Group—B-25s, and B-24s. They're mostly on bases over in the Hsiang River valley, south of the big Jap base at Hankow. They're trying to keep the Japs from chewing up the Chinese army—an exercise in futility. No, the Tenth Air Force, the India-Burma outfit, has some Mustangs, and you can bet Chennault will get his share. Come to think of it, I heard that the Fourteenth is forming a squadron at Kharagpur, just outside Calcutta. Betcha that's your new outfit. Get organized and train there, then deploy to China."

Ross frowned. "This begins to sound suspiciously like the way the Ploesti mission was put together: generals running in circles and changing their minds. We lost only sixty percent that day."

Kendrick nodded. "You're not far off. A couple of the B-24 crews at Kharagpur flew in that raid. There's a Colonel Halverson as well. I understand he started to China with a squadron of B-24s back in '42. Same idea as now, bomb Japan from China, but the Japs beat him to the base."

"This Chennault," Ross said, "he's quite the hero back in the States. What kind of guy is he?"

"He's a flyer's general." Kendrick sat up in his seat and showed a measure of enthusiasm. "I met him once at Kunming. His guys hadn't had PX supplies, steaks, or U.S. booze for over a month. He wanted to know if we were carrying any, and if so, who the hell was getting the stuff.

"Turns out, he wasn't being cheated. After the word came down to stockpile gas and ammo for the '29s, we haven't been carrying any goodies. He wasn't happy, but any general who will take the trouble to check up on things like that takes care of his troops."

Ross, gazing at the desolate terrain below with unseeing eyes, lapsed into glum contemplation of the future. Colonel Wilson's reaction to his statement that flying fighters might be "fun" returned to haunt him.

18 April 1944
Kharagpur, India

The nameplate was obviously hand carved. Ross admired the intricate swirls forming a rampant dragon coiled around the engraved words MILTON KING above smaller script that proclaimed King to be a major, U.S. Army Air Corps. Ross mentally added, and field-grade asshole.

He curbed his smoldering anger and waited while the sallow-complexioned officer let him stand before the desk as he perused Ross's 201 file. An apt description of King's features was "pinched," he thought. The man's face looked as though it had been placed in a vise at an early age, crowding his dark, beady eyes close together and reducing his nose to a knifelike protuberance. King had a habit of smoothing his straight black hair—slightly longer than regulation, and plastered to his skull like a helmet—as he read.

After Ross had thrown a snappy salute and rendered the customary, "Captain Colyer, reporting for duty, sir," the major's curt, "Stand at ease, Captain," had wiped the broad smile from Ross's face. Nothing had transpired since to induce a feeling of budding friendship with his new commander.

Major King tossed the folder aside, leaned back, and inserted a dark brown panatella between thin lips. "Well, shit," he said. "I need a qualified operations officer. I coaxed the general into sending an emergency requisition—insisted on a Blue Streak priority—and what the hell do they send me? A cub. A guy just out of school.

"I have a dozen new pilots on the way. I have fifteen new P-51Bs being unloaded in Calcutta right now, and exactly thirty days to get the squadron combat ready."

Ross spoke through stiff lips. “I’m sorry to be a disappointment to you, Major. But, with all due respect, I’m confident I can have your pilots combat ready as soon as anyone else. After all, I was ops officer for my B-24 outfit for a short time, I graduated tops in my instructor pilot course, I saw combat in the ETO, and I aced the Mustang transition course.”

King snorted. “Your record as a bomber pilot doesn’t impress me, Colyer. The way they hand out medals in the ETO is a joke, and a Purple Heart at Pearl doesn’t say much for your fighting skills, either. Nor does the fact that you diverted to a neutral country when you got into trouble on the Ploesti mission. As for your fighter experience, you’ll find flying here is a bit different than boring holes in the traffic pattern over Texas.”

“Sir, the man who passed my air-to-air work, a Major Cipolla, served with General Chennault’s ‘Flying Tigers.’ He’s a tough instructor.”

“That AVG was a bunch of drunks,” King sneered. “We have only a few of them left around. I’m surprised that your man is still alive.”

Ross didn’t trust himself to respond. He stood silently while the major continued. “No, as soon as I saw your personnel records, I got the general to give me Captain Oscar Holt for my ops officer. Holt has more than fifty missions under his belt. As far as I’m concerned, that makes him senior to you. You’ll be ‘C’ Flight commander.

“At any rate, you, Holt, and I will go to Chabua tomorrow. This base is too crowded for us to fly training missions from, so the ATC will let us squeeze into one of their bases six hundred miles northeast of here in Assam. That’s the jump-off point for the Hump run. The general let me have three B models until we get our new ones, so we’ll set up there and get ready for the rest of our planes and crews. You may even get an operational mission or two, flying escort for the transports across the Hump.”

Chapter Seven

22 April 1944
Chabua Army Airfield, India

Ross stood at Capt. O. B. Holt's shoulder and watched the new ops officer trace their route on a map spread on the ops counter. "We don't have the fuel or spare parts to support a regular training program, Ross, so we'll combine your theater orientation with an armed recce flight. This line, here, is the northern route from Chabua over the Hump to Kunming, China. Today, we'll cap the circuit to about here, at the Burma border. Things are quiet just now. But every so often the Japs will sneak a couple of Zeroes up from their bases around Myitkyina. They like to hang in the foothills and hit the transports from below, so keep your eyes down more than up. At the same time we're supposed to watch for any unusual surface activity—truck convoys, troop movements, and the like. No engagement, however, unless we bounce enemy aircraft.

"The Japs own Burma—and all of Indochina for that matter. They have closed all roads from our ports in India to China, so the ATC airlift across the Hump is China's sole existing lifeline. If you go down in Burma, you've had a real bad day. The Burmese, with the exception of some hill tribes, are Jap sympathizers and will hand you over without a second thought. The valleys are jungle like you never believed existed. Cobras, hungry tigers, goddamn python snakes that can swallow a small cow, mosquitoes that carry every disease they can load up with, temperatures in the nineties, and three hundred inches of rain a year."

"I can see that the forty-five automatic and foot-long pig-sticker they gave me at supply ain't just window dressing," Ross muttered.

"Bet your ass. If you do luck out and walk out of the jungle, you're in ten-thousand-foot mountains with two tribes of headhunters. The few Hump pilots who walk out after being shot down tend to drink a lot more than they used to."

Holt folded the chart and stuck it in a knee pocket of his flight suit. Ross couldn't avoid noticing that the captain's bars were brand-new additions to his well-worn garment. "Ross, I gotta say this." The ops officer studied the floor as he spoke. "I know what's happened, and I know it must piss you off. To get a hurry-up assignment for a job that's immediately jerked out from under you—well, I know it wouldn't set well with *me*. I'm going to do the best job I know how. I just hope you will come to me first if you have a bitch."

"In other words, don't undermine your efforts with the other pilots behind your back," Ross replied. "Don't worry. The situation between King and me is my problem. I'll handle it in my own way, and I won't let my personal feelings screw up the job you face. You've finished fifty missions over here. When you talk, I'll listen. Fair enough?"

It seemed to Ross that Holt's stocky figure relaxed slightly; his chubby features, resembling a pixyish cherub, split in a grin. He extended a hand. "We'll get along. I got that feeling."

Major King trudged inside the ops shack and wiped his sweaty forehead. "Whew," he grumbled. "I thought Calcutta was bad, but it was paradise compared to this hellhole. Mosquitoes so big they could be CAA certified, the heat, lousy chow, and living in tents, for Christ's sake. I'll be glad when we get organized and move out."

The disgruntled CO strolled to the counter and glanced at Holt's map. "Well, Colyer, looks like you're going to get the dollar tour. Don't let him get lost, O.B." The major flashed a sardonic grin and walked into the adjoining room.

Ross, ignoring the inane chatter of the personal-equipment NCO, drew his flying gear in a daze of cold rage. He recalled his hostile reception at the RTU. Colonel Thompson's initial comments had been scathing, but the man had shaken Ross's hand at the graduation party and growled, "I was wrong about you, Colyer. Anyone who can stick it to Cappy in a dogfight is good—damn good. It cost me a forty-pounder of Red Label, though, and for that I'll never forgive you."

Thompson had been tough, but at least he had been objective. King, the supercilious sonofabitch, came across entirely different. There seemed to be a personal, more than professional, motive in his sarcasm. Okay, Major, Ross told himself, one day—one day it's going to be just me and you, head to head at thirty thousand feet. You're not the man Colonel Thompson turned out to be; you'll never have the good grace to apologize. But we'll know, just between the two of us, that I waxed your ass in simulated combat.

Ross trudged across the searing, gravel parking ramp toward the '51. He regarded the aircraft's Form-1 with dismay. Red diagonals covered the first two pages—items requiring repair or replacement but not constituting a safety-of-flight restriction. He scanned them quickly: Canopy seal leaks, fuel pressure gauge inop, left windshield quarter panel cracked, excessive background noise on low-frequency radio, outside air temp gauge missing, gun harmonization overdue. . . . Ross stopped halfway through and gave the crew chief a quizzical look.

The grizzled NCO shook his head. "Parts, Cap'n. There ain't a plane on the line what don't need a major overhaul. I do my best."

Ross grinned. "I'm sure you do, Chief. I'll do my best not to put any more dings in 'er." He let the glum-expressioned sergeant help him get strapped in. As he did, Ross felt earthbound cares slip away. The old magic returned, as it always did, like the feel of pulling on a favorite pair of hunting boots. He ran the before-starting-engine checklist with quick familiarity and spun a forefinger in the ground crew's direction. The big in-line engine caught on the first revolution and settled into a stuttering rumble. He grinned; the crew chief might be hampered by a shortage of parts, but the power plant was clearly not a victim of neglect.

He saw Holt's ship waddle onto the taxiway. Releasing the parking brake, Ross added power and swung in trail. The plane lurched and bumped over the uneven clay and gravel surface. And they tell me this is one of the better strips, he thought, shaking his head. Takeoff should be a real thrill.

Braking to a stop in the engine-run-up position, he waved to a clutch of turbanned construction workers, forced to the sidelines until after takeoff. The grinning, brown-skinned natives squatted alongside an oxcart, their sole means of transporting the broken rocks and gravel needed to fill the ever-recurring potholes. A pot bubbled above a small fire—tea undoubtedly.

Chest-high tea shrubs lined both sides of the runway. During the last century Scottish planters, Ross learned, had carved their tea plantations out of the jungle covering the narrow Brahmaputra River valley. Beyond the swirls of dust and smoke obscuring the horizon lurked the majestic Himalayas.

His headset crackled. "Alleycat Flight, cleared for takeoff. Over."

The lead ship eased onto the runway. "Alleycat rolling," Holt drawled.

Ross added power to maintain position off lead's left wing. The Mustangs, as if happy to be free of their unnatural environment, skipped over one last runway patch and clawed for altitude. Ross heard the gear thump into the up-and-locked position and eased the throttle back from METO power. After catching a glimpse of the gaggle of mud-stuccoed, thatch-roofed buildings making up the base, he followed Holt's turn toward the snowcapped peaks emerging above the haze layer. Suddenly they were in blinding sunlight. The orange disk hung in a cobalt blue dome like a vengeful, omniscient orb.

Ross switched radio channels as the tower operator advised, "Cleared to Spyglass on channel D, Alleycat. Good hunting."

He diverted his attention from Holt's aircraft long enough to scan the instrument panel. All the gauges—at least those still operational—were in the green. A steady red light on the left console verified that his guns, armed immediately after takeoff, were ready. The altimeter passed through ten thousand feet. The oxygen automix's little blinking eye told him that he was receiving an adequate supply of that life-sustaining gas.

Still climbing, Alleycat Flight crossed the first range of jagged peaks. Ross guessed that the snow line existed down to about the eight-thousand-foot level. Beyond, towering peaks soared well above the Mustangs' fifteen-thousand-foot altitude. The view was breathtaking. Hurricane-force winds whipped streamers of diamondlike ice crystals from needle-sharp pinnacles. He tore his gaze away from the spellbinding panorama. Watch the lower valleys, he told himself disgustedly. Don't be a total green bean on your first sortie.

As if to reinforce his vigilance, Spyglass interrupted the silence with a crisp, "Alleycat, this is Spyglass. Bandits reported in sector Baker-

King at ten thirty-seven local. Flight of four at medium altitude, course south-southwest. Over."

Ross heard Holt's laconic, "Roger, Spyglass. Alleycat will be overhead in one-five minutes. Stay tuned for further exciting developments." Then, "Tuck it in, Two. Looks like we may get some action after all."

Minutes ticked by. Ross divided his attention between holding position on Holt and scanning the jumbled landscape below. "Tallyho, Two. Two o'clock low," Holt called out. A hesitation, then, "I'm breaking now. Cover me."

Ross allowed himself time for a wry grin. Holt's reassurance that he respected Ross's flying ability hadn't kept the fifty-mission veteran from voicing a last-minute emphasis on standing operating procedures. After allowing a two-hundred-yard interval to develop between his ship and lead, he followed, searching all the while for the target.

There they were! He was about to tangle with the vaunted Zero for the first time. He felt his spine prickle. The two tiny crosses quickly grew to be recognizable. Damn, they looked almost exactly like the AT-6 Texans he'd flown at Kelly. Holt, closing fast, was almost in firing range. The pair of enemy fighters seemed oblivious to their peril.

Ross watched, fascinated. A thought jarred him. Spyglass had reported *four* aircraft. They were closing on only *two.* Where . . .? He swiveled his head and searched the sky above. *Good Christ,* here they come! Noses down, the pair of Zeroes flying top cover hurtled toward the attacking Mustangs. "Alleycat One, break left *now!* Bandits six o'clock high—coming in."

He saw Holt stand his ship on one wing. Ross threw his own control stick forward and to the left and peeled into a corkscrew dive. From the corner of his eye, he glimpsed something flashing past. Okay, you bastard, he exulted, you overshot. He sucked the stick into his gut, entering a turn that caused his cheeks to sag from g forces and contrails to form off both wingtips. Get inside his turn. He can't stop his dive soon enough to get an altitude advantage. He'll be a sitting duck.

Through the gray mist of approaching blackout, he spotted his quarry. The Jap had managed to pull out of his screaming dive and was streaking almost straight up. Ross's gunsight pipper was closing, but too slowly. He tightened his turn and heard the war-weary Mustang groan in protest. There—a long shot, but give him a burst. Rattle him; maybe he'll do something stupid. Ross felt the jarring concussion of his four .50 calibers. Red tracer rounds arced slowly toward the fleeing Zero. They were going to fall short—damn! *No*—his heart leaped. The very last of his burst impacted in the cockpit area. He saw something fly loose and flash briefly in the brilliant sunlight.

The moment for a sure kill was lost, however. The Zero was increasing the interval. Don't try to climb with a Zero, he recalled Holt admonishing. Anyway, Colyer, you're a wingman. Where the hell is your lead? You're supposed to be covering his ass. Ross split-S'ed and searched for movement. He spotted the dogfight almost immediately. Holt was holding his own with the three swooping, rolling attackers. He appeared to be edging toward the relative safety of a valley, but the Zeroes had him boxed. Ross crammed the throttle forward and streaked toward the lopsided contest.

Holt was jinking in random directions—short, jerky movements. The Zeroes were unable to set up a planned attack, but it was only a matter of time until O.B. ran out of maneuvering room. Ross decided to concentrate on breaking up the chase rather than try for a kill. He held his fire until the rearmost Jap plane filled his gunsight, then loosed a long burst ahead of the lead ship. The startled Zero pilots reacted as he'd hoped, wheeling into a steep climbing turn.

Ross watched them flee with mixed emotions; he'd done his job as a wingman, diverting a threat to his element leader, but the thought that he'd passed up an almost certain air-to-air victory rankled. He'd rejoined on Holt's left wing before he realized that he had just taken part in his first dogfight with a real enemy. Okay, Cipolla, thought Ross, it's like I tried to tell you, you're full of shit. I did it: I had my shot and took it. Not a confirmed kill, but a possible ain't too shabby for a beginner.

Ross tugged the sweaty helmet from his head and started disconnecting oxygen and radio leads. He felt his body sag as the recent infusion of adrenaline drained from his muscles. Holt had already deplaned and stood at the wing root, his round face split in an ear-to-ear grin. "Get your ass out of that crate and let me buy you a drink, Ross. I got some bourbon stashed away. It's worth a fortune, but I'll cheerfully give you what's left. My ass may not be worth much, but it's all yours, 'cause you saved it."

22 April 1944
Somewhere Above the Himalayas

Lieutenant Nakano Yusaki's world revolved and shrieked in a strange and frightening manner. Something was wrong—terribly wrong. It was his mother screaming. He had fallen from the giant eucalyptus tree that shaded the garden. No, it was the same . . . but somehow different. An icy wind whipped his face. He willed himself to open his eyes against the blast to determine its source. The effort was too much. He rolled his head to one side, trying to escape the discomfort.

Where was he? Suddenly the answer to that puzzle became a matter of utmost importance. This time he managed to flutter his eyelids. He glimpsed an empty void. But no, an uneven white border appeared beneath cobalt blue emptiness. A mountain range, etched against the sky. He could hear a throaty roar above the cold, screeching wind. He was in an airplane. Awareness returned with a confused, jumbled rush. Of course. He was flying his sleekly beautiful Mitsubishi Type 0.

He was in danger. Realization that the airplane was out of control stabbed him like a white-hot needle. Focusing on the bit of swimming background visible to his right, he determined that the fighter was in a gentle, spiraling dive. Instinctively he grasped the control stick. Slight pressure to the right and back resulted in a gratifying return to equilibrium. He squinted at the instrument panel. Fuzzy disks, their edges overlapping, seemed to be in their customary locations, but the dials were hopelessly blurred.

Why was the engine noise so loud? Snatches of memory flitted across maddeningly sluggish thoughts. He'd been attacking—diving at nearly full throttle toward an unsuspecting enemy plane. The big radial was still bellowing at full power. He reached for the throttle with his left hand. Nothing happened. Try and strain as he might, there was no reaction. He glanced at his arm and saw that it hung inertly at his left side.

Angry not only at the arm's refusal to cooperate, but at his lack of understanding as well, he reached across with his right hand and snatched the power lever to a point midway on the quadrant. The engine settled into a less strident note, but the howling noise remained. Trying to locate its source, Yusaki realized that the windshield was missing. Its gaping open frame funneled a torrent of frigid air into the cockpit.

He'd been hit. The fact came as a surprise. It had never happened before. Enemy fire had punched small wounds in the fragile skin of his aircraft during previous attacks, but he had never considered that it might happen to his tough, young, perfectly conditioned body. How bad? He saw no blood. He felt no pain—just the infuriating inability to *think.* And the left arm—he tried again, without success, to force it to move. He attempted to place his left foot on the rudder bar. It too remained immobile. A moment of panic swept through him—quickly replaced by fear, a hitherto unknown emotion. He must land the aircraft. He would return at once to the base and see the doctor.

Where *was* the base? In which direction? He must decide what to do. But he felt overcome by lassitude—an overwhelming desire to sleep. First he would close his eyes and rest. But he was uncomfortable, his seat belt an annoying restraint. That wasn't right. He should be feeling weight on his buttocks, the belt just a reassuring pressure. Through bleary eyes, he saw a shadowy mass flit overhead. Only it wasn't overhead. He was inverted, hanging by his seat belt. The shock cleared his mind. He rolled the wings level, then aligned them, and the nose, with the horizon.

Was he going to die? Was he to become one of those familiar suppurations dotting the desolate mountain slopes? A crater? That's all that remained after an eruption of dirt, rocks, and metal caused by an eight-thousand-pound aircraft impacting at 300 MPH, followed immediately by an orange fireball topped by billowing black smoke.

No! There materialized a fleeting vision of his venerable father sternly admonishing his young son that a man's life in the afterworld was determined by the manner in which he died. Bushido, the code of the Samurai, demanded that a warrior die in battle. The alternative was suicide. Anything less than returning from battle wounded but unvanquished was dishonorable. He must find a place to land—and survive.

Where, and how severe, was his wound? He explored his body with his right hand. Legs, torso, arms—all were unscathed. Extension of the search to his head disclosed a long rent in his flight helmet. Probing the area produced the first pain he'd experienced. His fingers came away smeared with greasy-feeling blood. A fist-sized opening in the rear canopy confirmed that a projectile had entered there, grazed his head, and exited through the now-missing windshield.

The discovery of his serious but not necessarily fatal wound heightened his impaired ability to deduce and reason. He associated the paralysis of his left arm and leg with the blow. Very well, he could still land the sturdy craft safely. But where? His vision had improved, but the all-important instrument indicators and numbers were still indistinguishable.

Fly south. After takeoff the formation had flown north toward the route followed by the American transports. The mountain ranges lay roughly on a north-south axis. He scanned the terrain passing uncomfortably close below. There was a definite pattern to a row of jagged crests. He was crossing them on a perpendicular course. East or west? Shadows—they would appear on the eastern slopes in the afternoon. The sun was almost directly overhead, however.

The mountain ranges led to the base. Proud of his ability to recall such details, he turned right. If the mountains grew more rugged, he'd have guessed wrong and would reverse course. A map—he could orient himself by landmarks. He extracted the aeronautical chart from the holder beside his right leg. Peering closely, he discovered that not only were the details blurred beyond recognition, but blood from his hand had further obliterated the pattern of swirling lines and names. He threw the useless document to the floor.

Yet another concern surfaced through his disorganized thoughts. How much fuel remained? How long had he flown aimlessly, out of control, in the area of his crippling encounter? He abandoned efforts to remember their time of takeoff, elapsed time en route, how much fuel remained. . . . The reserve tank contained enough gas for an hour's flying time. When the main tank ran dry, he'd switch. If a landing strip didn't appear within that time, then, and only then, would he consider a wheels-up landing.

The situation was under control, he exulted. But while Yusaki was congratulating himself on surviving his brush with violent death, a lance of excruciating pain nearly caused him to pass out. Situated above his right eye, the agonizing pangs stabbed like a red-hot poker. His kendo training failed to dispel the torture; he wished for blessed oblivion.

Yusaki's seat belt prevented involuntary contraction to the fetal position. His father's stern visage returned. Never surrender. Fading into and out of periods of agonizing semiconsciousness, he guided the unfaltering airplane on an erratic course away from the inhospitable Himalayan landscape.

A flash of sunlight on water penetrated the pain-induced haze of awareness. A sizable river existed only thirty miles from the base, he recalled. Could it be? He summoned his last vestige of willpower and turned the Zero toward the glittering expanse. The young pilot sobbed unashamedly with relief. The horseshoe bend was unmistakable; its open end pointed directly at the runway.

What had been a determined effort to return his airplane, and himself, intact, became an obsession. He mustn't fail. Biting his lower lip to stifle a scream, he ignored the blinding pain induced by physical exertion as he reached across his body and switched to the reserve fuel tank, then depressed the landing gear lever.

The undercarriage dropped into position with a satisfying *thunk*. Yusaki could restrain himself no longer. Pointing his crippled fighter toward home, he screamed at the top of his lungs, "Banzai, banzai, banzai."

25 April 1944
Yokosuka Navy Hospital

Lieutenant Nakano Yusaki screamed again. He was somewhat surprised that he could hear the prolonged, reverberating yell. The piercing cry had emerged without conscious effort. He couldn't ever recall having expressed weakness in such a manner. But, then, he couldn't recall pain that remotely approached the excruciating level he'd just experienced. He felt a wetness at his crotch and knew he had committed the ultimate humiliation.

"Shut up!" the blurred face directly above his own shouted. "You move once more like that and you will be blind in that eye for life. Concentrate on the little light, I tell you."

The surgeon hadn't wasted a moment after first politely inquiring about the health of his father, Admiral Nakano. Yusaki heard him mutter imprecations as he scraped dead, stinking flesh and pus from the head wound. "Butchers. A horse doctor could have done better. A field hospital they call themselves. Bah—they should be sent to prison for such work."

After completing his exam, the grim-faced surgeon seated himself on the steel table. "There is no need for you to put on street clothes," he informed Yusaki. "I'm operating immediately. You have a serious infection. There is an abscess dangerously near the optic nerve; that is what is causing your pain. I will prepare you for the worst. The surgery must be performed without anesthetic. The relaxing properties of painkilling drugs will spread the toxin. Total blindness would be the inevitable result."

Yusaki dug his fingernails into the chair arm and braced himself. Blindness in one eye would end his flying career. He focused on the tiny spot of light and tried to ignore the shiny steel blade entering his peripheral vision.

Chapter Eight

25 April 1944
Chabua Army Airfield

Ross followed the example of older hands, Air Transport Command crews, and transferred his glass of canned grapefruit juice to his canteen. The acidic liquid would await the addition of locally distilled gin. An essential source of extra vitamin C demanded by life in the tropics, the juice was almost never consumed at mealtime, but saved for later use as a mixer. He forced down the remainder of his breakfast—powdered eggs, fried Spam, and "toast"—with valiant effort. "My God," he grumbled to the long-faced lieutenant seated across from him, "is it always this bad?"

"Nope, some days we have 'shit on a shingle.' You mix some curry powder with it, and you can hardly tell it isn't fit to eat."

Ross shook his head in disgust, donned his flight cap, and let the screen door to the ramshackle mess hall slam behind him. Even during the worst days at Benghazi, the cooks had provided fresh eggs for the combat crews.

Should he return to his tent first, visit the latrine, or make the daily trek to ops before the heat started to build? With another day ahead totally devoid of meaningful activity, one had to ration life's more exciting moments.

He decided to forgo the mandatory daily check of the bulletin board in operations. He'd drop in later to see if maybe they had moved his name forward to fly one of the infrequent recce missions along the

Hump route. He and Holt had been objects of envy for having tangled with four enemy fighters. Only Major King had withheld congratulations. A sarcasm-tinged, "I hope you aren't expecting another medal after letting all four get away," conveyed his opinion of their encounter.

Ross paused on his stroll along a path leading through neglected portions of the old tea plantation—displaced to accommodate airfield construction—and wistfully watched a heavily laden C-87 lumber into the haze of heat and smoke. His suggestion to King that he be allowed to check out in the transport version of his old B-24 had been met with flat refusal. Damnit, he *had* to do something; he'd managed to log only six flying hours since his arrival. While he sat on his butt, the C-46 and C-87 crews logged more than a hundred hours a month hauling drums of av-gas and bomb fuses across the Hump.

Trudging into the *basha* he shared with an ATC pilot, Rex Turner, he regarded a battered paperback, then tossed it on his tentmate's bed and swore softly. What a hellhole. The room was accumulating heat as the sun reached its zenith. Outside, the damn mosquitoes, including the deadly anopheles, made recreational pursuits impossible. He turned and grunted a greeting as his saturnine, weary-faced roommate entered.

"Bored?" Turner asked with a grin.

"I'm climbing the walls. Would you believe I seriously considered going on a cobra hunt yesterday?"

"What?"

"Yeah. A native saw one along the path that goes into the village. A pair of crazy bastards were on their way after it with loaded forty-fives."

Turner shook his head. "They're crazy, all right. Some of those babies get twenty feet long, and meaner than hell. I can't offer you anything that exciting, but I'm maxed out for the month—a hundred and twenty-eight hours. I'm on my way to ATC ops to file some tech orders, just for something to do. Want to come along?"

"Anything," Ross replied. "Let's go."

"You seen the transport side of the field?" Turner asked as they scuffed along the dusty track.

"No, I've stuck to the fighter section—too damn hot for sight-seeing."

"Well, let's detour past the loading area. Might see something you won't see back in Michigan."

Turner ambled toward a stationary train. Ross followed and observed, "Damn, those are the smallest railroad cars I ever saw."

"You're looking at the Calcutta-Assam Express—narrow gauge. Takes five days to travel five hundred miles, and that includes crossing the Brahmaputra by barge-ferry. It carries damn near everything we get here. We inherited it from the British; they built the line to carry tea from the plantations you see everywhere." He chuckled. "The Brits and their tea. I was past here one day and saw the train crew brewing their 'spot of tay, y'know.' Quick and simple—they just draw live steam from the boiler."

They ducked between two cars and Turner continued, "But here's what I wanted you to see." Ross gaped. An elephant, guided by a sleepy mahout, was loading fuel drums into a C-46. Slack-jawed with astonishment, Ross watched the beast pluck a full, fifty-five-gallon drum from a flatcar. Then, after balancing the barrel atop six-foot tusks with its curled trunk, it turned and plodded to the nearby airplane. The battered, travel-stained drum was deposited inside the gaping cargo doorway with the gentleness of a mother tending her month-old baby.

"That's Annie," Rex advised. "She does that all day, every day, without ever dropping one. They have others, but none as good as Annie. Old John L. Lewis would have apoplexy if anyone tried that stateside, don't y'know?"

The tech order chore complete, Turner took a more circuitous route back to the *basha*. Panting in the close, humid air of the path, the pair stopped in a relatively cooler spot. "Whose troops are those I've seen unloading the past couple of days, Rex? Indian soldiers?"

"Naw," Turner replied. "Chinese. Stilwell is bringing them over—two divisions, I hear. After he upgrades their training, he moves them to Burma where he's trying to reopen the Burma Road. Christ, I hope he succeeds. If he could run the Japs out of Myitkyina, we'd be able to refuel there and take the low-altitude route to Kunming."

"What kind of soldiers do they make?"

Turner snorted. "Crazy ones. I'm lucky, I've only had to carry one load. But let me tell you what happened. We had this flight engineer who was a real nag about keeping 'his' airplane clean. He hated to haul passengers because they left such a mess.

"We took on a load of Chinese troops in Kunming and sarge got it through to the officer in charge that anyone making a mess was in deep trouble. 'You gotta puke, do it in your helmet,' he instructed.

'Then open the jump door and throw it out. Understand?' He went through the whole routine in pantomime and the lieutenant nodded.

"Well, we hit turbulence, naturally, about an hour out. Sarge came running up front screaming, 'One of those crazy sonsabitches has *jumped* out!' Turned out the poor bastard had actually jumped. He puked into his helmet and the lieutenant did exactly what sarge had showed him—threw the puke, soldier and all, into the jungle."

"Rex, come on, you don't expect me to believe that."

"'Struth. Another incident—I didn't see it, but I landed shortly after it happened—is wilder than that one. This homesick soldier in east China stowed away in the wheel well of a P-40 he knew was going to Kunming, where he lived. God only knows how he got himself curled up in there without getting crushed when the gear was retracted. But he did. He couldn't hang on during landing, however, and came tumbling out on the runway. One little scratch—I saw him."

Ross was laughing almost too hard to talk. "Did they send him back?" he choked out.

"Nope. They shot him. Not for going AWOL, but because he lost his rifle when he stowed away. Most of their armies only have about one rifle for every two troops, so that was inexcusable. This whole damn country is like that, Ross," Rex complained morosely.

They intercepted the road leading through a fringe of the encroaching jungle to the village. "That looks interesting," Ross said, indicating a cleared trail leading into the dense growth. "Where does it go?"

His companion grunted. "No place you want to go. Elephant path. Probably been there a thousand years. Whole damn country is covered with them. Don't go exploring. You meet a wild elephant—they're around—and one of you has to get out of the way. Guess who always loses?"

Ross shook his head. "Wonder whatever possessed the British to leave a cold, cloudy island for this place?"

"Tea, so I understand," Turner replied. "They made fortunes growing the stuff. For several years English ships took opium to China to trade for it; the Chinese had a lock on the tea business—a strict embargo on young trees and seeds. Well, they got to fighting among themselves and a ship's captain smuggled out enough seeds to start his own plantation. Conditions here are ideal, so India soon took over the English market."

"You're a regular damn encyclopedia, Rex. Where did you pick up all this stuff? College?"

Turner sighed. "I've been in this armpit of the world more than a year, remember. Studying history is about the only thing that's kept me from dancing naked around bonfires during the full moon."

Ross laughed. "Well, thanks for the guided tour. I'm going to check the bulletin board, then have lunch. See you later."

Captain Holt stood in front of the chalkboard copying entries from a clipboard. He turned as Ross entered the rattan-walled, thatch-roofed ops shack. He was actually grinning, the first expression of pleasure Ross had seen for a while. "Hey, Ross, come in. I was about to send a runner looking for you. We're finally in business."

Ross brightened. "A mission?"

The pudgy ops officer chuckled. "Better than that—we got *airplanes.* A dozen of 'em. They're in maintenance at Kharagpur and are due out next week. Our new pilots are waiting in a hotel room in Calcutta."

"All *right,*" Ross said enthusiastically. "Let's get 'em up here."

"We're about to do that little thing. As soon as we get the word, you and I catch an ATC bird to Calcutta. We'll test-hop the birds, let the new pilots have one circuit around the field for a checkout, and fly the entire bunch here."

"Okay, anything you say. I was on my way to the chow hall. What say we walk into the village and celebrate? I understand there's a Chinese restaurant in town that's been cleared by the flight surgeon. The owner swore by all his Chinese gods to cook everything long enough to kill all known types of bacteria. Interested?"

Ross could smell the village even before they emerged from the jungle. One moment they were walking between green walls; the next, they were traveling a wide, dusty street between shops—bedraggled, open stalls, covered by slabs of sheet metal—and structures with woven rattan walls and banana leaf–thatched roofs. The fragrance of exotic condiments vied for predominance with the odor of charcoal fires and open sewer trenches. Ross eyed with amused interest the first native women he'd seen since his arrival at Chabua. They were dressed in voluminous folds of rough cloth, faintly resembling the saris he'd seen in Calcutta. It was impossible to tell if the Assami females were young and pretty or old and ugly. None gave the slightest indication that they were aware of his scrutiny.

The Chinese restaurant proved to be an odoriferous cubicle with four bamboo tables and chairs, presided over by a moon-faced Oriental. Lunch appeared with only the briefest attempt at conversation. There was no menu, Ross had been told, and the fare seldom varied. The proprietor slid a shallow bowl filled with rice and a meat and vegetable concoction in front of Ross. After swallowing a large spoonful, he gasped and grabbed for his cup of tea. "My God, what is this stuff? I'm on fire."

Holt grinned. "Real Indian curry," he replied. "Don't think Mexicans have a monopoly on high-octane chow. Pile on some more of those chopped bananas and coconut, or order a bottle of the local beer. That will take your mind off the spices, I guarantee."

After eating in silence for several minutes, Ross asked, "O.B., I know I told you that I wouldn't bring Major King into our conversations, but I'm damned if I can figure the guy out. What's bugging him? Do you know?"

"The major is going to be a good CO," Holt replied slowly. "He knows flying and does things by the book. You ask what's bugging him. Well, I know one thing that he's highly pissed off about. You may have noticed, he doesn't wear any personal decorations—just theater and campaign ribbons. He flew about twenty missions in North Africa, then thirty-some out of Italy. He doesn't have a confirmed kill. He claimed two and two probables, but none were confirmed.

"It happens a lot to wingmen with a lead who hogs the easy kills. Then, when they do nail one, there's nobody around to see it. Just coincidence, but them's the rules. He didn't even get an Air Medal for total missions because he moved from the Eighth Air Force to the Twelfth to the Fifteenth, and none of them put in the paperwork. He has a request for review in Washington, but you know how that goes. This all came out when I suggested putting you in for a probable kill and an Air Medal for that business with the Zeroes.

"Anyway, I suspect that's why he has a hard-on for you. A Silver Star and DFC, the Air Medal with four clusters, and a Purple Heart—he'd give his left arm for a collection of fruit salad like that. I guess it's gotten to be an obsession with him. He watches you, in case you don't know. He asked just the other day if you had ideas of using your record to make him look bad. So," O.B. paused and shrugged, "I'm not taking sides, Ross. I get along with the man, but you saved my ass the other day. I'd just hate to see you blunder into something without knowing the score."

"So that's it," Ross mused. "The bastard thinks I'm after his job. Well, you may think he's a good CO, but I disagree. Mark my words, his obsession, as you call it, will get someone killed. Maybe him."

They toured the bazaar after lunch. O.B. passed on his entire Assami vocabulary, consisting of *Teek nay* (it's no good) and *Teek hai* (it is good). Ross eyed the displays of cheap, poorly crafted jewelry and gaudy clothing, but lost interest after the third shop. They now stood before a stall with an array of shallow wooden bowls filled with dull-colored stones.

"You like to buy some jade? Rubies? Opals?" O.B. asked.

"Just might. Never thought about it," Ross answered.

"Guy I knew at Tinsukia says he knows the stuff, claimed he picked up a real bargain here. He talked the old man into dragging some stuff from under the counter. This is mostly junk. One pilot even bought a piece of red glass. They told him it was a priceless ruby."

Ross shrugged. "Why not ask?" he said. He leaned over the counter and with his finger pantomimed a necklace around his neck.

Dark eyes regarded him impassively for several moments. Then the turbanned head nodded almost imperceptibly and the owner stepped to the rear of his tiny stall. When he returned, he unfolded a scrap of dirty cloth and exposed its contents.

Ross examined a crudely fashioned ring—a chunk of polished green stone set in what appeared to be aircraft aluminum. He picked up another slab of what he assumed was jade with a tiger with a misshapen neck etched on the flat side. He discarded both, then caught his breath. The third item was a small figurine, a three-dimensional carving of a woman draped in the graceful folds of a sari. Her face, partially visible beneath a cowl, was formed with only a few deft strokes of the carving tool. The artist had nevertheless produced a placid, benign expression. Closer examination, however, revealed a Mona Lisa–like smile.

Ross's first reaction was Ruth. . . . No, it was too subtle for the outgoing, gregarious nurse. Janet Templeton. Yes, it caught Janet's personality perfectly. He had to have it. Perhaps it would assuage the slight pang of guilt he harbored for avoiding her. After fifteen minutes of arm waving and indignant *Teek hai* and *Teek nay,* he left with the figurine safely tucked into a shirt pocket. Turner was shaking his head. "Seven dollars is more than that guy makes in a month. You're ruining the place."

30 April 1944
Seattle, Washington

Janet handed her rivet gun to the pimply faced youth behind the half door to the tool crib and received a fiber disk in return. Snapping her proof that she had returned the tool to a ring on her belt, she asked, "Do you have any more of those Lucky Strikes, Moe? I'm down to smoking those things that taste like old cabbage leaves."

The youngster made a furtive check for curious ears and muttered, "Got a half carton in my locker. Meet me in the stairwell by the admin section in about ten minutes. I'm just getting off duty."

"A half carton?" Janet raised her eyebrows. "Wow, what did you do, hijack a truck?"

"Naw, I won't be needing them. Passed my physical. This is my last week here; I report Monday morning. After that I can get all I need at the BX."

"So you went ahead and enlisted. What does your mother think about that?"

"Aw, she put up a fuss when she had to sign the permission slip, but like I told her, it's better to join now while I can get into the navy, than to wait and be drafted into the infantry."

Janet removed the confining bandanna from her hair and combed the short, tangled tendrils with her fingers. "The war could be over before you're drafted, Moe; you just turned seventeen. Sailors get shot at too, you know."

"That's just it, Miss Janet," the sallow-faced boy replied. "I might not get to see any action if I wait."

Janet compressed her lips and turned away. Men, she thought. So damn anxious to see action. They never think about the wives and mothers who spend sleepless nights followed by longer days waiting for a Western Union messenger . . . then change the blue star in the window to a gold one. BT had left her without a thought for her feelings, but then BT had considered himself immortal. Even Ross treated the war as his own personal challenge.

She moved toward the time clock, oblivious to the cacophony of jarring sounds that had so intimidated her that first night. She waggled little waves of recognition to people she knew and exchanged ribald pleasantries with men who never tired of impressing her with their manly charm. Behind her, the midnight-to-eight shift had already started working. Sounds of machine-gun-like bursts of rivet guns and the whir of air drills filled the cavernous building, where chattering workers swarmed over the skeletons of B-17 bombers. A loudspeaker blared, "Mike Brodsky to the engineering office, please. Repeat, Mike Brodsky, you're wanted in engineering."

She caught sight of Peg Hopper's blond mop of curls and crossed to join her. "Hi, Peg. How did things go in final assembly tonight?"

The full-bodied blond's eyes flashed. "I could cheerfully stick that rivet gun in Ed Voorhies's you-know-what. Made me drill out and replace two entire rows of flush rivets. My lead man had a fit. If that big lug thinks I'll date him just because he's an inspector, he has another think coming."

Janet chuckled. "I can't imagine why he would think you're available. You're such a shy little thing."

Peg tossed her head. "Talk's cheap. I like to have fun. This job is boring enough as it is, without having to be checking that your halo is on straight all the time. Well, are you coming to the Rendezvous Room with me?"

"Peg—good God, we haven't had a full eight-hours' sleep all week. I'm out on my feet. I'm going straight home, take a hot bath, and collapse."

"Aw, Janet, those marine flyers will be there again tonight. We promised them we'd show up, remember? And that dark-haired one, Tommy, really has the hots for you."

"Tommy has the hots for anything that doesn't have hair on its chest," Janet replied dryly. "No, I'm going to pick up some cigarets from Moe, catch the bus, and sleep until noon."

"Okay, party pooper," Janet's roommate replied. "I'll try not to wake you." Peg left for the ladies' room where, Janet knew, she would change her slacks suit for a wispy chiffon thing she had folded inside a voluminous purse.

Janet shook her head and smiled as she watched the twitching hips, which even the baggy work uniform couldn't disguise. Peg was having the time of her life. The daughter of a vice president with Dole Pineapple in Honolulu, she and Janet had been classmates at the university before the war. Janet had often been the party-loving girl's alibi for all-night absences from the stern Hopper home environment. Peg's invitation for Janet to join her in Seattle had provided a much needed lift.

The bus was crowded, as usual, despite the late hour. The city never seemed to sleep. Plants operated with three shifts around the clock. Service and recreation industries—restaurants, bars, bowling alleys, movies—adjusted their hours accordingly. Janet saw patrons queuing up for a 1:00 A.M. showing of *For Whom the Bell Tolls* at a local movie house.

Her thoughts turned to the future as she trudged up the sidewalk toward the three-story Victorian house she called home. "Aunt Ruby," as the landlady's tenants called her, had converted the old mansion to a boardinghouse for working girls. The rooms were comfortable and cozy, the food was good . . . and the rules were strict. Aunt Ruby ruled her brood with draconian measures. No boys beyond the downstairs parlor, ever. No parties in the bedrooms. Booze—when one could obtain it—was allowed, but all drinking was restricted to the kitchen and the parlor. Pregnancy evoked an immediate invitation for the errant girl to seek other accommodations.

The harsh discipline imposed by the hard-faced, wasp-waisted matron—never seen without heavy makeup and hennaed hair—was ironic, if one believed the gossip. The story went that she and her husband had operated a casino in Reno before the war. Her spouse was bludgeoned to death during a holdup. The perpetrator, who resembled a familiar figure in the shadowy gambling community, evaded the police. But a week later, the alleged killer was found in a cheap motel room—nude and with his heart blown through his back by a single gunshot. The police investigation progressed no further than establishing that a slender woman wearing a long coat and a broad-brimmed hat had lured the man to the rendezvous.

No favor was too great to ask of Aunt Ruby. One girl had the misfortune of being arrested with a male companion sharing a hotel room. Aunt Ruby materialized at two in the morning with bail money. During the ride home she asked, "Were you selling?"

"He just gave me silk stockings and stuff," the wretched girl replied between sobs. Upon returning from work the next day, she found her bags packed and sitting by the front door.

So where do you go from here? Janet asked herself as she turned her key in the door. I haven't enjoyed life this much since I can remember. Doris Wilson was right; I'm free from having to conduct my life in a way that pleases others. I have my very own bank account, growing at a gratifying rate. There are men—young, handsome men—who need no more than a raised eyebrow to vow undying love and eternal companionship. Gay, frenetic parties underway around the clock, seven nights—and days—a week. If the hotel detective gives you a fishy look, you just stare him down.

It won't last, a little voice whispered. The war will end, probably in less than a year. The old order will return. The dashing, young men will revert to stodgy lawyers, bankers, and accountants. Or, more to the point, they'll return to jobs at plants turning out refrigerators and automobiles instead of tanks and airplanes. Where do you fit into that life-style, Janet Templeton, nee Richards—unmarried and approaching the ripe old age of thirty?

She softly closed and locked the door, then made her way into the dark, silent house. Deep in thought, she removed her shoes and mounted the open, curving stairway toward her second-floor—and suddenly very lonely—room.

1 May 1944
Kharagpur

Ross and O.B. dragged into a stifling barracks building just as a rosy twilight descended. "That had to be the worst day I can recall," Ross groaned. "My back has permanent curvature, I know. That gooneybird pilot had to be going out of his way to find that many bumps."

"Nobody said war was easy," Holt responded cheerfully. "You'll feel better after a shower and change. If you want to ride into Calcutta, we can eat at the British mess. It's the only place in this city that serves real, honest-to-God beef."

"Just hearing the word 'ride' sends me into shock. But beef? Now that's worth serious consideration. Where do they get it? Are they killing sacred cows on the sly?"

"Naw, it's shipped in. A battleship can carry a lot of steak. Okay, if you're game, I'll go right now and arrange transportation; that can be a major project all by itself."

Ross allowed the white-jacketed waiter to remove his plate, then leaned back and moaned with pleasure. "This is the way to go. What a meal. I haven't had a piece of meat like that since I left the States. And real coffee, no less."

Holt filled their glasses from a decanter of heavy port wine and lit a cigaret. "I guess it'll be a while before we see another one. We got a bunch of long days ahead of us. I just hope the pilots in this bunch won't need a lot of work."

"Yeah," Ross agreed. "Without plenty of av-gas, every hour in the air will have to count. You have a plan?"

"Sort of. Major King and I drew up a little syllabus. Flight commanders will give their pilots a once-over in a four-ship formation, a little rat racing, and such. Additional training will be on an individual basis, as required. I'm not expecting a lot of that. I'm told most have combat time in other airplanes. A couple are from a P-40 outfit in east China that ran out of aircraft."

Ross nodded. "We should get some idea on their trip around the pattern and the formation flight back to Chabua." He sipped his port. "O.B., I'm not superstitious, and I'm looking forward to getting the squadron operational, but I can't get rid of this nagging feeling that something isn't right. This place, Chabua—they all give me a spooky feeling."

Late the next morning Ross and O.B., each with a half-dozen twenty-minute test hops behind him, stood in the shade cast by a tarp stretched between four poles and scribbled initials on maintenance forms. A grizzled master sergeant scooped up the sheaf of papers and growled, "Okay, gentlemen, they're all yours. Acceptance checks and test hops all clear. When do you plan to leave?"

Holt wiped sweat from his forehead and tugged the sweat-drenched flight suit from his crotch. "First light tomorrow, I figure," he replied. "We'll give the new pilots a trip around the pattern this afternoon. If none of 'em auger in, we'll sign 'em off as checked out." He squinted at the parking ramp, which was drenched by brilliant, noonday sunshine. "If we don't all pass out from heatstroke, that is. Damn, and I thought Chabua was hot."

"It do get toasty," the NCO agreed. "I understand that when they laid this runway last summer, it was a hundred and forty degrees some days. But it don't seem you're the only ones crazy enough to be out today. Looks like we have company—important company." He nodded to where a Jeep was speeding toward them. A red metal plate in the license holder displayed two white stars.

The trio beneath the sheltering tarp drew to attention as a tall, lean major general stepped from the Jeep directly into the shaded area. A dark-skinned, hawk-eyed figure returned their salutes and asked, "Which of you is Captain Holt?"

"I'm Holt, sir," said O.B.

"Glad to meet you." The general's stern visage relaxed slightly, and he extended his hand. "Chennault—Claire Chennault. Reckon I'm your boss."

"Yes, sir." O.B.'s cherubic features formed a happy grin. "It's a pleasure and an honor to meet you. This is Captain Colyer, one of the 41st's flight commanders."

"Colyer?" The general cocked an eyebrow. He started to speak, then hesitated. "Are you the pair that tangled with four Japs over the Hump a few days ago?"

"Yes, sir."

"Zeroes, the report read. You sure they weren't Oscars? The Zero is a navy plane."

"They were Zeroes, sir." Holt's tone was positive. "I had plenty of opportunity to see three of 'em close up. Colyer saved my ass."

"Hmmm." Chennault stroked his lantern jaw thoughtfully. "That's interesting—damn interesting. Where's Major King?"

"He stayed at Chabua, sir. There's—uh—a problem with parking-ramp space for our new birds. ATC brought in more Dumbos; their cargo quota has damn near doubled."

"Damn." Chennault's already mahogany-hued features darkened further. "Wish I'd known that before I left Delhi. I didn't want to use an ATC base for shakedown. I'll have a word with Alexander before I leave here. Now, let's find a place to have some lunch. I want to talk with you boys, and give you a message for Major King."

Lunch consisted of Spam sandwiches and GI lemonade provided by a mobile, flight-line canteen. Chennault acted as if it were an everyday occurrence. Squatting just inside an open maintenance shack, idly brushing away flies in the heat, he talked as he wolfed down the uninspired fare. "Beauties, aren't they?" His eyes sparkled with pride as he surveyed the row of gleaming, factory-new Mustangs. "Are they flyable?"

"Yes, sir," Holt responded. "We just finished acceptance test hops this morning. Guns haven't been bore-sighted or harmonized, though. That's something else Major King is trying to work out with ATC. We'll give the new pilots a trip around the pattern this afternoon and take a dozen back to Chabua with us. I understand three will be left here as replacements."

Chennault grunted. "Tell King I said to get those guns sighted in if he has to use the fucking headquarters building for a target. And here's what else I want you to tell Major King; he'll get it in writing after I get back to Kunming, but that may take a week.

"Stilwell has his ass in a sling in Burma. He was to cruise into Myitkyina and have the airfield ready by now, but the Japs have two crack divisions in the area. He's screaming for photorecce flights. The Tenth is flying balls out providing him ground support, so I got snookered into agreeing to use our new B models from the 41st to do some overflights while you're shaping up for the move east."

"How far east, sir? Which base?" Holt asked.

The general gave the eager ops officer a lazy smile. "Down, rover. You'll know soon enough. In the meantime, get your squadron whipped into shape. Now I don't want any misunderstanding about the photorecce business. There is no reported Jap air activity around Myitkyina, so you should be able to get all the pictures that three-star platoon leader wants. But don't, and I mean *do not, under any circumstances,* get suckered into providing close support. You'll fly with hot guns, but use them *only* if you get jumped by Jap aircraft—no strafing. Those airplanes are needed for more serious work. Is that clear?"

"Yes, sir," Holt replied. Unabashed by Chennault's previous rebuke, he added, "Does that mean we'll be escorting the Superforts against Japan?"

The general's eyes flashed dangerously, then he grinned once more. "Heaven forbid. If and when those big, awkward fuckers get that far, they'll have to rely on that marvelous, new central-fire-control system to keep the Jap fighters away. While they do that, we'll be winning the war on the ground—chewing up any Japs trying to move south toward Indochina. Okay, enough of that. What I've just told you isn't for publication, by the way."

The rawboned two-star stood and looked wistfully at the parked fighters. "God, I'd like to take one of those babies up for a quick trip. Take my advice, gentlemen, don't ever become a general. It takes all the fun out of things."

Ross and O.B. watched the fiery Fourteenth Air Force commander stride toward his parked Jeep. Holt's expression was one of reverent awe. "What a guy," he breathed. "It's easy to believe all those stories about the AVG. There goes a fighter pilot's general."

Ross chuckled to himself. I get the impression I'm not the only one at odds with Major King, he mused. The thought of that asshole wearing three stars makes me sick.

Chapter Nine

5 May 1944
Chabua Army Airfield

Major King spread the sectional aeronautical chart on the ops counter and pointed to a red grease-pencil line. "General Stilwell's X Force is stalled here," he said. "The Japs are supposed to be here, in the Jambu Bum Mountains, in considerable force. The Chinese troops are taking both artillery and mortar fire every time they stick their heads up.

"Stilwell's thinking of bypassing the strongpoint by advancing down the Mogang Valley, then striking at Myitkyina from the west. He wants to know if the Japs have fortified positions along this route. We'll make our passes at five thousand feet, one mile apart. Here, at Inkangahtawng, we shut down the cameras and head for Myitkyina. We'll use the rest of our film to shoot pictures of any fortifications we find around the city.

"There hasn't been any enemy air activity reported there for several days. The boys in Calcutta say there's no heavy AA guns—just the usual twenty- and forty-millimeter stuff. Our two-ship formation should get in, get pix, and get out before they know we're there. We'll make the run at four hundred miles per hour indicated, so they'll only have about four minutes to get organized. Any questions?"

Ross shook his head. Inserting his own folded map in a knee pocket, he asked, "What if the ceiling is below five? We still fly a spread formation?"

"I'll make that decision during our descent into the target area. All I want you to do is maintain formation and follow instructions," King replied.

Ross glanced at Captain Holt, who was observing the briefing with a quizzical smirk. Why did that egotistical asshole King have to select *me* as a wingman? Ross wondered. You can bet he has some ulterior motive. He hasn't spoken a half-dozen words to me since we came back with the airplanes. Oh, well. I can put up with anything, even getting shot at, to get away from this sorry, stinking place. He forced a grin at his CO. "Fair enough. I'm ready when you are."

Ross's smoldering resentment at King's attitude faded as the two P-51s snarled their way above the angular, emerald-hued landscape. They skirted a ridgeline where a dozen or so thatch-roofed huts filled a small clearing—a Naga village described by the ATC pilot. Headhunters, for Christ's sake—a race of people whose hobby was collecting the heads of their enemies. There were thousand-pound tigers that could throw a full-grown man over a shoulder and travel at a dead run, chronically ill-tempered elephants, and snakes ranging from the poisonous twelve-foot king cobra to the two-foot but even deadlier krait. It was hard to believe that the benign-looking terrain below could shelter such violence. The full-throated roar of the Mustang's engine never sounded more comforting to Ross.

They swept across another, higher, range of peaks. A broad valley lay exposed, looking as evenly manicured as a golf course. Ross's lips tightened. Talk about a surprise. That apparent "carpet" was made up of eighty- to one-hundred-foot trees—rain forest where the sun never shone. Blood-sucking leeches up to six inches long, swarms of biting, stinging insects; he shook his head. The bloodthirsty Japs began to seem the least dangerous threat.

They flew over another mountain range and another, broader valley. The gleaming thread of a major stream meandered its length. Ross scanned his map: It was the Chindwin. Across the next rapidly approaching range, King would be starting his descent. A wry grin tugged at the corners of Ross's mouth. Secretly he'd hoped the ferret-faced major would screw up somehow—miss a checkpoint or something. Someday . . . He scanned the cockpit. Fuel selector on fullest tank, oxygen flow okay, camera armed and on standby; it felt great to be flying a plane with zero write-ups.

He saw King's ship nose down and increased the interval between their wingtips. His airspeed built past 380 MPH. They were below the tops of the Jap-infested Jambu Bum Mountains now, and details of the valley became more distinct. The speeding fighters whipped through a layer of broken clouds and emerged over the target area. Ross slid farther left and toggled the camera switches. Unbroken green terrain flashed beneath the streaking Mustangs, then Inkangahtawng's river dock area was behind them.

With the camera off, he slid into normal formation and saw King set course for Myitkyina. He frowned as he observed the altimeter sag toward three thousand. The Japs had an airstrip at Myitkyina. The town was a major interchange for road, rail, and river traffic. It was bound to be defended; three thousand feet put them within range of 20mm fire. A pall of smoke and haze ahead confirmed that they were dead on course. He checked that his camera was on standby.

King's voice crackled in his headset—the major's first transmission since departure from Chabua. "Break left, Two. Get pictures of the perimeter and rejoin me east of the city."

Ross watched the lead ship turn right and shrugged. Follow instructions, the man had said. A ragged checkerboard of buildings replaced verdant jungle, and Ross heeled left. Camera running, he followed the poorly defined outer city limits.

The built-up area passed from view off his right wing. Ross shut down the camera and nosed up, searching for his flight leader. He stiffened. There was no mistaking the red and orange balls arcing across the horizon south of town. Shit! King had blundered into an antiaircraft battery. Where was the damn fool? As wingman, Ross should be flying cover for him. He cursed silently and rolled right, straining for a glimpse of the low-flying P-51.

"Two, this is Lead. Rally south of town—angels three. We have an airfield full of parked airplanes down here." King's voice was shrill.

What the hell? Ross vividly recalled Chennault's grimly outthrust jaw, his biting, "*Do not, under any circumstances,* get suckered into providing close support." He'd heard Holt repeat the ultimatum verbatim. He hesitated, then keyed his mike. "Uh—Lead, this is Two. I'm east of the target, orbiting the rally point. Uh—your transmission was garbled. Over."

"Goddamnit, Colyer, get your ass down here. There's a dozen Bettys on the ground, all in a row. I got three on my first pass."

"Major, I—"

"I said *now,* Colyer. That's an order." King was screaming into his mike.

Ross groaned. Oh, for Christ's sake, he lamented to himself. He flipped the fighter into a diving turn and crammed the throttle to its forward stop. He made a hasty scan of the cloudless sky, hoping against hope to see enemy fighters lurking in ambush. He confronted nothing more than an empty blue dome. A flash of reflected sunlight gave him King's location. Ross executed a sweeping turn and transmitted a clipped, "Two, in position. Do you intend to make a firing pass?"

"Damn right. Ducks on the pond. We'll torch 'em all with one more pass. I'll take the first ones, you take the far end. Twelve enemy bombers in one mission—that's damn near a record."

Ross clenched his jaws and took up his strafing interval. A glance at the airspeed indicator revealed that the needle was well past the red line. Okay, he muttered to himself, let's get this business over with and get the hell outta here. He snapped the safety wire holding the master armament switch in the OFF position. A red light replaced the green SAFE one.

The airstrip loomed dead ahead. Three furiously burning hulks confirmed King's claim. Milling figures surrounded the remainder of a row of neatly parked, twin-engine airplanes. From the corner of his eye, Ross saw the blue-white flashes of large-caliber gunfire. His stomach knotted as he recalled the plain southwest of Ploesti, his crippled B-24 lurching barely fifty feet above a gun emplacement. He suppressed the memory with a savage, Concentrate on your gunsight, Colyer. That's history.

Shuddering concussions from his four wing-mounted .50s told him he'd squeezed the stick-mounted trigger reflexively. He touched the rudder and watched the row of tracers move left. They stitched their way through two sitting bombers. Then he was streaking across the field boundary. Back pressure—where's Lead? He felt but didn't hear a quick series of impacts. He was hit. The thunder of the big Packard-built Merlin didn't falter. He breathed easier. He was home free.

Ross saw King break left, away from the city, and followed, clawing for altitude on a course toward home. Sweat trickled from his armpits, making a chilly track down his side. That had been close. The idiot! he raged to himself. Not only disobeying a direct order, but returning to a target alerted by his first pass.

He scanned his instrument panel and froze. He hadn't escaped unscathed. A white arrow indicated that his engine coolant temperature was near the upper limit. Major Cipolla's admonishment flickered in his mind. "This bird will take a lot of punishment and still get you home. It has one fatal flaw, however: Get hit in the cooling system, and you have exactly eight minutes before the engine seizes up. There's not a damn thing you can do to extend engine life. Eight minutes—you can count 'em."

Ross keyed his mike. "Lead, this is Two. I've been hit. Coolant leak. I'll have to put 'er down." He chewed his lip and waited. He repeated his transmission after waiting a full two minutes. There was no response. He drew a deep breath and searched the broken, mountainous landscape ahead. A million dollars for a rice paddy; damnit, don't these people grow *anything* on level ground? He heard—felt—the engine begin to labor and checked the altimeter. Three thousand feet above ground level. He'd have preferred five or more, but this was it. Ross angrily rolled the crippled Mustang inverted and jerked his oxygen mask free. After jettisoning the canopy and releasing his seat belt, he let the rushing slipstream suck him clear. Tumbling head over heels, he located the ripcord. He felt a violent jerk as the chute opened, then he was swinging above an endless vista of treetops.

Lieutenant Otis Farnsworth lowered his binoculars and scratched his unshaven chin. The distant rattle of gunfire had brought him to the promontory, his favorite observation post. He'd identified the fleeing aircraft as Mustangs. From where? he wondered. The American planes pounding Jap positions in the valley were usually either B-25s or P-40s. Then he saw that the rear ship was trailing what appeared to be white vapor. As he watched, its canopy spun away and the pilot tumbled free.

A white canopy bloomed, contrasting sharply with the solid green valley floor. Farnsworth turned to the brown-skinned, near-naked man squatting alongside. He raised his eyebrows in an unspoken question.

The man spat a stream of blood-red betel juice and said, "Bad. Many Japanese by river. They see parachute." He held up his right forefinger. "One hour."

Farnsworth studied his Kachin guide while he decided what to do. The eight-member OSS detachment had remained undetected thus far. Three teams were poised to sever the major rail line traversing the valley below. An effort to rescue the downed airman could lead to discovery, and not only place the detachment members' lives in danger, but scuttle their sabotage plans.

"Can you find the American flyer?"

An expressionless nod.

"If Japanese find him first, can you help him escape?"

The answer was a sharp look, a shrug, and upturned palms.

"The man must be taken north—far north to Lisu country. He must not know that other Americans are here. If taken by Japanese, he can be made to tell. Understand?"

The Kachin frowned. Farnsworth sensed disapproval. No member of his tribe would abandon a brother, the guide's expression seemed to say. He trusted the big, red-haired man, however. Nodding, he stated, "I take two men."

Farnsworth hesitated. The guide could only mean that their radioman and the lone Kachin trained to plant demolition charges would go with him. He felt a twinge of the guilt implied by the Burmese native, however, and simply nodded, not trusting himself to speak.

Ross watched the unbroken mat of treetops rush to meet him. He searched for a break; there just *had* to be a clearing. At the last moment, he thought he detected a tiny sliver of space between three trees. He yanked furiously on his risers and tried to steer toward it. He was several feet short when his feet struck the first foliage. Crossing his feet at the ankles and covering his face with his forearms, Ross plunged into the tangle of vines, tree limbs, and panicked wildlife.

This isn't so bad, he thought. The heavy growth is actually slowing my fall. A jolt on his leg straps dashed his optimism; he came to an abrupt halt. Peering between crossed forearms, he made out the jungle floor a dismaying twenty to thirty feet beneath his gently swinging flying boots. A glance overhead revealed the parachute canopy firmly snagged on a thigh-sized limb. He hung, twisting and swaying like a 180-pound plumb bob.

Determined effort to set up a pendulum-like swinging that would bring him within reach of a tree trunk was to no avail. A pair of chattering monkeys watched his thrashing movements. "Oh, shut the hell up," Ross snarled. What should he do? Unsnap the chute harness and free-fall to the ground? A broken leg, or worse, would be a death warrant. Where the hell were those wrist-sized vines Tarzan was always swinging on?

Frustration grew as he dangled helplessly between the jungle canopy and floor. He was soon bathed in sweat, the fetid heat enveloping him like a warm, wet blanket. He studied the tree trunk again. It was his only means of descent. Something, a rope or a tree limb, was needed to bridge the ten-foot gap. Parachute risers. If he could reach as far as three feet over his head, cut a number of them, tie them together . . . He extracted his survival knife and set to work.

Thirty minutes later, Ross sprawled on the surprisingly clear jungle floor. The task had been simpler than he first thought. He ended up cutting all the risers on one side. The resulting imbalance moved him several feet toward the tree trunk. Pumping like a kid on a swing, he was finally able to grasp the vines growing there.

Now what? Ross surveyed his surroundings with increasing dismay. As his eyes adjusted to the eerie green-tinged gloom, he began to realize the full extent of his difficulties. In all directions a maze of trees, vines, and head-high, fernlike vegetation reduced visibility to a matter of yards. Scraps of a long-ago lecture, entitled "Survival in the Jungle," returned. "Don't do anything immediately after a crash landing or bailout," the instructor had told his bored audience. "You'll be in shock, whether you realize it or not. Sit down and regain your ability to reason. Inventory your possessions. Treat injuries first, then plan your next actions. Do not discard anything. Your parachute, for example, can provide lifesaving shelter."

Ross contemplated his chute, tangled hopelessly more than a hundred feet above his head. Forget that. He eyed the harness—the small emergency medical kit. Idiot! Why hadn't he removed it while he'd had the chance? He considered climbing the vine-wrapped tree to recover the precious medication. It would require too much time. He must start walking—get away from this creepy place. North—away from Jap soldiers.

Which way *was* north? A compass. Every crew member carried an escape kit: a flat, plastic box containing items needed to survive in hostile country. He extracted his from a knee pocket and ripped it open. Locating the tiny compass, no larger than a button, he watched the dot on its rotating disk settle to a stable reading. Relief that he knew his directions reduced him to near-tearful elation.

The afternoon passed in a blur of frenzied effort to cover ground. Twice he was on the verge of panic; he would never live to see civilization. He was *hundreds* of miles deep in the impenetrable morass of tropical growth. When it grew too dark to see the compass, he crawled into the crotch of a monstrous tree trunk. He tried to nibble a square of emergency ration from the escape kit, and discovered that his exertions had left him totally dehydrated. Burning thirst notwithstanding, he fell into exhausted sleep.

Awakening was both an abrupt and painful experience. Ross found himself sprawled on the jungle floor, gasping with pain. Awareness of his surroundings came slowly. More than pain, his first conscious perception was a consuming thirst. He floundered weakly. Water—he *must* get to his feet and find something, anything, to drink. His struggles ceased as he discovered two pairs of canvas boots with rubber soles only inches from his face. He raised his gaze slowly, stopping when it reached two broadly smiling, olive-hued faces. There was neither sympathy nor compassion in either.

Shrill, singsong imprecations, in a language Ross recognized with a chill of dismay as Japanese, emerged from the taller of the two. Shapeless, mustard-colored coveralls and floppy forage caps bearing red stars confirmed his worst fears. A well-aimed kick to his midsection drove him to a more-or-less upright position.

Ross's shoulder holster and .45 automatic were first to go. His captors' disposition seemed to improve as they gleefully examined the weapon. His wristwatch went the same route. One of the soldiers patted him down while the other held a carbine at his throat. The search netted the soldiers his escape kit, cigaret lighter, and a crumpled half pack of Lucky Strikes. They immediately divided the latter and put them to use.

Producing a length of harsh, hempen rope, the chattering pair lashed Ross's hands behind his back and prodded him forward, along the path he'd made the afternoon before. They rewarded his croaking plea for water, emphasized by opening his mouth, with a blow to the back with a rifle butt. He recovered, stunned and dizzy, face down in the dank, stinking jungle floor.

Screw it, his fuzzy inner voice advised. They're going to kill you anyway . . . after they torture the hell out of you. Just lie here and get it over with. He roused at the sound of two jarring thuds, followed by strangling, gargled cries. Ross forced his head upright. From the corner of an eye, he saw his captors writhing on the ground in the grasp of two half-naked, brown-skinned figures. The struggle was short. The savage-looking attackers leaped to their feet; the uniformed Japanese lay in inert mounds.

His jubilation faded as he obtained a better look at his rescuers. One, with a wicked-looking, machete-like knife in hand, straddled Ross. Good God, he thought wildly, talk about out of the frying pan. . . . I've been rescued by a pair of goddamn headhunters! Then, instead of his neck, he felt his bonds being severed. Powerful hands helped him to a standing position. "Water," he croaked.

"Okay," a cheerful voice replied. Ross gaped in astonishment at the sound of quite good English. The ferocious features confronting him were spread in a wide grin, exposing lips and gums stained black by betel nut juice.

"You—you speak English?" Ross managed to ask.

"Sure thing, sir. Come." The man led Ross to a vine-covered tree trunk. Selecting an arm-sized vine, he cut it cleanly with one blow. Handing the raw end to Ross, he added, "Drink."

The vine produced a trickle of clear, surprisingly cool liquid. Ross gulped thirstily, letting the lovely stuff splash over his unshaven cheeks, which were swollen from insect bites. His thirst partially slaked, he turned to see that they had been joined by a third man. The new arrival, smaller and younger looking, spoke to Ross's benefactor in rapid, urgent-sounding tones.

The first man scowled. "Come quick. Japanese bawstids look for you in all places." Ross, still groggy and trying to understand the swift, bizarre sequence of events, could only nod. He noticed that the need for immediate action didn't prevent their stripping the dead Japanese of everything having potential value, including the canvas and rubber boots. They returned Ross's belongings without comment—the .45 with some reluctance, he thought.

The English-speaking native indicated that Ross must follow carefully and not disturb the jungle growth. "Leave false trail," he explained as the younger man trotted off in the opposite direction, slashing a path with his blade.

"Where are we going?" Ross asked, panting.

"To airplane place," the man answered without slowing. He made flying motions with his arms. "You go back to own people."

Ross, trotting to keep up, considered at some length what he'd heard. "Airplane place" could only mean an airfield—one not in Japanese hands. How did this man know where Ross's "own people" might be? "How far to airplane place?" he asked.

"Four day—maybe five day." The man squinted at the horizon for a moment and cheerfully added, "Maybe two week."

7 May 1944
Camp Oboe, Burma

Lieutenant Farnsworth listened to the squatting Kachin's message and scowled. "Can he walk at all?" he asked.

The native shrugged. "Some. All time shit and vomit. Weak like baby."

"He can't make it to Fort Hertz, then?"

An emphatic negative head shake prompted the lieutenant's disgusted, "Damn. Well, that's it, you'll have to bring him here. The operation is set for three days from now. We'll have to move north then; the

Japs are going to swarm in here like mad hornets. When you contact the base tonight by radio, tell them that the American flyer is too sick to travel. We will advise them of a new arrival time when we can figure a way to get him there."

Farnsworth watched the little group straggle into the clearing. The pilot was in a bad way, he had to concede. Head down, forcing one foot in front of the other, he was unaware of his surroundings until the Kachins restrained him. His head rose slightly and swung from side to side as he took in the scene through half-closed eyes. "Hi," Otis called brightly, "you look all in. Let's get you up this ladder and inside where you can get the weight off your feet."

"An American?" Ross's voice sounded confused.

"Unless Milwaukee has seceded from the Union, I am," Otis said cheerily. "Now, up and inside with you. I'll have Honcho brew up some of that vile stuff the Kachins use for dysentery. We'll get some food inside you that will stay down, and let you have about twenty-four hours of sleep."

Ross used every ounce of remaining strength to climb the four ladder rungs leading to the elevated *basha*. He flopped on the bamboo floor and mumbled, "I don't understand."

"Good. Let's keep it that way. What you don't understand, you can't blab," Farnsworth replied unsympathetically. "Concentrate on this: Three days from now you're going to walk out of here. Nobody's going to carry you. If you can't keep up, we'll leave you behind."

Ross's fever-bleared eyes flared briefly. "I don't know who you are, but fuck you. I can manage." He promptly slumped back and closed his eyes.

Farnsworth regarded his unwelcome guest with wry amusement. The guy wouldn't survive a week in the jungle. Then again . . . he had guts. You had to give him that.

9 May 1944
Yokosuka, Japan

Yusaki's exposure to wartime civilian life started with the ride home from the hospital. The family sedan, a prewar American Plymouth, emitted choking clouds of noxious smoke as it chugged along at barely twenty kilometers per hour. It had been converted to burn charcoal, his father explained. Even at that, their's was one of only a handful of automobiles. Only the fact that he was a military personage and his position as leader of their neighborhood association allowed him to operate a motorcar.

They traveled streets congested with every form of unmotorized transportation Yusaki had ever known—and some he hadn't. Pedestrians moved more slowly than he remembered, and their faces were wan and drawn. The usually gay, animated conversation one heard on a busy street was missing. The clatter of wooden clogs sounded like a herd of sheep crossing a wooden bridge. Leather shoes, even canvas ones with rubber soles, were priceless items, his mother explained.

Yusaki was shocked to see the dilapidated condition of his parents' home. His dazed, pain-racked condition had blinded him to it when he first arrived. Her voice choked, head averted to conceal her embarrassment, his mother said, "If you will excuse us now, we must change clothing. My silk kimono and your father's wool suit are reserved for special occasions. The only cloth available now is a blend of scarce cotton, tree bark, and wood pulp. It is called *sufu*. Wait in the garden, Yusaki, and enjoy the fresh air and sunshine. I will join you after I change."

The subdued young pilot felt self-conscious in his neatly tailored uniform and leather boots. That his father, an affluent, respected figure in the city, should be reduced to living little better than a peasant was hard to accept. Why? It was to be expected that the war would curtail luxuries, but basic foodstuffs? Clothing? Fuel and electricity?

Yusaki stared at the carefully tended garden. He recalled it as a place of serene beauty, with its arched bridge crossing a gently gurgling stream, delicately shaped cedar trees, and cherry trees just bursting into bloom.

A rectangle of raw earth he remembered as being filled with a prolific growth of chrysanthemums showed shoots of what could only be vegetables. A symmetrical imbalance bothered him until he realized that the towering eucalyptus tree that grew opposite the ancient mulberry was gone—a stump cut cleanly to the ground provided mute testimony to his parents' source of heat during the winter.

Yusaki frowned as he recalled the weekly political orientation lectures at Nanking. The Japanese were rising to the challenge of war with America, they were told. The essentials of life were in plentiful supply, but most chose an austere life-style to show support for their sons and husbands on the fighting fronts. Had his father experienced crippling financial reverses? Was he too proud—mother too ashamed—to write of their adversity?

The possibility only added to his churning turmoil. He was grounded! The peripheral vision in his right eye was below the minimum requirements for flying duty.

Yusaki had welcomed the news that he was to return to Yokosuka for medical treatment. The hospital was close to Tokyo and gave him a rare opportunity to visit with his parents. He went straight home after arriving on an army hospital plane.

His mother had screamed when he entered the carefully tended garden. "My son, what have they done to you?" Tears flowed as she grasped him in a fierce embrace.

"It is only a scratch," he protested stoutly, concealing the fact that his mother's action had set off a stab of pain that nearly caused him to crumple. "I've been returned to a hospital with better surgical facilities as a precaution."

"You look terrible," she whispered, backing off to better see the blood-encrusted bandage covering most of his scalp. "What happened? The admiralty told your father you were being returned here for medical treatment, but we didn't dream . . ."

Yusaki cut short an explanation as his father's aged but still erect figure appeared in the doorway leading from the house. He forced himself to bow and mutter, "Honorable Father. It gives me great pleasure to see you again."

The senior Nakano's rigid, unbending expression barely flickered. "Your injury appears to be worse than I was led to believe, my son. A battle wound?"

"Yes, Father. An engagement with an American fighter plane. I did not conduct myself with distinction."

"Battles seldom go as planned," the admiral conceded. "To be wounded in combat is never disgraceful. I will speak personally with the head surgeon."

Yusaki's memory of the remainder of that first evening was blurred. The only clear vision he retained was that of his sixteen-year-old cousin, Fukio. No longer a girl, she was a mature woman of breathtaking beauty. Raven black hair coiled atop her cameo-like face, a slender but well-formed body beneath a flowing kimono—an almost overnight transformation, it seemed. He was embarrassed by the open adoration he detected in her demurely averted gaze. Despite his discomfort, he vowed to see her again at the first possible moment.

* * *

His reverie was broken by his mother's return. Fukio was with her. Yusaki's eyes burned with shame as he saw them step into crude, wooden clogs. They wore nearly identical dresses of coarse, shapeless blue fabric. No mention was made of tea as they seated themselves opposite him. "Dinner will be limited in both quality and quantity," his mother said. "I was able to get ten grams of polished rice on the black market." She blushed and looked over her shoulder. "Don't tell your father its source. As leader of the neighborhood association, he becomes angry when friends boast of not having to do without. But otherwise we would have *nukapan*—a horrible dish of fried wheat flour and rice bran. My sister says it looks like delicious custard, but it tastes bitter, smells like horse dung, and makes you cry when you eat it."

Yusaki grew restless. The talk of shortages was depressing. He stood and announced, "I must have exercise. Fukio, will you accompany me on a walk around the old neighborhood?"

The girl blushed prettily. "I would be honored to walk at the arm of one of our brave fighting men." Madam Nakano smiled happily as she watched the young couple exit through the garden gate.

The pair walked in silence, Yusaki staring at the ground, his features dark and brooding. "Fukio, our people are starving—living like animals," he blurted. "Aren't you terribly unhappy?"

"I do without things cheerfully, cousin Yusaki, that you may have the means to save our country," the girl replied softly.

Yusaki's scowl deepened. He recalled stories of shortages of almost everything the army needed to win in Burma. A sense of foreboding swept over him; he would never see the day he could ask for this heavenly creature's hand in marriage. He reached for her and roughly crushed her to his breast, his hungry lips bruising her own.

Thrusting the startled girl away, he rasped, "I may not return from this war because I will never shame you or my family by surrendering. If I do return, I will claim you. If not, remember me as one who loved you."

Dinner was a subdued affair. Yusaki ate sparingly, ashamed that he was consuming more food in one meal than his parents would have in a normal day. Fukio also toyed with her food, but for another reason. Unusual color painted her ivory-hued cheeks; she would not meet Yusaki's gaze.

Yusaki's thoughts returned to the present at his mother's words: "The surgeon performed a near miracle in just saving your sight. To be discharged after only two weeks' convalescence is most unusual for surgery such as yours. You will have time to regain your strength at home before returning to your station."

"I'm sorry, Mother. I report for duty tomorrow. And I won't be returning to my old station," Yusaki responded. "I can no longer fly an airplane. Do you not understand?" His voice rose. "My career is finished." He turned toward his father with an anguished look.

"If the ladies will leave us, I have need of a private conversation with my son," the old admiral said stiffly. Yusaki's mother and Fukio rose at once. After bowing in obeisance to the senior Nakano, they turned toward the door, but not before Fukio regarded the young flyer with brimming eyes. Yusaki resisted a sudden urge to embrace the lovely girl, to pour out his frustrated disappointment.

His father cleared his throat and announced, "Your flying career is not ended, Yusaki, unless you *request* nonflying duty."

Yusaki's wan features wrinkled in a puzzled frown. "I do not understand. Keen vision is a prerequisite for a fighter pilot. The doctor said the optic nerve was nicked during surgery. My condition is permanent."

The elder Nakano shook his head. "While it would be unwise, dangerous even, for one to fly combat with impaired vision, it is less critical in the case of an instructor pilot."

"An *instructor?*" Yusaki's voice was shrill. "Instructing whom? To do what? I have neither the experience nor the training to teach others to fly."

"I talked with the commandant at Tsuchiura—your old flying school. He remembers you; you were an honor graduate. He will be most happy to have you join the school."

"But—but, my eye. I cannot—"

"The surgeon and Commander Honekawa insist that your vision is adequate for noncombatant duty," his father interrupted. The old man sighed. "Yusaki, you may as well hear it from me. The war does not go well for us. Pilots, fighter pilots especially, are desperately needed."

"But they told us just the opposite," Yusaki protested. "The factories are building as many as twelve planes per day. Surplus navy squadrons are being assigned to land bases."

"Assigned to land bases because there aren't enough carriers to fly from." Yusaki noticed that his father suddenly looked much older. The normally direct, piercing gaze was faded, his voice and expression were melancholy. "Word reached navy headquarters only last week of a great sea and air battle. Our recent losses include four carriers and more than five hundred airplanes—and crews. The aircraft are easily replaced; the carriers and pilots are not. Pilot training must be greatly accelerated."

"I—I scarcely know what to say, Father. Instructing is a terribly important task. An instructor is responsible for ensuring that the student is trained to cope with any situation. To fail in one's duty could cost a life. Can I adequately meet these demands? My vision—do I dare risk failure?"

The old man's eyes blazed. "You are a Samurai, Nakano Yusaki. The blood of warriors courses your veins. There is no task too difficult, no challenge too formidable for a Nakano to undertake. You will report to the commandant at Tsuchiura tomorrow. You will not fail."

Chapter Ten

10 May 1944
Somewhere in Burma

Ross's eyes were swollen nearly shut by insect bites. With difficulty, he could make out that they were leaving the hilly scrub jungle and entering a level meadow. The thoughts of easier footing drove him to increase his pace to catch up with Farnsworth and the Kachins. His elation was short-lived. The "meadow" was matted with grass higher than his head and with blades that cut exposed skin like razor-sharp knives. He floundered knee deep in stinking mud and rotted leaves.

After what seemed hours, he almost stumbled headlong into the others; they stood waiting on an animal path that offered a respite from the swampy terrain. Farnsworth gave Ross a speculative look. "We'll have four or five hours of this stuff. We're exposed and can't stop for camp. You up to it?"

"Don't worry about me, Farnsworth. I'll be right behind you," Ross grated. The lieutenant merely shrugged and strode away.

Put one foot in front of the other, Ross told himself. The game trail had twisted off to their right all too soon. Don't worry about the next step, or the next; just concentrate on taking this one without stumbling. Ignore the insects; don't think about the burning, stinging rash in your crotch. Just tug one boot from the foul, sucking mud, move it in front of the other one, and shift your weight. The skin-withering sun mercifully passed behind a cloud. Its scorching discomfort was replaced by pouring rain, immediate and heavy, that made breathing difficult. Ross could hardly see the Kachin fifty feet in front of him.

Ross lost track of time. Nothing mattered but reaching the higher ground he glimpsed through slitted eyes from time to time. He was surprised to find Farnsworth halted at the edge of a wide trail. The grass forming its border was fire blackened. The smell of burned vegetation hung in the heavy air like acrid fog.

"Japs," Farnsworth said tersely. "They make these paths with flamethrowers. This one was made this morning."

"Well, at least it makes for faster going," Ross gasped.

"No way. Damnit, it adds hours to the trip—hours I can't spare."

"How so?"

Farnsworth grunted without answering. "All right, let's move out."

Ross discovered that his last few steps had been on firm ground. He looked up in pleased surprise. The rain had passed on and the sun was edging toward the crests of some jagged-topped hills. A cooling breeze flowed toward them. Farnsworth fell back to walk alongside. "The worst is behind us, Colyer. We'll be in those hills by dark and pitch a decent camp." Ross nodded, too exhausted to speak.

He came close to throwing in the towel when they halted at the foot of a steep incline. "If it weren't for the Nips, we could have gone an easier way," Farnsworth explained. "As it is, we have to go about a half mile straight up that slope before we make camp. If you can't hack it, I'll have the boys carry you."

Ross concealed his dismay and glared. "Nobody's going to carry me," he snarled. "Just point the way."

Without the stimulus of anger, he would have quit, he admitted to himself. The slope was pitched upward at a forty-five-degree angle. It was covered with tangled ferns and head-high brush—most bearing thorns. Ross watched the Kachins thread their way through the vegetation with little apparent effort; Farnsworth followed in their wake.

Ross's feet failed to support him, however. He clenched his teeth and crawled. Surprisingly, the space beneath the growth of briars was relatively clear. He tugged himself forward on knees and elbows. Farnsworth and the Kachins watched him crawl into the clearing a half hour later without comment.

He sprawled full length on turf covered by springy moss and ferns.

It was heaven—the most expensive Beautyrest innerspring couldn't have felt better. Farnsworth stood over him. "Cold camp, I'm afraid. The Japs are all around us. Now, we're going to eat, rest a couple of hours, then leave you. We have a job to do.

"There's a river just on the other side of this row of hills. A railroad bridge crosses it. We're going to blow that bridge tonight. That's our sole purpose for being here. Jap patrols are out, looking for you mostly. If we aren't back by daylight, rest up tomorrow, then head north by northwest along this ridgeline. Stay out of the river valley. The rail line runs there and you're bound to blunder into a patrol.

"You're about three days from some friendly villages. You'll find some paths; follow them and you'll run into friendly natives. I'm leaving all our supplies; take what you think you'll need. If the Japs catch you—well, good luck."

Ross sat and fumbled with his boots. "I'll be okay," he mumbled. "First I have to dry out my socks and boots. They must have sprung a leak; my feet are soaked." He drew off the boot and choked back a horrified scream. Fully a cup of blood poured from his boot. His lower leg and ankle were covered with ugly, bloated leeches.

12 May 1944
100 Miles South of Fort Hertz, Burma

Ross and Lieutenant Farnsworth slumped alongside the faint path the group had followed all afternoon. The half-dozen Kachins squatted in a circle and passed around slices of their seemingly never-ending supply of betel nut. The little band had emerged from the jungle-choked valley about noon and had been climbing since. Ross breathed deeply of the relatively dryer, cooler air. "My God, but it's good to be out of that hellish mess. Those leeches—I can still feel the damn things. How do these people stand living down there?"

Farnsworth grunted. "Put 'em in a New York slum and they'll probably ask you the same thing. Look, Benjy has gone ahead to a village just over the next crest. He'll tell the headman we're here and make sure it's safe to enter the village. We'll spend the night there, then tomorrow you'll be picked up by plane and flown to another base where an ATC plane can fetch you."

"The hell you say?" Ross sat upright, his bone-deep fatigue and burning heat rash mottled with insect bites temporarily forgotten. "Tomorrow? Why didn't you tell me sooner?"

The chronically morose lieutenant sighed. "Colyer, I've tried to convince you that you're a liability. The Japs have been on our ass since we blew their railroad bridge. If they catch you, you'll talk. Believe me, they have techniques guaranteed to loosen any tongue. We have to turn around after we deliver you and go back down there. I'd have trouble sleeping nights if I thought they learned from you where we might be—the location of our bases and friendly villages."

"Okay, okay," Ross said irritably. "You've made your point—once a day at least. But"—he looked toward the forested slope—"I don't see anything that looks like an airfield."

"Wait and see. Look, I know I've been on your ass pretty hard. But this is a business where any slipup is usually fatal. I'll say this, you've been a real trooper. I know that dysentery leaves you like an old limp rag. I'd figured on the boys having to carry you—part of the way at least. They like you, you know, and they don't have much tolerance for weaklings."

Ross chuckled. "Two compliments in one day. That's a world record. Now, I'll tell you that I'm forever in your debt for hauling me out of that situation back there. Somehow I think those Japs had slightly different plans for my future."

Farnsworth treated Ross to one of his rare smiles, a lopsided grimace. "We try. That's the reason the Kachins are on our side. The Japs butchered entire villages when they came this way. These boys don't forgive and forget very easily."

"Are they really headhunters?" Ross asked. "They seem too happy-go-lucky to be bloodthirsty killers."

"You better believe it. I saw one hut with a rack that covered an entire wall. It was full. They don't kill indiscriminately, though. It's almost always a tribal war type of thing."

Ross watched the squatting natives finish rolling betel nut slices inside a green leaf and chew it as they talked. "Do you suppose it's that stuff that makes them so damn bloodthirsty?"

"Hardly, they've been using it since they were off the teat," Farnsworth answered. "I gave Honcho holy hell for feeding it to you. He was surprised and hurt. Said he wanted to make you feel better."

"He sure as hell did that," Ross responded ruefully. "I would swear I saw one of those big tigers I hear about."

"You had your chance today, you know," Farnsworth told him with a lazy grin.

"Really? Where? When?"

"Shortly after we started climbing. One of the buggers stalked us for almost two hours. This is big tiger country—*really* big ones. The natives in this village we're headed for claim to have killed one that measured five feet from shoulder to forepaw."

Ross's eyes grew wide and round. "A goddamn tiger—*stalking* us? How do you know?"

"Benjy claims he can smell 'em—probably can. He dropped back and kept an eye on it until the cat saw something it thought was easier game. He was probably getting out of his territory as well."

Benjy's return terminated the conversation. The village was free of enemy threat and would welcome Farnsworth Sahib and his party.

Farnsworth, with Ross at his side, led the little column of swaggering warriors into the village. It appeared to Ross that most, if not all, the population was on hand to greet them—a rousing welcome for visiting heroes. Ross surveyed the village as the headman, attired in festive costume, rattled off a long speech. The man boasted a headdress of bamboo fronds painted to resemble feathers, as well as several necklaces. He would, in any other setting, look garishly out of place, Ross mused. He obviously considered Farnsworth an old friend.

Ross examined the arrangement of *bashas,* mounted three feet above the ground as protection against unwelcome furry and scaly visitors. They were well made and immaculately maintained. Low fences, a lattice woven of split bamboo, surrounded most. The "street" they traversed was swept clean. The center of attraction, however, was a temple. The structure boasted a tower almost three stories high and was surrounded by a shoulder-high wall of mud bricks.

The chattering throng ushered their visitors to an area sheltered by a woven-rattan top and with log benches around the perimeter. Smiling young women, looking almost Western with faces uncovered and breasts chastely draped with colored cloth, poured a potent beverage from hollow bamboo tubes. Exhaustion reduced Ross to a zombielike trance, and he barely remembered being steered to a remote hut.

Farnsworth was sitting outside the *basha* drinking coffee and smoking a cigaret when Ross awakened. "You missed a good party last night," the OSS officer said with a grin. "Nothing like a combination of a little booze and betel nut to get things moving. I'm not sure I'm going to be able to get my troops on their feet and underway before noon."

Ross decided he felt better than he had any right to, and helped himself to the coffee Farnsworth had brewed. "Any idea when that airplane will be here?" he asked.

"Honcho was on the radio before the party got out of hand last night. Weather cooperating, it should be here by noon."

"I'm ready. Where will I go next?"

"A base called Fort Hertz. It's about an hour's flying time from here. An ATC C-47 will pick you up in a few days, and presto, you'll be back with your squadron at Chabua."

"Can't be any too soon. Where is the field from here?"

The OSS man smiled. "You're looking at it."

"How's that?"

"I said you're looking at it. Keep an eye on that group of men just beyond the temple."

Ross watched, a puzzled frown wrinkling his forehead, as four villagers approached a bamboo hut. They lifted the crude structure from the ground and carried it to the edge of the forest. Others repeated the process again and again before Ross comprehended what was happening. The broad, well-kept "Main Street" he'd admired the night before was a goddamn *runway.*

"Pretty tricky, huh?" Farnsworth asked, obviously pleased at Ross's reaction. "The headman's idea. The Japs watch the villages from the air; they know we depend on light planes for supplies. Anytime we try to hack out a landing strip, they shoot it up. All they see here is a collection of huts. The fake *bashas* weigh maybe sixty to eighty pounds, and it takes about a half hour to create a runway."

"I'll be damned," Ross muttered admiringly. "It still isn't very long. What kind of plane do you use that can land and take off in . . . hell, it can't be more than five hundred feet?"

"It's a Gypsy Moth we talked the Brits out of. A fabric-covered biplane with two open cockpits—you'll love it."

"That remains to be seen," Ross said. "I flew a plane like that in primary flying school—the Stearman. As I recall, it was only slightly more comfortable than a freight car. But"—he cocked his head—"we'll soon know. Your pilot's early."

"What?"

"He's early. I can hear him. I've lived around airplanes too long to mistake the sound."

Farnsworth leaped to his feet. "Oh, good Christ, *no!* That can't be our plane." He yelled through cupped hands and ran toward the group removing the runway camouflage.

Ross couldn't identify the plane that cleared the range of hills north of the village and roared toward them, but it wasn't American, and its intentions plainly weren't friendly. "Get down, you damn fool!" he screamed at Farnsworth, then rolled beneath the scanty shelter offered by an elevated *basha.*

Farnsworth was caught in the open. Ross saw the single-engine craft level off less than a hundred feet above the ground and streak above the first cluster of huts. Two black objects tumbled from between its fixed landing gear.

Facedown in the dirt, covering his head with crossed arms, Ross heard two ear-shattering blasts—felt hot air, rank with the biting smell of cordite, rush past with hurricane force. The fragile structure above him disintegrated. Deafened, numb with shock, he reared his head in time to see Farnsworth's lower body flopping hideously in the still-raining debris. The OSS man's head and upper torso were missing.

He could dimly hear screams of pain and anguish; somewhere a woman wailed piteously. He saw dazed villagers emerge from cover and wander aimlessly among the dead and injured. He leaped to his feet and rushed toward the dust-choked scene. "Get under cover!" he yelled frantically. "Get out of sight, damnit. He'll be back!" His English words fell on unheeding ears. Ross scooped up two half-naked children standing alongside an inert woman who leaked blood from a dozen places, and raced for cover offered by the nearby forest.

The Jap pilot wasted no time, racking his plane into a tight turn and taking up a reciprocal course. Crouching behind a tree, Ross watched the sleek, forest green craft, a red "meatball" prominent on wings and fuselage, rake the hapless villagers with 7.7mm machine-gun fire. He could see the helmeted pilot crouched over the controls. The man faced forward, concentrating on avoiding trees rushing toward him at the clearing's edge. "Damn you!" Ross yelled helplessly. "Look *back.* Look at the helpless women and kids you've mangled. You call yourself a *fighter* pilot?"

Ross stood in the shadow cast by a huge bamboo tree and watched the OD-painted biplane brake to a stop at the primitive airstrip's far end. The pilot gunned the engine and trundled to where Ross and a dozen natives huddled. The pilot removed his goggles and helmet and regarded the group with tight-lipped anger. "How did Otis get it?"

Ross stepped forward. "He got caught in the open; there was no warning whatsoever."

The pilot pounded his thigh with a gloved fist. Surveying the stricken village through the smoke still curling from burned huts, he asked—

speaking to himself it seemed—"How? How in the hell did those bastards find out? That's what I'd like to know."

"You mean you don't think that Jap pilot just stumbled across the runway? They'd just about cleared it, you know," Ross ventured.

"Hell, no, it was no accident," the pilot growled savagely. "You can hardly find this place when you know where you're going, much less by luck. Some stupid bastard blabbed, not here necessarily, but as far away as Calcutta. The Burmese hear everything—and they pass it on to the Japs. Okay, which of you is the radioman?"

Honcho stepped forward.

"You're to stay around here. A new team leader will be airdropped within the week with new orders. Give Farnsworth a Christian burial; a Catholic priest is on his way from another village." He eyed Ross and rapped, "All right, whatever your name is, crawl in. You'll find a helmet and goggles in the side pocket. Let's get the hell out of this place."

Chapter Eleven

20 May 1944
Chabua Army Airfield

The smiling, sandy-haired major extended his hand. "Captain Colyer? I'm Jeff Baxter, intelligence officer for the 354th Air Transport Wing. Have a seat."

Ross sat down in the only chair visible, facing the major's desk. "Thanks. What can I do for you?"

"Well, the flight surgeon has given you a clean bill of health after your little stroll through beautiful Burma, and I understand you're leaving for Kunming to rejoin your squadron. I'd like to ask you a few questions about your experience."

"Oh?"

"Yes, we got the okay from Fourteenth headquarters to debrief you. We like to talk with walkouts to see if we can pick up any tips to pass on to our transport pilots. We're interested in where friendly natives can be found, the route you took, and so forth."

"I'll do what I can," Ross responded warily.

The major fitted a printed form to a clipboard. "Okay. The report filed by your CO states that you were shot down about thirty miles from Myitkyina."

"That sounds about right."

"Now, what happened? I'll take you back over events with some specific questions, but first I'd just like for you to tell me about your experiences without interruption."

"I came down in jungle. My chute got tangled in trees, and I had to climb down. I walked north that afternoon and slept on the ground near a big tree that first night. The Japs found me the next morning. Before they could get me away from the scene, three natives rescued me. They led me through the jungle for two days before I came down with dysentery. They took me to a camp where a Lieutenant Farnsworth took over and led me to another village, where I was picked up by a light plane and returned here."

Baxter gave a short laugh. "Now that comes close to being the shortest account of a walkout I've heard. I'm afraid we're going to have to ask for some more specifics. Let's start with the target. Your squadron commander said you were out of position during a high-speed strafing pass and flew over an AA battery. Can you recall seeing the gun position?"

"I beg your pardon?"

"The gun emplacement. Did you see more than one? Was it a multiple mount? Twenty millimeter? Forty?"

"No, not that," Ross snapped. "What was that bit about my 'being out of position'? Let's have that again."

Baxter selected a single page from the folder before him and read, "Colyer appeared to have trouble holding formation. He was unable to get in position during the first run, so I was forced to make a second pass at the row of parked bombers. This time he lined up outside the field boundaries. I didn't see the ground fire and was unaware he was hit until he advised me by radio." The major raised his eyebrows questioningly and asked, "Is that the way you recall it happening?"

Ross felt blood suffusing his neck and face. "Not exactly." He had difficulty forcing words past taut throat muscles. "Look, Major, I'm sorry, but can we put off the rest of your debriefing until I've had an opportunity to talk with Major King?"

Baxter frowned and scratched his jaw. "Well . . . I'm not sure I understand, but can we at least go on with your walkout? That's what I'm really interested in." He indicated a wall map. "Can you trace your route on the map?"

"I'm afraid not."

Baxter's frown deepened to a scowl. "Colyer, look. The lives of pilots shot down over that area could depend on information you can provide. Why are you reluctant to help me?"

"First of all, Major, I don't have the foggiest idea where I was at any given time. Lieutenant Farnsworth was worried that I'd be able to provide just those details if the Japs got their hands on me again. He went to great lengths to keep me unaware of where we were and where we were going. The only location I can identify for certain is Fort Hertz."

"Oh, for Christ's sake." Baxter tossed his pencil to the desk in disgust. "Those OSS types are paranoid. I know they debriefed you at Fort Hertz, but they refuse to share intelligence with us. What you can tell me may save the life of another pilot. Can't you understand that?"

"Maybe they aren't as paranoid as you think, Major." Ross's voice hardened. "The Japs bombed and strafed the village where I was picked up just hours before the plane arrived. Farnsworth was killed during the attack. The OSS pilot was mad as hell. That landing strip was beautifully camouflaged; he claimed that the Japs could never have found it by accident. Perhaps your security isn't as tight as it could be."

Baxter's sunburned features took on a deep crimson hue. "I resent the hell out of that, Colyer. I think it's time we terminated this session—unless you want to cooperate, that is."

"It isn't a matter of cooperating, Major," Ross responded. "I honestly don't know the details you want. But I'll say this. I'm not sure I would tell you if I did. If there's nothing more, I'd like to be excused . . . sir."

"Go right ahead," Baxter grated. "But don't think you've heard the last of this. I rather think your CO is going to have some pretty pointed questions for you."

You don't know the half of it, Buster, Ross thought grimly as he stalked into the energy-sapping afternoon heat. *I'm* going to have a few questions for *that* bastard as well.

21 May 1944
Chabua Army Airfield

Ross rolled out of the Jeep into a steady downpour. He grabbed his B-4 and duffel bags from the backseat and sloshed inside the dimly lit operations building. Dashing rainwater from his flight suit, he walked toward the dispatcher's counter to where a husky individual with curly brown hair was scowling over a sheaf of paperwork. "Lieutenant Butler?" Ross asked.

The bulky figure turned. "Yeah, I'm Butler. You must be our passenger. Captain Colyer, is it?"

"That's right."

"I understand you're an old B-24 pilot turned fighter jock. I envy you. You picked a helluva night to cross the Hump, but I guess you've been in heavy weather before. We're going to get bounced around right good—the monsoon's settin' in."

"So I see," Ross replied, taking an instant liking to the weary-faced young pilot. "If the C-87 is anything like the Liberator, it will be cold, leaky, and rattle like a bucket of scrap iron."

"Right on all counts. Wish I could let you take the right seat; I've got a green copilot this trip. But ATC regs are real iron-assed about that. You'll be on the flight deck, however. They used the room for the upper turret to put in four bucket seats. And you'll have company—a couple of Chinese army officers. They haven't shown up yet. Maybe they won't. You can't ever tell with that bunch.

"They're topping up the mains just now. It'll put us over gross takeoff weight, but I always like a cushion with ice out there. This bird gulps gas like it was good booze. C'mon, we'll hop a crew truck and go see how things are coming along."

As the battered truck jounced through muddy puddles, Ross leaned across the bed. "What're we carrying?"

"Same as usual. Ten thousand pounds of av-gas in drums and about a ton of bomb fuses. They've been flying our ass off lately. I understand they're stockpiling supplies for the B-29s—for whenever those elite bastards decide they're ready to bomb Japan. I'm sorry I won't be around to see that, but another fifty hours and I'm gone. I'd just like to be a little mouse when those guys who've been boring holes over Kansas prairies get a look at flying conditions over here. She-e-e-it." He flashed a wolfish grin at Ross in the gloom.

The plane's overhanging wing provided a brief respite from the steady rain as they climbed out of the back of the truck. Ross regarded the aircraft's bulk, faintly outlined by lights that the ground crew had placed to illuminate the refueling process. It seemed larger than he remembered. With huge twin vertical stabilizers, four oversized engine nacelles, and shoulder-high landing gear, added to the high wing extending from the top of her slab-sided fuselage, she resembled a crouching, prehistoric monster. He silently congratulated himself for manipulating his switch to the sleek P-51.

Ross walked around the clattering auxiliary power unit and crawled aboard. Scrambling onto the darkened flight deck, he saw that the copilot was already strapped in. The instrument panel's array of red, green, and amber lights cast just enough light for Ross to see the man's grinning face turned in his direction. "Welcome aboard, Captain. If you'll just take that seat there, you'll find a headset plugged into the intercom. Your chute and an extra oxygen mask are there as well."

Butler clambered up the boarding ladder as Ross was strapping into his chute harness. The pilot flung his own chute, map case, and oxygen mask into the cockpit and adjusted the shoulder-holstered .45-caliber pistol with its added sheathed hunting knife. Below and to Ross's left, the radio operator called, "Just got a pilot report, Lieutenant. Weather's rotten to Paoshan—clearing to Tsuyung. Kunming, up and down—mostly down."

"Thank you for those encouraging words, Sully. Keep listening until you can give me some good news. Arky, where the hell are you?"

A wizened, wet, fatigue-clad figure materialized out of the night and called out cheerfully, "Right behind you, Lieutenant. Tanks are checked, pins are out, and the fireguard's standing by."

"Okay." Butler turned back to the front and tapped the copilot's shoulder. "Bruce, call the tower for takeoff. Turning number three."

"Hold it," the engineer called. "Looks like our other passengers just drove up."

"Okay, hustle 'em on board," Butler growled. "Get 'em strapped in. If they have chutes, try to explain how to use the damn things. Just hope one of 'em can understand simple English."

"I can do that if you want to get started, Lieutenant," Ross said.

"Thanks, Captain. Arky, get back up here and let's get on the road."

Ross directed the pair of nattily uniformed officers to empty seats. "Do you speak English?" he asked.

One of the identically dressed pair smiled. "I am much pleased to understand many of your words, sir."

"Okay. Have you flown before?"

Two close-shaven heads bobbed in unison. Ross showed them the seat belt latch and called over his shoulder, "Hey, Engineer, don't these guys have chutes?"

"Naw. The Chinese army won't provide 'em none, and we don't have all that many for our own use, Captain. The Chinks don't care. They don't consider a life to be worth the hundred bucks a parachute costs."

Ross shook his head. "That's it, then. We're as ready as we'll ever be back here." Christ, if we should have to bail out, could we actually just wave good-bye and jump? he wondered. He switched his comm selector to radio and stood at the copilot's shoulder, watching the familiar routine of preparing for takeoff.

A Jeep, the words FOLLOW ME spelled out in lights on its rear, led them through the murky darkness to the takeoff position. When Butler started his run-up, the vehicle sped off down the runway. At the far end it turned until its headlights were barely visible.

"Hey," Butler exulted, "we can see the whole length of the runway tonight." He turned to Ross and added, "It's the only visibility check we have, but mostly he does that to be sure there aren't any cows on the runway."

Butler completed the engine run-up and keyed his mike. "Chabua Tower, this is Triple Six Eight, ready once more to defy gravity. Over."

"Roger, Triple Six. Hold your position. We have a Dumbo on final. After takeoff you are cleared to climb to ten thousand feet over the Victor George beacon before proceeding on course."

As Bruce read back their clearance, all eyes turned toward the runway's rain-obscured approach. A shaft of brilliant blue light bored straight up into the rain—the ceilingometer. It didn't require a reading of the theodolite at its base to see that the cloud base was less than three hundred feet. The C-46's landing lights swam into view, followed almost immediately by a splashing touchdown. "Not bad, not bad at all," Butler murmured. "Okay, crew, prepare for takeoff. All crew members will be on oxygen from the ground up."

Ross watched Butler coax the overloaded ship into a shallow, climbing spiral. The airspeed hovered at minimum safe climb speed, and the rate of climb never exceeded four hundred feet per minute. Damn, he thought, a B-24 with full combat load did better than this. We are *really* loaded, well beyond design limits. Nevertheless, he envied Butler, melding mind, muscle, and machine to obtain performance never envisioned by Consolidated's engineers. It was a heady experience, and he longed to switch places. Being a mere passenger was such a helpless feeling.

Forty minutes later, with the altimeter indicating ten thousand feet, Butler rolled to a heading of 114 degrees. The ADF needle swung to the rear as the VG beacon fell behind. Before them stretched five hundred miles of torturous terrain and weather. The Naga Hills just ahead were only twelve thousand feet, Ross recalled, but just to the north, peaks reared to eighteen thousand to twenty thousand feet in the storm-torn blackness.

Arky took advantage of the stable air to heat coffee and beef bouillon in a tiny galley. The Chinese officers accepted theirs—served with a couple of questionable-looking mess hall cookies—with pleased smiles. Keep smiling, Ross said to himself; all hell is going to break loose shortly. He glanced out the windshield. In the space of a heartbeat the driving rain had changed to snow. The flashing green navigation light marking the right wingtip was a barely visible glow.

They were running through boiling cloud tops now. Through occasional breaks, a half moon provided glimpses of angry thunderheads, piled to altitudes of forty to fifty thousand feet above the Naga range. Then the breaks closed over. The turbulence increased in short, jolting tremors. Ross heard Butler call for windshield defrosters and wing deicers. He tensed. The high-lift Davis wing was an engineering marvel, but just small amounts of ice could turn it into a slab with about as much lift as you'd get from a wooden plank.

A series of shattering crashes battered the aluminum skin only inches from his right shoulder. The Chinese would have sprung from their seats had they not been restrained by seat belts. Bruce, the green copilot, uttered a startled yelp. "Prop ice," Ross heard Butler explain in a casual tone. "Advance the props about a hundred RPMs to throw off the buildup, then return 'em to cruise. You'll probably have to do that every ten minutes or so." Ross gave his fellow passengers a reassuring nod and grin. He could have added that the time to worry was when the stuff *didn't* break loose.

Concern for the building load of ice fled as the big transport bucked like a wild horse and lurched into a near-vertical bank. Glancing forward, Ross saw the gyrohorizon exceed its limits and tumble into meaningless gyrations. The rate-of-climb indicator showed they were dropping at two thousand feet per minute. He watched with increasing concern as Butler wrestled with the controls in an effort to regain a level attitude. To maintain even flight with only the basic needle, ball, and airspeed instruments in turbulence such as this required consummate skill. The slightest misjudgment could result in either an excessive nose-up attitude and subsequent stall, or nose-down flight with the airspeed exceeding the plane's structural limits.

The swirling air currents, set up by 100-MPH winds spilling over the Nagas' eastern slope, ceased as suddenly as they began. Triple Six Eight entered serene, moon-bathed air. Butler returned the ship to an even keel, caged and reset the gyrohorizon, and signaled for Bruce to take the controls. The brawny pilot crossed to the galley, drew a cup of coffee, then settled into the empty seat beside Ross.

"Keeps you on your toes," he observed, sipping his coffee. "They say that on a clear day you can stay on course by following a trail of aluminum across this stretch. North of here are some really big mamas. One called Mount Tali gets a lot of pilots who are blown off course on this leg. Mount Everest is up there—twenty-nine thousand feet. Some of the guys, cruising at thirty, swear they've seen other peaks, ones that don't show up on the charts, two to three thousand feet higher than their flight altitude. It's a bitch, all right. No offense intended, but I've heard you fighter and bomber boys call the ATC the 'Army of Terrified Copilots' and 'Allergic to Combat.' She-e-e-it."

Ross clapped a hand on Butler's shoulder. "Not this fighter jock, Lieutenant, no how, no way."

Butler grinned and yelled to the radio operator. "Hey, Sully, what do you hear from Kunming?"

The RO disconnected his oxygen mask and climbed to the flight deck. "Nothing good, Lieutenant. There's a stack over Roger Queen beacon. It's taking about an hour to get down."

"Aw, shit," Butler exclaimed disgustedly. He turned to Ross. "See why I add gas on a night like this?" He tossed his paper cup into a trash receptacle and returned to the cockpit.

Ross clamped the headset to his ears and listened to Butler's conversation with Kunming Tower. "Descend to twelve thousand, Triple Six Eight. Hold over Roger Queen beacon. Expected approach time: zero-one-four-four. Current Kunming weather: ceiling three hundred feet, indefinite, visibility one mile, lowering to one-half mile during rain squalls." Ross shrugged. Kunming's runway elevation was six thousand feet. With planes stacked at five-hundred-foot intervals, that meant five aircraft were ahead of them. He mentally congratulated Butler for his foresight in adding extra fuel. Even with that reserve, they would have less than an hour's endurance remaining after starting their approach.

The traffic controller's unemotional drone as he directed individual planes to progressively lower altitudes lulled Ross into a lethargic doze. One exchange, however, brought him wide awake. "Kunming Tower, this is Seven One Three, holding at seven thousand five hundred. I'm down to emergency reserve fuel. Request an expedited approach. Over."

"Roger, understand, Seven One Three. Stand by. Seven Seven Niner, Kunming Tower. Over."

"Seven Seven Niner here, Tower. Go ahead."

"Seven Seven Niner, Kunming Tower. Continue holding at seven thousand, south of Roger Queen beacon. I'm letting an emergency in ahead of you. Over."

"Hold on there a minute, Dad. This is Seven Seven Niner, and I'm looking at a red warning light on my right main. I can't wait any longer to start my approach."

"Understand, Seven Seven Niner. Start your approach from your present position. Call final approach. Over. Seven One Three, descend to seven thousand. I will expedite your approach."

"Uh, Tower, this is Seven One Three. I don't know about this. What is present Chengkung weather? Over."

"Chengkung is presently reporting one thousand feet broken, visibility two miles with drizzle. Over."

"I think I'll divert, Tower. We have enough fuel to reach Chengkung if we go now. I don't like this hanging around."

"Roger, Seven One Three, understand. You are cleared from your present position to the Chengkung airfield, to land at pilot's discretion. Be advised of high terrain ten miles north of your route. Over."

A strange voice broke in. "Wally, this is Bob. You ever landed at Chengkung? Over."

"Negative."

"Well, it's a fighter strip—four thousand feet, unpaved. Suggest you make a pass at Kunming. Over."

"Uh—thanks Bob, but I think I'd rather take my chances VFR. I'm letting down now to—*what the hell*—"

"Wally! Seven One Three, this is Seven Oh Four. Over. Come in, Wally."

After unbuckling his seat belt, Ross sprang to his feet and stood between the pilots' seats. He heard the Kunming Tower operator make repeated attempts to raise Seven One Three, then, his voice sounding strained, say, "Triple Six Eight, you are cleared to descend to seven thousand. Report reaching. All aircraft holding for approach to Kunming, be advised the field is presently below ADF landing minimums. Reported visibility now one-half mile with fog and drizzle. Break. Triple Six Eight, advise your intentions. Over."

Butler pounded the control wheel with a clenched fist. Stripping off his oxygen mask, he raged, "The damn fools. Will they never learn? Oh well . . . Tower, Triple Six Eight. Will continue my approach. Over."

"Roger, understand. Do you have ILS equipment installed, Triple Six? Over."

"Uh—roger, Tower. We have ILS installed."

"Roger, Triple Six. You are cleared for an ILS approach to Runway One-seven. Call outer marker inbound. Over."

"Well, shit," Butler muttered. "What the hell do I do now?"

Ross realized with a sinking feeling that the veteran Hump pilot had never flown an ILS approach. He gulped and asked, "Uh, Lieutenant, have you made one of these recently?"

"Fuck, no," the glowering pilot snarled. "Never had time for training flights. I've heard about the stupid thing, but guys I talk to don't trust it."

"Look, Lieutenant, I went through the instrument instructor's course—flew maybe fifty. Would you like for me to talk you through this one?"

Butler scowled thoughtfully. Finally he snapped, "Beats maybe busting our ass. Screw the regs. Bruce, switch places with Captain Colyer. And watch what he does; maybe we'll both learn something."

Fifteen minutes later, Triple Six Eight slid over the field boundary and touched down in a shower of spray. Butler let the big ship roll to the runway's far end and turned to where a FOLLOW ME jeep waited. He glanced sideways at Ross and growled, "If you weren't so damn ugly, sir, I'd kiss you."

Chapter Twelve

22 May 1944
Kunming, China

A cheerful, "Welcome back from the vacation," made Ross look up from the paperback he was reading. He confronted O. B. Holt's grinning countenance. "Orderly clerk told me you signed in at some ungodly hour this morning. Thought I'd drop by and see if you still had all your necessary parts—like a head." The chunky ops officer stuck out his hand.

"To say I'm glad to get back would be an understatement," Ross replied. "And that business about a head is no joke. I met some really mean campers out there. Hey, I like this climate. I can actually breathe. Can't say much for the quarters, though. Whose idea was it to build them on the parking ramp?"

Holt chuckled. "I wouldn't get too comfortable. This is the transient hostel. The 41st is based at Chengkung, about thirty miles from here. Not exactly a garden spot, but better than Chabua. C'mon, let's go into town; we can talk over breakfast. You'll love the food here: bacon, fresh eggs, fresh bread, even *steak*. Then, tomorrow, you can ride the supply truck with us back to CK. I talked my way into coming on a scrounging mission. A lot of things we don't have—like Kotex, would you believe? As you'll find out, gasoline and oil are like gold here. We strain engine oil through Kotex and reuse it."

Holt led Ross into a hotel dining room and selected a cloth-covered table. The din was deafening. "Chinese have to be the noisiest goddamn people on earth," O.B. commented. "They talk constantly, and at the top of their voices. Forget anything you ever heard about the 'inscrutable' Oriental."

Their orders placed, Ross asked, "So how's the squadron coming along? Christ, I'll be glad to get back in a cockpit."

Holt rearranged his teacup and chopsticks. He didn't meet Ross's eyes as he replied, "Oh, there are problems. For one thing, we don't have fuel for training missions—no spare ammo for gunnery practice. We've flown exactly six four-ship sorties since we've been here. Not a single enemy sighting. Everyone is gearing up for the B-29s. General Chennault isn't talking, but rumor has it that we'll only be here until they have bases ready for us farther east."

"Are those the *only* problems?" Ross asked, pinning Holt with a shrewd look.

"Ross, we agreed from the start that I would stay out of your problems with Major King. I avoid discussing you with him when I can, but I hear talk. Anyway, he's replaced you as 'C' Flight commander. You're going to be the squadron training officer."

"I see." A waiter brought their food to the table, and Ross dug into his ham and eggs and ate with obvious pleasure. After washing a mouthful down with aromatic green tea, he asked, "So what did the good major have to say about our mission over Myitkyina?"

Holt stared directly at Ross. "The major says you broke off the run early and blundered into antiaircraft fire."

"Interesting." Ross chewed thoughtfully on a piece of bread. "And what did he say about violating General Chennault's direct, and explicit, order to avoid ground support operations—losing a wingman in the process?"

"He said the general chewed his ass something awful at first. He finally convinced the old man that a dozen Jap bombers, all parked in a row, were a target too juicy to pass up. He claims ten of them destroyed, and it's been confirmed."

"So, he has ten confirmed kills. Great. Maybe he'll relax a bit now."

"Ross," O.B. asked peevishly, "what the hell *did* happen?"

"You don't believe the man?" Ross arched his eyebrows in feigned surprise.

"Goddamnit, I don't have a choice. He reported you as a probable KIA. Said you went down in the jungle, in an area swarming with Japs. Said there was no way you could escape."

"Somehow, I didn't think he expected me to reappear," Ross said, his tone deceptively mild. "Look, O.B., I really shouldn't talk about the mission until I've been properly debriefed . . . *and* talked with Major King. But one thing I'll tell you now, I did *not* chicken out over the target. You can take that to the bank."

Holt visibly sagged with relief. It was evident he had not wanted to pursue the issue. "I knew it," he muttered. Then he brightened perceptibly and patted Ross on the shoulder. "Okay. Two of the guys came with me on the supply run. We'll go to Billie's tonight and celebrate."

"Billie's?"

"Yeah. It's just like being back home. Great food, drinks—it's the favorite hangout for crews. We'll make a night of it and sleep on the way back tomorrow. Just now I have some scrounging to do. Why don't you look the town over, catch up on some sleep, and I'll meet you here around five or six?"

The afternoon went rapidly. Ross strolled the city's narrow, dirty streets, gawking like a rube at the county fair. The noise level was unbelievable—and the smells. Pungent spices; sickening, greasy smells of cooking at outdoor stalls; trotting coolies carrying yokes with two buckets of human waste, leaving a line of brown stench: The blend was somehow evocative of romantic, faraway places.

Old women hobbled on doll-like bound feet; cruel-faced opium sellers lurked in doorways; ragged urchins ran through the crowds hawking soiled, rice paper–bound magazines and cigaret butts retrieved from the cobblestones. Ross paused by an early-opening nightclub—doors open as a concession to the afternoon's warmth. Barely visible in the club's gloomy interior, a four-piece band rendered an enthusiastic, if slightly jazzed-up, version of "White Christmas." A diminutive girl dressed in a red silk sheath sang in a shrill, tinny voice: "Anh may ah yore Chrisma sa be why."

The unseasonal rendition was a tribute to the Americans, he realized. Uniforms made up a good part of the press of humanity negotiating the cluttered scene. Chinese passersby invariably smiled and bobbed a friendly greeting. Most added a singsong, "*Ding hao.*" Engrossed by the colorful panorama, Ross realized with surprise that he would have to hurry to meet O.B. and the others.

Billie's three floors were packed with happy, shouting customers. A table of Chinese mah-jongg players, most more than a little inebriated, dominated a balcony overlooking the first-floor dining area. The jubilant shouts of winners rose above the losers' moans of anguish. They laughed and slapped each other on the back as counters changed hands at a feverish pace.

Holt led Ross through a miasma of exotic spices, cigaret smoke, perfume, and sweat. He stopped in front of two American pilots seated at a table. "Fellows, meet Ross Colyer. Ross, this is Gib Tyson and Walt Deardorf." Ross shook hands with both men and slid into a chair. He accepted a menu and, without hesitating, selected Southern fried chicken, mashed potatoes, and hot biscuits.

Lieutenant Tyson, in his early twenties, had short blond hair, pale blue eyes, and an impish pink face. He grinned and said, "So you're the guy who got lost in the woods. That must have been a real wild ride."

"Not much riding," Ross replied with a smile. "One helluva long walk, though."

The waiter returned with their first round of drinks—rice wine in small porcelain cups. Ross took a sip, swallowed, then drank the remainder in one gulp. "Hey, this stuff's not bad."

"Yeah, but don't get carried away with it," Tyson cautioned. "It packs a wallop. And above all, don't get involved in a drinking bout with a bunch of Chinese. You get your drink and right away one of them will yell, '*Gom-bay.*' That means bottoms up. To stop making toasts is to lose face. The crazy bastards keep it up until they usually end up *falling* on their faces."

The waiter appeared with their orders and set the steaming food before them. "I can't believe this," Ross marveled. "Is it as good as it looks?"

"Every bit," Tyson answered. "A little home away from home." They all attacked their meals with gusto.

After doing justice to the best food he had tasted since leaving Miami, Ross turned his attention to the fourth member of the group. The captain, Deardorf, he noticed, hadn't spoken a word other than an acknowledging grunt when he shook hands. He was older than the others, Ross judged. His dark, fleshy face wore a chronically brooding expression. He wore his black hair longer and more fashionably cut than the standard GI brush cut. Ross nodded toward the pilot's row of ribbons and observed, "I see this isn't your first tour."

"That's right."

Holt spoke into the silence that followed the cryptic response. "Yeah, Walt is an old China hand. He flew P-40s in the AVG. Went back to the States when the Air Corps integrated the contract operation. Applied for a return to active duty and asked to come back."

"How about that," Ross said. "So this is old stuff to you."

"That's right." Deardorf took a sip of wine before continuing. "I have your old job—I'm 'C' Flight commander. Does that bother you?"

Ross blinked. Deardorf's faintly hostile attitude had taken him by surprise. He saw Holt watching the exchange with narrowed eyes. "No," Ross replied cautiously. "After all, I never got a chance to meet most of you. Anyway, with your experience, I'd say 'C' Flight is lucky to have you."

Deardorf pushed back his empty plate and lit a cigaret. "I understand you're going to be the training officer. What kind of training do you plan to do?"

"I haven't had a chance to discuss that with O.B. and Major King yet."

"We don't have enough gas or ammo for training missions."

Ross was keeping his genial attitude with increasing difficulty. "Then I guess my job will be an easy one," he joked.

Deardorf tossed back the rest of his wine and signaled for a refill. "I thought maybe you had it in mind to teach us some combat tactics." Ross saw that the swarthy-faced pilot was feeling his drinks—probably had a head start, in fact. "Like strafing attacks," Walt added. "You get a lot of experience strafing in a B-24?"

"Walt," Ross said, keeping his voice even, "if for some reason you're trying to piss me off, you're succeeding. Now, I feel sure we can arrange a little head-to-head contest on a mission. Until then, I suggest you shut up. The last AVG veteran I took on in simulated combat got his ass whipped."

Deardorf's eyes blazed in surprised anger at Ross's blunt response. "The hell you say. Just who might that have been?"

"My squadron commander at RTU—Major Cipolla. He flew with the Tigers. You know him?"

"*'Cappy'* Cipolla? Hell, yes, I know him. You took *him* on one-on-one and came out on top?"

"That's what I said."

"I don't believe you."

Ross felt his self-control slipping. "If you're calling me a liar, Deardorf, then you have a choice: Either apologize or we go outside."

Holt held up a restraining hand. "Hey, hey, you two. This is a party. If you two mix it up and break a hand or something, the general will have Major King's ass—and the major will have *mine* for letting it happen."

"Okay, so I was maybe a little bit out of line. I'm sorry," Walt muttered darkly.

"I overreacted myself," Ross admitted. He extended a hand across the table.

Holt breathed a sigh of relief. The pair's insincerity was evident. As ops officer he wouldn't dare condone an unauthorized dogfight, but he'd sure as hell like to watch.

23 May 1944
Chengkung Army Airfield, China

Major King's office reflected some NCO's effort to create an impression of businesslike efficiency. A wooden desk, chairs cleverly crafted from packing crates, even handmade IN and OUT boxes were products of Chinese workmanship. A slatted-bamboo blind adorned the only window overlooking the gravel landing strip. The dragon featured on King's nameplate seemed right at home. A wall painting of a flying tiger left much to be desired in the way of professionalism, however.

King smoothed his straight black hair with a quick movement that indicated irritation. "Like I said in my report, Colyer, I had no idea where you went down. Otherwise, I'd have turned around and capped you. At any rate, if you had been in position during the firing pass, you wouldn't have sustained damage. I did not, by the way, officially record your reluctance to follow orders. While we're on that subject, that's the reason I replaced you as flight commander. Lieutenant Deardorf is an experienced fighter pilot, and, ah, can be counted on for aggressive leadership."

Ross had difficulty breathing. His chest felt as if constricted by steel bands. Watch it, Colyer, watch it, he admonished himself. This is no time to blow up and start a shouting match. His voice finally emerged, sounding like a badly tuned radio. "I will request assignment to another squadron, Major. I'm sure you will be pleased. Perhaps my replacement will be more, ah, aggressive. I'll have it on your desk tomorrow morning."

"Don't bother." King's close-set eyes glittered. "I will disapprove it. Don't act like a spoiled child, Colyer. It's time you learned that a chest full of medals doesn't entitle you to a free ride to anywhere. You'll earn your promotions in this outfit, just like any other rookie. And don't get ideas about going behind my back. General Chennault is aware of your attitude."

"Very well, sir." A blind impulse to strike back prompted Ross's next words. "I'm scheduled to be debriefed by Fourteenth Air Force intelligence tomorrow. In the interest of accuracy, since you couldn't observe the entire sequence of events, I'll request that he obtain a statement from the OSS officer who watched the attack."

King's already pinched features tightened. "Tread carefully, Colyer," he said, his voice barely above a whisper.

"Absolutely, sir," Ross answered brightly. "While I'm here, Major, could we discuss a flight-training program? I have some ideas."

The squadron CO's face assumed a speculative look. Ross could almost see the wheels turning. Was there, in fact, a witness to their attack at Myitkyina? "OSS?" King asked idly.

"Yes, sir. They've dropped sabotage teams behind the Jap lines. They blew two railroad bridges while I was walking out."

"I didn't know that. Well, until we have an adequate supply of fuel and ammo, I can't see much point in discussing a training program," said King.

"Sir, during the short time I've been around the new pilots, I've noticed a serious lack of instrument-flying skills. Just last night I heard the story of two fighter pilots landing here with empty tanks. I've completed an instrument instructor's course, Major. I believe I can do something about that."

"What, specifically?"

"Since we're restricted on sorties anyway, why not divert one flight to a Calcutta base after a mission. They have plenty of fuel there. I could schedule perhaps a week of instrument training, then return here after a mission launched from a Calcutta base."

"I'll present it to Fourteenth ops," King said curtly. He returned to his paperwork, then looked up and added, "Since you're assigned directly under me as training officer, report here every morning—and keep me advised of your whereabouts."

"Yes, sir." Ross stopped short of saluting and took his leave. He had trouble keeping a straight face. Let that bastard have a few sleepless nights until he discovers that Farnsworth is dead. Who knows? He might never find out; that OSS outfit is very closemouthed. In the meantime, I'll bet money he lets me alone.

23 May 1944
Seattle

Janet read the headline ALLIED BOMBERS POUND BERLIN with unseeing eyes. The microfilmed V-Mail letter tucked in her dresser drawer upstairs swam before her eyes, obscuring the printed words. From Ross, it read:

Dear Janet,

Doris Wilson sent me your address. Congratulations on your job! I know you must be having some bad days. Nothing like a job to take your mind off your loss. I've always had a soft spot in my heart for the old B-17. Sorry it took so long to answer your letter, but I've been moving around quite a bit. I can't tell you where I am just now, but I'd rather be back in Texas. I'm writing this to tell you to expect a package one of these days. It's a little trinket I picked up in a bazaar yesterday. It reminded me of you. Maybe you'll see why when you open it. Will sign off now, these little V-Mail forms don't give you much room. I PROMISE to look you up when I come back.

Sincerely,
Ross

Damn him, she raged. If he wasn't going to say anything, why did he even write? She had gone over the scrawled words a dozen times, searching for some hidden meaning between the lines. She had settled on the "trinket." What could it be? More important, why would he select a gift for her? What could remind him of her? If it was something like a foreign-made cooking utensil, she'd kill him. Didn't he know that she had wanted to have the conversation with him she'd had with Doris? She had *no one* with whom to share her really private thoughts, not even Peg.

Janet looked across the breakfast table to where her still sleep-drugged roommate struggled with a cup of coffee. "Okay, bright eyes," she snapped. "You wanted the day shift, now up and at 'em. We have five minutes to catch the bus."

"Oh, my God," the bleary-eyed blond whimpered. "I'll look like a witch tonight."

"What's so special about tonight?" Janet asked, gathering up her purse.

"The *Treadwell* is in port." Peg brightened. "Those guys throw the best parties—they're *all* crazy. Duane Swoffard is throwing a bash for them at his house. You'll come, won't you?"

About to wither Peg with a scathing retort about her nightlife, Janet hesitated. Finally she said, "Yes. I think I will. It might be fun."

* * *

Janet paid the cabdriver and followed Peg up a winding front walk to an imposing, two-story home, constructed from weathered, unpainted redwood. The side facing the Puget Sound was a solid row of windows, with French doors opening onto a brick patio. Fully thirty people, a blend of khaki and brilliant party colors, mingled there, most locked in tight embraces dancing to the strains of "Don't Fence Me In" blaring from a portable record player.

Delighted squeals greeted Peg and Janet, followed by a flurry of introductions. "Hamp, Duke, meet Peg and Janet." "This is Tony, girls. Watch him, he has three hands." Janet soon lost track of names and faces and accepted a glass of what appeared to be fruit juice. One sip told her it had other ingredients. She took a second look at the crowd and felt faintly overdressed in her flowered-silk frock. Most of the girls wore tailored slacks and peasant blouses. The men were hardly distinguishable from each other—lean, sun-browned faces and navy khaki adorned with gold aviator wings.

Except one. A dark-complected man—naturally dark, not sun-darkened, she noticed—stood beside the punch bowl exchanging wisecracks with a pair of laughing girls. His nose was slightly off center, as if it had been broken and poorly set. His hair was a riot of tight black curls, and he wore civilian clothing—light blue gabardine slacks and a navy blue crewneck. He met Janet's brief glance, then, after a parting sally to his entourage, strolled toward her.

"Hi, I'm Duane Swoffard," he drawled. "Don't believe I've seen you around this crowd's watering holes before."

"Oh, hi," Janet said, extending her hand. "I'm Janet Templeton, Peg's roommate. You're right, you *haven't* seen me before. I don't seem to have either the time or the energy to keep up with that girl. This is quite a party you're putting on."

"Yeah. Cliff Nicholson"—Swoffard paused and pointed to a sandy-haired pilot wearing the two-and-a-half stripes of a lieutenant commander—"and I went to school together. His ship's in port for retrofit, so I'm having a little get-together for his squadron. Care to dance?"

He was an excellent dancer, Janet observed, but before they could resume the conversation, a pink-cheeked ensign cut in. Soon she was caught up in the party mood and found herself having a delightful evening.

The sun dropped from view, its spectacular demise going unnoticed by the revelers. Shortly, the evening chill drove the party inside a cavernous living room. A blazing fire, kindled in a natural-stone fireplace, plus steady consumption of alcohol-laced punch, soon elevated the party to frenetic levels. The temperature rose in proportion to the volume of laughter and shouted conversation.

Janet glanced at her watch—it was midnight already! Her alarm was set for six-thirty. Swoffard materialized at her side as she searched the crowd for Peg's bouncing blond hair. "Having fun?" he asked.

"Oh, I can't remember such a great evening. But"—she made a rueful moue—"I'm a working girl. I'm looking for Peg to tell her I'm calling a cab, not that I expect her to come with me."

"Look, I know what you mean about not keeping up with this crowd," her host said. "I'm feeling a bit ragged around the edges myself; this party started early this afternoon. Why don't we go to a place I know for scrambled eggs, then I'll run you home, okay?"

"Oh, I couldn't ask you to leave your own party."

Swoffard laughed. "Don't give it a second thought. This bash will go on until daylight, and I'll never be missed. C'mon, I'm suddenly ravenous."

Janet caught Peg's eye and made walking motions with two fingers. Peg, observing Duane guiding Janet by the elbow, pursed her lips and favored her roommate with a lewd wink.

Janet closed the front door behind her and leaned back against it, suffused with a warm, happy glow. I must get out more, she told herself. I'm getting into a rut—work, sleep, work, shampoo my hair, sleep. . . . That party was fun—what great people. The wild, exuberant navy pilots—and that handsome Duane Swoffard. She sobered. Now there was a man to take seriously.

The drive to the little waffle house, the midnight breakfast, and the drive home had passed in a euphoric blur. Not one suggestive remark, not one crude brushing of hip or breast, just a brotherly peck on the lips at the door. She'd accepted his suggestion for dinner tomorrow evening—damn, *this* evening, it was two o'clock—without giving it a second thought. She slipped off her shoes and tiptoed up the dark, echoing stairway.

As she scrubbed off her makeup, Janet mentally played back their conversation. He had money—quite a bit of it. They rode in a baby blue LaSalle convertible and his clothing had that feel of expensive wool and silk. That huge house was his, and he had a live-in housekeeper. He had been rejected for military service; a football injury had left him with a trick knee. He had his own business—a vague reference to trucks and government contracts.

She laid the hand towel on the lavatory console and frowned at herself in the mirror. And what else did she know? They had talked nonstop. She remembered telling him a great deal about herself. But, in the final analysis, although he had talked a great deal, she knew precious little about Swoffard as a person. She shrugged. Oh, well . . .

Duane Swoffard was very much in Janet's thoughts later that morning as she took her place in the line waiting at the tool-crib window. Was this guy real? He was fascinating; still, civilians made her feel ill at ease, somehow. All of her life, she'd talked, flirted with, and dated guys in uniform. Well—she shrugged—it promised to be an interesting summer.

At the window Janet fumbled for the fiberboard disks clipped to her belt. "An air gun, drill, and a three-sixteenths drill bit," she said, passing two chits through the protective grill's opening.

"Yes'm, Miss Janet," a familiar voice replied. "Comin' right up."

Janet raised startled eyes. "Moe!" she exclaimed. "Whatever are you doing here? I thought you reported to the navy last week."

"I got rejected, Miss Janet. They sent me back home."

"Why? I thought you'd passed all the tests and everything."

"They found something wrong after I reported in," the youth replied sullenly.

"Oh, I'm so sorry, Moe. I know how badly you wanted in. What was it?"

"Nothin' much. I'm gonna take care of it, then they'll *have* to take me."

"Well," Janet replied easily, "I know you're disappointed, but I'm glad to see you back. Now I can get decent cigarets again." She flashed the morose-looking tool-crib clerk a warm smile, gathered up her tools, and wormed through the press of bodies toward where B-17 number 42375 squatted beneath a skeleton of scaffolding, nearing completion.

"Hi," a petite brunette said in greeting. "I'm Ellen, and I'm your partner today. This is just my third day; hope I don't slow you up too much."

"I'm sure you won't," Janet replied good-humoredly. "We're doing the tail assembly today, I see. Gosh, you're tiny enough to walk around inside that tail gunner's compartment."

Ellen giggled. "I always hated being short, but it's what got me the job."

"Okay, let's get at it," Janet replied. "The usual procedure. I'll drill twelve holes and insert the rivets. Just have the bucking bar against the next rivet down when you hear me stop driving the previous one."

Janet's mind wandered as she fell into the now familiar routine. Thankfully Ellen wasn't a talker, so the business of attaching aluminum skin to the frame members went smoothly. Then, as she stepped back to cast a critical eye at her last row of countersunk rivets, a voice from behind called, "Janet Templeton?"

She turned to confront a uniformed security guard. "Yes, I'm Janet Templeton. What can I do for you?"

"An emergency, Miz Templeton. Come with me, please, quickly."

"An emergency? What's wrong? My family?" Visions of the day the telegram arrived telling her of BT's death flashed through her mind.

"No, ma'am. Nothing like that. You're just wanted in the office; hurry, please."

Janet trotted into the corner office housing the plant security chief to confront a half-dozen grim faces. "Mrs. Templeton?" a beefy, florid-faced man asked.

"Yes, I'm Janet Templeton. What's wrong?"

"Plenty," was the cryptic rejoinder. "D'you know Moe Moskowitz?"

"Moe? The boy in the tool crib? Yes, I know him. Why?"

"He's gone berserk—plain nuts. He's barricaded himself in the tool crib. He's got six sticks of dynamite strapped around his waist. Says he's gonna blow the whole damn plant to smithereens. Not only that, he's got a woman in there with him."

Blood drained from Janet's cheeks. "Moe?" she whispered. "Threatening to blow up the place? I can't believe it."

"Well, you jolly well better believe it," the perspiring man replied. "He says you're the only person he'll talk to. Now why would he say a thing like that? You a good friend of his, maybe?"

"A friend, I guess," Janet replied. "But a *good* friend? I only know him from checking tools in and out."

"Well, for some reason the fruitcake insists on telling nobody but you what he wants," the angry security chief grumbled.

A middle-aged man with an anxious look stepped forward. "I'm William Justin, Mrs. Templeton, the plant manager. You mustn't feel obligated to do this, you know. It's a most serious situation; we believe the man is perfectly capable of doing what he threatens. No one will blame you for refusing."

"I—I hardly know what to say," Janet stammered. "Moe wouldn't knowingly harm me—or anyone else, for that matter. What should I do?"

"Well, make up your mind, for one thing," the red-faced guard captain said. Blodgett, Janet read on his name tag. "We keep screwing around in here, he's gonna get nervous and set that stuff off."

"That's quite enough, Captain!" Justin snapped. "We're evacuating the plant, Mrs. Templeton. We'll do everything in our power to protect you, but you must realize you will be in danger."

"Of course. I'll speak to him," Janet said. "Does anyone know what happened to bring this on?"

"I just talked with personnel. It seems that when he reported for induction into the navy, a psychiatrist determined that his psychological profile was unacceptable for military service."

"Them personnel people should have *their* heads examined for putting a looney back on the payroll," Blodgett snarled. "Now, if you're ready, ma'am, we'll slip this army flak jacket over you. If things do blow, it'll at least give you some protection. When you get in there, try to see what he intends to detonate the stuff with. Talk to him about it in a loud voice so we can figure out what we're up against. Don't get squarely between him and the door. We got an army sharpshooter standing by. He'll have Moskowitz in his sights the whole time. If you see that the guy can't explode the dynamite by reflex—like he has to light a fuse or something—brush your hair back with your right hand. Then drop to the floor. Our man will do the rest."

Janet crossed the now empty, echoing cavern of the assembly hangar in a daze. She halted at the checkout window and called, "Moe?"

"That you, Miss Janet?"

"Yes, Moe. What on earth are you doing?"

"Don't come inside, Miss Janet. I don't want to have to hurt you, too."

"What is it you want me to do, Moe?"

"You tell those sonsabitches upstairs to clear my record. They told the navy doctors something that made 'em turn me down. They lied. Tell 'em that if they don't take it back, I'm gonna blow up the place—I'll show 'em."

"Moe." Janet detected a tremor in her voice. She clenched her hands to stop their trembling and said more firmly, "I don't believe they did that, Moe. I know some of those people—Kathy, the payroll clerk; Bob, in the timekeeper's office—they're nice; they wouldn't lie about you. Why don't you let that poor girl in there with you come out? She must be terrified. I'll go get the plant manager himself to talk to you."

"*No!*" Moe's voice seemed to be bordering on hysteria. "I want *you* to tell me it's gonna be all right—that I can be a sailor like I wanted."

"I'll do what I can, Moe, but believe me: No one is going to make any promises as long as you have that girl in there. I'll tell you what, let me take her place. I can talk with you just as well in there as from out here." Janet gasped as the enormity of what she'd just done dawned.

"Oh, no, Miss Janet. I couldn't do that. If I *do* have to blow everything up, I want you to get out of the building. I'd never do anything to hurt you; you're always nice to me. This bitch is not a nice person; she called me a draft dodger. I *ain't* a draft dodger, Miss Janet; you know that."

Janet stood frozen, at a loss as to what to do. She saw Blodgett wigwagging madly from her left. He was trying, with charades, to tell her to get Moe to come to the open window. Her thoughts raced. That girl's life was at stake, and her own as well. One expertly placed shot, and the threat was ended. All she had to do was coax Moe to come into view. She could easily talk him into it, she was certain. *He trusts you!* an inner voice screamed. He's just a poor, sick kid.

She ignored Blodgett's wild gesticulations and stepped squarely in front of the open top-half door of the tool crib. Her spine prickled; she tried to forget that unwinking eye of the sniper's weapon behind her. "Moe," she said, her voice friendly and casual, "if you do explode that dynamite, you'll never get into the navy; you know that, I guess."

"No matter. They'll be sorry they lied about me."

"Moe, your mother will be sorry, too." Janet waited for a response. After a long silence, she continued, "You have a phone in there. Why don't you call your mother? If you *do* blow everything up, it will be her last chance to talk to you."

Janet had decided that the boy wasn't going to respond, when he said, "What will they do to me if I come out?"

Chapter Thirteen

24 May 1944
Tsuchiura, Japan

"I am Lieutenant Nakano Yusaki. You see before you a Mitsubishi Type Ninety-six fighter plane. During the next four weeks you will learn the function of every control, you will know every aspect of its behavior in the air, and you will master takeoff and landing."

Yusaki regarded the dozen eager-faced cadets hanging onto his every word and hesitated. *No!* he wanted to scream. This is murder. No one—not the most experienced flight instructor on earth—can prepare these young men for aerial combat in four weeks. He swallowed hard before continuing.

"After you have mastered the Type Ninety-six, you will receive familiarization flights in the Zero-sen and move to your operational units for combat training. Today, you will learn to start the engine. Then, after observing my technique on takeoff, you will execute simple maneuvers in the air and perform a landing. Cadet Tonaka, you will be first. The others of you wait beside the hangar and take your turn in the sequence given you this morning." Unable to face his charges further, he turned and strode toward the waiting airplane, Tonaka trotting in his wake.

Yusaki had almost rebelled after Commander Honekawa's briefing. "The syllabus calls for twenty hours of air time, two hours of navigation, two hours of meteorology, and one hour of formation flying. The course is of four weeks' duration," the commander had said, his face without expression, his voice grim.

"I—I don't understand, sir. These cadets haven't attended ground school—haven't had so much as an orientation flight—and I am to make proficient pilots of a class of *twelve* in four weeks' time?"

"That is correct, Lieutenant Nakano. This is an accelerated course. Operational units are seriously undermanned. The students will be given additional training by their squadron commanders."

"With all due respect, honorable sir, that seems scant training for a combat pilot. I recall logging nearly two hundred hours in the Zero before joining my squadron."

To Yusaki's surprise the commander allowed the criticism of a superior officer's orders to go without reprimand. "You will do your best, Lieutenant. We must provide four hundred pilots to defend key islands within striking distance of Tokyo by American superbombers. The new units are to be in place not later than June tenth."

Yusaki stifled further objections, saluted, and departed. His father had warned him that the war was not going in Japan's favor, but this was monstrous. American bombers within striking distance of the home islands? Islands to be defended by young, poorly trained recruits—most no more than high school children? He felt a chill course down his spine. The slaughter that would occur when pilots whom he, Nakano Yusaki, had trained went up against hardened veterans was sickening to contemplate. His mouth set in harsh anger. "Additional training with their operational units," indeed. It would be a learning process few would survive.

24 May 1944
Kunming

Elliott Sprague crossed his legs and settled into a more comfortable position. Situated in a spacious house donated by a former Chinese merchant-prince, General Chennault's office bore scant resemblance to the Spartan quarters most military commanders occupied. Comfortable sofas and armchairs were grouped around a low table; an expanse of triple windows overlooked a rolling, manicured garden. Only the subdued bustle of daily office routine in the background reminded a visitor that serious business went on here.

The room's two-star resident lounged behind a heavy table of solid teakwood and regarded his visitor with lazy interest. It would be an intriguing session, he decided. Sprague bore all the earmarks of a cunning manipulator. He reminded Chennault in many ways of one of Chiang's scheming warlords. The general, a master chess player, advanced a pawn. "When do you plan to launch your first mission, Elliott?"

"That's one of the things I wanted to talk with you about, General. As I see it, your air force is dedicated to accomplishing what I see as the main objective—taking away the Japs' source of arms and manpower. All this hand-to-hand fighting in jungles just plays into their strength. I believe we must coordinate use of the VHBs very carefully.

"I talked with General Wolfe before I left. In strictest confidence, sir, we don't see eye to eye on this. I'm afraid that Stilwell has planted some idea of using the B-29s in a tactical role. I was surprised to see the Joint Chiefs change their minds about control of VHB operations, but maybe they anticipated something like this if Stilwell had final approval."

"And you advocate immediately pounding the Jap home islands." Chennault's words formed a statement, not a question.

"Most definitely. But when I start, I want to hit them one day and, before they recover from that, hit them the next day, and the next, until they hurt." Sprague smashed his right fist into the palm of his left hand.

"We can only do that from Chengtu," he continued. "Until we are able to operate from there, I want one or more . . . call them shakedown missions. What target would help you most? One that would give us a realistic, long-range objective, but still not be impractical for green crews?"

"What targets are you getting from the JCS?" Chennault parried.

Sprague scowled. "A harebrained idea to confuse the Japs. They flew a Superfort to England. Announced that the B-29 hadn't lived up to expectations for range and would be used in the ETO after all. They want us to haul cargo across the Hump and call the plane an 'armed transport.' Fly into Chengtu with full tanks, drain, and add to the stockpile all but enough gas to get home—a stupid idea. Our pilots need high-altitude formation training, not practice as aerial truck drivers."

Chennault concealed the fact that he was fully conversant with the plan—was, in fact, in favor of it. "It might be an opportunity to work out the bugs in the R-3350 engine, Elliott," he observed mildly. "I understand you had problems with it on the way over."

Sprague flushed. "Green crews," he snapped. "It's a good engine, but all the more reason to get some high-altitude formation experience."

"Hmmm. Yes, I see what you mean. Tell me, does the JCS target list include any in east China?"

Sprague shook his head. “None, sir. It would be overkill to put the VHBs on shipping, troop concentrations, and the like. My God, a single ship can flatten one of those little towns.”

Chennault gnawed his lower lip. “I see. Well, I wouldn’t exactly call Hankow, for example, a ‘little town.’ The Japs are using it as a major command-and-control point. Airfields, dock facilities—the Yangtze is their main supply route. They’re launching a major drive south from there. Frankly, I’m worried about my bases in the Hsiang River valley. A B-29 sweep would sure take a lot of pressure off them.”

“That’s out of the question, sir. First, General Arnold is adamant about not using B-29s to bomb Chinese targets. Second, it would mean operating out of Chengtu—using materiel stockpiled for missions over Japan.

“By the way, I’d sure like to meet the generalissimo and his wife while I’m in China. I understand they are quite a pair. Since we’ll be depending on the Chinese army to defend Chengtu, I’d like to discuss arrangements, informally of course, and impress upon him that our Superforts can cripple the Jap land armies by wiping out their factories. Do you think you could arrange an introduction?”

Chennault’s hooded eyes concealed his amusement as Sprague’s casual question exposed his visitor’s real purpose. The wily veteran chess player mentally moved his knight into position for a flank attack. “I believe that might be arranged, Elliott. Tell you what. Why don’t you let me show you the facilities at Chengtu, then we’ll hop over to Chungking and meet the generalissimo. Will you need Wolfe’s approval?”

Sprague hesitated. “Uh, no, I see no reason to bother him. K.B. hasn’t adapted well to the climate in Calcutta. He’s pretty well leaving things up to me until he gets back on his feet. Off the record again, sir: K.B. is having a little problem accepting the fact that Wild Turkey and the tropics don’t mix well.”

Chennault pursed his lips. “Sorry to hear that. They can be a lethal combination, all right. Well, I’ll get on the radio and arrange things. Is tomorrow morning okay? We’ll use my B-25. This will also give the commander of my new P-51 squadron a chance to see his next home. Which reminds me, one of his pilots flew on the Ploesti raid with you. Maybe you’d like to meet with him?”

“Of course. What’s his name?”

“Colyer. Captain Ross Colyer. Interesting guy—got shot down over Burma and walked out. Do you know him, by chance?”

Sprague's carefully guarded manner slipped. "*Colyer? Ross* Colyer?" He quickly recovered his composure and added, "Yes. Yes, I know Colyer. He's a P-51 pilot? And here? I'll be damned. I would indeed like to see him. We have much to reminisce about. Yes, I certainly do recall him. As you say, sir, he is a *most* interesting guy."

24 May 1944
Chengkung Army Airfield

Major King regarded Ross with a shrewd, faintly distrustful gaze. "Colyer, maybe we should talk more often," he said thoughtfully.

"Anytime, Major. What would you like to discuss?"

"Your friends, for one thing."

"Oh?"

"Yes. Do you know a brigadier general by the name of Sprague?"

Ross's eyebrows rose fractionally. "General Elliott Sprague?"

"The same."

"Yes, I know him. He was my wing commander in England."

"I see. Well, you're about to meet him again. He's here—in Kunming, anyway—and he wants to see you."

Ross couldn't conceal his mirth; his shoulders shook with silent laughter. "Well, as a guy I once knew told me, 'It's a small air corps, isn't it?' When and where is this meeting to take place?"

"I just talked with General Chennault. General Sprague would like for you to have dinner with him tonight. He's sending transportation for you."

"How thoughtful. I'll try not to stay out too late."

"Don't be a wiseass. There's more."

"Oh, oh," Ross responded warily.

"Yes. Sprague and Chennault are making a quick inspection trip to Chengtu and to Generalissimo Chiang Kai-shek's headquarters in Chungking tomorrow. General Stilwell has an inflexible rule that any time a general officer flies within range of Jap fighter bases, the flight must have fighter escort. I'm going to have a look at what may be our next base. You're going because Chennault says you'll go, not because I selected you."

"Major, why won't you approve my request for reassignment? I'm useless to you—a training officer with no training to do. I haven't had an operational mission since I was shot down."

"Don't be impatient. You'll have a chance to earn another medal before the war's over. In the meantime, watch what you tell your high-ranking friends. Your life could be worse, you know."

Ross tucked his Mustang into position off King's right wing as they drilled their way upward through the swirling morning mist. King was a good pilot, he acknowledged to himself. Give credit where credit is due. The major flew with a sure touch and made it easy for his wingman to keep in tight.

His thoughts drifted back to the previous night's dinner with Sprague. Ross had to admit he was baffled. Afterward, he had examined the discussion from every angle, looking for hidden meaning and innuendo. It still appeared to be just another instance of two people who had shared danger getting together for drinks and dinner. No way, he thought. Sprague was a devious sonofabitch. He wasn't the type to have dinner with a lowly captain—especially one he'd once promised to court-martial for insubordination—just for old times' sake. He would turn another card someday.

The flight broke through the mist; a solid carpet of benign, fluffy cloud tops stretched as far as the eye could see. King picked up the slower, twin-engine Mitchell bomber with Sprague and Chennault aboard and leveled off at twenty thousand feet. With throttles retarded, they swung into lazy, shallow turns to maintain position. Ross was enjoying himself. Chances of encountering a stray Jap fighter were nil, and he let the sheer pleasure of being back in a cockpit take over.

Two hours later, Ross set the parking brake, cut the switches, and turned the ship over to a stolid, unsmiling Chinese mechanic. Two armed soldiers took up immediate position, he noticed. At Chennault's invitation, Ross and King joined the inspection tour conducted by a harassed-looking colonel wearing the twin-castle insignia of the army's Corps of Engineers.

After weeks of looking at nothing but rugged mountains, Ross felt a new sense of freedom as he regarded the flat, admittedly dreary, landscape. He caught up with the clutch of senior officers in time to overhear the colonel apologize for making the party walk. "Gasoline is precious," he said. "Every drop is hoarded. Until we get crew accommodations finished, some walk as far as two miles from their quarters, and that's *all* ranks. The trucks you see run on charcoal and require a crew of three coolies to keep the fire going."

"Understandable," Sprague reassured the man crisply. "I'm more interested in the runway, just now. It appeared to be well beyond the five-thousand-foot mark when we landed. When will you have seventy-five hundred?"

"Two to three weeks, General."

They strode toward the uncompleted end of the runway. Ross blinked. The ground was practically invisible, obscured by a swarm of humanity. Men of all ages, women, even children of no more than ten or twelve formed a seemingly orchestrated ballet conducted by tall men wearing long, dark cloaks and mandarin hats. Singsong chants and laughter, punctuated by an occasional shout, formed the musical score.

The party paused beside a pyramid of small chunks of granite heaped at least twelve feet high. Ross noticed that each rock was of a uniform size. A chain of sinewy workers, some with wheelbarrows but most with two baskets suspended from a shoulder yoke, made never-ceasing inroads on the pile. Ross guessed that none carried less than a hundred pounds. At the other end of the chain, a thousand hands swiftly placed the stones into level layers that would have defied a journeyman bricklayer to duplicate.

Ross moved to the rear of the heap to investigate a staccato pounding and discovered the pyramid's source. Countless numbers of strawhatted workers squatted beside piles of larger, irregularly shaped rocks. Ross watched a gray-bearded man select one and with practiced rhythm reduce it to three smaller pieces. A hoop of hempen rope, slung to his waist, failed to pass over a segment of one. After two sharp whacks the correctly sized stone was tossed into the stockpile.

Sprague asked, "Do you mean that runway we landed on is nothing but loose *rocks?* Hell, I've landed on worse concrete strips." Ross detected a note of awe.

"That's right," the colonel replied. "These larger rocks are covered with another layer of smaller gravel mixed with clay, and rolled. See those rollers?" He pointed to where two stone cylinders, fully six feet in diameter, trailed four columns of straining coolies. "They weigh six tons and are hand carved from a single boulder. We have an abandoned steamroller, filled with rocks, that weighs even more. It takes two hundred and fifty men to pull the damn thing."

Major King spoke for the first time. "My God," he breathed. "How many people do you have out there?"

"On a good day, ten to twelve thousand," the colonel answered casually.

"The provincial governor furnishes all our manpower. He conscripts them from farms and villages; some travel as far as a hundred miles. They live in those little huts covered with bamboo mats you can see over there. They stay a while, then go home to harvest crops or whatever and are replaced by others."

"What a country," King said. "What do these people have to look forward to?"

"Old age," the colonel observed dryly. "Which isn't easy to come by over here. Life is cheap. About a month ago one of the coolies pulling a roller got tangled in his harness and fell. Well, to get one of those babies moving from a full stop isn't easy. It takes an additional hundred men and help from pry bars. They didn't stop—just rolled right over the poor bastard. Okay, let's go look at one of the POL revetments, then we'll have what passes for lunch."

The revetment was identifiable only by a truck unloading fifty-five-gallon steel drums. Four coolies rolled one down a ramp, secured it in a sling between two poles, then hoisted the ends of the poles onto their shoulders. With their straw sandals slapping in the packed dust, they trotted beneath a canopy of woven bamboo mats covered with a thin layer of dirt. "We have a dozen like this scattered around—earthen dikes with camouflage on top," the colonel explained. "I don't have to tell you that this stuff is valuable. You might not realize it, but we have two machine guns trained on us right now. Try so much as to light a cigaret, and you won't get to take the first puff."

Stooping to read lettering on a drum, he added, "This one was loaded in the port at Houston, I'd say at least four months ago. Drums are usually offloaded at Karachi, then sent across India—fifteen hundred miles—by train to the terminal in Calcutta. You know the rest—up the Brahmaputra valley by narrow-gauge rail, and over the Hump by air.

"From Kunming it's a different story. If you cross the road leading here when you take off, if you can call it a road, look carefully. You won't see a railroad with tank cars. You won't see many trucks on the highway, either. You'll see coolies rolling the drums by hand or hauling them in two-wheeled 'Peking carts,' contraptions as old as China itself. They've modernized some by putting old truck tires around the rims, but they're still pulled by pygmy Mongolian ponies.

"You'll even see two coolies with a drum slung from a gin pole between them—three hundred and fifty pounds of gasoline inside a fifty-pound drum. Seventy to seventy-five days that takes. Sometimes one or both of the pair that started out dies along the way. When you fuel up for your first mission, General, you'll be burning fuel faster than all the Chinese out here can replace it.

"Wang, here, has one of the few alcohol-burning trucks around. He's getting rich—hey Wang?"

The happy-looking trucker bowed. "Wang has many hungry mouths to feed, Honorable Colonel. It is a long and difficult trip I make, and the alcohol is terribly expensive."

"Sure, sure, you old fraud," the colonel joked. "Well, unless you want to see the bomb dump, that's the tour, General. Shall we have lunch?"

Chennault, silent to that point, replied, "I believe we can forgo the dump. You've seen one, you've seen 'em all. What do you think, Elliott?"

"Uh—oh sure, General. We still have that trip to Chungking to make."

Ross saw that the unusually subdued Sprague was impressed. Ross yielded to impulse and asked, "How many drums of that fuel do you suppose it takes just to start and warm up four of those big 3350s, General?"

Sprague glared, then strode away without answering. Ross thought he detected a twinkle of amusement in Chennault's piercing gaze.

25 May 1944
Chungking, China

General Sprague ate with quick, forced movements. His stomach growled with hunger. "Lunch" at Chengtu had been a kind of stew with bits of meat that defied chewing. "Water buffalo," his host explained laconically. He had looked forward to a sumptuous meal in Generalissimo Chiang Kai-shek's private quarters, but the mound of unappetizing, nameless vegetables—there seemed to be no meat in it—staring up at him from the plate was an even greater disappointment.

Chennault had explained that the evening meal would be taken *en famille* to demonstrate the generalissimo's esteem for his American allies. Too bad they didn't have one of those boring state dinner parties I've heard so much about, Sprague thought wistfully; perhaps there will be a mountain of exotic desserts to fill in the gaps left by this garbage. He raised his eyes to find Madame Chiang regarding him. Her look suggested she had read his thoughts.

Sprague turned his attention to Chennault's conversation with the generalissimo. "The situation worsens daily," the hatchet-faced two-star rasped. "We were unable to prevent forces driving south from the

Yellow River from linking up with the Sixth Jap Army moving up from Hankow. With this supply line secure, they will consolidate, then march south. My bases in the Hsiang valley are at risk."

Chiang waved a slender hand in dismissal. "General Yuang is one of my most able commanders. He assures me that the Japanese advance has been contained. He will counterattack very soon now."

Chennault slowly shook his head. "I agree that General Yuang is a great commander. We speak frequently, and I have the utmost faith in him. But he labors under an assumption that my planes can provide massive air support. That is an erroneous assumption. My own supply situation is critical. The simple fact is, I am almost out of gasoline."

"How can that be?" the generalissimo asked, frowning. "Is not your airlift across Burma providing more tonnage than ever before?"

Chennault, the chess player, mentally brought a bishop into play. "It is. But demands increase faster than the flow. The bases at Chengtu, for example. A tremendous amount of fuel and bombs must be in place before Elliott, here, can attack the Japanese home islands with his new Superfortresses. In the meantime, my planes must do with less. I talked with Casey Vincent at Kweilin only yesterday. His bombers sit in their revetments with only enough fuel to evacuate, if necessary. He can launch no more than four to eight fighter sorties per day."

The Chinese leader bent an icy stare in Sprague's direction. "Who says this must be?" he queried.

"General Stilwell is responsible for the allocation of supplies," Chennault responded smoothly.

"Stilwell." Chiang made the word sound like an expletive. "The man is blind to China's plight. Tell me, General Sprague, will your new bomber bring an end to this cruel war?"

"It is the ultimate weapon, Generalissimo," Sprague said, dredging up his favorite briefing demeanor. "Capable of placing both high-explosive and incendiary bombs with great accuracy, using radar to pinpoint targets by night and through an overcast, flying above the reach of enemy fighters, it will level Japanese industrial centers. Their flow of arms and men to China will drop to a mere trickle within a matter of weeks."

Chiang's aristocratic features assumed a skeptical expression. "When will you fly your first mission?"

"As soon as the runway at Chengtu is completed. No later than the second week of June."

"How many planes?"

"The operational plan calls for a hundred-plane effort, sir."

"Then the answer appears simple." Chiang gave a dismissive shrug. "Use only fifty airplanes for your first raid. Provide General Chennault with enough fuel to support my armies." He appeared to lose interest in the matter and turned to Chennault. "I wish my soldiers in Burma to have fresh watermelons every day, Claire. We Chinese love watermelons, and I understand they are plentiful there. Could you impress General Stilwell with my concern?"

Sprague, stunned by the disaster's swift development, sat speechless as the conversation turned to more mundane affairs. He was roused by Madame Chiang's soft question.

"General Sprague, would you care to join me for a tour of our gardens? We are quite proud of them, and they are truly beautiful by moonlight."

"Uh, yes, ma'am," Sprague stammered. "Of course. Generalissimo, would you excuse me?"

Chiang waved a hand without answering, and Sprague followed his slender, elegantly gowned hostess onto a broad, tiled patio. He was struck by her extraordinary beauty as she turned to face him. Reflected moonlight gave her ivory-hued features, capped by a coil of jet black hair, the appearance of a delicate porcelain figurine. She extracted a cigaret case from her evening bag and murmured, "It occurred to me that you might enjoy a cigar while I smoke an after-dinner cigaret."

"I certainly would," Sprague replied fervently. He produced a light for her cigaret and extracted a cigar from an inner pocket.

"Since the generalissimo's illness during his captivity, he abhors tobacco smoke—likewise liquor. I apologize for the absence of wine with dinner, but"—she shrugged a bare shoulder—"he is much concerned for his health. The dinner, for example—hardly American fare. I can arrange for the cook to prepare you a sandwich, if you like."

"Oh, no—no, the dinner was excellent, Madame."

His hostess uttered a tinkling laugh. "You are not a convincing liar, General. I went to school in your country, you know. You Americans are so open, so lacking in guile. The Orient must be a confusing place for you."

"I'm not sure I understand, ma'am."

"The generalissimo. You must think him a terrible fool. Take his simplistic solution to your supply problems, for example. Do not be misled. He created the first and only unified government China has known since the Manchu dynasty. Created it from a bewildering array of fragmented, warring factions. True, he has not the Westerner's grasp of large-scale military strategy, but he achieves his ends in more subtle ways.

"He knows full well that his recommendation will not be followed completely. But the seed is planted. General Stilwell will worry, afraid that we will enlist President Roosevelt to support reallocation of your precious resources. Who knows?"

"Ma'am," Sprague responded, "massive strikes at the enemy's industrial base is the only sure way to finish the war. Do you not agree with that?"

"Not entirely," was her serene reply. "Consider: No amount of destruction from the air will eliminate the need for an invasion of Japan. Just now, Japan has more than one million men committed to conquering our country. If they became available for defense of the home islands, they would extract a horrible toll of American lives. Besides, if our armies collapse, you will have no bases from which to launch your attacks. Your president realizes this, General." She stubbed out her cigaret. "Shall we rejoin the others?"

Sprague followed Chennault down a hallway to their rooms. The conversation following his and Madame Chiang's return to the dining room and the ensuing good-nights were a blurred memory, overridden by implications of that brief discussion on the patio.

Chennault paused outside the door to his room. "I never travel without an emergency supply of Pinch, Elliott. Care to join me for a nightcap and a last cigar?"

Sprague nodded grimly and followed the cheerful two-star inside. He collected his thoughts as Chennault poured generous measures of Scotch and settled onto a deeply upholstered, Western-style sofa. Raising his glass in response to a silent toast, Sprague spoke first, his voice tinged with anger.

"General, you set me up. Why didn't you give me the entire picture before I blundered into this absurd situation?"

Chennault chuckled. "Elliott, please. I was as surprised as you were at the outcome of our little visit. As for briefing you ahead of time, how could I have prepared you? Tell you that the Fourteenth is flat on its ass? Hell, Vinegar Joe knows that—or should at least. Anyway, I'm very interested in the result of your little tête-à-tête with Madame."

"Now *there's* a broad to watch," Sprague growled. "She's a shifty one, and a helluva lot smarter than her husband. But about this business of dipping into Chengtu stocks—K.B., the Joint Chiefs, they'll never in hell go along with it."

"And you, Elliott?" Chennault's voice was soft. "Given absolute control . . . what would you do?"

Sprague realized that his glass was empty. He crossed to the dresser and sloshed it half full. His mind raced. He was on the fringe of unprecedented opportunity; he could feel it. A leapfrog to—not a wing, not a division—a whole fucking numbered air force. But he needed time to think. "If I was in absolute control, we wouldn't be in this screwed-up situation," he mumbled.

"Possibly," Chennault agreed. His voice hardened. "Elliott, we're on the verge of losing China—believe me. I can save her. The Japs are pouring everything they have into this drive south. They're putting up as many as two hundred planes at a time. We're knocking them out of the air like flies. Once we have uncontested control of the air, we can turn them. The Chinese army will hold. But we can't do it without that gas you have stashed at Chengtu.

"Look, send an urgent message to Wolfe. Tell him that you want him to ask Stilwell for orders making you commander of an advance echelon at Chengtu, that there are problems you can handle only from there. I'll send a report of our trip confirming it. Once you're at Chengtu, I'll send all my B-24s up there. Give 'em full tanks, plus a bomb bay full of drums. That will give Casey Vincent enough gas at Kweilin to keep his fighters up for at least two to three weeks. By that time, we'll have chased the Jap air force out of the sky."

"Let me think about it, General," Sprague finally muttered. "Oh, and thanks for the Scotch, sir." He rose and departed without further comment.

Alone in his room, Sprague stripped and sat in bed, propped in a sitting position by pillows. Okay, he thought. Chennault is at odds with Stilwell, but in favor with the generalissimo and his wife, who both hate Stilwell. The Chiang Kai-sheks are cozy with the president. What if they pressure Roosevelt into ousting Stilwell and giving Chennault his job? If Chennault is obligated to me, I can have the Fourteenth.

Great. But in the meantime, I have to make a name for myself with the '29s. His furrowed brow relaxed, and a pleased smile curved his lips. Of course. The answer was there all the time. He'd just left her moments before.

Chapter Fourteen

26 May 1944
Loyang Airfield, China

Lieutenant Nakano Yusaki listened intently to the hard-faced army colonel's welcoming speech. "It is a tribute to our glorious leaders that units and aircraft of our services are trained for more than one specific purpose. You brave pilots of the Imperial Navy and your excellent airplanes will serve the emperor on land with the same distinction your brothers demonstrate flying from aircraft carriers. Consider your attachment to the China Expeditionary Force an honor."

Flight Sergeant Takuma, seated next to Yusaki, risked a stern rebuke to whisper, "And to whom do we pay tribute for the fact we have no aircraft carriers to operate from?"

Yusaki scowled. Had it not been explained that losses of carrier-based aircraft and crews were far lower than expected? That now-surplus assets were being attached to army units? Takuma's words bordered on treason. Only from his father had Yusaki learned the sobering truth. Project Ichi Go was a desperate effort to stave off disaster. Over-water shipments to Indochina fell under constant attack from the American navy and their bombers based in China. A land route from Peking to Hanoi must be established. In so doing, they would also destroy the American air bases in the Hsiang River valley. The Japanese Sixth Army had already forged a route from the Yellow River to the salient containing Hankow, but the toll of airplanes and pilots lost during that drive had been tremendous. The sturdy Zero was to even the odds. Therefore, they had rushed all Zero-qualified pilots to Hankow by air transport. Commander Honekawa waived Yusaki's restricted vision with a stroke of the pen. His job as instructor at Tsuchiura had lasted one day.

Yusaki returned his attention to the harsh-voiced briefing officer. "Despite the success you've had attacking the American air transports in Burma, a more urgent task prompted your relocation. The Americans plan to attack the home islands from bases in China with a new superbomber. The first squadron of these giant, long-range craft is already waiting in Calcutta. They are more than twice the size of the Liberator and have double the range. They thus pose an unacceptable threat.

"There is a dual purpose to our augmentation of the expeditionary force's air arm, however." He crossed to a wall map and traced a heavy black line that followed an irregular course across eastern China. "Our base here at Hankow is key to the movement of our forces south to link up with our army in Indochina, and west to secure what we feel certain to be bases intended for use by the American B-29s.

"Hankow is presently in a tenuous situation. Fighters and bombers of the American Fourteenth Air Force constantly harass shipping along the Yangtze River. They likewise hamper our advance against the Chinese ground forces holding south of there. Only a trickle of essential supplies is reaching Hankow by barges traveling the Yangtze, operating during the hours of darkness only. Our task is to seek out and destroy the American air capability, and to deny them the bases at Chengtu and those south of the Yangtze along our drive to Hanoi."

Senior Lieutenant Subachi, a section leader, broke the ensuing silence. "What types of aircraft will we face, sir?"

"Presently, their twin-engine B-25 and four-engine B-24 bombers, escorted by P-40 fighters. There are recent reports of an improved fighter, however—the P-51." The colonel paused and stroked his chin. "The fighter aircraft are inferior to the army's Hayate and your Zero-sens, but the pilots are experienced. The bombers, likewise, are flown by veterans and are heavily armed. You face a formidable enemy."

Yusaki's jaw muscles tightened. There was nothing inferior about the Mustang *he* had encountered.

The colonel returned to the map. "Your first sortie today will consist of escorting bombers to the American airfield at Hengyang. On the return trip you will seek to destroy concentrations of enemy troops that impede our advance down the Hsiang River. Section leaders will brief you on specific aspects of your mission."

The colonel stepped down and exited without the customary inspirational send-off to men going into battle. He looked almost sad, Yusaki noticed.

Lieutenant Subachi assembled the twenty fighter pilots making up that day's formation and assigned aircraft numbers, radio procedures, and formation positions. "Expect determined opposition," he warned them. "The Americans can ill afford to lose their northernmost base."

Yusaki felt excitement build. "You will lead a four-ship element," Subachi explained to him. "You are more experienced than most of the recently arrived pilots. Petty Officer Sasai will be your permanently assigned wingman. He has keen eyes and is a good pilot, and his sole duty is to protect your blind side."

The exuberant young pilots trooped outside to watch the bombers take off. The speedy fighter escort would follow after a one-hour interval. Yusaki wore a puzzled frown as, one after another, the bomb-laden force roared into the air. In the lead were seven Mitsubishi Type 97s. The lumbering, lightly armed heavy bombers were followed by a dozen Aichi D3A Type 99s. All were obsolete models. The Aichi had distinguished itself during the attack on Pearl Harbor, but with its fixed landing gear it was terribly slow and vulnerable.

Repeated blows to the huge gong suspended outside the operations building warned the waiting pilots that start-engines time was ten minutes away. The excited, grinning pilots raced for their planes. With a parting shout of encouragement to Sasai, Yusaki leaped onto his Zero-sen's wing and let a sober-faced mechanic help him strap in. It was a nearly new machine, he noticed, as were all the others. The dark green paint, with brilliant, red-orange rising sun insignia displayed on fuselage and wings, was free of oil and dirt. A sobering thought temporarily dampened his high spirits: Perhaps the planes did not survive combat long enough to acquire the grime of repeated use.

He quickly ran through a before-starting-engine check. Fuel tanks full, fuel-air valve open, radio on and working. The two 7.7mm machine-gun breeches, protruding through the upper fire wall, were ready for arming: He gave a thumbs-up signal to the ground crewman. A green flare arced from the tower, and Yusaki made a cranking motion to start the engine.

Yusaki joined the train of waddling fighters—so graceful in flight but so awkward on the ground—emerging from concealed revetments. Inching forward as the snarling craft streaked skyward one by one, he moved into takeoff position at the flagman's signal, then added full throttle. The reassuring surge of power never failed to stir him. Gear up, find the assembling formation, slip into his assigned slot: It all flowed smoothly.

The twenty-ship armada droned southward in pursuit of the bomber stream. Yusaki felt uncomfortable with the formation; the planes were tightly bunched. In Burma they had quickly learned that such a formation invited a head-on attack by the P-40s. Numbers lost their advantage, as only one ship at a time could fire at an attacker. The remainder were unable to alter course and aim without running into, or shooting at, a comrade.

Also, there they had flown in two columns, weaving in a scissorslike path. An enemy attacking one element found himself directly in the sights of planes in the parallel, crossing column.

He was unhappy with their altitude, as well. The bombers were at eight thousand feet, the fighter cover at thirteen. The P-40s, when they struck, would come from above. Using their heavier craft to an advantage, they would make one slashing pass and outdistance the more maneuverable but slower diving Zero.

Yusaki shrugged. The air staff must know what they were doing; perhaps the Americans used different tactics up here. He looked across at Sasai, who was holding perfect formation, and, shading his eyes, pointed emphatically upward. Sasai nodded his understanding, and Yusaki reached for his map. A distinctive bend in the river indicated that they were approaching the target. He rechecked that both the 20mm cannon and two 7.7mm machine guns were armed.

Excited voices chattered in Yusaki's earphones. Someone had broken the strict order for radio silence to report sighting enemy planes. Yusaki swiveled his head left; Sasai would have to be his eyes to the right. There they were! Exactly as he had feared. Four dark-painted shapes, their noses displaying evil sharks' mouths, flashed through his range of vision. They had been lurking far above. He saw the telltale dark stream of expended shell casings trail behind. He glimpsed a flash of orange flame up ahead—then another, and another.

The tightly knit formation started to come unraveled as three Zeroes tumbled out of control. "Break up, you fools," he yelled into the empty cockpit. "Roll, dive, get on their tails." Horrified, Yusaki watched the group leader nose over and lead the still-compact formation in a futile effort to catch up with the streaking P-40s, which hadn't deviated from their primary objective—the dive-bombers.

This was madness! he thought wildly. We will be shooting at our own ships. He clamped his jaws. Orders or no, he would do what he knew to be right. Yusaki led his flight of four away from the formation. Adding full power, he leveled and streaked straight ahead, above the confused swirl of airplanes below.

The attackers would hit the bombers just as they had struck the bunched Zeroes, slashing through the formation with guns blazing, shooting only at those directly in their path. Then, he knew, they would escape straight ahead to re-form and return for a head-on attack. He would be waiting for them, he thought grimly.

Yusaki led his small flock into a lazy orbit directly over the airfield. He counted six Aichis spinning toward the ground, trailing plumes of flame and smoke; another blew up in midair. The bomber formation was in total disarray. Fewer than a dozen managed to straggle across the target to loose their bombs. Random geysers of dirt marked releases toggled by panicked, disoriented pilots. The damage they caused would be repaired overnight. No parked aircraft were visible.

Movement south of the field caught his attention. There they were, on the deck, using speed built up during their diving turn. This time they were heading directly at the gaggle of Zeroes. Yusaki signaled to the pilot on his left to break off and attack in pairs. He stood his plane on one wing and peeled off, hoping desperately that he didn't lose his wingman.

He set up an intercept course. The P-40s would be devoting their full attention to the Zeroes ahead, which were trying desperately to re-form. The Americans would have to nose up to attack. He felt supremely confident of a kill. But no! The Americans were far from being combat novices. The trailing pair had spotted the danger diving from above and behind. They whipped into a climbing, twisting turn. Within seconds, Yusaki was looking head-on at a spinning prop and that hated row of white teeth set in blood-red jaws.

He cursed his impaired vision. The correct tactic was to flip his nimble fighter into a tight turn—a turn that the heavier, slower P-40 could not duplicate. He would lose Sasai in the process, however, leaving his wingman exposed to certain death.

Still out of range of his enemy's .50-caliber guns, he loosed a burst of cannon fire. He had little hope of scoring a hit, but perhaps the stream of tracers would frighten the P-40s into breaking off the attack. He was disappointed. He saw the leading edges of their wings erupt in red sparks and dove to escape. The ships passed each other, separated by only inches. Yusaki could see the American pilot clearly. His heart leaped. The shark-nosed craft was trailing smoke; a piece of metal fluttered in its wake. He *had* damaged his opponent.

Yusaki racked his ship into a tight turn. Return and finish the job, he exulted. He saw Sasai still in position. Good boy, I must compliment him, but where are Three and Four? Headed north once more, he confronted nothing but empty sky. Their attack successful, the enemy ships had disappeared—even the crippled one. Finally, far in the distance, Yusaki saw an array of black dots limping home.

Senior Lieutenant Subachi watched Yusaki enter the ready room and approach with his face set in an angry scowl. "Sir—" he started, but Subachi halted the disgruntled pilot's outburst with an upheld hand.

"You disobeyed orders, Lieutenant Nakano. You left the formation at a time when your experience was needed. I will overlook your mistake this time, but *never* do it again."

Stung by the rebuke, Yusaki sprang to rigid attention. "Sir! Do I have permission to speak?"

"Permission granted."

"Sir. We learned in Burma to fight the enemy in small elements of one and two ships, and to take advantage of our superior speed and climbing ability at high altitude."

"Be at ease, Yusaki. Sit down, please," Subachi said, his voice weary with resignation. "In Burma you flew with experienced pilots. Today, fewer than five of our group had ever *seen* the enemy. The security offered by a tight formation lets them gain confidence."

"But, sir. We allowed only *four* enemy fighters to destroy . . . how many of our attacking force?"

"Twelve bombers and fourteen fighters returned safely, Yusaki."

"We lost *thirteen?*"

Subachi nodded. Yusaki could only stare in shocked amazement.

The senior lieutenant continued. "The official report will state that we encountered a superior force and only through valiant effort allowed our bombers to inflict heavy damage."

"But—but that isn't *true,*" Yusaki whispered.

"It is true because the official report states that it is true. Yusaki," Subachi's voice faltered, "Japan's back is to the wall. Ichi Go must succeed. Today's survivors will fly better tomorrow. Tomorrow's survivors will fly even better the next day. What we lack in quality, we must compensate for with numbers. Actually, I am surprised that we encountered only four defenders today. And, for the first time in weeks, we haven't been visited by their bombers. Perhaps we *are* winning. Now, have lunch and report to the ready room. You may be called upon to fly again today."

Yusaki stumbled to the door. He paused to watch a truck disgorge two dozen young, laughing men—boys, actually—sporting flying badges.

26 May 1944
Chengkung Army Airfield

Ross rolled to a stop alongside Major King's ship, set the parking brake, and let out a sigh of relief. The last half hour had been touch and go. Low clouds and a fine drizzle had kept them on the deck from a hundred miles out. The terrain was unfamiliar. Luckily, a glimpse of the heavily traveled Old Burma Road gave King the fix he needed for an approach. Ross opened the canopy and let Master Sergeant Wilkes, the crew chief, help him disentangle the hoses, cables, and straps that are essential to flight. He stepped into the fine rain and surveyed a scene filled by trotting GIs, rumbling trucks, and a hundred coolies, all seemingly imbued with grim purpose. "What the hell's going on, Chief?" Ross asked. "Spring housecleaning?"

"Word is we're buggin' out, Cap'n. Plus there's two big missions slated for tomorrow. That's all I know. Hope to hell y'don't have a bunch of write-ups. This bird is scheduled for a daylight takeoff."

"The hell you say," Ross replied. "Naw, nothing worth grounding her—sure wish you could get the leak in that canopy seal fixed, though. I got soaked climbing out yesterday." He leaped to the ground and jogged after Major King, already striding toward the ops shack.

They were greeted by a sweating, pink-faced O. B. Holt. "Glad you're back, Major. All hell is breaking loose."

"Fill me in," King responded in clipped tones.

"Okay. First off, we have movement orders east to Hengyang. The Japs are pouring out of Hankow like bees from a hive—going through the Chinese troops like shit through a tinhorn. Chungking is screaming for air support, which Vincent can't give 'em because he's out of gas.

"So—act two. ATC has agreed to refuel the next eight C-87s out of stocks here and take their loads on east. Problem is, they won't go north of Kweilin without fighter escort. That's where we come in. We fly top cover, land at Hengyang, and stay there. All but four, that is."

"Where are *they* supposed to go?" King snapped.

"Well, it seems the Japs are not only headed south, they're also spreading west, along the north bank of the Yangtze. Chungking is in total panic; they see a real threat to the capital. Fourteenth ops thinks differently. Colonel York is of the opinion that they're headed for the B-29 bases at Chengtu. Either way, you're to send one flight to the strip at Hsinching to fly recce along a route the Japs are apt to take. That's just the sketchy outline. Colonel York wants to see you the minute you land. He'll fill you in."

"O.B., I want you to take 'A' Flight to Hsinching; you'll be detachment commander," King said as he stripped his flight suit and donned Class A's. "From what I saw on this little trip, you'll have your work cut out for you. I'll explain later. Alert the crews going east. Colyer, you'll go with me to Hengyang. As of now you are also the squadron supply officer. That's going to be the name of the game from now on. The CO who can scrounge the most gas and spare parts is going to be the one setting records for kills."

Ross glared at King's departing back, then hiked his buttocks onto a tabletop. Regarding the floor between swinging flight boots, he said, "I gotta get out of this goddamn outfit, O.B. I swore I'd grit my teeth and take anything that bastard could dish out. But this is the last fucking straw—*supply officer.*"

Holt straightened from packing records into a shipping carton. "I know how you must feel, Ross," the chunky ops officer responded. "But things will change; they have to. The guys in the squadron, those who know you anyway, respect your judgment and flying ability."

"All except Deardorf," Ross observed bitterly.

"Look, Walt respects you. It's just, well, I hate to say it, but he thought you chickened out on that mission to Myitkyina."

"*Thought?*"

"Uh—I had a long talk with him."

Ross looked up and grinned. "The hell you did? Okay, thanks. Well"—he leaped to the floor—"enough crying in my beer. I'd best alert the troops, and get an idea what supplies we can take with us."

"Thanks, Ross. You won't regret this, I hope. Deardorf has 'C' Flight on a sweep over Bhamo. They're due back in about an hour. I'll give them the word when they check in here."

Ross frowned. "An hour from now? O.B., have you looked outside lately?"

"Well, no. What's going on?"

"Weather. We were on the deck coming in. It's apt to be down to a hundred feet in an hour."

Holt rushed to the door. "Holy shit!" he exclaimed. "Where the hell did that come from?"

"It's moving in from the north. The major and I got in just ahead of it."

Holt scratched his jaw. "Well, Walt's an old hand out here. He'll find somewhere to put in."

"Really? O.B., I know he flew with the AVG, but is he a good instrument pilot?"

"Hell, I don't know. You know the way it is. Fighter pilots don't do much flying on the gauges."

"Well, 'C' Flight is about to. With a CFR forecast for their return, they'll be at altitude coming back. If they get caught above this, well . . ."

"Damn," the ops officer muttered.

"Tell you what. I'm going to the tower and try to raise them. Maybe they can sneak in underneath if there's a hole southwest of here."

"I'll go with you."

Ross and O.B. strode into the little second-floor cubicle that housed the primitive tower facilities. "You heard anything from Blue Flight?" Holt asked the operator.

"No, sir. They ain't due for another forty-five minutes."

"Try to raise them on D channel."

"Yes, sir." The corporal picked up his mike. "Blue One, this is Hilda. Over."

Tension filled the ensuing silence. Finally, a drawled, "Blue One here, Hilda. Go ahead."

Holt took over the mike. "This is Ops, Blue One. What is your position? Over."

"Uh, 'bout thirty minutes out."

"What are your weather conditions? Over."

"We're on top at sixteen, O.B. It's pretty solid. What's our forecast for landing? Over."

"Maybe as little as a hundred and one, Blue One."

A pregnant silence followed. Then, "Roger, gotcha, Hilda. Guess I'd best start lookin' for a hole."

Ross stepped forward. "May I?"

Holt silently handed him the mike. "Blue One, have you flown enough instruments to lead a flight down through this?"

"I'll get down, don't sweat it, son," came the curt response.

O.B. grabbed the mike. "Answer the question, Blue One," he snapped.

"Okay, okay. Not for some time, I reckon."

"All right," said Ross, taking over again. "Reduce power to maximum endurance and stay on course at your present altitude. I'm going to meet you overhead and lead you in. Do you copy?"

"I copy, but I don't like it."

"Trust me, Blue One," Ross shot back. "Hold your heading and altitude. I'll call back in about fifteen minutes."

Ross wheeled to find O.B. frowning at him. "Ross, how the hell are *you* going to find your way back?"

"I've got an idea. Corporal, have you heard anything from Piano Player?"

"General Chennault's B-25? Yeah, he's working Kunming for an ADF approach."

"Great!" Ross cried. He keyed the mike. "Piano Player, this is Hilda Tower. We have an emergency. Over."

"Roger, Hilda. Go ahead with your message. Over."

"Piano Player, we have a flight of four fighters caught on top. Can you lead two of them down on your approach? Over."

"Uh, I have two code ones on board, Hilda. I'm afraid not."

"Ask them," Ross snapped.

"Roger. Stand by."

Moments later the trio in the tower heard General Chennault's gravelly voice: "Hilda, what is the nature of your emergency? Over."

"We have four fighters trapped above this weather," Ross replied. "I can lead one down on each wing. Can you do likewise? This stuff is too thick for me to try four."

"Who am I talking with?"

"The flight-training officer for the 41st Squadron, and I have a green instrument rating."

"I see. What is your plan?"

"If you will orbit the Kunming beacon above the overcast and start firing flares in about ten minutes, I'll join up on you. We'll hold there until Blue Flight homes in on your flares."

"You're apt to have airplanes scattered all over the landscape," Chennault argued.

"It's that or have the flight bail out, I'm afraid, sir."

"Very well. Call me on channel B when you're airborne."

Ross wheeled toward the door. He called over his shoulder, "O.B., raise Kunming. Have them send two men to the approach end of the runway with flare pistols. When they hear engines, tell 'em to start shooting flares to make an arc over the touchdown point." Holt looked confused. "It's an old trick we used in England," Ross added.

Ross's Mustang poked its nose into bright sunlight. He glanced at the altimeter—twelve thousand feet. It was going to be a long trip down. He scanned the sky to the east, spotted an arcing red-green flare, and turned in that direction. Within minutes the distinctive profile of the twin-tailed B-25 was clearly outlined against the cottony cloud tops. He keyed his mike. "Blue One, this is White One. Do you read?"

"Loud and clear, White One. Estimate I'll be at your location in one-zero minutes. We're still at sixteen thousand. I'm readin' forty gallons of fuel left. Blue Three has slightly more'n thirty-five. Over."

"Roger, Blue One. Piano Player is orbiting the Kunming beacon at thirteen, firing red-green flares. You can start your descent. Call when you have us in sight. We'll be landing at Kunming, Runway One-eight. The altimeter at Kunming is twenty-nine-point-two-eight. Ceiling obscured, visibility one mile in light rain, wind is light and variable. Since Three and Four have less fuel, they will join Piano Player and start an immediate descent. One and Two, form on me. We will start our descent as soon as Piano Player calls clear of the runway. Copy?"

"Copy all, White One. We have your flares in sight."

Ross grinned. Deardorf might be a horse's ass, but he could fly—and he didn't panic. There must be four tight sphincters over there, but the guy sounded like they were discussing a stroll to the club for a drink. He watched Three and Four break off, tack on the B-25's wings, and disappear into the clouds. The die was cast. He keyed his mike. "Okay, troops, we'll spiral straight down from where Piano Player disappeared. That's the radio beacon, one mile north of the field.

"I'll hold a half-needle-width turn and set up a five-hundred-feet-per-minute descent. Stay tight; this stuff is thick. You'll probably get disoriented in this spiral—get the feeling I'm leveling off, climbing, even turning in the opposite direction. Glance at your gyrohorizon if you get vertigo. It will show you your true attitude. If you lose me, level your wings and climb back on top straight ahead; I'll climb back up and we'll try again. The runway isn't wide enough to land all three abreast. When you see yellow flares, drop into trail and land on your own. I'll touch down long and get the hell out of your way, okay?"

He heard a clipped, "One, roger." "Two, roger." Rolling into the shallow orbit, he cursed to himself. Damnit, *why* can't they devise an autodirection radio set for fighters? Or *why* can't they at least set up some kind of four-legged radio range at the bigger bases that we can pick up on our coffee-grinder sets? And *why,* for Christ's sake, don't they teach fighter pilots to fly better instruments in single-engine advanced pilot training?

His mental muttering was interrupted by a voice in his earphones. "White One, this is Piano Player on the deck with both chicks safe and sound. Be advised we broke out at about two hundred feet. Good luck. Over." Ross acknowledged, reduced power, and rolled into a gentle, descending spiral.

The altimeter unwound with agonizing slowness. Damn, it was dark inside this stuff. He pivoted to see Blue One in position on his right wing, wingtips almost touching. A glance to his left showed Two in good position as well. It was tempting to increase his rate of descent, but with only a one- or two-hundred-foot ceiling, he dared not make any sudden moves when they broke out underneath. He mentally blessed the light wind. Hopefully they would emerge from the clouds within a mile or two of the runway.

At five thousand feet, Ross breathed more easily. While he mentally rehearsed the final approach, they sagged through one thousand. Seven hundred, six—he resisted the urge to peek outside; he wanted to give his wingmen the steadiest ride possible. Four hundred, three—he caught a glimpse of a ragged cloud base—a slight break, then trees. Rice paddies appeared through the rain-beaded windshield. A yellow flash lit up the murk at eleven o'clock. *We got it made!* he exulted as he dropped gear and flaps.

Parked in front of base ops, Ross left his canopy closed while he filled out the Form-1. A rapping on the canopy made him look up. Deardorf stood on the wing, his face devoid of expression. Ross swung open the Plexiglas covering and squinted against the rain.

"Piss on the paperwork, Colyer. Get out and let me buy you dinner and drinks, heavy on the drinks part."

Ross grinned and joined the taciturn pilot on the ground. "Okay, I'm a fuckhead," said Deardorf. "You know your stuff. That was a nifty piece of work, and I'll fly your wing anytime. Truce?"

Suddenly the day seemed brighter to Ross. He extended a hand. "With an offer like that, I'll follow you anywhere . . . Walt."

Chapter Fifteen

27 May 1944
Kunming
General Chennault rolled an unlit cigar between thin, grimly set lips. "Well, Elliott, what have you decided about the loan of some gas from Chengtu?" he rasped.

"We both know what that 'loan' depends upon, General." Sprague's voice was bland, but his gaze was shrewd.

"Yeah." Chennault's granitelike features cracked in a glacial smile. "I'll do my part. My secretary is typing up the report right now. It'll be in the pouch on board your airplane this afternoon. Two questions remain, however: One, how convincing can you be when you get back to Kharagpur, and two, will you follow through after you get to Chengtu."

Sprague flushed. "I gave you my *word,* General. You'll get your gas. As for K.B., well—he'll come around. I'm betting I'll be in Twenty Bomber Command's ADVON within a matter of days."

"Don't make it too many days, Elliott. I received a message from Casey Vincent the night before last, after you left. The Japs appear to have their sights set on two big raids in as many days. With a secure supply line from Peking to Hankow, they're pouring troops over it—artillery and tanks, as well. Casey was only able to launch eight—think of it, only *eight*—P-40s. He's looking at dry tanks.

"They scored like crazy, however. It looks like the Japs are throwing green pilots into the drive, but without our close air support, the Chinese can't hope to stop them on the ground.

"Now, I'm sending the 41st from Chengkung to Hengyang—before they're ready actually—to give those yellow bastards a look at some Mustangs. All but one flight—it will go to Hsinching, outside Chungking. The generalissimo is nervous as hell. They remember what the Jap bombers did in '38. I put real pressure on Stilwell to let some transports take their Hump cargoes right on through to my eastern bases. That'll take the pressure off for a few days—no more."

Sprague nodded. "You were busy that night, weren't you, sir? One other thing before I go. If we're to work closely, I'd like to have one of your people attached for fighter liaison. Can you spare me someone?"

Chennault sat silently for a moment. "It's possible."

"Good. I had in mind Captain Colyer, the one who led those fighters home yesterday. He served under me in the ETO, you may recall. I know him, and we think alike."

Chennault grunted. "He's a good man, all right." After another pause, he added, "But I'll tell you what, Elliott. I'd rather give you a field-grade officer; it's a pretty responsible job. Major King is a helluva good man, but, frankly, he's easier to replace than Colyer. Casey has a senior major at Kweilin who is overdue for promotion and needs command time on his record."

Sprague nodded. "I was impressed with King—fair enough, sir. I'd best get on my way, though. I have a full night's work ahead of me when I get back."

Chennault walked Sprague to the door. As his visitor disappeared, he turned to his secretary. "Susie," he rapped, "locate Colonel York. If he isn't flying, I want to see him."

Colonel Sam York, his seamed, wolfhoundlike features streaming sweat, paused in front of General Chennault's desk. "Yes, sir, General. You wanted to see me?"

"Yeah, Sam." Chennault waved the perspiring colonel to a chair. "You look hot."

"About to melt. I'd kill for a bottle of cold American beer."

"If I had any, I wouldn't share." Chennault grinned. "How's the move progressing?"

"On schedule. The gooneybirds with the ground crews, spare parts, and such were airborne about an hour ago. Holt and 'A' Flight are strapping in—should be on the ground at Hsinching well before dark. The rest of the squadron is alerted for a daylight departure tomorrow."

Chennault grunted. "Good. Look, Sam, I don't want you to fall to the floor, kick your feet, and scream, but I'm making some last-minute changes."

York groaned but didn't speak.

"That brigadier who just left—Sprague?"

"Yes, sir."

"He can be a problem."

"The B-29s?" York asked.

"Right. Because he's outside the chain of command over here and has the Joint Chiefs behind him, he thinks he can dictate his own terms."

"Such as?"

"He's sitting on top of all that lovely gas at Chengtu. He doesn't want to share. Hell, he can't possibly launch a mission 'til sometime next month. If Casey Vincent doesn't get a shipment before then, we'll be handing the Japs Chengtu on a platter. So Casey is going to get what he needs. I had to make a pact with the devil, but it's done. Anyway, this guy had the unmitigated gall to up the ante with a little bonus for himself. He wants a 'fighter liaison' type at Chengtu."

"What the hell for?" asked York.

"You can bet your ass it isn't for the reason he gave me. He wants to have a pipeline into my headquarters. With a straight face, he asked for Colyer over at the 41st. Colyer flew with him on the Ploesti raid. Can you believe that? How damn stupid does he think I am?"

"So what are you going to do?"

Chennault flashed a wicked grin. "I dealt him a card off the bottom of the deck. I gave him Major King."

"*What?* King? Sir. My God, he's in the process of moving the squadron to Hengyang."

"Anything else you'd like to tell me about my command, Sam?" Chennault asked, his voice caustic. "Now, don't go into overboost; let me finish. I had an interesting file on my desk when I got back: intelligence debriefings from both King and Colyer, his wingman that day over Myitkyina. They don't agree worth a damn. And you know what? I believe Colyer. Let me tell you why. King ignored my direct order *not* to engage the enemy on those reconnaissance missions. He gave me a convincing story right after the mission about not being able to pass up a fat target—I had to agree. I'd have probably done the same thing myself. But it still pissed me off, so I did some checking. The little bastard lied to me. Listen to this from King's Fourteenth Air Force debriefing:

Q: What was Colyer's position when you started your run over the field, Major King?

A: Off my left wing trailing by about a hundred yards—standard formation for a strafing attack.

Q: Then what happened?

A: Colyer seemed reluctant to hold position. He slid farther to the left until he was over the airfield's perimeter. That was when he flew into antiaircraft fire.

Q: Did you see him take a hit?

A: Not actually—I was pretty busy engaging targets at the time.

Q: When did you first realize your wingman was in trouble?

A: Well, he didn't respond to my radio calls. I didn't think too much about it. I'd had trouble calling him into formation after my first pass.

Chennault looked up, his expression grim. "Right there, he contradicted himself. At the squadron mission debriefing he said there was no ground fire on his *first* firing pass. And that's what he told me later. Colyer's account confirms what King told my boys. Colyer stated that he observed ground fire *before* King called him to join up for *another* pass."

The general closed the folder and slammed it onto the desk. "I'm having orders cut right now relieving him of command and attaching him to Twenty Bomber Command. At the same time, I'm cutting orders making Whizzer Weibel, over in Casey Vincent's headquarters, CO of the 41st."

"I see." York mopped his head with an already saturated handkerchief. "You talk to Casey about this?"

"Naw, no time for that. He'll be glad to see Whizzer get a squadron. Weibel is one of my old AVG pilots. He'll flat tear those Jap Zeroes apart."

"I dunno, General," York replied slowly. "I talked to Casey when I was out there last month. Whizzer's been fighting the booze. He's been off the operational roster for some time. Nothing official, but he missed a couple of alerts, and Casey came down hard on him."

"Whizzer is bored, for Christ's sake. He used to fly two—sometimes three sorties a day. With the fuel shortage, he just doesn't have enough to do. Give him some responsibility, and he'll shape up. Now,

I'd like for you to go to Hengyang with the squadron and get it set up. Weibel will be there by Friday, I'd guess."

"Yes, sir. It's your show. I'll go pack." York's homely features wore a worried frown as he took his leave.

Elliott Sprague watched low clouds envelop the VIP C-54 and settled back with a self-satisfied smile. Things had gone better than he'd expected. Chennault hadn't been the only one busy that night in Chungking. Two handwritten letters caused a bulge in Sprague's breast pocket. His aide would be on this same airplane headed for Washington within hours after landing at Kharagpur—with the letters tucked securely inside his briefcase. The one addressed to Sen. Broderick Templeton—stamped PERSONAL AND EYES ONLY—started out:

Dear Senator Templeton,

I hate to presume upon our acquaintance so soon after your son's tragic death, but I've encountered a situation I believe warrants your committee's attention. I've just returned from a tour of our bases in China, during which I was privileged to have dinner with Generalissimo and Madame Chiang Kai-shek. . . .

The other, marked PERSONAL AND EYES ONLY for Lt. Gen. Clint Wolfenbarger, read:

Dear General Wolfenbarger,

Sir, it's time to call out the fire department! This CBI mess is unbelievable. I just made a swing through our east China bases and had a meeting with Generalissimo and Madame Chiang Kai-shek. Unless some major changes are made, and fast, we'll never carry out the JCS plan to put a hundred bombers over Japan before summer. Now, you know me, I speak my mind without pussyfooting around. K.B. is floundering. It's his old problem, I'm afraid. He's drinking heavily and losing control of the situation. My own estimate is that our best effort will put no more than fifty planes in the air.

Then there's Chennault. A wonderful guy—treated me royally. But, damnit, he's still living the period when the AVG was in its heyday. His pilots spend more time in bars and whorehouses than in the cockpit.

I see only one immediate solution: Put *all* air operations under the Twentieth Air Force with a commander in New Delhi coequal to Stilwell (who, I learned from the Chiangs, is causing them no end of grief).

As always, I'm giving you my best effort, but it's an uphill battle.

Sincerely,
Elliott

6 June 1944
Hengyang, China

Ross broke hard left, retarded the throttle, and watched his airspeed bleed off to 180 MPH. The nose swung through the runway's reciprocal heading, and he dropped half flaps. Glancing to his left rear, he saw the other three members of his flight stringing into the landing pattern. Rolling level on final approach, he felt the gear thump into the down position. Two green lights winked on, and he lined up for touchdown. Landing long on the left side of the runway to reduce the effects of prop wash on those touching down behind him, he checked the instrument panel clock.

Fifteen-twenty—enough daylight remained for yet another sortie. While the fliers gulped down coarse sandwiches and cups of tea in the ready room, the ground crews would refuel the four Mustangs, and they could be airborne within thirty minutes. No need to replenish the ammo cans; he looked disgustedly at his still-taped gunports.

Those sneaky yellow bastards—the Japs know all about our fuel crunch, Ross thought. They launch formation after formation of dive-bombers, at least two or three each day. When the shark-nosed fighters come up to meet them, they turn tail and flee north, leaving a few Zeroes circling lazily at thirty thousand feet or thereabouts to cover their retreat. Another victory without a shot being fired; the Americans waste another sixteen hundred gallons of priceless av-gas.

He waited for the other pilots to join him before entering the ready room. "Ross," Cal Evans, a rosy-cheeked, red-haired second lieutenant, grumbled, "when are we going to stop this stupid business? Let's put together one big mission, go up there, and wipe that goddamn Hankow off the map."

"Our number-one job is to destroy the Jap air force," Ross replied, his voice sagging with weary resignation. "Besides that, we don't have the gas to put up a 'big' mission, and the bombers don't have fuses for what bombs they have left. That infusion from Chengtu is damn near gone. A convoy left Kunming two weeks ago, and that means another two weeks before we can even fly a full schedule." The four gaunt-faced men trooped inside.

Major Weibel leaned against the counter, a canteen cup of grapefruit juice at his elbow. Oh shit, Ross muttered to himself, I wonder how many of *those* he's already consumed? The CO wore a rumpled flight suit with white, sweat-formed salt rings at the armpits. Ross had never seen him in another uniform. Lank straw-colored hair was in need of a barber's attention. His narrow, normally pinched face was blotched and puffy.

"I see your gunports are still taped, Ross. The usual?" Weibel inquired.

"Yeah, a dozen Vals stooging around. They ran before we could even get a good look at them. I dunno, Major. We gotta think of something different. How'd the P-40s make out?"

"Two sampans and a truck, but twenty-some horses. Ain't that a knee-slapper? Three-hundred-fifty-mile-per-hour airplanes fighting a goddamn force of horse-mounted cavalry—and losing. This bunch was a good ten miles closer than yesterday. I don't know. I think I'll run down to Kweilin tomorrow and talk to Casey. Shit, back when we were flying out of Rangoon we just tore into those bastards anytime we saw one. Maybe he'll let me put up some B-25s as decoys, then ambush the bastards."

Ross guessed the major had at least three of those cups of grapefruit juice—laced with the locally produced, triple-distilled rice wine—under his belt; he was back flying with the AVG again. "I don't see any balls on the pole, Skipper. Does that mean an all clear for the day?"

"Maybe—maybe not. The warning net north of here is shot to hell. The Japs are rolling it up as they come. They can be within fifteen minutes of here before they're spotted. Stand by for another hour. If they don't run up two or three balls by then, call it a day. First, let's go over to my office. Want'a talk to you."

They crossed the dusty strip separating the ready-room shack from the main cantonment in silence. Ross glanced again at the empty air raid warning pole. A single three-foot red canvas ball hoisted to the top meant enemy aircraft had been seen or heard within 180 miles of the base. Two balls indicated that they were less than a hundred miles away. A three-ball alert was reason to head for cover. Primitive but effective, he mused.

Inside the major's cluttered office, Weibel tossed a soiled, sweat-stained shirt from a chair and indicated that Ross should sit. Weibel slumped into the chair behind his desk and took a long pull from the canteen cup. "Ross, this business of being both CO and ops officer is getting to me."

Ross concealed a smile. The major's sole operational mission had been with the 67th in his beloved P-40—a sweep to beat up some shipping on Ting-tung Lake. "You going to bring O.B. back from Chengtu?" he asked.

"Nope. Holt is needed up there—doing a damn fine job. But he can be detachment commander without also being squadron ops. Besides, he's coming up for rotation. No, you're the ranking captain, so as of tomorrow you're my ops officer."

Ross blinked and covered his surprise by fishing a limp cigaret from his sweat-soaked pocket. "Uh—well, Major, I'll do the best job I know how for you."

"I'm sure you will, Ross, I'm sure you will. Now, how do the pilots shape up? I haven't been with them long enough to get a good fix on the boys. You happy with Deardorf and Axel as flight commanders?"

"Totally," Ross answered firmly. "Look, I haven't flown with all of them yet, myself. Major King kept me—ah—busy with other jobs. Then I spent two to three weeks walking out of Burma. I'm impressed with what I see, but, damnit, there's never been enough fuel to do any training."

"Yeah, a real pisser," Weibel agreed. "Now, when we were in Burma—hell, there wasn't any need for training. A new man fought Japs from the day he showed up. We learned in a hurry that way."

"I can believe that," Ross replied. "But there's one thing I do know, and it worries me. These guys, none of them, can fly instruments for sour owl shit. With the weather we have over here, it's going to get someone killed. It damn near got Deardorf and his flight at Kunming."

"Yeah, I heard about that. Chennault himself was impressed with the job you did. But, goddamnit, Walt should have his butt kicked for ever getting into that situation. A fighter's place is on the deck—see where you're going, not trying to read a goddamn bunch of dials and gauges."

Ross sighed unobtrusively. "Well, if we *ever* have a few gallons of gas to spare, I'm going to change that. Ten hours each can make all the difference. After that, there's no reason we can't scrounge some five-hundred-pounders, hang them on, and make a nighttime sweep over the bases at Hankow. Hell, if we can't knock them out of the air, let's catch 'em on the ground. But, shit, the way these guys fly instruments, we'd probably lose more on the trip than we'd destroy on the ground."

"Now wait a damn minute, Ross." Weibel's voice reflected alarm. "At night? With the weather we have around here? Oh, no. We tried that once in Burma—a total goddamn disaster. Now, I'll probably be in Kweilin in, oh, three to four days. You'll be in charge, but don't—and this is an order—*don't* go trying some foolish stunt like that."

Ross trudged inside the semiprivate cubicle he shared with Walt Deardorf in the run-down hostel. Walt was already sprawled on his bed, stripped to shorts, and half asleep. "You don't have to come to attention when I enter a room, Deardorf, but I think you should show a bit more respect to your ops officer," Ross growled.

The recumbent pilot opened one eye. "Is someone standing behind you?" he mumbled.

"Just God, that's all. I'm one of the chosen."

The eye closed. "You should know better than to accept one of Whizzer's concoctions. They make you brain dead."

"No shit. He just dropped it on me. I'm replacing Holt; O.B.'s due for rotation."

Deardorf sat upright. "It's about time, that's all I got to say. I know the story about you and Major King. I don't know how you kept from strangling him. Well, let's go to town. This calls for about a dozen Gom-bays."

"My thinking exactly. First I'm going to take a shower. Then, since we're not on the alert roster tomorrow, I propose we have a *real* drink. I have four fingers of liquid gold I've kept hidden from the rest of you greedy bastards—genuine twelve-year-old Scotch. After that I suggest we proceed to a location suitable for the occasion, like Mama Wong's."

The accumulated fatigue after four days of standing alert from dawn to dusk fell away as Ross entered the shower room. It was the one place in that primitive land where he could forget the hellish drain of danger and deprivation for thirty delicious minutes. This place should be enshrined like a temple, Ross thought.

Even its appearance was relaxing. Roughly ten by ten feet in size, each shower cubicle was equipped with a stone hearth with a hole in its top. A fifty-five-gallon drum rested there, filled with water always at exactly the right temperature—another mystery. Ross disrobed, handed his clothes to a smiling Chinese boy, who always looked as if he thoroughly enjoyed his job, and stood in the center of the room. The attendant lowered a large wooden bucket hanging from the ceiling by a rope and pulley and, using a huge wooden ladle, filled the bucket with water from the drum. After hoisting the container over Ross's head, the boy tugged on an attached cord and exposed several holes drilled in the bottom of the primitive vessel. The water came streaming out.

Several minutes of luxurious lathering followed. The attendant lowered the empty bucket, refilled it, and raised it back to the ceiling. After Ross had rinsed off, the boy bowed and handed him a towel. Life looked better. It was one of the few instances, Ross mused, when an American and a Chinese knew exactly what the other was doing.

Entering the hostel, he was greeted by pandemonium. A shorts-clad Cal Evans pounded down the hall toward him, yelling, "Have you heard? Tyson just heard on his shortwave—we've invaded France! It's going on now. We crossed the Channel and have a beachhead."

Ross was able to conceal his queasy stomach and pounding head only with great effort the next morning. He saw Major Weibel off to Kweilin without remembering a word said. Afterward, he dashed to the nearest parked Mustang and sucked pure oxygen for several minutes. The reputed restorative properties of the gas were greatly exaggerated, he decided. It fell in the same category as feeding an inebriated man black coffee: All you ended up with was a wide-awake drunk.

On the way back to ops he checked the air-raid warning pole; the hated ball hung like an accusing omen. He groaned and trotted to the ready room, where the alert flight was assembling for briefing. Lieutenant Axel, the flight commander, grinned when he saw Ross. "My, my, I detect signs of debauchery, Captain. That must have been some celebration. Congratulations, by the way."

Ross mumbled his thanks and scanned the ground observer reports. There were only two—both reporting breaks in the overcast fifty miles north. Damn, he thought, before long they would have to start flying a dawn weather recce.

General Chennault's vaunted early-warning net was coming unraveled. Since its inception in 1942 the primitive arrangement had kept the Japs from catching AVG units unprepared. Coolies, professional men, anyone with access to a radio transmitter or telephone relayed word of enemy aircraft movement to Chennault's communication centers. A typical sighting would read, "heavy engine noise in sector Baker Fourteen." The grid also provided weather observations and was instrumental in locating downed flyers. To the north, the Japanese advance was efficiently rooting out the corps of observers.

Ross turned and gave the customary, perfunctory briefing. "Remember, airborne targets only. Zeroes have first priority. If you see a fat truck convoy or barge, okay—but no frontline stuff. Leave that for the P-40s." He looked outside, where early morning fog still hung above the adjacent Hsiang River. "Watch that weather—and don't get caught on top. Have a good time."

Ross stood in the doorway as the flight assembled and raced down the uneven runway. He saw Axel's lead plane disappear into the fog and frowned. Damn, the stuff was heavier than usual. Still frowning, he heard a muffled *whump*. An orange glow illuminated the fog bank. Oh, good Christ! A midair. He pounded to the shack housing the base's only fire truck.

The crash truck, a weapons carrier mounting a water tank, was already rolling when Ross grabbed a rear tank support and swung aboard. One of the grinning Chinese firemen steadied him and shouted, "Hold on, Captain, sir. Chou, he go velly fas'."

"Velly fas'" was an understatement, Ross concluded. "Hell-bent" and "insane" were more fitting terms. The driver apparently believed that the accelerator had only two positions—off and full throttle. He adjusted forward speed by clashing the gears into a different ratio. All four wheels left the ground as the sturdy vehicle leaped off the runway and roared toward a narrow dike separating two rice paddies.

Fog closed around the speeding truck with no discernible effect upon Chou. Ross felt the rear end slew as they left the dike and plunged into the sodden, malodorous rice paddy. Only then did he see a flicker of flames from the Mustang.

Even in four-wheel drive, the crash truck, with a full tank of water, progressed less than fifty feet. Chou, eventually convinced he could go no farther, removed his foot from the accelerator. Ross jumped to the ground and found himself knee-deep in ooze. He floundered around the mired vehicle toward its front end.

The Mustang was in two pieces. The tail section pointed skyward; a wing and part of a fuselage lay buried a few yards farther on. Spilled gasoline still burned with yellow, smoky tongues. Ross watched a half-dozen coolies, awed by the sudden disruption of their work, wading toward the scene. The thought that he was looking at the wreckage of only one plane suddenly occurred to him. Where was the *second* one?

Angry shouts from behind him overrode the chattering of the fire truck crew and the coolies. He turned. A dozen more blue-smocked workers were gathered on the dike. They had subdued one of their number and were kicking and beating the screaming figure as he sprawled in the dirt. Ross turned to the fireman who had shared the ride with him. "What are they doing?" he yelled.

The man shrugged. "They say man is Nippon spy. He cause American plane to fall from sky."

"Oh, nonsense. It was a midair collision. Tell them to stop."

His interpreter shrugged. "They not do, I think. He is a bad man. Soldiers come now anyway."

An American Jeep slid to a stop at the mob scene. A Chinese officer and three men sprang to the ground, guns ready. "Thank God," Ross muttered, and started wading toward them.

It was impossible to make himself heard above the babble. Ross shouted until he was nearly hoarse. At last the fireman joined him and caught the officer's attention. They engaged in a rapid-fire, singsong exchange. The fireman turned to Ross. "Is true, he say. People saw him. He raise hands and shout—plane blow up and fall."

"Oh, for Christ's sake." Ross shook his head. "What are they going to do now?"

"Shoot him, I think."

"*No!* Look . . ." Ross thought furiously. "Tell him—tell him the man is an American prisoner. It was an American plane; *we* will shoot him."

Another exchange—longer this time. Then, "He say okay. You don't have gun; use his."

Ross felt he was beyond surprises. He crossed his arms and assumed his most officious position. "No, only American soldier police can kill prisoners. Put the man in the Jeep. Take us to the base. I will see to the shooting myself."

Ross's throbbing headache returned. What a mess; he tried to assemble his jumbled thoughts. He grasped the fireman. "Get help from these workers. The pilot must be in the cockpit. Get him out and bring him to the base. Another plane is probably down. I will send men from the base to start a search for it and the pilot. Understand?"

The man nodded vigorously. Infused with delegated authority, he commenced giving orders. Ross joined the Chinese soldiers in the Jeep.

Their hapless prisoner cowed in the rear, two .303 Lee Enfield muzzles inches from his head. The vehicle started toward the base, the triumphant captain erect in the front seat, Ross hanging over the rear, and the third soldier seated on a front fender.

Ross's first act after entering operations was to grab the field phone and call the tower. "This is Captain Colyer. Are you in contact with Red Flight?"

"Yes, sir. Lead is aware that one of his aircraft crashed on takeoff. He is continuing on his mission."

"*One?* Are you sure it was only one?"

"Yessir," the tower operator replied. "He says he's proceeding with a flight of three."

Ross slowly returned the phone to its pouch. *Damnit!* The kid had just plain lost it when he entered the fog bank. This was the last straw. This bunch was going to learn instrument flying if it took the last drop of gas on the base. He turned to confront the hard-faced captain and his abject prisoner. "Shipley," he yelled.

"Yes, sir," the ops clerk responded from behind his counter.

"Get Captain Deardorf down here—on the double!"

Ten minutes later Ross faced his roommate. Scowling as hard as his aching head would permit, he shouted, "Round up four presentable-looking men and an interpreter. Then go to Weibel's quarters and get two of his oak leaves. Pin them on: *You* are about to hold a court-martial."

Walt regarded Ross through bleary, bloodshot eyes. "I *told* you that stuff Whizzer mixes up would make you crazy," he mumbled.

Ross ignored the confused pilot's pathetic condition. "Put on a good show for the captain, here," he added with feigned anger. "Yell, wave your arms, then sentence this poor bastard to be executed. Explain to the captain that our only firing squad is in Chungking. I'll cut orders putting this guy on the next gooneybird going there . . . to report to Major King for further disposition."

Chapter Sixteen

13 June 1944
Hsinching Airfield, China

The Chinese army band ended its national anthem with a flourish and launched into a shrill rendition of "The Stars and Stripes Forever." The addition of gongs and bells to the score made Sprague wince. God help us all if anyone ever teaches them the *1812 Overture*. They'll use live ammo in the cannons, sure as hell, he surmised. Resplendent in a carefully preserved Class A uniform, the general marched one pace behind and to the right of Generalissimo Chiang Kai-shek. Madame Chiang, in the shade of an umbrella carried by an attendant, provided a regal touch at the generalissimo's left elbow.

Striding along the parked row of B-29s, crews standing at attention in front of nosewheels, the generalissimo was clearly in his element. Sprague mentally congratulated himself for coming up with the ceremonial touch. He only wished the crews made a more military appearance. He'd heard from Major King that there had nearly been a mutiny when he'd ordered the men to wash and iron their flight suits immediately after landing the previous night. However, they still made a rather scruffy appearance. He hoped that the Chiangs didn't notice the sullen expressions.

The reviewing party reached the last of the thirty Superfortresses, which stood with its bomb-bay doors open and a boarding ladder erected at the nose entrance. The aircraft commander stepped forward and saluted as the generalissimo's entourage approached. "If the generalissimo would care to inspect the aircraft, Captain Hall will oblige, sir," Sprague announced crisply. "Captain Hall and I will pilot the lead ship in our history-making first mission against the Japanese home islands."

Chiang's face lit up. "I would very much like to," he enthused. "These, indeed, Elliott, are most impressive machines. They seem almost too large to become airborne."

Sprague wisely refrained from informing Chiang that the takeoff process did indeed present a major problem; only 68 of the 150 bombers parked around Calcutta had managed to reach the Chengtu bases. Instead, he said, "Before you board, please observe what Mister Tojo can expect us to leave at his doorstep the day after tomorrow." Leading the way beneath the open bomb-bay doors, Sprague pointed upward. He watched the generalissimo quickly count twenty thousand-pound bombs filling the double bomb bays. Sprague did not explain that before the mission, the ground crews would unload more than half of the bombs and install long-range fuel tanks, giving each bomber a capacity of nearly nine thousand gallons of av-gas.

Sprague joined Madame Chiang in the shade cast by a seventy-foot wing while Captain Hall guided his distinguished guest into the bowels of his flying behemoth. Favoring Sprague with a bemused smile, she said, "As the American girls at Radcliffe might say, 'You put on a great show, Elliott.' You *do* know how to impress my husband."

Sprague affected shocked innocence. "Please, Madame Chiang, I only gave this demonstration to provide a measure of reassurance that America will do its part in driving the invader from your shores."

"In the meantime, the Japanese armies advance steadily," his madonna-like companion responded tartly.

"Their inroads will be short-lived, Madame," Sprague protested. "Seventy-two hours from now, their steel industry will be a shambles. In order to supply their Pacific fleet, the flow of arms into China will cease virtually overnight."

"One would think that a visitation of destruction upon their capital city would more effectively hasten their desire to negotiate," Madame Chiang observed with a shrewd glance.

"That theory was disproven by General Doolittle's raid, Madame," Sprague replied firmly. "The Japanese learned a bitter lesson and are stronger because of the attack."

"General Doolittle's tiny force was a token effort, General. In the meantime, I, and the generalissimo of course, would rest easier if Claire was provided enough fuel and bombs to support our armies in the Hsiang valley."

"Madame Chiang!" Sprague exclaimed, his voice reflecting shock. "*I* lived up to *my* agreement. We are launching roughly half of our intended force. After providing General Chennault with the requested fuel, scarcely enough av-gas will remain to top off even one bomber after this mission."

"And when will the *next* mission be flown?"

"Even now, B-24 bombers, converted to flying tank cars, are arriving at Kharagpur. In addition, a hundred of our B-29s will be stripped of armament and used as cargo carriers. Our bases around Chengtu will be resupplied as rapidly as humanly possible."

"How soon?"

Sprague frowned. "Perhaps a week—perhaps longer. Much depends upon General Stilwell."

"Stilwell?"

"Yes, Madame. The general is doing his best, I'm sure, but he is forced to divert large amounts of materiel to the campaign to liberate Burma. Last month's Hump tonnage was not adequate to satisfy General Chennault's needs—exacerbated of course by the new Japanese offensive."

Madame Chiang dropped her suave demeanor. "General, I must remind you that *I* am commander of the Chinese Air Force," she snapped. "True, we are a weakened, poorly equipped force, but I still receive daily briefings. I understand that your B-29s are unproven in combat. They may or may not accomplish what you claim. You are hitting the steel manufacturing plants in the southern tip of Kyushu because you do not have the range to strike Tokyo. Now, what must be done to save my country?"

Sprague drew a deep breath. He returned Madame Chiang's set look with a wry smile. "You are given to straight talk, Madame. Did you learn that in America? Where is the Oriental guile you spoke of when last we met?"

"All things have an appropriate time and place, General. This is a time for, as you put it, straight talk."

Sprague smiled, but his eyes assumed a flinty look. "Very well. The American forces require a severe streamlining. Air power is the only thing that can save China from being overrun: a combination of close ground support for your armies and long-range pounding by the Superforts. A supreme commander for air, at least lateral to Stilwell—or his replacement—must be installed in New Delhi. The air bridge across the Hump will provide for all, *if* intelligent allocation of resources is made."

"You said 'Stilwell—or his replacement.'"

"Yes." Sprague swallowed hard. This was dangerous ground, but the iron was hot. Strike now, damnit! he thought excitedly.

"Whose approval is required for such a drastic reorganization, Elliott?" Madame Chiang's expression was a picture of innocence.

What a woman, Sprague marveled. A time for straight talk, a time for . . . He forced her to meet his direct gaze. "President Roosevelt's," he stated flatly.

"I see." Her eyes hooded briefly. "Our armies badly need the American lend-lease aid—guns, artillery—being blocked by—ah, someone. What is your feeling about that, Elliott?"

"If I were in New Delhi, with sufficient authority, I would release that materiel tomorrow, Madame."

There was no verbal response this time, just a hint of a twinkle in her swift glance. Madame Chiang turned and uttered a girlish laugh. "Look at the generalissimo," she said. "He acts like a child who's just come from the sweetshop. Did you enjoy your guided tour, dear?"

"An astonishing machine," Chiang replied. "Did you see me in that gun barbette? One man can sit there and aim and fire from any gun turret the plane carries. And a radar bomb-aiming device—just like seeing the target with the naked eye. This plane is our salvation, my dear wife."

"I'm sure it is," Madame Chiang replied gaily. "Now, General Sprague insists that we visit their officers' club. I warn you"—she laid a coquettish hand on her husband's arm—"I plan to smoke a cigaret and enjoy a real American martini with General Sprague. This is a cause for celebration."

"I'm afraid that our accommodations are humble indeed, Generalissimo," Sprague said as the party moved off. "However . . ." He would never recall what he said after that. His head was spinning with the enormity of what he had just set in motion. He started mentally composing a carefully worded dispatch to Sen. Broderick Templeton.

14 June 1944
Seattle

"Janet Templeton, report to personnel. Janet Templeton. Report to Miss Kingston in personnel."

Janet disconnected the air hose from her rivet gun and compressed her lips. Damn, of all mornings. Her head throbbed. Four hours' sleep—and that damn punch and alcohol concoction. Getting to work that morning had been an ordeal.

The smiling brunette seated behind a sign reading ALICE KINGSTON said, "Go right in, Mrs. Templeton. Mister Osgood is waiting for you."

Lawrence Osgood had a moon face and a bald spot surrounded by limp blond hair. Prominent green eyes twinkled behind round, steel-rimmed spectacles, giving him the appearance of a faintly amused barn owl. Janet decided she liked him as he invited her to be seated.

"Mrs. Templeton, how nice to meet you." When Janet only nodded, he continued, "That was a very gutsy call you made in the hostage situation last month. Everyone else was scared stiff. I congratulate you."

Janet smiled. "Thank you. The truth is I was scared out of my wits as well. But Moe was always such a nice boy; I'm glad things turned out the way they did. I hope the doctors can help him, someday, be a normal person."

"Well, someone with more horsepower than I've got will have more to say about your little demonstration of courage, Janet. I've been intending to speak with you anyway. Tell me, how do you like working for Boeing Aircraft—may I call you Janet?"

"I enjoy my job, Mister Osgood; and please, by all means, call me Janet."

"Ah—yes, thank you. Have you ever considered doing something besides assembly line work?"

"Well, no, not actually. You see this is my first job ever. Is my work not satisfactory?"

"Oh, eminently so. Yes, your foreman gives you excellent ratings. It's just that, well, your personnel record shows you to be a college graduate. We just wondered . . ."

"If I feel that manual labor is beneath me?" Janet finished for him with a faint smile. "No, Mister Osgood. I lost my husband last August—he was a bomber pilot. I have close friends overseas. Without wishing to sound trite, I feel I'm doing something for my country."

"Indeed you are, Janet, indeed you are. And we are all proud of the excellent job you and others like you are doing. But there are other jobs in which you can make a contribution to the war effort—an even more significant contribution."

"Oh?"

"Absolutely. I can't tell you a great deal about the position we have in mind here just yet. It's office work, day shift only, and in a highly classified area. You would be working with our engineering staff—in an administrative capacity, of course—and it carries a, ah, rather handsome salary increase. Are you interested?"

"Of course." Janet flashed a smile. "Day shift? A quiet office? A raise? What do I have to do?"

"Nothing further for the time being, Janet. I will note your interest, and we will interview you again, possibly several times. Some of the questions will be, ah, quite personal in nature. Will that create any, ah, problems?"

"I'm an army brat, Mister Osgood. My husband had a top secret clearance. I'm familiar with the routine."

"That's excellent. So many don't, you know—understand the need for in-depth background checks, that is. Now, Miss Kingston will give you a form to complete. I hope to be seeing you again, quite soon."

The somber, subdued atmosphere of the Hotel Ste. Germaine's dining room failed to dampen Janet's bubbling spirits. Duane had barely seated himself across the white linen–draped table when she burst forth: "Guess what? I was interviewed for a promotion today! A real important job. Oh, I do so hope I get it."

Swoffard's features spread in a wide grin. "How about that?" he said enthusiastically. "Congratulations. This calls for a celebration. I'm sure I can persuade Henri to part with some of that French champagne he hoards so jealously."

"Oh, no," Janet demurred. "It's way too soon. I have to go through more interviews, have a background security check and all. It could take weeks."

"Background check?" Swoffard gave her a sharp look.

"Yes, there's a building they call the Big Pit. You see load after load of stuff going in, but nothing ever comes out. It's where the hush-hush research goes on. Oh, I'm so excited."

"And well you should be. Look, let's have that champagne right now, for good luck. When you do get the job . . . well, I'll have a banquet in your honor."

Janet's glow lasted throughout the meal, an elaborate seven-course affair. The coldly formal atmosphere of the restaurant apparently discouraged the hordes of rowdy servicemen from invading its regal environs, she noted with private mirth. Real, rare roast beef, pure butter—Janet mentally ticked off fifty red ration points. She squelched a pang of jealousy as she observed that Swoffard was obviously well known here. How many other women has he wined and dined at this table? she wondered. Over velvet-smooth brandy and coffee she posed the question in a teasing voice.

She saw a flicker of annoyance cross Duane's darkly handsome features. He recovered quickly. "You can be assured that the number of lovely, gracious women I dine with are all too few, Janet. That's why I will treasure this moment."

"O-o-h, nicely put, sir. You do have a way with words. No wonder you appear to be highly successful in your business. Are many of your customers, clients, or whatever, women? You didn't mention exactly what line you're in."

Swoffard traced the outline of his broken nose—a gesture she'd noticed he used when thinking—and regarded her with a lazy smile. "I seldom see the end user of my goods and services," he replied, "but I imagine there are women among them. Which brings me to something you mentioned earlier—your security background check. I understand they inquire into your associates in some detail. It might be best if you didn't include me."

"Oh?"

"Yes. You see, I have several government contracts, some of them involving classified projects. Any hint of collusion or influence must be avoided. It could prove embarrassing to both of us. Do you understand?"

"I'm not sure I do," Janet answered, one eyebrow raised quizzically. "I'm not involved in any form of contracting."

"Well, you know," Duane explained offhandedly, "those nosy parkers see war profiteers lurking under their beds. I'll tell you what, just mention that you attended a party at my house—if they even ask you, that is."

"I won't make any false statements, if that's what you're asking, Duane," Janet said firmly. "But since I *don't* know what it is you do, I can honestly say you aren't a *close* associate."

Swoffard flashed a winsome smile. "That's using your head—just so you include a qualifying 'yet.'"

"I'm speaking of history. The future is another matter," Janet murmured.

Peg was perched on her bed, painting her toenails, when Janet returned. "Well, you're looking all flushed and high school–girlish," the blond observed. "I'd guess the evening went well." She glanced at the clock. "It's too early to speculate that it was a home run, however. Unless"—she cocked a quizzical eyebrow—"the backseat of that convertible is roomier than it looks."

Janet blushed. "Peg, you have an evil mind. Duane is a perfect gentleman."

"Uh-huh. Look, I don't want to throw cold water on this, but something about that guy isn't kosher. He appears to me to be a man who gets what he wants—by one means or another. It may be your warm, tender body; then again it might not be. Ask him to introduce you to his mother. That's the acid test, believe me."

15 June 1944
Hengyang Army Airfield

Ross heard the throaty roar of straining radial engines before he saw the boxcar-sized airplane. It was low—and in trouble. He stood outside the tower on its narrow platform, sweating it in. He'd been there since the tower operator had advised him that a B-29 had requested an emergency landing. He focused his binoculars on the distant speck. The plane's right wing, cocked high, supported two feathered props. The ship had to be from the raid on Japan. Axel had led a sweep over Hankow as a diversion.

Ross heard the radio loudspeaker inside squawk, "Hengyang Tower, this is Zebra Two Seven. We have the field in sight. Request emergency equipment stand by. We have wounded on board. Confirm your runway is five thousand feet long. Over."

"That's affirmative, Zebra Two Seven," Ross heard the operator respond. "Be advised that there is a drop-off at the far end. I have you in sight. Emergency equipment is standing by; you are clear to land."

Ross winced at the operator's reassuring message. He shifted his gaze to where the emergency vehicles were, indeed, "standing by." The weapons carrier with its four-man crew, and a white-clad medical technician crouched over the steering wheel of a Jeep, were poised in front of the ops shack. Nearby, a half-dozen Chinese mechanics leaned on their bicycles. You poor sonsabitches, he thought. There was no chance of stopping the big bomber on the rain-slicked, clay-and-gravel runway.

The stricken plane was lined up in a good landing attitude, he observed. After the wings leveled, the tricycle landing gear emerged. "That guy knows what the hell he's doing," Ross muttered aloud. Compared to the sleek P-51s and P-40s, the huge bomber seemed to dwarf the entire field. He thought fleetingly of trying one more time to rouse Major Weibel. Forget it, he decided.

The Superfort cleared the boundary and touched down on the extreme approach end in a shower of muddy spray. Ross saw the nose bang to the runway and the flaps come up. Atta boy! he mouthed. Dump that lift the flaps provide. Get all your weight on the main gear and tromp on those binders.

It looked to Ross for a time as though the pilot might pull it off. Then the plane seemed to accelerate. "Oh, shit!" Ross yelled aloud. "Fucking hydraulic failure." Fifty feet of nose disappeared off the runway's far end. The bomber came to rest with its tail pointed skyward at a forty-five-degree angle. "Please, God," Ross shouted as he raced past the tower operator, "no fire. *Please,* no fire."

Chou was going for a new speed record, Ross observed as he leaped into the waiting Jeep. The pathetic assortment of rescue vehicles had roared from their station as soon as the plane's main gear touched down. He saw three figures drop from the aft escape hatch. By God, he did it, Ross exulted. I want to meet that pilot. He deserves a medal.

Two hours later, Ross faced the B-29's pilot across a trestle table in the otherwise deserted mess hall. "Captain Yancy, that was one helluva demonstration," Ross said. "You'd have made the turnoff if . . . what happened? Hydraulic failure?"

The exhausted pilot, his lean, handsome features sagging and his eyes glazed, merely nodded his acknowledgment and fumbled for a cigaret.

"I'm afraid I can't offer you much selection in the way of a meal. Eggs—I swear these Chinese hens must lay three a day—a piece of fried Spam, and some vegetables whose name I don't have the slightest idea. Captain Deardorf is taking some of your crew into town. It isn't too late for you to join them."

Yancy waved a hand. "Anything," he mumbled. "I'm too pooped to care."

"Okay," said Ross. "While we're waiting, I have something that may brighten your day." He extracted a quart-sized clay jug from the musette bag at his side.

The weary pilot showed interest. "Is that what I think it may be?"

Ross smiled. "Well, yes and no. It's alcoholic, but not apt to be like anything you're familiar with." He extracted a pair of tiny porcelain glasses and filled them with the colorless liquor.

Yancy reached for his eagerly and tossed it down. His eyes grew wide and round. Tears formed and he gasped. "My God, what do you call this stuff?"

"Triple-distilled rice wine. It packs a helluva jolt. Want another?"

"I feel better already. Sure, give me a refill."

"As I said," Ross continued, "that was a damn-near perfect landing. I used to fly '24s. I know a little about short-field landings."

"You're an old Liberator jock? So am I. Where did you fly?"

"The ETO. I was on the Ploesti raid. After my crew and I escaped from Turkey, they sent us home and I decided I'd rather do my second tour in fighters."

"Smart man," Yancy grumbled. "I flew a tour out of a bunch of places in the South Pacific. Had a chance to stay stateside and instruct. But, no, I couldn't pass up a chance to fly this new, invincible bomber."

"Problems?"

A Chinese mess attendant slid a tray of food in front of Yancy. The pilot chewed a mouthful and swallowed before answering. "More like disasters. You don't have *small* problems with this bird."

"The hell you say. Like what?" Ross refilled their glasses.

"Like engines that catch fire. Like sophisticated electronic gadgets that aren't properly sealed and collect dust and moisture. You see, this is the first time they ever cleared a plane for service without working out the bugs. *We're* supposed to be doing that. There are damn near as many Boeing and Wright tech reps in Calcutta as there are aircrew."

Yancy ate in silence for a time and tossed back his drink. He continued, "The 3350 engine has two settings—off and overheated. It's redlined at two hundred seventy degrees. With runway temperatures of a hundred to a hundred fifteen degrees, it always goes above that on takeoff. The engineer will hit the engine primer when one hits three hundred. The raw gas will cool it a bit, but you lose power with the overrich mixture. So where does that leave you?

"The engineers tell us that the valve lubrication system breaks down under that much heat and the valve stem snaps. The valve gets sucked into the cylinder—very hard on cylinders, that. The piston promptly drives the broken valve through the cylinder head on the next stroke and sprays raw fuel on a red-hot exhaust manifold. In about ten seconds you got a blowtorch out there."

"My God, and I thought the '24 had problems with engine fires," Ross said, shaking his head. "What do they plan to do about it?"

"Oh, they're screwing around with more cooling baffles and such, but they tell you with a straight face to fly in a manner to keep sufficient airflow over the engine. I'm serious—as if the greenest pilot in flying school couldn't figure that out. If you can level off right after takeoff and let your airspeed build to two hundred miles per hour, sure, you're in pretty good shape. But there's not a half-dozen fields over here that aren't surrounded by hills with clouds sitting on them.

"So, you got this sweat period. You lift off at about a hundred and forty-five and hope you can make two hundred without an engine catching fire. The engineer has to play those cowl flaps like a pipe organ. That's about the time you start picking up ice, and then you've got the same airspeed versus rate-of-climb dilemma all over again."

"That's hairy," Ross observed.

"Right. On the way back, they say you *always* have ice problems landing at Chengtu. Usually there's clouds up to about fourteen thousand. You pick up ice on the way down, but you have to let it melt off before landing. Otherwise your touchdown speed is too high, and you end up just like I am out there. Speaking of which, that thing has your runway closed. Damn, I'm sorry."

"Don't worry about it," Ross assured the bomber pilot. "It'll be out of there by morning."

"Yeah? Do you have any idea what kind of equipment it takes to move one of those big bastards? Especially one with a busted nosewheel?"

"We've got it, never fear. I just called the mayor. There'll be maybe five hundred coolies out there before dark. If they can't figure out a way to roll it—and I'm betting they will—they'll just call for maybe five hundred more and *carry* the sonofabitch." He chuckled at Yancy's pop-eyed reaction. "But you were talking about problems landing at Chengtu; I'm not sure I understand."

"Oh, yeah. Well, while you're stooging around letting the ice melt off your wings, the ice in the bomb bay is melting, too."

"Ice in the bomb bay?"

"Uh-huh. You see, there's no ice machine at Chengtu. Unless you like warm booze, you have to bring your own ice. We put buckets of water in the bomb bay to freeze while we're crossing the Hump. If you don't get the hell on the ground, half of it will be melted." It was Ross's turn to stare in amazement.

"Look, I just came from your sergeant with the flak wound," Ross said, changing the subject. "He's in good shape. Our medic gave him a shot, and he's sleeping. Tomorrow, we'll have one of the B-25s take him to Kweilin; they have a pretty good hospital there. As for the rest of you, we'll try to get a Gooneybird out of Kunming to pick you up."

"Whatever," Yancy agreed. "What a day."

"Do you know your bombing results yet?" Ross asked.

Yancy grimaced in disgust. "Not officially, but I doubt we even scared the yellow bastards."

"Oh?"

"Naw, we were supposed to bomb in four-ship diamonds. Some of us tried to tell the general that we couldn't make the trip in formation. It takes too much gas, and no one is going to overheat engines to stay in position. So we were a gaggle over the target. The MPI was overcast, so some tried to drop by radar. The rest dropped through holes in the clouds. God knows what they hit. It was a mess. I'm almost glad I'm here instead of at the debriefing. Sprague's probably throwing a foaming, falling-down fit right about now.

"It went just like our so-called shakedown mission to Bangkok last week. Ninety-eight birds took off. Fourteen aborted on the way to the target—engine problems. Forty-two ran low on fuel and landed at other bases. Five crashed on landing. Recce photos showed a total of eighteen bombs on target. I'd guess today's mission did about as well."

"How about flak and fighters?"

"I took what is probably the only battle damage to the whole effort. Number four blew up over the target. I had to let down to sixteen thousand, and, although the flak was light, I got nailed. That's what knocked out number three . . . and Sergeant Thorpe."

"Damn," said Ross. "When will you put up the next mission?"

"Depends on how soon we can resupply Chengtu. We're supposed to be self-supporting, you know. After ATC laid in the first stockpile, it's up to us. That's why I'm in no big sweat to get back there. I had a taste of hauling av-gas before this mission. We're getting some C-109s—B-24s modified as tankers that we call C-one-oh-booms—but we still have to use mission birds. Pile on every drop we can land at Chengtu, bomb-bay tanks included. Then, drain all except enough to get home. Someone figured out we're burning an average of six gallons to lay one gallon on the ground. Hell, one guy got to wandering around in thunderstorms, iced up to the eyeballs, and had to *add* fuel to get home."

Ross frowned. "Yancy, this isn't going to work. I'm sitting here measuring gas by the pint while you guys are practically throwing it away."

Yancy nodded somberly, then stood up, his face sagging visibly. "I'm out on my feet, Ross. If you'll point me to our hostel, I'm gonna get twelve hours of sleep."

Ross watched the exhausted pilot shuffle out the door. He eyed the earthen jug. Shrugging, he poured another drink. Damn, he muttered to himself. Why didn't I ask him how much fuel he had on board. He could easily have two thousand gallons—that would let me put up eight planes instead of four tomorrow. The thought made Ross feel better, and he strode off to give orders to drain every drop. That B-29 had made its last flight. With two thousand gallons—hell, he could do more damage with it than Sprague's entire fifty-odd plane formation.

15 June 1944
Loyang Airfield

Yusaki strode into the ready room and threw his cloth helmet atop the counter. Lieutenant Subachi hurried toward him. "Did you make contact?"

The young pilot made a sour face. "We *saw* them—if you want to call that making contact—three hundred miles north. The devils must have been at an altitude of nearly thirty thousand feet. They were traveling at a rate almost equal to our climbing speed. They are truly awesome machines, Lieutenant. Huge—the intelligence photos do not do them justice. I counted sixty. Our poor country—will we know where they struck and how much destruction they caused?"

"I expect not, Yusaki." Subachi's tone and expression were sad. "Those matters are not even permitted to be discussed."

Yusaki paced the room, slapping his gloves against his thigh. "I've been thinking, Lieutenant. The only thing holding up the army's advance south are the planes at Hengyang. Our bombers cannot get near the place. One plane, arriving just at dark, would take them totally by surprise. I could inflict more damage in that manner than our dive-bombers have managed during the past month."

Subachi squinted at the pacing figure. "'I' can inflict?" he asked.

"Yes, sir. One plane—deliver one bomb on the runway, then return and strafe any visible aircraft. I'll be gone before they realize what happened."

Lieutenant Subachi frowned. "Returning after dark, Yusaki? The weather—how will you find the field? Besides, you fly only with a wingman on your right; that's an order."

A breathless clerk rushed into the room. He saluted and stammered, "A thousand pardons, sir, but a radio message from the army in the Hsiang valley. One of the giant American bombers, sir. It landed on the airfield at Hengyang only a short time ago. It was badly damaged."

Subachi sprang to his feet. "I will notify the commander at once. Perhaps a strike could be scheduled for tomorrow morning. It would be good if we could destroy that plane before it is repaired and flown away."

"Sir . . ." The section leader wheeled at the sound of Yusaki's voice. The frustrated pilot returned Subachi's gaze with unswerving determination. There was no mistaking the message in his eyes.

Subachi hesitated, his face mirroring agonized indecision. Then his expression hardened. "Go," he snapped.

Yusaki leveled off at one thousand feet. Late afternoon sunlight filtering through breaks in the overcast would make following the river south child's play. He didn't permit himself to dwell upon the return trip. Surely there would be enough reflected light to follow the river, and he could fly through scattered rain showers. Lieutenant Subachi would see that they lit the flares when they heard his engine.

Yusaki smiled as a feeling of grim satisfaction enveloped him. At last! After weeks of running away like a cowardly cur, evading instead of engaging the enemy, he was about to press the attack—alone, unhampered by choking rules of engagement.

He reviewed his plan. The runway lay on a north-south axis. Timing his arrival for the last minutes of daylight, he would approach from the north and streak across the landscape like an avenging banshee. The two-hundred-kilogram bomb suspended beneath the stubby fuselage would land someplace along the runway's length while he located the big airplane. Its size made it impossible to conceal. He'd learned that the arrogant Americans hadn't even bothered to apply camouflage paint.

After crossing the field, he'd turn and make his strafing pass. The entire attack would consume less than five minutes. He would be on a north, homeward-bound, heading; pursuit would be futile. He gleefully envisioned the consternation that he would leave behind.

A distinctive bend in the river's course alerted Yusaki that he was only minutes north of the field. Deepening gloom made it necessary to snap on the map light to verify his position. He was exactly on course; Yusaki altered his heading, reduced power to mask his approach until the last minute, and allowed the plane to ghost downward.

A flicker of lights ahead, an unexpected bit of luck—once more the Americans had underestimated their enemy's ingenuity. He crammed on full power and curled his mouth in a savage grin. Blurred outlines of buildings emerged through the dusk, then a stretch of level ground, lighter than the rest—the runway. He raced over the field boundary at full power, less than a hundred feet above his objective. His finger tightened on the bomb toggle. The runway's approach end disappeared beneath the nose—*now!* He felt the aircraft leap upward. Then he saw it.

Yusaki gaped in astonishment, even in the heat of the attack. The monstrous bomber covered an entire corner of the field, its bare aluminum skin reflecting lights being used by a swarm of workmen. A mere glimpse, then he was hurtling into total darkness. Concentrating on his dimly lighted instruments for a moment, he entered a 180-degree turn and searched for his prize target.

Faint flickers of yellow-orange flame from the bomb detonation led him back to the field. The workers had extinguished the lights. Nothing could conceal the sheen of naked metal, however. He double-checked that the 20mm cannon was armed and lowered the Zero's nose.

Unmindful of the ruinous effect that a prolonged burst of cannon fire had on the barrel, he clenched the trigger. A stream of colored tracer rounds marched toward the barely visible B-29. A ball of flame erupted beneath him as he swept overhead.

Yusaki's elation knew no bounds. He forced himself to concentrate on locating the river and checked his watch. He possibly would have to employ dead reckoning to find the field at Hankow. Nevertheless, he laughed aloud at the thought of the celebration his triumphant return would evoke. Many cups of sake would be raised in his honor this night.

Chapter Seventeen

15 June 1944
Washington, D.C.

Lieutenant General Clint Wolfenbarger scowled at his champagne cocktail. The Portuguese ambassador had access to unlimited amounts of good booze. Why couldn't he pour something substantial, like Wild Turkey bourbon? The general looked around the brightly lit ballroom, searching for someone with whom to share his gripe. Wartime hadn't slowed this damn town one bit, he grumbled silently. Bare shoulders, expensive ball gowns, and gaudy uniforms crowded the gleaming parquet dance floor. Half of the posturing clowns should have LEND-LEASE stamped on their peacock-hued clothing, he thought grumpily.

"Clint. You don't appear to be sharing the festive celebration of . . . what *is* the occasion this time? The Portuguese wine harvest?"

The unhappy three-star turned to confront a tuxedo-clad man he recognized as one of Sen. Broderick Templeton's stable of aides—Wooster? Williams? No matter, they all looked and talked alike.

"The day they castrate the bulls, I think," Wolfenbarger snapped. "God, how I hate these things. 'I'll be unavoidably detained in the war room, Clint,' the chief says—a goddamn lie. Your boss pull the same stunt?"

"More or less," Williams—or was it Wooster?—replied in oily tones. "He did want me to talk with General Arnold, however. Since you're here in his place, I suppose I must discuss the matter with you, eh?"

"If you must."

"Yes. Completely unofficial and off the record, you understand."

"Why?"

The sleekly attired aide frowned. "Really, Clint. Your droll sense of humor is so refreshing. A matter was brought to the senator's attention that will probably amount to nothing—not something to call anyone over to the Hill about. Anyway, it concerns your General Wolfe, over in New Delhi."

"Yeah?"

"Did the general have a drinking problem before he was assigned to the CBI?"

"Are you implying he has one now?"

"Not really, but you know how those things start. The senator felt that the rumor should be squelched before it spreads—if it is a rumor, of course. Can I tell him you'll look into it?"

Wolfenbarger felt blood suffusing his neck. "You can tell him I'll check it out personally," he grated.

The young man strolled away, chuckling. "Day of castrating the bulls—that's very good, you know."

The general snatched a full glass from a passing tray and tossed it down in one gulp. Elliott, you bastard, what are you up to now? he wondered.

Before his ire had completely subsided, Wolfenbarger found himself boxed in by dancers. A tanned, manicured hand on his forearm prevented him from extricating himself. "Excuse me, General, I've been looking for General Arnold. Are you subbing tonight?"

Wolfenbarger recognized the speaker immediately: navy captain Frank Kirby, military aide to the vice president. "Good evening, Frank. Yes, the chief is in the war room tonight, I'm afraid."

"Too bad. Can you pass a discreet inquiry to him?"

"Of course."

"It concerns 'Vinegar Joe' Stilwell, in the CBI."

"Oh?"

"Yes. It seems that Madame Chiang Kai-shek has voiced dissatisfaction with the manner in which Joe is allocating supplies. She claims he's shortchanging the generalissimo's armies in China. Have you had any feedback from over there?"

"I know that General Stilwell is having the devil's own task keeping materiel flowing over the Hump. There will never be enough to go around, I guess."

"Yes, a touchy matter, I'm sure. Madame Chiang seems to think the situation could be resolved by placing an Air Corps officer in New Delhi, coequal to Stilwell. Give him command of all air operations—including targeting, supply priorities, and the like. Before we bring General Marshall into the discussion, we'd like to hear Arnold's views. Off the record, of course. Do you suppose . . . ?"

"Of course. I'll speak with the chief first thing tomorrow morning."

"Thank you, General," the leathery officer said, then wandered off.

Fuck you, you landlocked swabbie, Wolfenbarger raged. He glanced at his watch. Ten-thirty—almost another half hour before protocol would permit him to flee this goddamn nest of political intrigue.

16 June 1944
Hengyang Army Airfield

Ross emerged from the radio shack into early morning sunshine, his face a grim, unshaven mask. He thrust his hands into his hip pockets and surveyed the scene of organized confusion. More coolies than he could count were putting finishing touches on the bomb-cratered landing strip. His face twisted in a grin, rendered grotesque by streaks of soot and dirt mingled with sweat. To the approaching Major Weibel, he resembled an angry native warrior.

"Morning, Major," Ross rasped. "Some might call it luck to have a ready-made repair crew on hand. They didn't miss a lick after the B-29 blew—just grabbed shovels and changed jobs. Worked all night. We'll be able to launch a mission within the hour."

"Hey, that's great work," Weibel croaked. "You get any sleep last night?"

Ross eyed the disheveled, bleary-eyed major with bemused tolerance. He must have slept in that filthy flight suit again. "Not much," he replied, a laconic tinge to his words.

"I can't believe I crapped out during the whole thing." Weibel shook his head, a confused look on his face. "You should have woke me."

"I figured there was no need for both of us to be wiped out today. I can catch some sleep until noon. In fact, that's where I'm headed as soon as I grab some breakfast."

Ross concealed a grin at the woozy major's startled look. "Uh—yeah, sure Ross. You must be dead on your feet. I'll take over. What's the situation?"

"Well"—Ross gestured to where the B-29's blackened skeleton lay in a heap of scrap metal—"we don't have to worry about that beauty.

I've been on the horn to headquarters in Kweilin. As soon as the runway is open, they're sending a B-25 over from Ling-ling to evacuate the wounded sergeant. They'll take him to the hospital at Kweilin. Later today, a C-47 will pick up the rest of the crew—take them to Kunming, at a guess.

"Deardorf and 'C' Flight will go on alert as soon as they get that crater patched. I look for a raid today, probably before noon. They'll think we're out of action; you can bet that pilot reported heavy damage to the runway. I'd suggest you not launch until you think they're damn near overhead. They'll figure on coming all the way—catch us with everything on the ground. In fact, I've put everyone on standby. If they come, we may as well hit 'em with everything we have."

"Good thinking, Ross," Weibel mumbled. "We have enough gas for a max effort?"

"Barely. But we may as well burn it in the air as on the ground."

"On the ground?" Weibel's vacuous stare reflected bare interest.

"Yeah," Ross responded. "I was saving the worst 'til last. We're bugging out."

"Bugging out?" Weibel showed vague awareness. "You saying we're being pulled out?"

"That's right. The comm boys just finished decoding the order. We've lost contact with the Jap army. No one knows exactly where the hell they are, but they're not too far north of here. We're to hang tough as long as the gas holds out, but we're supposed to start rounding up trucks, anything that will roll, and begin moving the bulky stuff. They'll air-evac the rest in a few days.

"I figure we'll have dry tanks by about Thursday. We have exactly eleven thousand gallons on hand, and there won't be any more. That damn Jap!" Ross spat. "The B-29 pilot said he landed with at least two thousand gallons. Two more days we could have held out. We didn't have time to drain a drop."

"I'll be damned." Weibel was showing increased signs of comprehension. "Where do you suppose the Jap came from? It isn't like them to be out stooging around after dark. They have poor night vision, they're superstitious, they're rotten instrument pilots. . . . In all the time we were in Burma, I can't remember a single night attack."

"Well, this one apparently didn't learn to fly in Burma," Ross said grimly. "He laid that goddamn egg squarely on target, and only needed one pass to wipe out that B-29. Fuck it, I'm for some chow and the sack." Ross's voice was blurred with fatigue. "The flimsy from that message is in the radio shack if you want to read it." He stumbled toward the mess hall.

Captain Deardorf regarded Ross from across the mess table with a sympathetic expression. "You look like hell," he observed, taking a sip of coffee. "Be careful you don't bark. Somebody will think you're a stray dog. Probably take you home and feed you milk or something."

"Your deep concern is touching," Ross mumbled. "Look, here's the situation. . . ." He quickly related the morning's developments. "Tell the ops clerk to wake me if anything earthshaking develops."

"Sure," Deardorf responded. "Blow and go, huh? Wonder where? Oh, well," he added when Ross didn't answer. "Guess it makes no difference. We can burn all the gas we want then?"

Ross nodded.

"That'll be a pleasant change. What kind of shape is old Whizzer in this morning?"

Ross shrugged. "He's on his feet and talking."

"You're covering for him with Vincent, aren't you?" Deardorf asked softly.

Ross shrugged again. "Call it that, if you like. He's still a better CO drunk than King was sober."

Walt stood. He slapped Ross on the shoulder in passing. "You'll do to hunt with, guy. Sleep tight, your ass is safe with old Walt on the job." He grinned and strode out the mess hall door.

Ross followed moments later. Habit made him glance at the alert pole. Shipley, the ops clerk, was raising one ball. He waited. The fatigue-clad figure scurried back inside. A one-ball alert—fuck it, he thought wearily. Let Weibel deal with it. He trudged toward a bed—any bed, anywhere.

Ross stumbled from the hostel into the bright sun. The heat struck him like a giant hammer. He donned his sunglasses. The thought of a shower drew him on like a magnet. After hesitating, he decided to check with ops. The past five hours were a black void in his memory. He grinned—talk about the major sleeping through an air raid!

He could hear the yammering of jubilant voices while still a block away from the ready room. He scanned the flight line. Eleven Mustangs crouched in their shallow revetments. One was missing. He frowned and pushed his way inside the noisy ready room.

"There he is!" Ross heard a voice—Evans, he thought—call out excitedly. "Hey, Captain, you missed a turkey shoot. We clobbered 'em."

Ross spotted Deardorf, a broad grin on his face, and posed an unspoken question with his gaze.

"That's right, Ross. We waited for three balls. Scrambled nine and climbed to twenty-five thousand south of the field. Caught 'em with their pants squarely at half mast. We've tallied a dozen and still counting. Vals, Sallys, and two Zeroes."

"The hell you say!" Ross's grin slipped. "I only count eleven birds. Who's missing?"

The rowdy crowd quieted. "Tyson," Deardorf replied. "We saw his chute. It looked like he took a hit in the radiator. By the time the dogfight was over, we couldn't spot him on the ground, but we think he's south of the Japs. I imagine we'll be hearing from the warning net by dark."

Ross frowned. "Christ, I hope so," he replied. It was then he noticed that everyone was holding canteen cups. "I hope there's nothing in those cups but grapefruit juice," he snapped.

"'Sall right, Captain." Ross turned to see Major Weibel leaning on the counter, cup in hand. A wide smile split his somewhat blurred features. "Couldn't let the boys hit home runs without a little celebration, you know. Besides, you can bet that bunch isn't going to be back again today. Not for several days, I'd wager."

Ross swallowed the angry retort he'd been about to spit out. "Maybe," he acknowledged. "But let's keep a couple of guys on alert until dark, okay?" He turned back to Walt without waiting for Weibel's reply. "How much fuel did you use?"

"I figure we burned about four hundred gallons per bird," Deardorf replied. "That leaves us about eight thousand."

Ross nodded, his thoughts turning to something that had struck him when Weibel discounted a follow-up raid. That Zero pilot who had sneaked in last night—would *he* return? A good possibility, Ross thought. The guy must have been really pissed when it turned out he hadn't closed down the field. And, like a sheep-killing dog, he'd tasted blood. Yeah, he'd be back, if not that night, then the next night for sure.

The field phone jangled. Shipley answered, grunted a monosyllabic response, and hung up. He turned to Ross. "That was the tower. The B-25 coming to pick up the injured sergeant is ten miles out."

Ross and Yancy followed the four Chinese medical technicians as they carried the wounded airman from the dispensary. "You feeling okay?" Yancy asked.

"Sure, Captain. I wanted to walk, but these guys almost cried. The medic told me that they'd lose face if I didn't let them treat me like a real patient."

Ross stood in the shade of a wing and watched a pair of medics scramble from the B-25's bomb-bay entrance. I'll be damned, he mused—a woman. Not a bad looker, either. His gaze followed her as the team moved to the stretcher. As the nurse knelt and grasped the sergeant's wrist, feeling for a pulse, her profile was clearly visible for the first time. He felt as if Joe Louis had thrown his best punch—right to his solar plexus.

He looked closer. That patrician nose, the firm jawline, the short-cropped black hair—Christ, it couldn't be. When she turned to face Ross, he knew for certain; that pair of smoky gray eyes had haunted too many lonely nights. He felt a sudden urge to turn and run.

The nurse's eyes widened; she resembled a startled doe. The husky voice he remembered so well stammered, "Ross—Ross Colyer, as I live and breathe. My God, what a time and place to see you again."

Ross stood speechless, but finally uttered a strangled, "Ruth, I—I . . ."

"Well, get over here, you idiot. I can't leave my patient."

Their audience gaped in astonishment as Ruth seized Ross in a rib-crushing bear hug and planted a kiss on his still-moving lips.

"I didn't know you were a flight nurse," Ross said lamely.

Ruth laughed, a braying that bordered on hysteria. She wiped tears from her eyes; not all were tears of laughter. "In my outfit, nurses do anything that needs doing." They both commenced talking at once.

"Can you get to Kweilin? I'm at the hospital there." "What are you doing here? I thought you had orders for the ETO?" "Do you ever hear from anyone back at Kelly?" "Is it rough flying up here? I hear the Japs are on the move."

They fell silent and regarded each other with foolish grins. Finally Ruth said, "This is awful; I have to go. They've loaded my patient. Oh, Ross, can you *possibly* get to Kweilin? Even for just a few hours?" Her voice trembled.

Ross held the wet-eyed woman close and kissed her quickly. "Probably sooner than you think," he said cryptically. "Just don't go home without me."

He watched the B-25 trundle to the end of the runway. He was sure he saw a pale face peering out from the waist gun position. From behind him, he heard, "That's the trouble with you damn fighter pilots—always after us bomber pilots' women. Had you two met before today?"

Ross wheeled to confront Yancy's grinning countenance. He stifled an angry retort and barked a self-conscious laugh. "My sister—she's a nice girl. *You* stay away from her."

Ross watched the altimeter wind through twenty thousand feet. Plenty of altitude, he decided. Retarding the throttle and prop control to twenty-five inches and 1,700 RPM—the minimum cruise setting—he regarded the deepening hues of red and purple in the west with satisfaction. The timing was right; the weather was right. Already, dusk enveloped the landscape. To the north lurked scattered rain showers, but the field sat exposed beneath clear skies.

The tower operator had reluctantly agreed to stand by his radio. He would alert Ross at the first sound of an aircraft engine, then run like hell, Ross surmised. A puzzled squad of Chinese soldiers had likewise agreed to take up positions at the south end of the runway. Armed with nothing but Lee Enfield rifles, they posed the merest of threats to an attacker, but, he thought, who knows? One of them might get lucky.

He drifted into a lazy orbit north of the field. Its blacked-out area was visible only as a slightly paler blur in the surrounding countryside. He'd been tempted to leave a few lights on, but that would be a dirty trick to play on those sweating it out below. Tomorrow night he would set out some decoy lights a mile or so away. He searched beneath him for the faintest sign of movement. The guy would show no lights, he knew, but there wasn't anything the slant-eyed bastard could do about his exhaust flame.

C'mon, Charlie, he muttered to himself. Show your ass before it gets too dark for you to find the field. The name Charlie had sprung unbidden after the previous night's sneak attack. He recalled hearing of similar night intruders who struck out of early darkness. They were universally dubbed Bed-Check Charlie. Laughed at for their puny efforts, they nevertheless raised hell with sleep and morale.

Ross tried to conjure up a picture of the guy. Short, stocky, a cruel expression, sneering and snarling as he dove to the attack? He realized that he really didn't know what a "typical" Jap looked like. There weren't any in Justin Falls, where he grew up. The wanton killing by the plane that had attacked the Kachin village, and at Pearl Harbor—they didn't hesitate to deliberately kill women and children.

But he had to admire the guy's—Charlie's—ability as a pilot. That was no mean trick—finding a target in total darkness, through broken clouds, then creaming it. He's probably just a top-rate fighter pilot who got fed up with flying nothing but decoy missions, he thought.

His reverie was interrupted by a yell in his headset. "He's here! Goddamn, he's right over the field. Get the sonofabitch!"

Ross rolled into a vertical dive. *Damn!* How could the plane have gotten so close without being detected? As he streaked through ten thousand feet, an orange mushroom of flame erupted to his right. The sonofabitch did it again, he fumed. Okay. He tried to calm himself. Take it easy now, stay north of the field. He *has* to come back this way. He probably made one pass north to south, then turned around and made a strafing run headed north—and home. A second conflagration materialized. It seemed to be in the aircraft revetment area. It was!

He strained his eyes, searching for that telltale dot of blue flame. There, was that it? Yes, but he's in the wrong place—northwest, over the river. The blue spark faded from view. Of course, he cursed to himself, he only made one pass tonight, then hauled ass. Ross jerked the Mustang into a hard turn and headed for the now brightly illuminated field. No point wasting gas chasing the elusive quarry.

A shaken Major Weibel paced the ready room, talking in disjointed sentences. "All at once, he—he was just . . . First I knew, Hostel Four just blew up. I . . . He came across from the east, dropped his bomb, then strafed. Got one bird square and damaged 882 next to it. Four killed, they think—they're still searching. Ross"—his eyes grew wild—"damnit, we gotta *do* something."

"Okay," Ross said savagely, hurling his helmet to the floor, "we will. I'm going to Chengtu. I'm going to bring Holt and 'A' Flight back here. We're down to ten birds and a cripple. *And* I'm bringing back some fucking gasoline! I'm fed up with sitting on our ass counting fuel by the quart. I don't know how, but I'm going to take a raid to Hankow—at night. If that sneaky sonofabitch thinks he has a patent on hit-and-run, he's in for one big surprise.

"In the meantime, sir, put a patrol up every night at dusk. Wait until those fuckers get close before putting up our own fighters, like we did today. And, Major," Ross's voice took on a pleading note, "lay off the grapefruit juice, okay? If we aren't careful, we won't have anything left to evacuate."

"Yeah, sure, Ross, sure," Weibel mumbled. Both men looked at each other with mild astonishment written on their faces. Each realized a change in command ceremony had just transpired, as surely as if it had been accompanied by a parade and a marching band.

Chapter Eighteen

0620 Hours, 17 June 1944
Hengyang Army Airfield

Ross placed the message, scrawled in pencil, before a dull-eyed Major Weibel. "This is what I suggest you send Colonel Vincent, Major."

Weibel squinted and read the note:

> Night intruder attacks reduce combat-ready aircraft to nine. Without additional aircraft and fuel, evacuation is only hours away. General Tsu states he can contain enemy advance with close air support. Colyer en route Chengtu to retrieve four a/c dispersed there and arrange for emergency shipment of fuel.

"Casey isn't going to like this," Weibel protested.

"Probably not," Ross agreed. "But, damnit, sir, we *can* prop up the Chinese with ten planes a day flying three sorties each."

"I dunno, Ross—taking it on ourselves to do this. I'll send it, though. By God, this is what we'd have done in the old days, in Burma. Didn't have a lot of brass looking over our shoulder. If General Chennault was here, he'd do the same thing. Good luck."

0955 Hours, 17 June 1944
Hsinching Airfield

Ross cut the switches and scribbled entries onto the Form-1. A Chinese soldier made a thumbs-in gesture to indicate that the wheel chocks were in place. Ross released the parking brake and crawled onto the wing.

A grinning O. B. Holt stood at the wing root. "Ross, you old bastard. What on earth brings you this far from home?"

Ross leaped to the graveled hardstand and shook Holt's outstretched hand. "Probably in the process of getting myself court-martialed," he replied with a short laugh.

"Sounds interesting," Holt responded. "God knows we could use some excitement. Never thought I'd get bored out here, but we go out, we look, we come back, and say, 'Yep, they're ten miles closer today.' Haven't seen a Jap fighter since we've been here.

"And what about you? You an ace yet? Congratulations on finally getting the job you should have had all along."

"Thanks, O.B. No, I'm not an ace—far from it. All we've done is put up four planes each day. The Japs come south until they see us, then turn around and go home. They win every time because they have gas and we don't—it's frustrating. In the meantime, Tojo's little men just keep rollin' on. I figure we have less than a week before they overrun us, if we don't do something."

"That bad, huh?"

"That bad," sighed Ross.

"So what does this new CO, Major Weibel, plan to do?"

"Let's get out of this heat, and I'll fill you in. Got anything cold to drink?"

"You kidding? Half the guys here can't even spell the word 'ice,' much less remember what it looks like. C'mon, at least I can find you a cooler spot."

Thirty minutes later, Holt sat silently, staring at the ground. "That's grim," he said finally. "Does Fourteenth Air Force know you're taking the birds out of here?"

Ross grinned. "Not yet. I figure they'll get the word about the time the planes are halfway to Hengyang. Weibel promised to wait until this afternoon to send the message to Vincent."

"What do you think your chances are of getting more gasoline out of Twenty Bomber Command?"

"Pretty slim," Ross conceded. "I figure my only hope is to plead with our good Major King. I'm going to lay it out for him and, if that doesn't work, go directly to Chennault."

Holt uttered a mirthless laugh. "You can forget about King, Ross. General Sprague is at Chengtu. I attended a briefing over there this morning. He's raising hell, trying to get another mission launched over Japan. The POL situation was the main topic of conversation. He doesn't have half enough gasoline as it is. I'd say your chances just went from slim to none."

"Sprague is here? I thought he was in India. Oh, great; that's all I need. He'll blow a fuse about the fighters, too. Well, all I can do is beg. I'll wait until the flight is airborne before I go to see him. You got your rotation orders yet?"

"In hand, guy—day after tomorrow. I hop a ride on a C-109 going back to Kharagpur, then zingo. The mothers in Salina are already getting their daughters off the streets."

Ross grinned. "You're gonna miss the fun."

"Don't I know it. And I hate to, I honestly do—but I'll suffer through. Now let's get going; we've got work to do."

1410 Hours, 17 June 1944
Chengtu Airfield

Major King regarded Ross with a skeptical scowl. "I haven't heard a word about this, Colyer. I'm General Chennault's liaison officer; why didn't he arrange this through me? General Sprague is out measuring the POL inventory with an eyedropper. And he's going to loan General Chennault another eight thousand gallons? Something's fishy, very fishy."

Ross spread his hands. "Beats the hell out of me, Major. All I know is, Major Weibel told me to come up here, see the ADVON folks, arrange for a C-109 to make a run to Hengyang, and fly escort for it. You're going to support me, aren't you?"

"Not until I see something in writing from Fourteenth Air Force, I'm not."

Ross shrugged. "Well, you'll be too late. I have an appointment with General Sprague in twenty minutes."

"What?"

"Major, it's fourth down and there's about two minutes on the clock. Unless we get support, Changsha folks are going to be eating Jap leftovers within forty-eight hours. Vincent has already given orders for us to start sending the heavy stuff south and to be ready to fly out on one-hour's notice. Ling-ling will be history within a week. Doesn't *any-one* understand? East China is about to become Tokyo South. And it needn't happen. We have air superiority—*if* we can get off the ground. The Chinese army is hanging tough. If the Japs get stopped cold at the Yangtze—now—today, they'll never get regrouped. With the additional four birds, we can hold them in place until we get that C-109 tanker."

"Additional four aircraft?"

"Oh, yeah. Guess I forgot to mention it." Ross glanced at his watch. "'A' Flight should be touching down at Hengyang about an hour from now. They took off at noon."

King's eyes bulged. "'A' Flight? *Our* 'A' Flight? The detachment at Hsinching?"

"Yeah."

"Colyer, who the hell authorized *that* move?"

"Oh, I don't know that anyone actually *authorized* it in so many words," Ross replied in an offhand manner. "It's an emergency redeployment. They'll be sent back once the fire is out."

King leaped to his feet. He snatched up his cap and strode to the door, then he stopped. "You stay right here. Don't move. I'm headed for the radio shack. I want General Chennault to confirm this."

Ross shrugged. "Sorry. I may not be here when you get back. I'm due to see the general in ten minutes."

King's face turned purple. His mouth worked, but no words came out. Ross slammed the flimsy door as he exited.

Ross rehearsed his pitch to Sprague as he entered a mud-stucco building housing the ADVON staff. He stopped and blinked. Was he in the right place? No semblance of order existed. A bird colonel sat on one of the desks, a glass of amber liquid in his right hand. He was flanked by a pair of giggling Chinese girls. Everyone was standing and talking at the same time. A florid-faced major spotted Ross. "Come on in, Captain. Join the party."

"Party?" Ross asked.

"You better believe it." He snatched up a piece of yellow paper and waved it in Ross's direction. "Just came in. Orders making General Sprague acting commander of Twenty Bomber Command."

Twenty confused minutes later Ross faced a smiling General Sprague. "Congratulations, sir," Ross said as he dropped his salute.

"Colyer. Glad to see you. Sit down. Yes, perhaps I can get this ball rolling around here. Just like the old Seventh Wing in England, huh?"

Ross winced inwardly as he recalled the disaster following Sprague's "getting the ball rolling." "Yes, sir. I'm sure you will," he responded dryly.

"Now, what brings you to Chengtu? Checking up on your detachment at Hsinching? Those boys are doing a fine job over there. Couldn't do without 'em."

"Yes, sir," Ross replied with smooth evasion. "In a manner of speaking. But I won't take up too much of your time, General. What I really came for is to ask for another loan of av-gas."

Sprague's happy expression faded. "What's that? You want more fuel? This is the first I've heard of it. Did Chennault send you?"

"I didn't speak to the general personally, sir. The matter is quite urgent. If we don't get more fuel at Hengyang, we'll have to pull out by the end of the week. The Japs are moving south, and unless General Tsu's troops get close air support . . . well, that's the ball game."

Sprague drummed his desktop with blunt, hairy fingers. "Does Major King know about this?" he asked. "Where is he, by the way? This is the sort of thing he's supposed to handle."

"Major King isn't in his office, sir. They expect him back shortly, I think. This is an emergency, sir—a matter of hours, perhaps. Ops tells me there's a C-109 inbound. If you will just give your okay, I'll fly escort for him on to Hengyang."

"Out of the question, Colyer. I told Claire . . ." His voice trailed off; he seemed to be thinking furiously. Finally, he concluded, "Yes, out of the question. I'm in the process of launching another mission from here in a matter of days. What you're asking will mean one less plane in the formation."

Ross felt cold rage form a knot in his gut. Watch it, Colyer, don't go shooting off your mouth. Sprague's next words shattered that resolve, however.

"That one plane can inflict more damage on the Japs than your entire squadron," the general added in a patronizing voice.

"*If* it finds the target," Ross blurted.

"What did you say, Captain?" Sprague's voice was dangerously soft.

"Why, sir, I thought it was common knowledge that the raid over

Kyushu had some bad luck. What was it—fifty airplanes, and only about a dozen bombs on a primary target?"

"Who told you that? Someone, by God, is going to get court-martialed for leaking classified information."

"I'm sorry, sir. I overheard a conversation in a bar—in Kweilin, I believe it was. I'm afraid it's pretty widespread."

Sprague's face was a white mask—the beetling black eyebrows meeting above his nose. "Colyer," he grated, "few men have the ability to make me lose my temper. You are one such person. I should have followed my instinct and court-martialed you after the Ploesti mission.

"Now my gut feeling is that the strike report is *not* common knowledge. Somehow, you heard a rumor and are trying to blackmail me, by God, into jeopardizing my next mission by wasting precious POL. Furthermore, I don't believe that General Chennault knows you're here. This is probably some harebrained scheme you cooked up on your own." Sprague pinned Ross with a shrewd, icy gaze.

"Perhaps they were confusing it with the Bangkok mission, sir."

Sprague's pale features flushed flaming red. "You're dismissed, Colyer," he roared. "General Chennault will hear of your arrogance, believe me. Now, get out of my office."

1925 Hours, 17 June 1944
Hengyang Army Airfield

Ross trudged into the ops building and disgustedly threw flying gear onto a chair. Major Weibel's and Lieutenant Deardorf's expressions turned glum as they watched. "No luck, huh?" Deardorf asked.

"No gas," Ross answered shortly. "Did 'A' Flight get here okay?"

"That they did," Weibel replied. "Flew a sortie this afternoon."

"How much gas do we have?"

"Just under a hundred barrels."

Ross threw a quick glance at the major. He could swear the man was sober. "How about the evacuation? Looks like the civilians are headed south."

Deardorf barked a bitter laugh. "Go climb up on the tower platform and have a shifty."

Ross followed the pair up hand-hewn plank steps to a narrow perch supporting the primitive tower accommodations. The main road south skirted the base. It resembled a giant, squirming worm. Humanity filled every square foot, from verge to verge. Conical coolie hats, blue-quilted caps, and bared gray heads formed a multihued carpet. A pall of choking dust hovered overhead. Every conceivable manner of unmotorized transport was in use: bulging baskets dangling from shoulder yokes borne by straining backs; wheelbarrows; an occasional two-wheeled cart pulled by a water buffalo. One enterprising group had piled their possessions on an ancient truck and was pulling it along with ropes.

Ross saw an elderly woman, her face and bare arms appearing like twisted brown leather, stumble and fall. The aged, burnished yoke slipped from her neck. A cooking pot, assorted articles of clothing, and a sack of grain spilled from its baskets onto the roadside. Willing hands helped the woman to her feet, but the pitiful possessions remained where they fell. Their further conveyance was beyond her waning strength.

The refugees on foot made progress, however. Snail-like though their pace might be, they fared better than their compatriots electing to flee by rail. The five-car freight train sat motionless, its outline obscured by desperate-looking people clinging to every semblance of a hand and foothold. Seated on the locomotive's cowcatcher, packed on the roofs, even wedged on steel braces beneath the cars, the erstwhile passengers watched the shuffling pedestrian traffic with anxious eyes. Ross was struck by the absence of noise. Customarily, when two or more Chinese came together, the air was filled with their nasal chatter. The seriousness of their plight was underscored by the eerie silence.

"From the town," Deardorf explained. "We tried to get some alcohol-burning trucks from the mayor—even offered avgas. None are left. Even so, how would you ever get a truck through that mob? We got some stuff to the river, where the army commandeered a couple of sampans. But that's it."

"Okay," Ross said, "here's what I'd like to do. Major?" He looked at Weibel, the question unspoken. The major gave an almost imperceptible nod.

"If we gotta go, let's go out with a bang. Do the P-40s at Ling-ling have any gas left, do you suppose?" Ross asked Weibel.

"They launched a four-ship mission today."

"They also have bombs, right?"

"Yeah, but there haven't been any fuses east of Kunming for more than a week."

Ross nodded. "Here's what we're gonna do. . . ."

18 June 1944
Hengyang Army Airfield

Chinese houseboys, cooks, clerks, even the boys from the shower rooms watched the flurry of activity with excited eyes. The Americans were leaving. Why were they working so hard?

About midmorning, six P-40s, led by Major Weibel in a Mustang, broke overhead and landed in a cloud of dust. They rolled to the armament revetment, where the ground crews unloaded the two-hundred-fifty-pound bombs that the planes carried. A dozen Chinese squatted to one side, loading ammo belts with nothing but tracer rounds. Major Weibel, his hands not completely steady but his eyes clear, went from group to group, giving crisp instructions.

Ross spoke to a dozen curious faces in the ready room. "We can only put six planes in the air for this mission—that's all the gas we can muster. It leaves us just enough to refuel and head for Kweilin after we get back. This is our swan song, guys. It's a bitter goddamn pill to swallow. We could have stopped the slant-eyed bastards in their tracks, I'm sure of it. But . . . it's how the Russians finally got to Hitler—fire and fall back; leave nothing behind the enemy can use.

"I'm not asking for volunteers," he stated in flat tones. He began calling the roll, starting with Deardorf. Then, looking each man in the eye as he called his name, Ross continued, "Axel, Evans, White." He paused, then said, "Tyson, welcome back. Understand you rode a bicycle the last ten miles." After Tyson's grin and nod, accompanied by scattered laughter, Ross went on, "Do you feel up to a mission tonight?"

"Bet your ass, Captain. Never felt better," the serious-faced blond replied.

"That's it, then." He smiled at the array of startled faces. "Yeah, I said 'tonight.' This is going to be fun, gentlemen. Now, the rest of you get the tail numbers of the planes you'll fly out tomorrow, check 'em over, then help the Chinese troops lay demolition charges this afternoon. A gooneybird will be in tomorrow to take everyone else and our footlockers.

"All of you can stay for the briefing; we may need a backup at the last minute. Here's the target, gents." Ross turned to the wall map and tapped Hankow. "And here's the way we're going in. We'll go after dark. Don't raise your eyebrows. By tonight, the five of you I picked are going to be instrument pilots, or I'm going to kick your butts all the way back to Calcutta.

"I'll take you up one at a time for an hour each. I'll fly your wing. You will wear this." He reached behind the ops counter and withdrew a cap. The headgear resembled a baseball cap of woven rattan, except the oversized bill extended out ten inches or more. The Chinese fabricator had embellished the bill with the old AVG shark's mouth.

After shouts of laughter died down, Ross continued. "With this on, you can't see outside—only your instrument panel. I'll have hot guns and will shoot down the first sonofabitch I catch peeking. Now, here's the drill." He passed out sheets of paper.

"This is called the 'A' pattern. We'll use two hundred miles per hour for a base airspeed to save gas. You take up a heading of north and fly two minutes straight and level. You make a single-needle-width turn to the left—still level. Now, as you all know, a single-needle-width turn gives you three degrees per second. At the end of one minute and thirty seconds you'll have turned two hundred and seventy degrees, right? You'll now be on a heading of zero nine zero—due east. You hold that heading for two minutes, climbing at two hundred miles per hour at five hundred feet per minute. Then you make another two-hundred-seventy-degree level turn. Now you're headed south."

Waiting for the groans and muttered "Oh, shits" to subside, Ross added cheerfully, "You guessed it. You'll hold that heading for two minutes, except this time you lose that thousand feet at five hundred feet per minute. Next, you climb one thousand feet during your two-seventy—you'll have to adjust your rate of climb, right? Hold your west heading for two minutes, lower your gear and flaps, and descend one thousand feet during your last turn. End of pattern.

"You're making faces and calling me names, but when we finish, I want to see every turn come out exactly on time, on the correct heading, and at the correct altitude. I'll be generous and allow you five miles airspeed, plus or minus, and five degrees. If you flunk, I'll give one of the backups a shot. Walt, you're first in the barrel."

It was late afternoon when Ross touched down for the last time and taxied to the armament revetment, where he would have his gun bays filled with all-tracer ammo belts. Then he would face the group of sheepish, chagrined fighter pilots. He leaped to the ground, stretched weary muscles, and crossed to where Major Weibel was slumped on an empty ammo box.

"Will it work?" Ross asked.

Weibel flashed a weary but triumphant grin. "I believe it will. When it comes to fireworks, these Chinese are the best in the business. We've already rolled the P-40s back to revetments, or I'd show you. Sung Fe, the old master, took a Chinese grenade and taped it inside the bomb's fuse receptacle with twenty feet of fine wire coiled inside. He says your hunch that a grenade would explode the bomb is correct. We'll drop at about a hundred feet. The wire will pull the pin on the grenade, and five seconds later—blooey. If it isn't on the ground by then, it'll be damn close."

Ross felt the strain of a full afternoon of flying drop away. "All right!" he enthused. "Look, I'm going to debrief five, hang-faced pilots—they all *think* they flunked, but they really did damn well. Then I'll take a shower and flop till chow time. How about we set briefing for nineteen hundred with takeoff at twenty hundred. Can you have the P-40 pilots there?"

"Sure." Weibel stood, hesitated, then said, "Ross . . ." He stopped, then muttered, "Aw, the hell with it," and strode away.

Ross watched him go, a puzzled frown on his face. Now what the hell was he about to say? he wondered. But he knew. That bastard hadn't had a drink for two days. You don't suppose . . . ?

The sun appeared as a huge, orange ball as it entered the haze and dust hanging over the stifling river valley. It suffused the oppressive atmosphere with a flame-colored hue. The entrance to hell might look something like this, Ross thought as he approached the ready room. I wonder if it's an omen?

He had paused to observe the serpentine column of refugees still clogging the main road south. Where the hell are they going? he wondered. Do they *never* stop to sleep?

Ross pushed open the ready room's screen door and stepped inside. There were no ribald greetings; muttered conversations ceased. "Hi, boys and girls." His attempt to induce some levity fell flat. He crossed to where Major Weibel leaned against the ops counter and turned to do a quick head count. Ross frowned. "I count only five P-40 pilots."

"Count again," Weibel said in a low voice. "I'm going along. I'll be in a P-40—on your wing."

"What?" Ross's startled reaction was impulsive. "Uh—Major, you haven't been flying a lot lately," he added lamely. "Are you sure?"

"I'm sure." Weibel's voice had a new firmness. "I could give you a lot of horseshit about how I'm a changed man, how I've seen the error of my ways, but that's all it would be, horseshit. Now, get on with your briefing, Captain. That's an order. I'm still the CO here, on paper at least."

Ross recovered his composure and turned to face the assembled pilots. "You've all had time to study the photos and pick out your targets. We'll fly in pairs—a P-40, with its bomb, on the wing of a Mustang. We'll take off at two-minute intervals and follow the river. You're on your own finding the target. After you've hit it, circle north of the city and return to the river. There will be some nasty weather; rain showers and evening mist or haze are almost always up there. You lead crews keep a running time and distance check—penetrate weather by dead reckoning. You wingmen hang tight, and I do mean tight.

"Remember, strafe go-downs, sampans, and anything that your tracers will ignite. The P-40s will drop from about a hundred feet; that's the best altitude for your grenade fuses. And, of course, there's no safety device. If you get into trouble, pull up and hit the silk, because if you belly in, that bomb is going to detonate. If there are no questions, let's saddle up and ride."

Weibel fell into step with Ross as they crossed the parking ramp. The crunch of gravel beneath their boots could be heard above the constant din of the fleeing refugees. "Wonder if your Bed-Check Charlie will visit us tonight," Weibel asked.

Ross barked a harsh laugh. "That'd be ironic, destroying a field they're going to own in a few days. I hope he does. Even better, we might meet that sonofabitch headed this way down the river."

Weibel walked silently for a time. "Ross, you made this trip sound easier than it's gonna be. But I guess you know that."

"It won't be a milk run, that's for sure," Ross replied.

"This will be my last one, so I want to make it a good one," Weibel responded.

"Oh?"

"Yeah, I'm washed up. Casey gave me a break when he gave me the squadron. I blew it. I don't have the touch for dealing with people—for giving orders. I would never have had the guts to schedule this mission. We're going to lose some damn good men tonight. You know that, but you can rationalize it. I can't. Guess that's why I turned into a drunk."

"Aw, Major—"

"Don't give me any bullshit," Weibel interrupted. "I just have one request. If I buy the farm, ask Casey to put me in for a DFC, okay? Ask him to send it to Sal with a nice letter. She's always been so damn proud of me. Don't let her know that I turned into a bum."

The major slapped Ross on the shoulder and strode away toward his waiting P-40. Ross noticed for the first time that Weibel's flight suit was freshly washed and ironed. His boots were shined, and he walked briskly erect.

Chapter Nineteen

20 June 1944
Kweilin Airfield

The single silver star adorning Casey Vincent's collar sparkled with the unmistakable sheen that shouts "brand new." The dour expression the just-promoted general directed at Ross, however, was anything but sparkling. Stroking cheeks slack with fatigue despite their twenty-nine years, and covered with late-afternoon reddish brown stubble, he rumbled, "So you left Hengyang totally unusable?"

"Yes, sir," Ross replied. He sat erect, almost at attention, in the wooden chair facing the east China forward echelon commander. "I circled and watched the Chinese troops torch all the buildings and set off charges buried in the runway."

"It breaks my heart." The sad-faced general shook his head. "So much went into that base. At one time it was to be home for the Superforts."

"Yes, sir," Ross responded, "and it didn't need to happen."

Vincent's hooded eyes fixed on Ross like a cobra's. "I think you'd best explain that statement, Captain."

"With fuel, and fuses for the P-40s' bombs, we could have given the Chinese enough air support to hold. The fuel was at Chengtu."

"I wasn't aware you were an authority on tactics, Captain," Vincent observed sarcastically. "Perhaps that's what led you to make an unauthorized trip to Chengtu, to give misleading, possibly false statements to Twenty Bomber Command's new commander, and why you ordered the withdrawal of our detachment at Hsinching, all of which prompted a blistering request for an explanation.

"On the next day you violated standing orders limiting P-51 engagements to air-to-air combat and led a totally unauthorized offensive mission—depleting the 41st's entire inventory of fuel in the process—which resulted in the loss of three aircraft and pilots. Is that a fairly accurate account of your busy days?" He tossed a full-page radio message form aside.

"Ah, yes, sir. But it was a last-ditch effort, sir. One last—"

Vincent cut Ross off with an outthrust palm. "Later, Captain. You'll have an opportunity to explain, but now I'm waiting with bated breath to discover just what the hell was Whizzer doing all that time?"

"It was hectic, sir. The evacuation needed organizing, and getting the Chinese army and the mayor of Hengyang to cooperate was essential. Major Weibel felt that as squadron commander, he must handle those matters."

"I'm impressed. Because of those weighty responsibilities, Whizzer gave *you* the trifling job of trying to steal eight thousand gallons of scarce av-gas, of sneaking a fighter detachment from under the nose of an irate general, and of *leading* the most bizarre, unorthodox fighter mission of the war. Why, I want to know, did you fly lead instead of the squadron commander?"

"It was Major Weibel's idea to rig grenades for fuses, sir. He felt obligated to be the first to try one."

"I see." Vincent returned to scratching his bearded jowls. "Colyer, you're a goddamn con artist." He raised his hand again as Ross opened his mouth to protest. "Not yet—I'll tell you when. No, you gave that pompous ass Sprague a song and dance, and got away with it. But don't you ever—ever again, hear me—try to give *me* a snow job like the tale you're spinning now.

"Whizzer was a great fighter pilot—one of the old breed. Always flew by instinct—rules didn't apply. He never adapted to the Air Corps way of doing things. He drank too much. I gave him a chance to run a squadron against strong opposition. I was wrong. You covered for him—are still trying to. Now that we understand each other, tell me how Whizzer got killed."

Ross relaxed. "The mission was my idea," he stated flatly. "We spent weeks wasting gas trying to engage the Jap air force. They would start south; we'd go up to meet them; they'd turn around. When we got word to pull out, I decided to let the guys take one last shot where it might hurt.

"Anyway, it was a rotten night—overcast, with rain showers in the target area. Major Weibel and I were in the lead element. I located the dock area, and we started our run-in. Just then a battery of what must have been thirty-seven-millimeter stuff opened up off our left wing. There were five elements in the slot behind us. This one battery alone would have had a field day as they came past.

"Major Weibel called me on the radio to suggest that we change course and take out the gun position. We almost made it. I started firing from way out. We'd loaded the belts with nothing but tracer rounds, and it made quite a show. I thought it might throw them off. We were within a minute of drop time when I saw tracers hitting the major's ship. He still had control, it seemed to me, and he just dove directly into the gun emplacement.

"We lost the fourth element when the Mustang pilot got shot down. The P-40 on his wing flew into a rain shower and was never heard from."

Vincent steepled his fingers as he sat silently for several moments. "Had Whizzer been drinking?" he asked.

"No, sir. This mission seemed to fire him up. He hadn't had a drink for two days."

"I see. Colyer, was Whizzer a battle casualty? Or . . . ?"

"A suicide?" Ross said, finishing the general's question. "I honestly don't know. I've thought about little else these last two days. He had changed completely, but he either had a premonition, or had decided before takeoff not to come back—said he was washed up, that this would be his last mission. He told me to ask you to award him a DFC if he didn't come back—to send it to his wife with a nice letter. Any way you cut it, sir, he kept perhaps half the others from getting killed."

Vincent didn't hesitate. "He'll get the DFC. And I see no reason for these conjectures to go any further, do you?"

"No, sir, none whatever."

"Good. I'm putting you in for a DFC as well." Vincent's lips parted in a wolfish grin. "I'm not surprised at your shocked look, but as they say, it's a very fine line between a Medal of Honor and a court-martial. You were squarely on that line. I'm also not surprised that you didn't know the gun emplacement Whizzer took out was part of a ring of AA guns placed to protect a major storage depot—ammo, aircraft engines, small arms, the works. The sampans the others hit were unloading at a big fuel storage facility; the fires are still burning. The frosting on the cake, however, was the headquarters for their China expeditionary forces. It was next door to the ammo depot.

"In short, you hit the jackpot. Intelligence is still going over the recce photos, but my guess is you slowed up the Jap bastards by as much as a month—a month we badly need."

Ross sat, too stunned to speak. The general's dour expression returned. "Now, I suppose you think you're going to get the squadron," he growled.

"I—I wasn't expecting it really, no," Ross stammered.

"Good, because you aren't. I'm sending your stolen flight back to Chengtu. I'm tempted to send you with it, but I don't think you'd be too popular with that bunch up there, and I shudder to think of what devilry you might think up. So, with the 41st being understrength, I'm breaking it up and using individual pilots and airplanes as replacements for the 28th Group."

"General, *please.* We're a new squadron, true. There are a lot of rough edges, but we made a damn good account of ourselves."

Ross's anguished plea fell on deaf ears. "That you did," Vincent conceded, "but the need for pursuit and interceptors has passed. Your planes will be equipped with bomb shackles, and the pilots will get training in bombing and close air support.

"As for you, I'm assigning you to group ops. Now get that whipped-dog look off your stupid face. All our headquarters pilots are attached to squadrons for operational flying. You'll get your share of stick time.

"The birds we're getting now have a Bendix radio direction finder installed. No one here knows how to fly decent instruments, much less use the damn things. General Chennault remembered your name from a time you brought four fighters down that were trapped above the overcast. He's ordered you to set up an instrument-training course. Your pilots we debriefed yesterday say you did the job for them in one afternoon.

"And that isn't all. Someone in Calcutta sent us a bunch of steel tubes, only they didn't tell us what they were for. Well, the staff armament officer showed up last week. He found the Chinese playing games with them and had a hissy fit. It seems these things are rocket launchers—top secret stuff. He was horrified that they were just lying around out in the weather. Guess what—you have an additional duty: rocket-tube installer, experimenter, figuring-out-how-to-shoot-the-damn-things officer."

* * *

Ross sat on steps chiseled out of stone, leading down to the base hospital. Who the hell decided to build an airfield here? he wondered. The landscape resembled what the back side of the moon might look like. The rounded hills reared up from a flat plain like droppings from some mythical herd of gigantic horses. A few of the tops appeared to reach three hundred feet. Erosion, someone had told him. Millions of years of wind and rain had washed the soil away, leaving the black rock. Well, the freakish things might drive some geologist to a premature orgasm, but they sure as hell made for interesting instrument approaches.

They also made snug bomb shelters, he had to admit. Key installations, such as headquarters, the radio shack, and the base hospital, were all constructed inside caves chiseled by hand from—what else?—solid rock.

Ruth Lasher interrupted his ruminations. The sight of her stretching and savoring the fresh air caused his heart to turn over. Who else could wear baggy OD fatigues with a fashionable flair? He crossed to the tiny porch and grasped both her hands in his. Stealing a quick kiss, he asked, "Long day?"

Ruth's wan, oval-shaped face brightened. "Like most of them, yes. But I have tomorrow off. How did your day go?"

Ross groaned. "You had to ask. Let's go to the club, have a drink, and I'll tell you all about it, okay?"

They settled into rattan chairs situated in a remote corner of the veranda where a slight breeze produced a small island of cool air. A red-jacketed waiter appeared. "What I wouldn't give for a cold American beer, or a tall, cold gin and tonic," Ross lamented. "Do you have *anything* besides rice wine?"

"Yes, sah," the smiling boy replied. "We have very good whiskey. Brandy, maybe?"

Ruth shook her head. "No. Avoid that stuff like the plague, Ross. The Chinese believe that the only difference in brandy, Scotch, and bourbon is the color. God knows where they get the alcoholic base, but they just add more or less coloring to make whatever it is they think Americans prefer. It all tastes the same: awful. *And* lethal—we treat a half-dozen cases of alcoholic poisoning every month. I have a hunch they use the same alcohol for motor fuel. The local beer isn't very good, but at least it's safe."

Ross grinned. "Beer it is, then." The cheerful waiter, who had stood by silently grinning during Ruth's scathing indictment of his product, shuffled off. Ross reached across and grasped Ruth's right hand. "Let's take up where we left off," he said.

"You mean that ten minutes in ops yesterday or the ten minutes on the runway at Hengyang?" she asked.

Ross chuckled. "Don't be coy with me, girl. I mean where we left off back at Eagle Pass."

Ruth withdrew her hand. "As *I* recall, we decided we didn't have a future, Ross," she said quietly.

"*You* decided, my proud beauty, not *we.*"

"Ross, will you do something that's very important to me?"

"Of course."

"Very well. Will you promise to keep our—our friendship light and, well . . ."

Ross sipped his beer and made a face. "Wow," he exclaimed. "You mean I'm to keep my grubby paws off your warm and tender body," he responded, his voice flat and devoid of emotion.

"Ross, please. Don't be crude. As I said, this is important to me. Seeing you again has me confused. I thought I'd relegated you to my past. Your showing up out of the clear blue—well, it's disturbing. My resolve hasn't changed, Ross. I don't plan to make a career of the army; you do. Every time we work desperately to save some shot-up, mangled airman, my determination to never again expose myself to that state of constant apprehension deepens."

"What if I said I would get out and become a—a banker?"

"You'd soon hate me. You'd blame me for having to give up the most important thing in your life."

Ross drank deeply from his beer. This time he didn't grimace. "If that's the way you feel, then I guess we'd best shake hands here and now. I'll stay on my side of the field, you stay on yours."

"*Ross.*" Tears welled up in Ruth's eyes. "Don't you understand what I'm saying? I just need some time. I want you; oh, you'll never know how much. It's just that . . . Please don't hate me for being mixed-up."

"What's there to be mixed-up about?" Ross asked.

Ruth's bosom heaved as she took a deep breath. "Damnit, Ross, I've been seeing someone else." She went on hurriedly as she glanced at Ross's bunched jaw muscles. "He's a doctor—a Chinese doctor. He comes to the hospital three days a week. We've gone out together a number of times. He's a gentle man, Ross. He took his residency and internship in the States and plans to return there after the war." Ross had to strain to hear the next words. "Until I saw you last week, I thought that's what I wanted, too."

Ross stood and tossed some coins onto the table. "Shall I walk you to your quarters?" he asked.

After a silent, ten-minute walk, they stopped in front of the dark-timbered nurses' quarters. Ruth turned. "You once told me that you loved me. If you still do, do this for me, will you?"

Ross's tone was bitter. "You say *you're* confused. What am *I* to think? Am I supposed to say, 'Oh, that's all right, my dear. Go sleep with him for a while, then sleep with me for a while, and make up your mind which of us is best in bed'?"

Ruth's eyes blazed. "I'll forget you said that."

"I'm sorry. That was a dumb thing to say," Ross replied, shamefaced. Grasping both her shoulders, his voice firm, he added, "I do love you and, no, I won't insist on an answer here and now. But I can't live with this standing around while you pick petals off the daisy.

"I have to go to Kunming day after tomorrow, maybe on to Kharagpur. I'll be gone about a week. When I come back, I'll come here. Either have a table reserved at the best restaurant in town, where we'll have a polite farewell dinner, or have the bivouac gear you had at Eagle Pass that day sitting on the porch." He brushed her lips with his and strode off.

24 June 1944
Kunming Airfield

"There you are, sir, all set to go out and rearrange some landscape." The crew chief stood back and admired his handiwork.

Ross regarded the abomination hanging beneath the Mustang's wing, but with less enthusiasm. "That's the goddamnest getup I ever saw," he said, shaking his head. "Looks like some boilermaker had been drinking Chinese whiskey. Are you sure the damn airplane will even *fly?*"

He turned at the sound of approaching footsteps. A grinning lieutenant, attired in flying gear, stood behind them. "Hi, I'm Buster Wingate. I'm flying lead for you while you get the hang of these crazy firecrackers. To answer your question: Yeah, she'll fly—different, though. That's why I'm going along for your first trip."

Ross shook Wingate's hand and turned to look once more at the cluster of three tubes—they looked like lengths of stovepipe—suspended beneath each wing. "I still don't see why everyone is so excited about these things. They look kinda puny to me."

"Okay." The lieutenant's voice grew serious. "For one thing, you've got range. You can shoot from a thousand yards, so you don't have to fly right down the throat of some pissed-off Jap gunner. You get penetration. These babies are zipping along at about the speed of sound when they hit. They'll punch through protection that will deflect machine-gun fire. Once inside, fifty pounds of high explosive will raise all kinds of hell. We hear that the Jugs in the ETO are having fantastic results. The last and final advantage is that you're carrying only about three hundred pounds of armament on takeoff."

"Okay," Ross conceded. "How do you aim the damn things? Can you hit what you're aiming at?"

"They aren't as accurate as your fifty calibers, but they get in the vicinity of where you're aiming. Some of the guys put a wire loop on the cowling, but I'm not sure it helps.

"As long as we're up giving you some target practice, group wants us to make a sortie along the Salween River. We're looking for supply dumps, convoys, river traffic, or troop concentrations. Stay on the west bank; the situation is real fluid there. The Chinese have crossed in places, but we're not sure where.

"Select single, sequential release; you need to have aiming practice. I'm flying clean for two reasons. One: The Japs still put up a few Oscars in the valley. If we see any, get the hell out; head for home by yourself. Don't try to dogfight with those pods on. Two: You'll notice about a ten-mile-per-hour loss of airspeed, but more important, those things set up a burble around the Pitot tube. You can't depend on your indicated airspeed. For landing, stay on my wing all the way to touchdown and ignore your indicator. All set?"

An hour later, Ross heard, "Blue Two, this is Blue One. The river is dead ahead. Troops are reported dug in at the base of the first row of hills. We may take some small-arms fire. Ignore it, but if we see any twenty-millimeter stuff, I'll enter a racetrack and come back to give you a shot."

Ross acknowledged and concentrated on holding position, catching only fleeting glimpses of the terrain flashing five hundred feet below. The river appeared and immediately passed from view behind. Ross felt the familiar sense of remote objectivity take over. They were over hostile territory.

Wingate jinked left, and Ross saw small-caliber tracers arcing toward them. A terse voice sounded in his earphones: "Heavy stuff on our left. Hang tight." Ross followed his leader into a sharp turn as they reversed course. Returning to their original heading, he heard Wingate say, "The emplacement is on a knoll about a hundred yards south of a big clump of bamboo—there. Have at it."

Ross edged to his right to have maneuvering room and searched the benign-looking landscape. He saw it then; Wingate had sharp eyes, he decided. The barest disturbance revealing raw earth—he estimated it to be a good thousand yards out. Could these things carry that far? As he vacillated, twin rows of orange balls spurted from the knoll. Feeling like a Western gunslinger shooting from the hip, he pointed the nose toward the target and squeezed the trigger.

At first, he thought he'd had a misfire. There was no sound, no recoil. Then he picked up the rocket's fiery tail. It darted toward the knoll with unbelievable swiftness. It appeared to have virtually no drop, even at that range. Wingate broke up and left, then Ross caught the merest glimpse of a surprisingly large eruption of dirt toward the knoll's apex.

He heard Wingate chuckle. "Not bad, not bad at all for your first shot. You didn't get a direct hit, but you can bet they have their heads down. Okay, this bunch will be on their toes. Let's hop over the ridge and see if we can find their base camp."

Streaking over the rim of hills at treetop level, they found themselves above a sizable clearing filled with vehicles and milling figures. "Hot damn!" Wingate yelled. "Pay dirt. Select pairs this time. Give 'em hell. After you expend your ordnance, switch to your guns."

Twenty minutes later Wingate announced, "I'm down to reserve fuel, Two. Let's go."

Ross moved back into close formation and followed his leader in a steeply climbing turn. He craned his neck for a last look at the smoking scene of devastation behind. A dozen trucks sat drunkenly, spewing flame. Covered mounds of supplies either smoldered or had been strewn to the four winds. There were inert bodies, too. He shook his head in awe. Firing from safe distances, he'd seen his rockets wreak havoc within the clearing. His last one had found an ammo dump just inside the tree line. Four strafing passes with blazing .50 calibers had reduced the camp to rubble.

*   *   *

Still on Buster Wingate's wing, Ross felt the main gear touch down and rumble toward the turnoff. A smiling crew chief glanced at the empty rocket tubes and the smoke-grimed gunports, then quickly walked around the plane looking for battle damage. He gave a thumbs-up and yelled, "Looks like you scored, Captain."

"Did we ever," Ross called back from the cockpit. "I've never had my hands on anything like this rig." He clambered to the parking ramp and joined his grinning lead pilot, who was striding toward the ops shack. The bitter memory of seeing the base at Hengyang destroyed by their own hands momentarily marred his ebullient mood. Damnit, he cursed silently, with gas the B-29s burned on that one futile mission, and rockets, we could have chased the Japs all the way back to Peking.

28 June 1944
Kweilin Airfield

Lieutenant Colonel Lucas Henley, the 28th Group's ops officer, greeted Ross with a wry grin. "What the hell did you bring home? It looks like a flying pipe organ."

Ross crossed to the waist-high counter and talked as he closed his flight plan. "Colonel, you're looking at the goddamnedest fighting machine in all of China. I saw a two-ship element do as much damage as a half-dozen B-25s." He tossed a bulky envelope onto the counter. "Here are shop drawings, wiring diagrams, and such for the modification. The sooner the better. I can pass on what tips the armament boys at Kunming showed me. It only takes about four hours per airplane."

Henley's expression tightened. "We could sure as hell use a shot in the arm just now. The Japs are swarming south like locusts, and we're down to four sorties per week. Gas—the '24s haven't flown a mission for two weeks. The B-25s put up six airplanes last week. We couldn't fly escort, so they got clobbered. Ling-ling is doomed; we think it's surrounded. They've been supporting the fighting around the town of Hengyang. When they fall back, the Chinese main line of resistance is sure to collapse."

Ross frowned. "I don't understand. You're closer to Kunming than we were. What's happened?"

"General Vincent is on his way to Fourteenth headquarters right now to ask that very question. We got the 41st's airplanes, but we didn't get your fuel allocation. The suspicion is that Stilwell has pressured Chennault into giving priority to supporting his drive into Burma. Did you see any shortage of fuel at Kunming?"

"No," Ross replied slowly, "I didn't. And my shakedown mission was to the Salween."

"Just as we suspected." Henley's voice was grim. "Well, we can hang those rocket tubes, but the joke is, we don't have any goddamn rockets to shoot."

"Oh, for Christ's sake, Colonel. We may as well go home. Can't *anyone* see what the hell is happening? If east China goes, what the hell use is Burma to us? They'll chase the B-29s out of Chengtu, which won't be all that big a loss. Without bases around Hankow, they can't reach enough of the Jap home islands to do any damage to speak of—assuming the dumb fucks can even *find* Japan."

"That's right; you're an old bomber man, aren't you?"

Ross nodded.

"Okay, how do these rockets stack up against a B-25 in hitting shipping and harbor facilities?"

"They'd be deadly against targets like that. You can shoot from a long ways out, you get better penetration, and they're more accurate."

"Hmmm. And a Mustang burns less than half the fuel a B-25 does. I'm going to get off a flash message to General Vincent at Kunming. He can get enough of those small rockets on board his '25 to get us started. As soon as the gooneybird gets back in commission, we can use it to bring in more rockets. We may still be in business. If we can reduce the threat coming up from Hong Kong and Canton, maybe, just maybe we can hold the bastards at Ling-ling. Get cracking on hanging those rocket tubes."

"Yes, sir. But, sir, about my instrument-flying school . . . ?"

"Until we get enough fuel to put up combat sorties, forget it, Colyer. As of now you're lead pilot for the skyrocket brigade—the Fourth of July kids."

Ross emerged from the shower cubicle, dried himself, and put on his least wrinkled uniform. Okay, he asked himself, what am I going to find? Did she even keep tabs at ops to find out when I landed? If not—well, I guess that's my answer. He followed the well-traveled path from the ops side of the field to the hill concealing the administrative complex, oblivious to passing groups of chattering Chinese workers and airmen on their way to catch the bus into town.

His steps slowed as he approached the nurses' quarters. He turned off the main track and willed his eyes to penetrate the gathering dusk, then broke into long, swift strides. The unmistakable bulk of two OD duffel bags sat outside the door.

Chapter Twenty

11 July 1944
Cascade Mountains, Washington

Duane Swoffard kissed Janet's upturned nose and her closed eyelids, then moved to nuzzle her neck. Meanwhile, deft fingers unbuttoned the front of her V-necked ivory silk blouse. "You're so beautiful," he murmured. "I've longed to do this since that evening you appeared, like a dream, at my party."

Janet leaned back fractionally, eyes still closed, while he deftly removed the filmy garment. It fell to the floor with a sensuous rustle. She shrugged the straps to her camisole free, then felt her breasts escape their lacy prison. Her knees like jelly, she twined her hands behind Duane's neck to support herself.

She opened her eyes as she felt the necklace being slipped over her head. She started to protest, but the spell of the moment rendered her speechless. Nevertheless, a twinge of dissent followed as she saw the slender chain and its attached jade figurine—a dull reflection in the gloom—tossed casually to the floor.

No . . . she wanted to object. You shouldn't just . . . Oh, it's probably just as well that she isn't present during what is about to happen. Janet smiled faintly at the thought as she surrendered to the deliciously languorous process of total submission. The figurine's delicate facial features, partially obscured by a minuscule sari, maintained their Mona Lisa inscrutability, seemingly unperturbed by such shameful treatment.

*   *   *

Janet woke up first. Total darkness had replaced the soft dusk she last remembered. Duane slumbered beside her, his breathing deep and even. What time was it? Had they slept all night? Suddenly it seemed important to know. She eased from the bed and tiptoed to the bathroom. She closed the door soundlessly and fumbled for the light switch. Blinded at first by the glare, she squinted at her watch—eleven-forty.

An apparition in the huge mirror gracing half of one wall gave her a start. My God, *that's me,* she thought wildly. Naked, still standing in a partial crouch to read her watch, hair in total disarray, makeup smeared and splotched over puffy cheeks, Janet panicked. I can't let him see me like this. She grabbed a hand towel and soaked it beneath the cold water faucet. After three minutes of furious scrubbing, she felt better.

Carefully groping on hands and knees in the darkened bedroom, she retrieved the camisole. Then, rising to a kneeling position, she wriggled into its clinging folds. Her knee rested on something small and unyielding. The necklace—she scooped it up and slipped the chain over her head. The figurine slid between her breasts, its familiar weight restoring a large measure of self-assurance. Further search produced panties. Seated on the floor, she pulled them on, then made her way soundlessly into the living room.

His mountain cottage, as Duane had described it—four bedrooms and three baths—faced a sizable lake tucked between two modest mountain peaks. The living room, with rows of double-paned windows facing the panorama, was illuminated by a tiny, concealed bulb on the gleaming white stove in the adjoining kitchen. The steaks! They lay on the work counter—obscene-looking bloody lumps. The plan to light a fire in the natural-stone fireplace and grill them while sipping chilled wine had gone awry when she had felt warm lips caressing the nape of her neck.

She returned the meat to the refrigerator and eyed the empty, sticky daiquiri pitcher with mock indignation. *You* are the culprit, she told it silently. The shadow of a headache reminded her that the pitcher's contents had been a wicked influence. She drank a glass of cold water, gathered cigarets and lighter from the coffee table, and curled into the end of a long sofa facing the lake.

Well, it happened, just like you knew it would, she scolded herself. Are you glad, or sorry? Oh, don't be such a Pollyanna. It was like Doris had said: I'm single and self-sufficient. Why shouldn't I sleep with whomever I please?

Would you marry him? Good question. Heaven knows he's handsome enough, smooth, very intelligent—and rolling in money. They had fun together, plus, a big plus, he told her he respected *her* for her mature thinking, her ability to discuss worldly matters, her rise to a highly responsible job—that he was sick of the inanely chattering females in the crowd he mingled with. That, to her, had been his most flattering comment. But marriage? She honestly didn't know. Freedom, after BT's domination, had become a heady experience. She uttered a wry chuckle. Anyway, the question was moot—why even conjecture? *He* sure as hell hadn't mentioned the possibility.

She turned at the sound of the bedroom door opening. Duane stood there, barely visible in the half light. He wore slacks but no shirt. "Hi," he greeted her. "I missed you." He crossed to Janet on bare feet and kissed her lightly on the forehead. "Don't ever go away and leave me alone for that long again." He sank to the sofa beside her and laid a hand on her thigh. "Thinking?" he asked.

"Umm-hmm, sorta."

"Second thoughts?" he teased.

Janet laughed softly. "Second thoughts are for high school girls. We both knew what was going to happen when you picked me up this morning. Now, I have memories—fond memories."

Duane regarded her at some length, his head cocked to one side, his off-center nose and curly mop of hair silhouetted in the dim background light. "That was a most touching statement," he murmured. "I hope you soon have an entire scrapbook full of them."

Janet laughed again, gaily this time. "Not unless you feed me, you brute. I'm starved. Why don't I slip into some clothes and make a salad while you light the fire?"

"No, yes, and yes," Duane replied. "The salad and fire—great ideas. Dressing—not so great. I just want to watch your every move. Did anyone ever tell you how beautiful you are? I don't know which describes you best: a gazelle approaching a water hole, or a prowling lioness. You resemble both when you walk."

"You think I resemble an animal?" she chided. "Why not a flower? A lily? A wild rose? A sunflower?"

"No." His voice was devoid of its previous bantering note. "Never a flower, my dear. You have many attributes, attributes I plan to explore thoroughly, but flowerlike is definitely *not* one of them."

* * *

The salad was uninspired—warm, limp, and tasteless. The steaks were overdone and the wine tepid, but to Janet it was ambrosia. After demolishing every bite and heaping the dishes in the sink, she returned to the sofa. Duane seated himself on the floor and leaned his head into the hollow formed by her curled figure.

"What would you like to do tomorrow?" he asked lazily.

"Take a long walk in the mountains, swim in that frigid lake, lie in the sun, drink a pitcher of daiquiris, take a long nap, do steaks over the fire—"

"We did all that today," Duane interjected.

"Today was just practice," Janet drawled. "Perhaps tomorrow we can do it all better."

Duane turned his head and looked directly into Janet's eyes, crinkled by a mischievous grin. "Lady," he said, "you do have intriguing ideas. They warrant careful consideration."

He returned to his original position, his demeanor changed. "Janet, how would you like to be rich? I mean rich like in seven figures."

"I'd settle for a truckload of red ration points, another of real silk stockings, bourbon that didn't cause you to go blind, a new car—one with zero miles on the odometer—and my own private rail coach or a One-A airline priority," Janet replied promptly.

"I'm not joking."

"I'm not either," Janet retorted, her voice sharp. "I've seen what money—too much money—can do, Duane. It got my husband killed. I have a job I'm good at. I'm free to do as I please. I have a nest egg for my old age. What more can a million dollars do?"

"Put you in a different world," he answered dreamily. "Above the petty day-to-day annoyances. A world filled with beautiful people, and something new and exciting to do every day."

"I'm not sure I like the direction this conversation is taking."

"Look." He rolled to a seated position, legs crossed, his face suddenly set in harsh lines. "We will make an unbeatable team. You have brains and, if you'll admit it, ambition. I have the means. Working together we can have that million dollars."

"What are you suggesting?"

"Janet, we're winning this war; it won't last forever. There are millions being made every day it continues. When it ends, most of those opportunities will disappear. We *must* act quickly."

Janet's voice bore ominous overtones. "Are you talking of war profiteering?"

"You're using a label," he responded with a dismissive wave of his hand. "You sound as if there was something wrong with providing goods and services our country needs desperately to end this war. If it were wrong, the opportunities wouldn't exist, would they?"

"Go on."

"All right, so I buy low and sell high. That's the principle good business was founded upon. I've done well, but I'm earning peanuts compared to what's possible. For example: You work for Boeing Aircraft. You prepare technical reports. It's common knowledge that Boeing is working around the clock to build a bomber powered by jet engines. To shorten the war? Hell, no. That bomber will emerge as the prototype of a jet-powered, intercontinental airliner! They're using the taxpayers' money to foot the bill for technology. How much do you think companies like Lockheed and Douglas, just to name two, would pay to have a peek at Boeing's research?"

"Duane! That's monstrous. You want me to be a *spy?* And how did you know my job? I don't recall ever telling you exactly what I do."

"Oh, come off it, Janet. We aren't selling secrets to the Germans or the Japs. Your job? I make it my business to check out people I'm thinking of doing business with. Look, the big companies are stealing from the public. What's wrong with relieving *them* of a few pennies?"

Oblivious to her thunderstruck expression, he continued. "And that's just a start. What do you think will happen to these tons upon tons of valuable machinery, airplanes, and the like once the war is over? They'll be offered to the public for pennies on the dollar. Your father-in-law is a senator. Think what it could mean to the right people to be able to influence—"

Janet sprang to her feet. "I've heard quite enough, Duane. I—I . . ." She paused, eyes brimming with tears. Her voice choked but she continued. "You did a background check on *me?* Because you considered me a future *employee?* Didn't today mean *anything* to you?"

Duane stood also, a puzzled frown on his face. "Janet, hey, look. Maybe I put it badly, but we're talking millions. Sure I enjoyed today; we can have a hundred others just like it. But we're mature people; we can mix business with pleasure."

She strode toward the open bedroom door. Duane followed and watched as she yanked on slacks and thrust her arms into the sleeves of her blouse, ripping a shoulder seam in the process. "I want to go home," she grated as she slipped her feet into shoes. "*Now.* If you won't take me, I'll call a cab. If there are no cabs in this godforsaken wilderness, I'll walk, but I'm leaving."

Swoffard threw his hands heavenward, as if in supplication. "Okay," he sneered, "so I misjudged you. You're just another broad who thinks because she has a job, a college degree, and a nice pair of tits, she's hot stuff—you'll get the good life handed to you on a platter. Well, I'll tell you something: Until you can hunt with the big dogs, stay on the porch. Wait 'til I get a shirt on; I'll take you home. I can see now it would never have worked out with us."

"No, Duane, it would never—as you put it—have worked out with us," Janet spat. "Not only are you a cheap crook, you're a—an asshole."

Janet stalked into the living room to wait. She attempted to straighten her blouse and encountered the jade figurine. Regarding its enigmatic features, she murmured, "Ross, you said this reminded you of me. I just wish I knew what you meant."

29 August 1944
Kweilin Airfield

Ross trudged up steps formed from hard clay toward the ops building. The ungainly, two-story control tower reared alongside like a hastily conceived afterthought. Its sides of random slabs of mismatched wood and shed-type, sheet-metal roof contrasted sharply with the building housing operations. The latter boasted stuccoed walls and a tile roof, the eves all curling gracefully upward. The roof tiles, a seemingly ostentatious touch to a structure that might shelter cattle, were a prime example of the Chinese ability to work with whatever materials were at hand. He'd once watched a building under construction. A roof tile was formed by hand, the workman taking a rolled slab of clay and bending it lengthwise across his leg—simple, and the sun-baked clay would last a hundred years.

He paused at the door and glanced around. The other three flight members trailed close behind him. He shoved the door open and waved at the sad-faced corporal behind the ops counter as he crossed to the debriefing room. Lieutenant Colonel Henley sat on a tabletop, chewing a cigar and swinging his legs. He gave Ross an inquiring glance.

Ross ignored it and sagged into the nearest chair. "Colonel, turn off the damn spigot, will you? I never thought I'd see the day when

I complained about too much flying, but my ass is dragging out my tracks. What happened?"

Henley waved at the remaining flight crews straggling in. "One thing, General Chennault finally got the message across to Stilwell that east China was about to go the way of the dodo bird. The monsoon is tapering off, so stuff is crossing the Hump like never before. They waited too long, though," he added bitterly. "The Chinese army is beat to a frazzle. The Japs are hitting them at will, from all directions. We can't be enough places at the same time to give them close air support. Ling-ling is surrounded. How did you find things in the south?"

Ross scanned his notes. "You can scratch one coastal freighter and about six sampans. There's a destroyer in the harbor, though, that's putting up some wicked AA. It's going to be hard to take out. We'd expended our rockets, but it's going to take something with heavier stuff than we can throw at the damn thing.

"The B-24s left a lot of fires burning at Canton, but the railroad bridge the '25s took out last week is carrying traffic again. But, Colonel, this business about Ling-ling—why do we keep going south when the big threat seems to be in the north?"

Henley grunted. "The troops coming down from the north have their supply line stretched awfully thin. Our job is to keep them from linking up with the harbors at Hong Kong and Canton." He hesitated, then added, "If not from here, then from farther southwest."

"You're not thinking that Kweilin will go too?" Ross asked.

"Nothing is for certain in this business," Henley observed with what, to Ross, seemed an evasive air. "Okay, make out your strike report, then you are all to stand down for two days."

30 August 1944
Kweiyang, China

Ross let his bicycle coast to a halt before a weather-worn, whitewashed building set apart from the village's collection of mud-walled storefronts and dwellings grouped around an open-air market. Despite ducks and geese foraging for the occasional grain of spilled rice, and a pair of pigs roaming in search of something more substantial, the overall impression was one of neatness. The street showed broom marks; stepping-stones leading to the small inn's entry were still damp from recent scrubbing.

Ruth rolled her cycle into a slot made for the purpose and swung gracefully to the ground. "Well, this is it," she called gaily. "I'm sure that sign says 'Inn of the East Moon.'"

Ross stretched stiffened limbs and grinned. "You don't read Chinese any better than I do. More likely it says, 'Big Opium Sale—Today Only.' But I like the place," he added. Already he could feel the strain and fatigue of the past two weeks' grueling flight schedule draining away. It seemed hard to believe that such a sleepy, pastoral scene could exist less than five miles from Kweilin's frenetic activity.

Ross's uniform drew an immediate cluster of giggling, laughing children, crying "*Ding hoa,* Yank." No dirty, malnourished urchins these, he thought. Like everything else he could see, they reflected loving care. He gravely placed coins in outstretched hands, thinking, my God, may this place be spared if the damn Japs manage to get this far.

He untied musette bags from the bicycles, and led Ruth toward a doorway, resplendent in red lacquer with a friendly-looking dragon embossed in gold. A smiling girl with straight black bangs and short, square-bobbed hair bowed and greeted them in broken English. "This house is honored with your presence. Be so kind as to make name in book. Your room is waiting."

Ross lolled in the oversized, sunken bathtub and groaned with pleasure. Fully eight feet in diameter, filled to within inches of the top of its three-foot, wooden stave sides, the tub represented, to its bone-weary occupant, the ultimate in opulent decadence.

He watched Ruth add another bucket of steaming water through half-closed eyes. "Peel me some more grapes, woman. And send the dancing girls home. Then get back in here and scrub my back," he ordered.

Ruth uttered a throaty laugh and slid her nude body into the warm water. She half floated to where Ross sprawled on the submerged wooden bench and playfully shoved his head under the water. After he emerged, spluttering and shaking his head, she purred, "You're going to need more substantial fare than peeled grapes to survive the next two days, lover boy. And the dancing girls took one look at that ugly, hairy body, broke out laughing, and went home of their own accord."

Ross encircled Ruth's wet, slippery waist and drew her to his lap. "Liar," he mumbled between lips pressed against her neck, "my Greek-godlike physique is already a legend in these parts." He kissed her hungrily. "I will grant you the rare privilege of sharing my bed only after you tell me how you found this heavenly bathtub."

Ruth curled herself against him. "Reading the ads. This little inn is pretty well known, I understand. The Chinese interpreter sort of giggled when I asked her if she knew of a place to spend a quiet weekend. It wouldn't surprise me to find that the place has a certain reputation, in fact." She shook with silent laughter.

Ross's lazy smile froze. He pushed Ruth roughly to arms' length. "Is this the first time you've been here?" he asked harshly. "Did that Chinese doctor . . . ?"

Ruth's playful ardor disappeared. "Ross Colyer, that was uncalled for. In the first place, it's none of your damn business. In the second place, it hurts to discover that you think so little of me . . . that I would be so—so cheap as to taint this beautiful togetherness. After weeks of making love in places like the ambulance, a tent pitched on the side of a mountain, and that horrible, smelly place in town, I looked forward to this as a civilized interlude."

"Oh, damnit," said Ross in abject tones, "I'm a total idiot. Can you forgive me? It's just . . . You're right, it was none of my business."

Ruth dashed tears from her eyes. "I know you're on edge. This damn war—it brings out the worst in everyone. I won't forgive you. You don't forgive people you love; you understand them." She returned to Ross's embrace. "Do you suppose that bed is as uncomfortable as it looks?" she murmured.

1 September 1944
Kweilin Airfield

Ross swung onto the runway and braked to a halt while his wingman edged into position. He keyed his mike. "Hollywood Tower, Wishbone Flight ready for takeoff. Over."

"Cleared for takeoff, Wishbone One. Contact Hot Dog Control when fifty miles south of Ling-ling. Good hunting. Out."

After a final check of oil and coolant temperatures, Ross crammed the throttle forward and cocked a critical ear, listening carefully to the powerful engine's thundering response. Satisfied, he let the sluggish, ordnance-laden Mustang choose her own time to become airborne. Entering a lazy orbit at one thousand feet, he waited for Three and Four, now streaking down the runway, to join up.

Damn, he cursed silently. Ling-ling was probably doomed, according to the tight-lipped intelligence major: taking heavy incoming—from either artillery or tanks; four P-40s destroyed on the ground; refugees fleeing the fighting being slaughtered on choked roads leading to safety; the rail link cut south of the city. "Find those fucking big guns and take them out, or else Ling-ling is history," he'd said in parting.

Ross glanced overhead. The swifter, slick-winged P-51s would catch up by the time his attack force reached the target. The Japs were still putting up a token effort to crush the field's defenses from the air. The flight following him would fly top cover for the slower, less maneuverable, rocket-equipped planes. He could see the leading groups of refugees below. They looked like clots of black, dried blood on the reddish brown roadway. He thought fleetingly of the peaceful villagers at Kweiyang, and clamped his jaws.

He spotted his landmark and keyed the mike. "Hot Dog Control, Wishbone Flight here. Flight of four with full pods. What do you have for me? Over."

"You're a sight for sore eyes, Wishbone. We're taking incoming from at least four locations between the field and the river. Be advised you'll be laying your fire only a hundred yards or so in front of friendlies. Over."

"Gotcha, Hot Dog. We're on our way." Ross signaled for his flight to drop into trail formation and nosed over. The landscape blurred as the Mustangs howled across the battleground at a hundred feet, indicating in excess of 400 MPH. A glimpse of color—a half-dozen figures raced to spread an orange signal panel. Friendlies, he thought—closer to the river than he expected. Maybe the . . . shit! Those weren't Chinese troops. The sneaky yellow bastards had captured a signal panel and were using it as a decoy.

He led his formation into a sweeping turn. "Ignore the panel, Wishbone Flight. It's a trick. Let's spread out. I'll take this one; the rest of you look for big guns." He selected a pair of rockets and hurtled toward the orange marker. Please, God, don't let this be a mistake, he prayed. If this *isn't* a Jap trick, at least I'll be the one to blame. He streaked across the airfield. His thumb caressed the firing button. As he hesitated, a blue-white muzzle flash blossomed just beyond the orange marker. It was actually a relief: The thought that the gun was aimed at him didn't enter his mind.

Now! Ross felt a slight lurch as the missiles left their launching tubes. Dark specks, they sped toward the still-invisible target trailing a plume of flame. He jinked right to miss the debris that would soon follow. Impact—a jumble of dirt, tree branches, and dun-colored metal that shot skyward was briefly visible. Then he was climbing and turning to search for a new target.

"Tallyho," his headset crackled. "Got one. Looks like a tank maybe—dug in and covered with tree limbs. I'm starting my firing pass."

Ross extended his turn to make a pass parallel to the battlefront. He still hadn't spotted the friendly lines, but tracers—37mm stuff, he guessed—soon made the Jap lines easy to spot.

"Wishbone Two, this is Lead. Do you have me in sight?"

"Uh—I think so, Lead—just flying north between the field and the river?"

"Roger. Follow me in trail. I'll keep their heads down with a strafing pass. You look for targets for your rockets. Over. Three, I suggest you and Four do the same thing."

After ten minutes of hectic twisting and turning to avoid ground fire, Ross called, "Hot Dog Control, things are getting pretty nasty over here. They're getting our range. Do you have other targets?"

"You betcha. About ten miles north. Reported troop concentration."

"We're on our way!" Ross said excitedly. "Spread formation, Wishbone Flight. Throw everything you have at this target. Reserve fuel in twenty minutes. Over." Flying S turns to let the flight re-form, he scanned the countryside for a target.

A sharp, "Wishbone, this is Tallywhacker. Over," broke his concentration. This was his first contact with their top cover.

"This is Wishbone Lead, Tallywhacker. Go ahead."

"Bandits, bearing three-five-zero your position, high. We're going after 'em; keep your eyes peeled."

Before Ross could acknowledge, a disorganized sprawl of men, horses, and vehicles loomed ahead. "Use rockets on the trucks first," he snapped. Rolling slightly left, he zeroed in on three parked vehicles, their drivers scrambling for cover. Expending his last two rockets, he saw flames gush from two of them. He rolled into a turn and armed his .50 calibers.

"Wishbone, this is Tallywhacker," a shrill voice cried in his headset. "Bombers—Bettys—three of 'em low, trying to sneak past you to the east. Get 'em!"

Ross hesitated. Their mission was ground support; the rocket tubes reduced their maneuverability, although a baffle installed outboard of the rocket tubes at least gave them honest airspeed indications. But bombers, headed for the virtually defenseless airfield at Ling-ling, couldn't be ignored. He reversed his turn. Rolling out on an easterly heading, he spotted them immediately—big, lumbering shapes impossible to miss. "Bombers, twelve o'clock, Wishbone Flight. I'm starting a firing pass."

Closing rapidly, Ross selected the lead Betty. He would make a thirty-degree deflection from below and behind. Ignoring puny 7.7mm fire from the doomed bomber, he banked to lead his quarry. It filled his gunsight, and he squeezed off three short, rapid bursts; the Betty's right wing crumpled in a ball of flame.

His exultant whoop was cut short. "Wishbone Lead, this is Two. You took a hit. You're streaming oil—looks serious."

Ross's gaze flicked to the instrument panel. Already, the oil pressure gauge surged with ominous movements. "Take over lead, Two. I'm going to try and make the strip at Ling-ling."

"Roger," came the concerned reply. "We'll cap you 'til you're on the ground."

Ross reduced power to minimum cruise and took up a course toward the barely visible landing strip. The oil pressure gauge fluttered madly, then sank to zero. Seconds later, the oil temperature gauge started its chilling march toward the red line. Hang on engine, Ross pleaded. The runway took shape, tantalizingly near. He resisted the urge to set up a descent—hold altitude as long as possible. Another two minutes and he could glide to a dead-stick landing.

A minute passed; the oil temperature gauge's little hand was well into the red zone. But he had it made. Gear down, flaps down—the boundary flashed beneath the nose—cut the power and suck the stick into his gut.

Ross let the crippled bird roll off the runway into the dry grass. A pair of fatigue-clad figures raced toward him. He swung the canopy open and stepped down to meet them.

"What's the problem, sir?" a perspiring three-striper asked.

"Took a hit in an oil line somewhere. Do you suppose it's possible to improvise a fix that will get me back to Kweilin?"

"Shit, Cap'n—sir." The sergeant glanced nervously over his shoulder. "The Chinks just fell back to their perimeter positions on the north an' west sides. We're in the process of gettin' the hell out. Those yellow bastards just keep comin'—there's only a handful of us left. The birds are all up. Soon's they land, we'll refuel an' send 'em south. The major's still here. He'll take the last men out in the B-25 over there. It's loaded with bombs that he'll dump on the runway after takeoff. Everythin' else—buildin's, fuel an' ammo dumps—have charges set an' ready to blow."

Ross had trouble curbing his impatience. "Okay, okay," he finally broke in. "Can you at least take a look? It may not be serious—any kind of fix that'll hold for an hour's flight."

"I dunno, sir. We got no spare parts for a Mustang. Got nothin' to tow the thing with—have to work on it right here. If the Nips see a plane sittin' out in the open, they're gonna do anythin' they can to take it out."

"Can't you at least jerk the cowling and have a quick look?" Ross snapped.

"Well—I guess so." The two men removed screwdrivers from side pockets and crawled beneath the oil cooler. A distant rattle of automatic weapons fire ripped the silence. Ross thought for a minute that his reluctant mechanics would bolt. They steadied, however, and moments later the senior of them yelled, "It's an oil line, all right, Cap'n. Looky here, this 'uns damn near cut in two."

He wiped oily hands on the grass and crawled back alongside the landing gear. "No way are we goin' to find a replacement. Looks like you're stuck here with us."

"Damnit," Ross muttered angrily. He crept to where he could better see the offending line. "Isn't there some way to reroute the sonofabitch—put a clamp around it or something?"

"No, sir," the sergeant replied emphatically. "That there's an eighty-PSI line. She busts loose in flight an' you're in real trouble. No, sir, I wouldn't want to be responsible for some half-assed repair job that might get someone killed."

Ross heard his voice rising to a shout in spite of his diligent effort to remain calm. "What the fuck do you think I'm in now, if not trouble?" he raged. "Look, I'm not asking you to be *responsible*. Just *try* to fix the goddamn thing."

The sergeant, somewhat taken aback by Ross's outburst, scowled and muttered, "Smitty, go get Chou. The major calls Chou his secret weapon," he said grudgingly as the other mechanic trotted toward a row of buildings. "Chou can do things with a pair of pliers, wire, a scrap of tin, and maybe some electrical tape that you wouldn't believe."

The pair crouched in silence, wincing once at the sound of a heavy exchange of small-arms fire; it sounded closer. Once, Ross thought he heard the distinctive buzz of bullets disturb the air above them. Confused shouts, in both English and Chinese, blended in the distance. A number of invisible insects struck up a conversation in the dry grass. Ross scowled—stupid creatures. You'd best be digging instead of talking.

Minutes later, Smitty returned with a diminutive, blue-smocked Chinese trotting alongside. The sergeant grabbed an arm and tugged the slight, bespectacled man to the ruptured oil line. "He don't speak English," Smitty offered. "But damn if he don't seem to understand most everything you tell him."

The Chinese, hunkered beneath the aircraft, seemed to suck his teeth as he surveyed the damage. Finally, he reached inside a leather bag he carried and extracted a neat coil of wire, pliers, and a length of rubber hose.

"That's ordinary radiator hose, you dumb shit," the sergeant exploded. "That line carries eighty pounds of pressure at eighty degrees centigrade. It won't last five minutes."

The Chinaman exposed a row of widely gapped teeth in a broad grin, nodded, and ignored the GI mechanic. Ross watched, fascinated, as the man trimmed the hose to fit, then painstakingly wrapped it with wire that he tugged tight after each turn.

"Smitty, go get a drum of oil," the sergeant ordered. "Mind you, Cap'n, I'm not responsible for when she blows, but if you're dead set on tryin', well . . ."

Ross had his hand on the starter switch as Smitty cranked madly at a hand pump thrust into the twenty-gallon oil drum. The sergeant crouched several feet to one side, keeping an apprehensive eye on the field boundary. After what seemed like hours, the private replaced the oil filler cap. Ross held his breath; start, damn you, he breathed.

Three minutes later, he applied what he judged was only enough power to get the Mustang airborne, one eye on the oil pressure gauge. He glimpsed a column of horse-mounted troops as he lifted from the besieged runway. I should make a firing pass, he thought; the least I can do for those poor bastards back there. He dipped the nose and loosed a long burst of machine-gun fire. Unable to see any results, he nevertheless felt better as he nursed the patched-together ship toward home.

Chapter Twenty-one

13 September 1944
Kweilin Airfield

Lieutenant Colonel Henley paced the floor of the debriefing room with quick, angry strides. "Gross stupidity," he snarled, stopping in front of the desk. "Just when it's beginning to look like we have a chance to hold, the dumb asses strip us of our most effective weapon—the rocket ships."

Ross, along with Deardorf and Lieutenants Evans and White, slouched in uncomfortable chairs waiting for the irate ops officer to vent his wrath. All showed signs of long, consecutive days of grueling, close air support missions.

At last, Henley exhausted his extensive reservoir of profanity. "We've been ordered to reinforce the detachment at Hsinching. Twenty Bomber Command has a new boss—Major General Curtis LeMay. He's a hotshot from the Eighth Air Force. Apparently he's dead set on making headlines. He's launching a hundred-plane raid with the B-29s and has them assembled at fields around Chengtu.

"Well, the Japs are moving west. They are within range of Chengtu—hit Kwanghan yesterday. The brass are wetting their pants. The thought of losing those Superforts on the ground has thrown them into total panic. So, who gets called on to put out the fire? Why, the only outfit that stands a chance of stopping the Jap linkup."

Ross mentally raised his eyebrows. So Sprague didn't get his command—interesting. I'll bet he's livid, Ross mused with no small amount of glee. He listened more closely.

"Anyway," Henley grumbled, "Colyer, you'll take four birds with rocket tubes to Hsinching. The four slick-wings already there will fly top cover for you. You'll be detachment commander and will leave tomorrow morning. We have to send crew chiefs and a couple of armament types. They'll follow on the gooneybird that will take a load of spare parts and rockets for you. Okay, get a good night's sleep. I'll see you here at oh-four-hundred."

Ross reached across the table and covered Ruth's right hand with both of his. "You look especially desirable tonight, Captain Lasher. What say you to a visit to the ambulance? I'm sure the emergency gear needs to be inventoried again."

Ruth's eyes took on a mischievous twinkle. After the ever-smiling waiter had taken their orders for beer, she asked, "Shouldn't you be saving yourself for a weekend at Kweiyang? You're due for a stand-down, I believe."

"That's just it." Ross made a face. "There aren't going to be any more weekends at Kweiyang for a while."

Ruth's smile slipped. "Why not? What on earth has happened now?"

"I'm being sent west—to Chengtu," Ross grumbled. "The Japs seem hell-bent on taking out the B-29s."

Tears welled in Ruth's eyes. "I should know better," she lamented. "I tell myself over and over, 'live one day at a time, Lasher. Don't make plans; don't get accustomed to happiness—it won't last.'" She squeezed Ross's hands and sighed. "I'll bring a blanket," she said softly.

14 September 1944
Kweilin Airfield

Ross stumbled toward the mess hall. His sleep-fogged mind registered bustling activity. Most buildings displayed lighted windows, and vehicles dashed about at breakneck speed. He could hear the muted roar of ground crews preflighting aircraft engines on the far side of the landing strip. Had he overslept? he wondered. Regarding his watch with bleary eyes, he discovered that it was, in fact, only 0330 hours.

The mess hall was crowded, an excited babble of voices vying for supremacy with the clatter of trays and silverware and the shuffling of feet. Ross saw Colonel Henley deep in conversation with a pair of headquarters-type majors and sauntered over. "Good morning, Colonel. What's all the excitement about?"

"Oh, good morning, Colyer. Glad to catch you here. Your redeployment is canceled. Find your other three pilots and give them the word: officers' call here in the mess hall at oh-four-thirty. You'll be flying a sortie immediately afterward, so check your planes for full loads. I'll brief you at ops before you take off." The harassed ops officer hurried off to accost a just-entering NCO.

Ross, accompanied by the other three members of his flight, stumbled through the cloying, humid darkness toward the flight line. He found his Mustang and dumped his parachute, oxygen mask, and helmet into the open cockpit. Squatting beneath the wing to watch a pair of sweating armament specialists working by the dim light of two flashlights, he asked, "What the hell kind of a load is this?"

"Standard load for all birds this morning, Captain." The weary noncom paused to wipe his forehead. "We been out here since midnight, removing the drop tank and hanging frag bombs on that shackle, plus rockets and full ammo cans. I'd say you won't be going far—with just your internal tanks."

"I've heard all kinds of rumors," said Ross. "What do you hear?"

"I hear the yellow bastards are at Chuanchow and moving south. We might haul ass."

Ross snorted. "I'll believe that when I see it. Hengyang, Ling-ling—they were just small fields. But Kweilin? General Vincent's headquarters? You better believe he'll have us all in the trenches throwing rocks before he'll pull out of here." Nevertheless, Ross wore a frown as he trekked back to officers' call.

Brigadier General Casey Vincent looked haggard and old. One would hardly believe that the man was the youngest general in the Air Corps, Ross observed. The general stood on a mess table and scanned the sea of intent faces. "Guys, we've been had," he rasped. "I've never questioned my orders, and I'm a firm believer in the adage 'If you work for a man, then for Christ's sake work *for* him. If you can't, find another job.' With that in mind, I'll just say that if we'd had this glut of fuel and supplies six months ago, we wouldn't be pulling out of Kweilin tomorrow."

He waited for the sound of sharply indrawn breaths to subside, then continued. "That's right. Today will be our last mission flown from here. General Stilwell, with General Chennault's reluctant agreement, has decided that we can't hold this place. When you finish your last sortie, you will land at Chihkiang—except certain of you who will be briefed separately at takeoff.

"There will be talk that the Chinese army folded and left us unprotected. That's bullshit. They folded, all right. Worn to the dropping point, without enough to eat, without supporting artillery, and—the bitterest pill of all—without adequate close air support, they've made the Japs pay dearly for every foot of ground on their way south. General Tsu's right flank just collapsed. That division has four thousand men; they share two thousand rifles. Some may say that's 'folding.' I have a lot of other, more fitting terms.

"Let's make today a day the Japs will remember for a long time. Now, their task force is poised for their final drive, ninety miles north of here at Chuanchow. If our information is correct, the idiots are bivouacked in the Hwangshaho Pass." Vincent's smile was bleak as he observed, "I do believe they'll regret selecting that location. They're creatures of habit. They'll strike camp and assemble in marching order by first light. They have never been attacked at this juncture; ergo, it can't happen. Well, just when that pass is light enough to see a hundred yards, our entire group will be in orbit at twelve thousand feet, ten miles east behind the mountain range. I don't believe it necessary to paint the rest of this picture.

"You will fly two sorties . . . but I won't deprive Colonel Henley, your mission leader, the pleasure of assigning specific targets. Good hunting."

Ross taxied toward the far end of the runway in total darkness—the group's first-ever mission to depart before daylight. He followed Colonel Henley's dimly visible Mustang into takeoff position, using light from a dozen parked trucks to orient himself with the centerline. Behind him he could see the remainder of the group groping its way down the narrow taxiway. Each plane's crew chief sat on a wing to provide forward visibility so the pilot wouldn't have to taxi in S turns.

Henley's lead ship started its takeoff roll. Ross followed, keeping the red, portside navigational light in view. He felt, more than observed, the thundering fighter break from the ground. *Gear up, reduce power, stay tucked in,* he reminded himself. *Christ, I hope nobody augers in with vertigo.* Vincent had agreed to this nighttime departure only after Henley assured him that Ross's unpopular instrument-training classes had prepared the pilots for the tricky operation.

The lead flight leveled off at twelve thousand feet. Having extinguished their navigational lights after lift-off, Ross maintained position solely by reference to Henley's blue exhaust flame. The colonel had emphasized the horrible fate that lay in store for anyone who failed to maintain radio silence.

As the false dawn painted the eastern sky gray-pink, Ross swiveled his head. His heart surged while he counted a cluster of black dots visible against the pale background. He couldn't make an accurate count, but most of his fledgling instrument pilots had made it. He focused on Henley's ship and waited for the hand signal. The faint lines of the mountain range had grown more easily discernible.

Ross saw the helmeted figure to his right raise a clenched fist, then drop it. Simultaneously, the first rays of sunlight winked off his canopy as he rolled into a vertical, diving turn. The first two flights were supposed to hit the south end of the pass. The next two would attack the north end. Para-frags would hurl their deadly hail of steel into troop formations massed for marching. With both ends of the pass blocked, the process of decimating the trapped army would commence. We're going to look awfully damn stupid if that pass is empty, he decided.

As Ross held a forty-five-degree dive, his airspeed edged past the 400-MPH mark. The altimeter unwound with startling swiftness. Even with the throttle retarded, the huge Rolls-Royce engine bellowed in protest. He double-checked to see that the manual bomb release was within reach of his left hand and widened the interval between him and Henley. It was time to search for a target.

Vincent's intelligence report was dead on. Black forms milled below like ants emerging from their hill. Okay, level slightly, slow down—the tiny para-frag bombs have chutes attached to slow their descent and ensure that they detonate *above* the target. Ross did a double take. My God, those are *horses*—not several, but literally hundreds, he thought in amazement. No wonder the Japs made so much progress in this primitive land. While we were pounding rail, truck, and water traffic, they could stay on remote trails and move at night without fear of detection.

He tugged the bomb release cable and felt his clustered para-frags drop clear. He saw Henley, slightly ahead and to his left, do likewise. Both immediately broke up and hard right; Blue Charlie Flight, assigned the valley's north end, would be approaching head on.

Dust and smoke soon made it difficult to select specific targets. Ross expended his rockets, seeing covered cargoes of ammo on horse-drawn carts and wagons explode with fiery, death-dealing destruction of its own. Then it was just a matter of dropping into trail behind another plane and blindly raking the chaotic scene with .50-caliber fire.

By the time Henley broke radio silence to announce that it was rally time, Ross was mildly sick to his stomach. The carnage below defied description. Entering initial approach for landing at Kweilin, he was shocked to discover that the savage attack had lasted a mere one hour and ten minutes from takeoff to landing.

Colonel Henley, coffee cup in hand and grinning from ear to ear, yelled, "At ease! Listen up, now. You've had your warmup, and a damn fine show it was. Estimates run from several hundred to a few thousand troops, not to mention the weapons, that no longer pose a threat. Now for the encore.

"We're standing by for a one-ball alert. With every tenth person in the city a Jap spy, we sent a few troops into town last night to spread the word that we were out of gas and couldn't get a mission in the air. We're betting that the Jap air force bases at Hong Kong and Canton won't be able to resist an all-out effort. This could be the biggest damn ambush since Custer at the Little Bighorn.

"Stand by in your cockpits. As soon as the ball goes up, take off and rendezvous at twenty-five thousand, twenty miles east. I want everyone to maintain strict radio silence. Sit up there until you hear General Vincent give the word."

The two dozen pilots resumed elated accounts of the just-completed mission. Henley read off names of former 41st Squadron members and waved them into the debriefing room. His demeanor grew somber. "You boys won't be going to Chihkiang," he said. "I'm afraid this is a parting of the ways. The 41st is being restored to active status and reassigned to Hsinching. Captain Colyer will be acting commander.

"The message is clear, I'm afraid. East China is being written off the books. We'll hang tough and fight a rear guard action, but with no idea of stopping the yellow bastards. This morning's work notwithstanding, there's nothing between them and Canton but a handful of poorly armed, exhausted Chinese troops. We can't do it all from the air.

"If there's action later this morning, land here. We'll destroy the base tomorrow morning after you take off. One thing is for certain, the Superforts are our last chance to hit the Japs where it hurts most. See that they get that chance." The usually ebullient ops officer turned and walked away, flat-footed, his shoulders sagging like those of an old man.

Ross accepted the pilots' shyly proffered congratulations and handshakes with an offhand, "No big deal, guys. You heard him say 'acting.' No way are all those headquarters-type majors going to sit back and let a company-grade officer have a squadron. Major King is at Chengtu, remember? He'd be the smart money bet for the job." The pilots sobered and trooped wordlessly toward the parked airplanes.

By ten o'clock Ross had decided that the wily Japs weren't going to take the bait. A shame, he mused, after the Chinese soldiers had set dummy airplanes made of straw and bamboo in highly visible locations. It was ironic, too, that there was no reason to repel the expected attack. What existed after today must be destroyed tomorrow morning. More than five hundred buildings, he'd heard at breakfast. Okay, so let the enemy destroy what they would have to restore.

About to call out to Deardorf, slumped against a landing gear in the shade of the plane's wing, he saw the familiar red ball start its ascent. "Okay, everybody," he yelled. "*Jing-bow.* Get your asses in the air. We're getting company."

Ross led the twenty-one Mustangs in a wide circle above clumps of puffy cumulus. The field at Kweilin sprawled in the building heat with no visible movement. By straining, he could make out the dummy fighters scattered among the parking hardstands. To an approaching bomber pilot, they would be the equivalent of a kid finding the door to the toy store unlocked.

His headset crackled, and he jerked to attention. Who the hell was breaking radio silence? He listened in disbelief; the exchange was in *Japanese.* The tone was lighthearted; a snatch of laughter was unmistakable. The arrogant bastards, he raged. They must believe they're on a holiday—using *our* frequency, for Christ's sake. He searched the horizon until his eyeballs burned from the strain. C'mon, he pleaded. Let's get on with it.

At first he thought his eyes were playing tricks on him. But, no, the black dots above the horizon formed a definite pattern. They didn't dissolve after close examination. He spotted another group beneath and to the left of the first. He turned and made a pointing motion to Evans, his wingman. The redhead nodded and pointed north. Ross blinked. *Two* groups—one coming north from Kai-tak and White Cloud, the other approaching on a southerly course, probably from repaired runways at Ling-ling and Hengyang. It was without a doubt the largest armada the Japs had launched in months. They must have put everything in the air that would fly, he conjectured.

The indistinct dots acquired distinguishable shape. He counted by tens and twelves—good God, there must be eighty or ninety! Now the two streams were joining and forming for battle. Larger planes, Bettys and Lilys, were breaking into a huge racetrack pattern that Ross guessed to be at about eight thousand feet. Somewhat lower, forty or fifty planes, which he identified as Val-type dive-bombers, headed directly for the field in echeloned elements. Four-ship vees of Zeroes and Oscars scissored above the others at sixteen thousand or thereabouts.

Their attack pattern became clear. The dive-bombers would lead, destroying antiaircraft defenses and catching any fighter defense on the ground. The heavy bombers would follow, with the fighters flying top cover throughout. Well planned, Ross admitted. Except, you dumb fucks, you've never looked into the sun.

When to hit them? he wondered. The heavies would be sitting ducks while the dive-bombers were doing their job. The time to hit dive-bombers was during their dive. Get the fighter cover between you and the bombers, then zip through their formation shooting at anything in front of you. Disrupt the fighter formation, make two passes at the bombers, and get the hell out.

Which strategy would Vincent use? Ross wondered. After double-checking his gun switches, he waited. His pulse raced. He saw the Vals tip over and start their run. Now, he urged. Let's go. The only thing he heard in his headset was the occasional festive-sounding comments of the marauding Jap pilots. The first wave released their bombs and streaked skyward, leaving behind red-centered eruptions of dirt and buildings.

Ross realized that his fascination with the attack had resulted in an unconscious descent. He quickly led his formation back to its original orbit.

The second wave created added havoc. All of the dummy fighters were ablaze, aided by cans of gasoline planted inside by the Chinese. Ross had to admit they looked real. He chafed with impatience as the heavy bombers dumped tons of high explosives on the living quarters and operations complex. Damnit, General, he thought anxiously, they're gonna haul ass any time now. Let's *go.*

The attackers, caught up in a feeding frenzy of unopposed destruction, made strafing run after strafing run. The top cover could stand it no longer and swooped down to add their guns to the hellish game.

Ross began to worry. Radio silence was necessary, but what if the general's radio had failed? What if one of the fragmentation bombs had found the cave sheltering the headquarters? For that matter, how safe were the ground personnel awaiting evacuation? Ruth and the medical staff caused special concern. He fingered the mike button on his throttle. I'll wait until I see the first one head away from the target, he decided. Then, orders or no orders, I'm going after them.

Ross spotted two of the heavies forming on the wing of another. He tensed. This was it. They were heading out. His thumb was on the mike button when he heard Vincent shout, "Now, Tigers! Nail their asses."

Ross flipped into a diving turn. A glance backward showed the others following suit. A stream of two-ship elements streaked toward the gaggle of fighters, now obligingly re-forming into a tightly knit formation. Choosing individual targets, firing short bursts only when a meatball-adorned plane filled the gunsight, the Mustangs slashed through the astonished, still-disorganized enemy like starving piranhas.

Ross saw two Zeroes disintegrate as his tracers impacted squarely in their cockpit areas. From the corner of his eye, he saw Evans send one tumbling earthward trailing flames and smoke. Then he was in the midst of the stream of dive-bombers. Again, surprise was total. None made the slightest move to evade the deadly hail that his four .50 calibers spat in carefully aimed bursts.

Seconds later, a certain and a probable Val to his credit, Ross eyed the tempting fat targets presented by the heavy bombers. Reluctantly, he ignored them and entered a three-g Immelmann turn into the sun, clawing to regain altitude. The scattered Zeroes and Oscars must not be allowed to recover their wits.

"Charlie Baker and Charlie Dog Flights, take the bombers," he rapped. But the Zeroes had reacted faster than he'd anticipated. He watched them dash south without making any attempt to re-form. Pursuit was out of the question, he observed disgustedly. But taking time to survey the scene, he counted twenty flaming wrecks dotting the hilly terrain, and that was just within his immediate view. In the distance, he saw a dozen Mustangs swirling amongst double their number of slower dive-bombers. Dazed by the swiftness and totality of their victory, Ross led the unengaged elements toward the field. Had the ferocious attack left enough runway intact to recover the mission?

He flew over the field at five hundred feet and surveyed the damage: only one bomb crater at the runway's far end. He chuckled and swung around to enter an initial approach. The bloodthirsty bomber pilots had expended their cargo on buildings and the dummy planes—things that Vincent would burn or blow up.

The devastation was sobering. With a faintly sick feeling in the pit of his stomach, Ross regarded the smoldering heap that had been the tower and operations building only an hour before. The hostels were still burning. He heard the crackling pops of stored ammo cooking off. The smell of petroleum-fed fires and burning wood made breathing a gasping effort. The conflagration made the day even hotter than usual. He breathed a sigh of relief as he saw more and more people emerge from the shelter of caves.

The ships of the 41st came straggling in. Seven, eight—two still in formation made ten. He scanned the empty sky. Had they lost any? Had the others diverted to Chihkiang without losing a single plane? Incredible. Even if they had lost one or two, the mission would undoubtedly go down in the books as the biggest victory of the war. They would probably never get an accurate count, but forty to fifty destroyed seemed a conservative estimate.

A voice spoke from behind him. "The miserable sonsabitches. I wish you could have killed every single one of 'em." General Vincent, his face twisted in a bitter scowl, stepped alongside Ross. "I suppose I should take the view that they saved us a lot of miserable, heartbreaking work—destroying our own base. But I find damn little to feel good about. Your boys did a magnificent job, by the way. That bunch will be a long time licking their wounds."

"How about our own casualties?" Ross asked, his voice tinged with anxiety.

"No accurate head count yet, but as far as I know, everybody is hale and hearty. Including the nurses," he added dryly.

Ross grinned. "Thank you, sir. I was sweating it out up there. You don't know how hard it was to sit back and watch. I was beginning to think you'd been hit—weren't going to give us the word."

"I *do* know how difficult it was," Vincent said, surveying the burning buildings around them. "Now do you understand *why* I waited until the last minute?"

"I figured it out as I was on initial approach," Ross said with a rueful smile. "Fuel. Both groups were a long way from home. After they finished working over the field, they didn't have enough fuel left to engage and still get back."

Vincent's smile was bleak but pleased. "Exactly—a trick I learned from General Chennault." He slapped Ross's shoulder. "C'mon, we have work to do. I see that the Chinese are already filling in that crater. As soon as they finish, a pair of gooneybirds and my B-25 will arrive from Kunming. We have to load them tonight and lay charges to blow anything our slant-eyed friends left standing."

Ross hurried across the rubble-strewn, still-smoking airstrip toward the remaining structures built inside the caves. He was close to trotting as he approached the hospital. A dozen dazed medics milled just outside the door, faces slack and eyes blank. "Any casualties?" Ross blurted.

"I—we don't know, I guess," a dull voice replied.

"Has anyone seen Captain Lasher?"

"Uh, yeah. I saw her packing some stuff—second door on your right."

Ross's knees almost gave way as he saw Ruth, stooping over a crate, arranging medical supplies. She turned and rushed into his open arms. "Oh, Ross. Oh, my God. You're safe. I can't ever remember being so damn scared—for you, and for myself. It was awful. My ears are still ringing. It just went on and on. The building shook, windows shattered, dust and smoke were everywhere; I almost ran outside just to be able to breathe." She buried her head against his shoulder.

"It's okay, gal. Everything's okay," Ross reassured her, patting her shoulder. "There'll be a gooneybird in here shortly. You'll load tonight and take off for Chihkiang tomorrow morning."

"All except me." Ruth stepped back and regarded Ross with an enigmatic grin.

"Except you?" Ross frowned. "What do you plan to do?"

"Fourteenth Air Force ordered one doctor and one nurse to go to Chengtu to augment the dispensary there. I volunteered."

Ross's face was a study in delight mixed with apprehension. "You *what?* You *volunteered?* That place is apt to be the next one fighting for its life. You'd be a helluva lot safer at Chihkiang."

"I'll give you three guesses why I'm willing to take the risk," Ruth purred.

Ross grinned in spite of himself. He grabbed Ruth and squeezed until she yelped, "Hey, you're breaking my ribs. Save the rough stuff until tonight. I've cleaned out a room that still has a bed."

20 September 1944
Chungking

Elliott Sprague halted his restless pacing and glared at the immaculately manicured garden, ignoring its serene beauty. A white-jacketed houseboy approached and bowed. "Madame Chiang will join you quite soon, General," he advised.

"Good. Thank you," Sprague growled. "Do you have any Scotch in this house?"

"No, sir. The generalissimo does not serve alcoholic beverages in his personal residence. Tea, perhaps?"

"Okay, okay. Make it tea then." The stocky, uniformed officer resumed his pacing. Damn woman, he muttered to himself. She didn't come through. Wish I could tell her what I really think of this musical comedy setup. She, Clint Wolfenbarger, Senator Templeton—I've put my neck on the line, and they didn't deliver. He paused as the slim, elegantly gowned figure of Madame Chiang glided through the door.

He bowed. "Madame, so kind of you to see me on such short notice. I apologize."

"I'm always pleased to see you, General—any of our American friends, of course. My secretary said you have something of an urgent nature to discuss."

"Perhaps urgent isn't precisely correct," Sprague responded. "Distressing would be more apt."

"Oh? And how may I help?"

"Madame, General Curtis LeMay was appointed to command Twenty Bomber Command. I had been—er—led to believe that *I* would remain in that capacity. I wondered if you could perhaps enlighten me as to why I was replaced."

Madame Chiang arched her finely penciled black eyebrows. "*I,* General

Sprague? Assignment of senior American military officers is hardly a matter upon which *I* would be consulted." She uttered a small, tinkling laugh.

"Then I was misled," Sprague replied harshly. "It was my belief that you did, on occasion, render advice on matters that concerned the defense of your country."

"Only on most infrequent occasions." She waved a delicate hand in airy denial. "And even then, only in most general terms. Nothing as specific as, say, military personnel matters. And seldom are my suggestions acted on. The matter of lend-lease items our poor country needs so badly—they are still holding them in India for some inexplicable reason." She favored Sprague with a saccharine-sweet smile.

"Quid pro quo, eh?" Sprague barked a short laugh. "Had I been in a position to influence lend-lease allocations, perhaps I could have lived up to *my* previous offer."

"Perhaps, General." Madame Chiang's affable manner grew chilly. "Then again, perhaps not. Almost certainly not, I believe. It is said in certain places that you have, ah, Machiavellian qualities that create a degree of mistrust in your stated motives."

Sprague grew beet red. "I beg your pardon?" he said through stiff lips. "May I ask *what* 'certain places'?"

"Places that count, General. A rumor that you perhaps misstated General Wolfe's—shall we say, state of health?—was poorly viewed. An entirely baseless rumor, I'm sure. I must ask you to excuse me now. I have a prior appointment. Please, make yourself comfortable. Finish your tea; smoke a cigar if you like. Good day, General."

Chapter Twenty-two

16 October 1944
Hsinching Airfield

Ross stood at parade rest, his jaw set in stubborn lines. General Sprague lounged behind his ornately carved teakwood desk and regarded the 41st Squadron's acting commander with an icy glare. "Major King is assigned to my headquarters as fighter liaison, Colyer. Regardless of what you *think* your mission is, Major King will exercise operational control. Fuel is scarce, and I don't want to see a drop wasted, is that clear?"

"I'm sorry, sir," Ross replied in clipped tones. "Headquarters Fourteenth Air Force issued my movement orders, and those orders designate *me* as squadron commander. My mission statement charges me with providing air defense for the airfields used by Twenty Bomber Command. I will respond to all requests falling into that category. Anything else, such as escort duty for the VHBs, must originate with General Chennault."

Sprague resembled a stalking wolf as he leaned forward and grated, "That will be taken care of, I assure you. My staff is at this moment drafting a radio message to General Chennault that clarifies your mission, and at the same time recommends that Major King replace you as commander. If you cooperate, I may suggest to Major King that he assign you as operations officer. But we are launching one hundred B-29s tomorrow morning across territory contested by an estimated four hundred Jap Zeroes. I demand fighter protection."

Major King was seated in a side chair, a smirk on his pinched features. "Ross, if even *one* B-29 is lost to enemy fighters, I'll happily testify at your court-martial for insubordination."

"I'm *not* being insubordinate, Major," Ross replied with weary resignation. "No one has given me a lawful order. Furthermore, the intelligence brief I received states that fewer than *forty,* not four hundred, Zero and Oscar fighters are in the Hankow area—our fighters' extreme operational radius.

"Half of my P-51s are equipped with rocket-launching tubes that render them unsuitable for an interceptor role. Your B-29s are in far greater danger of being destroyed on the ground by artillery and enemy bombers than they are of being shot down. My brief clearly assigns first priority to destruction of rail transportation. Both the Japanese land armies and their advance airfields depend on that rail link back to Peking and Hankow." Ross paused and turned back to face Sprague.

"So you see, sir, until Fourteenth Air Force changes my orders, I must insist on scheduling sorties against rail facilities. I might add that we have destroyed twenty-two locomotives on ten sorties this week."

"Who besides your own pilots can verify that, Colyer?" King sneered.

"Why don't you go ask the Japs, Major," Ross snapped.

"All right, you two, knock it off," said Sprague, sounding exasperated. "Major King, will you leave us for a few minutes? I have a private matter to take up with Captain Colyer."

Sprague stripped cellophane from a cigar, frowning in deep thought as a chagrined Major King strode from the office. The general didn't light the cigar, but used it instead as a pointer to aim Ross to the vacated side chair. "Colyer," he asked pleasantly, "do you stay awake nights thinking up new ways to defy me? I sometimes wonder if we're fighting the same war."

"No, sir," said Ross in clipped tones. "But surely you can see my point. What would *you* say if General Chennault ordered your crews to bomb, say, Hankow instead of Japan?"

Sprague lit the cigar and puffed until it was burning evenly. "You should have been in the judge advocate's office, Colyer," he said with a sigh. "You pick winners to back. Claire Chennault is hot merchandise just now. I'm just another old has-been, fired for trying to do my job. I guess I can't blame you for choosing his side over mine.

"General Stilwell, the fancy-dan crowd in the War Department, the generalissimo, yes, even Chennault," Sprague continued. "I stepped on too many toes trying to save China. Old K.B. did a number on me when he returned to Washington. Because he couldn't meet Arnold's schedule, he blamed me. Stilwell got mad when I went over his head to get the supplies I needed to hit the Jap home islands in force, and he gave Chiang a load of crap; everyone knows that the Chiangs are tight with President Roosevelt." Sprague slumped, chin on chest, his face appearing older and furrowed with care.

Ross frowned. "Sir, believe me, there's nothing personal in my objections. Despite the intelligence estimate you have, I *know* there aren't more than the forty or so Jap fighters between here and Hankow. Damnit, sir, I've been there."

Sprague's smile was tinged with sadness. "I don't doubt your figures, Ross. Actually, the four hundred estimate is King's. But a fighter escort will buck up the bomber crews immensely—remember Germany? More than you know is riding on tomorrow's mission. It's my last one. LeMay is watching me like a hungry tomcat. If I can put a hundred planes over the target, inflict heavy damage, and all without losing a plane, I have a shot at getting a wing in the Pacific. I'm down, just now, but sure as hell not out. I can redeem my reputation in a combat outfit, but never in hell in someplace like Training Command headquarters.

"You can play a big part. In addition to making a show of force for the crews, you can relay weather conditions, the general appearance of the formation, and such to me in the lead ship. I trust your judgment, Ross. It will be like old times again—just like when we pulled the Ploesti mission out of the fire."

Ross felt blood suffuse his neck. Then his anger turned to amused contempt. Why, you goddamn old fraud, he thought. You went too far when you threw in the "old times" line. You know Chennault will never authorize an escort mission, so you tried to bluff me. When that didn't work, you decided to soft-soap me into violating orders.

Ross stood. "General, as much as I would like to help you for old times' sake, I have my orders. Now, if you will excuse me, I have a crew briefing to give."

Sprague didn't return Ross's salute. His face a furious white mask, his clamped jaws nearly biting completely through the cigar, he snarled, "Someday, Colyer, that arrogant disregard for authority will be your undoing. I hope to be around to help the process."

1620 Hours, 17 October 1944
Pingchang, China

Yusaki crouched in a corner of the dripping tent that housed the squadron's combined command-operations center. He scooped rice from his mess tin into his mouth and listened to the all-important radio set—their sole contact with headquarters. Senior Lieutenant Subachi stood, hands clasped behind his back, peering into the late afternoon gloom, intensified by a fine mist of rain.

"The raid was on coke production facilities at Anshan, Honorable Lieutenant," the radio operator droned. "More than a hundred of the big Superfortresses were counted. All of Kyushu was cloud covered, but they bombed anyway. Most bombs fell away from the important targets, but one complex of ovens was destroyed and two were slightly damaged. Four enemy bombers were downed by antiaircraft fire and one by fighter attack."

Yusaki's head snapped up. "Only *one* downed by our fighters? Where were our home defense squadrons?" he asked.

Subachi spoke over his shoulder. "Scattered in rice paddies between here and Hankow, I fear. Most of our replacements during these past weeks have come from those squadrons. One group based near Tokyo remains to defend the emperor's palace."

"The bombers will return to their bases around Chengtu," Yusaki mused. "They will be weary but flushed with victory. Now, tonight, is the time to strike. Tomorrow, they will be gone, back to their lairs in India."

"Strike? With what, Yusaki?" Subachi inquired morosely. "Observe the weather. The few bombers we still have operational could never penetrate it."

Yusaki set his mess tin aside, his weary features contorted by a furious scowl. "Remember Hengyang, Lieutenant?" he asked. "The weather over Chengtu is reported to be much better. I can surprise them and be gone before they know it—just like before."

"No, Yusaki. You are the sole remaining veteran I have. Tomorrow, our bombers will return to Chengtu. Perhaps they will be more successful then."

"They won't and you know it, Lieutenant," Yusaki barked, then caught himself. "A thousand pardons for my outburst, Honorable Sir," he added quickly. "But they have more Mustangs now; they will cut the bomber formations to ribbons. Also, the Superfortresses will be gone by that time."

"Have patience, Yusaki. The army advances daily toward the bases. Soon they will be close enough to use their artillery."

"In the meantime the Americans will continue to bomb our homes, our families. We cannot allow that to go unopposed. One mission, Lieutenant, I beg of you."

2000 Hours, 17 October 1944
Hsinching Airfield

Ross leaned against the operations shack's ready room door and surveyed the bustle of activity. Seventeen B-29s squatted on the parking ramp, covered with swarming ground crews. Adding four thousand gallons of av-gas by hand to the thirsty birds from fifty-five-gallon drums would take most of the night. He could count only a dozen engines with cowlings still in place. Even with this frantic activity, he guessed that less than twelve would make the scheduled 0700 takeoff for India.

Twenty-four of the huge aircraft had occupied the same space only hours earlier. He shook his head in disbelief. They held the mission debriefing behind closed, guarded doors, but the news spread like melted butter. Five B-29s had been lost to enemy action; *twenty* were down someplace, either at one of the few fields still under Chinese control or in some rice paddy—burning, shattered hulks. Engine fires, fuel exhaustion—the list of contributing causes went on and on.

Walt Deardorf strolled toward him. Turning to watch the center of activity, he drawled, "Did you hear the strike report?"

"I did," Ross answered. "Eleven ships hit the primary. Forty dropped on targets of opportunity. The others? Most of them had mechanical problems and salvoed their loads on the way to the target."

The ear-numbing roar of four Wright R-3350s interrupted their conversation. The squeal of tortured tires contacting the stone runway announced touchdown of another of the huge craft. Ross could make out the words ESSO EXPRESS by the glow of the plane's taxi lights as it rumbled past. "Unbelievable," he said to Deardorf. "If he had good weather over the mountains and a tail wind, he'll off-load four of the nine thousand gallons he left Kharagpur with.

"Would you believe they have a hundred and fifty of those things? Bombers—combat airplanes—stripped and converted to flying tankers.

It takes that many to keep a hundred mission-capable birds on the ready line. This is insane."

"Well," Walt observed cheerfully, "at least we're getting our share. It's better than sitting on our ass at Hengyang and Kweilin measuring gas by the cupful."

Ross's response was cut short by the arrival of a dapper Chinese officer. "Good evening, Captain Li-jen," he called. "Are you out checking up on your boys?"

"Ah, good evening, sirs." The captain's round face broke into a smile; his black eyes twinkled with innate good humor. He preened his pencil-thin mustache. "Yes, we must be most vigilant tonight. So many airplanes on the field make it a tempting target for the Japanese."

"Yeah, the weather is favorable, too," Ross said as he scanned skies illuminated by a half moon playing tag with a handful of puffy cumulus. "By the way, Walt, do you know Captain Li-jen? He's commander of the antiaircraft brigade. Li, meet Lieutenant Deardorf."

The pair exchanged greetings, then Li-jen made his departure; he would get little sleep the rest of the night, Ross guessed.

"Well, I'm turning in early," said Ross. "I want to be on hand to see this bunch take off in the morning. Your birds all in commission? You should have a good day weatherwise."

"Yes, and yes," Deardorf replied. "Those rockets do make great locomotive killers. The Japs could patch fifty-caliber holes overnight. But a solid hit from a five-inch rocket, and it don't go no farther. Those engineers are catching on. They see an airplane, and they uncouple from the train, then go balls out for shelter. I think I'll hit the sack as well—try to get airborne before that gaggle clogs the place up in the morning."

Major King's pen raced across the paper, forming a scathing indictment of Ross's conduct. Chennault couldn't ignore it. Colyer was an arrogant bastard—he'd answer for today's B-29 fiasco. A fighter escort would have halved the day's losses. King knew he could count on General Sprague to back him up. Muttering to himself, King was oblivious to the presence of the stocky, flight suit–clad man who walked through the war room's open doorway.

"Is this Twenty Bomber Command's so-called war room?" a harsh voice rasped.

"Yeah," King replied without looking up, annoyed at the interruption.

"*Yeah?*" bellowed the intruder. "Major, I don't know where the hell you went to officers' training, but all the courses I know of tell you to stand and address senior officers as 'Sir.'"

King threw a startled glance at the bulky figure, only partially visible by the single kerosene lantern's feeble illumination. There was, however, enough light to identify the two silver stars pinned to the man's collar. King twanged to attention. "Sorry, *sir.* I—I didn't expect to see a general officer here, not this evening."

"Obviously. Do you know who I am?"

King strained to make out the man's features as he stammered a weak, "N-no, sir. I'm sorry, I don't believe we've met."

"Does the name LeMay mean anything to you?"

King felt icy fingers clutch his gut. "Yes, sir. Of course, sir. What can I do for the general?"

"You can start by telling me who you are and what it is you do around here," XX Bomber Command's commander growled around a dead, half-smoked cigar.

"Major King, sir. Fourteenth Air Force fighter liaison to General Sprague's headquarters. I—I don't believe General Sprague was expecting you, sir, or I'm sure someone would have met you. Did you come in on the Esso Express?"

"Fighter *what?*"

"Liaison, sir. General Chennault assigned me here to coordinate air defense for the bomber bases and fighter escort."

"Jesus H. Christ," LeMay said disgustedly. "Claire must have more men than he needs if he can spare field-grade officers for boondoggles. Yes, I was on the Express, and I'm not in the habit of advertising my visits. Now, can you tell me what went wrong today?"

King's eyes gleamed. "Well for one thing, sir, General Sprague didn't have the fighter escort he requested. The fighter OIC, Captain Colyer, refused to provide it. I was in the act of writing a message to General Chennault apprising him of Colyer's insubordination when you came in, sir."

"That's bullshit, Major. Fighters had nothing to do with today's sideshow. You obviously don't know fuck-all about what's going on. Maybe you *can* manage to run down Sprague, however. Tell him I'm here, and also tell him I want to talk to all of today's aircraft commanders—the ones who managed to find their way home, anyway.

"Yes, *sir!*" King hoped his relief in being dismissed didn't show.

"Oh, and Major . . ."

King turned to see LeMay peering at the desk the major had been using.

"Is this your desk?"

"Yes, sir."

"Maybe you'd better start cleaning it out. I have no need for deadwood. I'll send a message to General Chennault from the plane when I leave." LeMay paused to relight his cigar, then added, "Something just occurred to me. We've been raising hell to get a POL officer up here. Since you're already in place, maybe you can fill the bill. I'll suggest it to Claire—I'm sure he'll see it my way. Now, stop standing there with your mouth hanging open and get moving."

King reeled outside, almost colliding head on with a wide-eyed lieutenant colonel pounding toward the mud-brick, thatch-roofed war room.

Ross woke to the sound of the alert gong's reverberations and the muffled *pom-pom-pom* of 37mm antiaircraft fire. He sprang from his cot, shaking sleep-induced fog from his mind. What the hell? He peered at his watch. Ten-thirty—he'd barely gone to bed. The halting chatter of 20mm cannon joined the drumroll of gunfire. Air raid! He raced to the door and peered in the direction of the runway. He saw lights surrounding the parked B-29s winking off. Black forms scampered for cover.

He jerked on a pair of trousers and jammed bare feet into his boots. Goddamn! He found himself thinking more of the safety of his parked Mustangs than the Superforts. The howl of a radial engine at top revs ripped the darkness as he pounded down the hostel steps. He halted abruptly. You stupid ass, he told himself, where the hell are you going? Take cover. He threw himself onto the porch beneath the entry overhang.

He wasn't a moment too soon. A single-engine plane, dark against the moonlit sky and spitting blue exhaust flame, streaked overhead. As it passed from view, it loosed a small black object. Ross covered his head and waited.

The explosion, when it came, sounded less alarming than he'd expected—a muffled *thwump.* The sonofabitch, Ross raged inwardly; he's bombed the building complex first, and now he'll come back to rake the parked airplanes with cannon fire. Their polished aluminum skins make them impossible to miss. Ross heard the firing from the antiaircraft batteries increase in tempo. Sure enough, there the bastard came.

Adjacent buildings were silhouetted starkly against an angry red glow. To hell with it, Ross fumed, he's after the planes. He scrambled down the steps and raced toward the fire. Rounding the nearest building, he saw that the farthest hostel was engulfed. Orange, soot-tipped flames licked from a gaping hole in the roof. As he watched, two windows on the second floor exploded outward, raining shards of glass and fiery debris. A dozen shouting figures pounded toward the conflagration. Ross raced to join them.

He halted in front of the main entrance; searing heat reminded him that he'd forgotten to put on a shirt. While he hesitated, others bypassed him and raced into the burning building. "Get some water, ferchrissake," someone shouted. A jumble of excited voices added to the din. "Bring gas masks, flashlights—the place is full of smoke." "Hurry, the damn roof looks like it's going to fall in!" "Blankets—get some wet blankets." Then, "This is where the B-29 crews are bedded down."

That was enough. Ross dashed inside the building, oblivious to the flying sparks and choking smoke. Rushing through an open doorway, he grabbed the blankets from two empty cots and wrapped one around himself Indian fashion. He stopped on his way out of the room to let a shouting group of skivvy-clad men stumble down the hallway toward the clear night air. An indistinct figure, going in, crowded past them. He recognized Ruth, a wet towel covering her head and tucked into the neck of her fatigues.

Ross grabbed her arm. "Ruth," he yelled, "get the hell out of here."

The hard-faced nurse turned. "Ross! Oh, my God, what a nightmare." Tears formed little, sooty rivulets down her cheeks.

"Get out, woman, while you can. The whole place is about to collapse."

"There are men trapped upstairs, Ross. I can't just let them die." She stripped his hand from her arm and ran toward the stairs.

Ross's yells went unheeded. He stumbled after her through the press of fleeing, half-naked bodies. Upon reaching the second floor, he dropped to his hands and knees, gasping the relatively clear air. Ruth crouched alongside an inert body. She removed the wet towel from her face long enough to croak, "He's alive. Overcome by smoke. Get him out. There're others farther back."

Before he could protest, Ruth disappeared into the smoky inferno. Ross grabbed the unconscious man by the armpits and dragged him down the stairs. Dumping the victim unceremoniously outside the front door, Ross wheeled, intent upon returning to where he'd last seen Ruth. He had one foot on the lower step when a splintering crash from above caused him to freeze in midstride. The roof members, weakened by fire, could no longer support their sheath of heavy clay tiles. The entire second floor became a mass of sparks, flame, and smoldering timbers.

"*No!*" Ross became a wild man—shrieking and tearing away restraining hands. "No, I have to go after her. I can find her. She's going to be all right!" His last memory was of rough hands dragging him outside. Blessed oblivion descended like a gray mist.

Ross swam toward full awareness as if emerging from a sea of hot molasses. Some indefinable urge drove him to sit erect. He ignored lancing pain in his back and chest, and pawed at his eyes—everything was a reddish blur. Why am I wearing these mittens? he wondered vaguely. Cool, gentle hands pushed him back to a supine position. "Now, now, Captain. You're all right. Just relax."

He forced himself to focus on the source of the soothing voice. A Chinese nurse hovered over him. A nurse. Ruth! Memory flooded back. He struggled to sit. "Ruth," he rasped, "where is she? Is she all right?"

"Now, Captain," the voice grew firm, "you must rest. Lie back." The smooth brown face came into sharper focus. He could see tears forming in the almond-shaped eyes.

"She didn't make it, did she?" Ross asked dully.

"No, she was trapped when the roof fell in," the nurse replied in husky tones. "There was nothing you or anyone else could have done to save her."

"I see." Ross slumped to his pillow, powerless to do or say more. Dimly he recognized a hunk of aluminum hanging on the opposite wall. A red ball identified it as a piece of wreckage from a Jap fighter. He'd salvaged it at Hengyang. At least I'm in my own room, he realized, not the hospital.

The nurse seemed to read his thoughts. "All of the hospital beds are filled with more seriously wounded, Captain. I must return there when you feel you can care for yourself. You have burns, but they're not serious. You inhaled a lot of smoke, so your throat and chest will give you some discomfort. I'm leaving you a bottle of water; drink as much as you can. I'll check in on you later. All right?"

Ross nodded and closed his eyes. "What time is it?" he asked.

"Eleven-fifteen," the young woman answered. "A mess attendant will bring you lunch."

Ross forced himself to eat the thin soup and hunks of hard bread. He'd need all the strength he could muster to carry out his plans. He pinned the nervous Chinese boy who had brought him lunch with a harsh look. "Do you know Captain Deardorf, the fighter pilot?"

The startled youth nodded unconvincingly.

"Even if you don't know him, find him," Ross ordered sternly. "Tell him I must see him, chop-chop. Understand?"

The nod was more positive this time, and the boy scuttled from the room. Ross forced himself to stand. The room ceased spinning, and he took a few tentative steps. Not as bad as he'd feared—weak, but the pain was bearable. He paced the length of the room four times before returning to the bed to rest.

Ross was sitting, examining red, swollen hands, when Cal Evans poked his head inside. "Hi," he called tentatively. "Good to see you up and around. You had a near miss. The kid said you wanted to see Walt. He's airborne. Anything I can do?"

"Yeah," Ross replied in a hoarse whisper. "Come in and have a seat. Then bring me up to date."

"Sure." Evans regarded his CO with that wary look that healthy people acquire when they are around the sick. He sat on the edge of the room's only chair and cleared his throat. "Look, Skipper—about Ruth . . ." Ross nodded. "Uh—we—the guys, well . . ."

"I know, Evans, thanks. Now tell me what's going on. You say Walt's airborne? Did the bastard get any of our birds?"

"No, he stuck to the '29s. Burned two of them and disabled one more. Walt took off late, after nine o'clock, but we put up eleven ships. Five bombers left shortly before that. They lost some members of two crews in the fire. Everything else is getting back to normal."

"I see." Ross got to his feet and paced the room with increasing confidence and vigor. "Cal, would you find Captain Li-jen and the master sergeant who runs the weather detachment? I think his name is Aikens—Adkins—something like that. Have them meet me at fighter ops in a half hour, okay?"

1600 Hours, 18 October 1944
Hsinching Airfield

Captain Deardorf and Lieutenant Evans wore angry scowls as they faced Ross. The atmosphere in the ops briefing room crackled with tension. Captain Li-jen and Sergeant Adkins maintained an uneasy silence as they observed from across the room.

"Damnit, Ross, you can't do this," Deardorf exploded. "It's crazy. You're doped to the eyes with painkillers. You'll be damn lucky just to get off the ground without killing yourself. You aren't going. I can try it, Evans can try it, but you, by God, are staying on the ground—if I have to hog-tie you."

"My goodness," Ross observed with deceptive mildness, "maybe I *am* doped up. For sure, I'd have sworn that *I* was the one who gave the orders around here."

"That's bullshit, Ross," said Walt. "Don't give me that commanding officer–subordinate crap. This goes deeper than that. You saved my ass once, remember? Now, it's my turn. You want to charge me with insubordination? Okay, have at it, but you may have to add an assault charge on top of it."

"It's something I have to do, Walt," Ross stated flatly. "Can't you two understand that? I'm responsible for her getting killed. She was happy—engaged to a doctor. She hated the danger, the killing—she lost her first husband at Salerno. Then I came along and talked her out of it. No," he smiled, more of a grimace, and added, "a long time ago I had to enforce an order at gunpoint. I'll do it again if necessary, by God. Now, what's it to be?"

Head down, Deardorf scuffed at the floor with one boot toe. "You don't even know if the sonofabitch will come back tonight," he countered sulkily.

"He'll come," Ross said. "I thought all afternoon about this. I'll bet money it's the same pilot we saw at Hengyang. Same tactics, same timing—he's damn good. The Japs don't have too many pilots left who can pull off a stunt like he did. Just like before: He's tasted blood; he'll be back for more. When he comes, by God, I'm going to be sitting up there waiting."

Deardorf raised his arms in a sign of surrender. "Have it your way. What's the drill?"

Ross turned to Li-jen and Sergeant Adkins. "You two all set? Any questions?"

"No, sir," the NCO replied. "Just tell us when to set up. The best I can estimate, the weather is right. We'll have a broken deck overhead—bases about four thousand, tops at seven or less. The heavy stuff that was east of us yesterday is moving out, so he won't have any trouble getting airborne. With a half moon, I don't think it could be much better."

"Great," Ross said. "Captain Li-jen?"

The Chinese officer wore a broad smile. He was the only enthusiastic one around, Ross observed. "Yes, sir," Li-jen replied. "My men grumble; they feel they lost much face last night. But they will do as ordered."

"Glad to hear that," Ross responded with a faint grin. "I'm going to have enough to worry about up there without having to sweat out being shot at by our own guns. Okay, let's get some chow. Takeoff will be just after sunset."

Evans gingerly helped Ross into the cockpit, clamping his lips when he saw Ross wince. "You gonna fasten the straps?" he asked.

"Just the seat belt." Ross grunted and shifted to relieve the pressure on his back. The nurse had applied an ointment and wrapped his torso with three layers of gauze, but it still hurt to move. He'd decided to forgo any painkiller stronger than aspirin, however. Deardorf was right: Airplanes and dope were a lethal mixture. He considered the parachute harness. Evans stood by to help him buckle up.

"Just do the leg straps," Ross said finally. "If I get into trouble, I'll snap the chest straps together before I go. I'll probably pass out when the chute opens anyway. My goddamn hands worry me as much as anything. With these gloves on I can hardly find the mike button and gun trigger."

"It still isn't too late, Skipper," Evans told him, his face creased by worry lines. "I'm suited up and ready."

"Just stand by that radio," Ross responded. "I know the bastard has our tower frequency, but I'm betting he doesn't have crystals for the channel used by the '29s."

"I'll be here, Captain. And Ross . . . aw, shit. I just wish I was flying your wing." He clapped Ross on the helmet and leaped to the ground.

Ross taxied in easy S turns toward the runway's far end. The blackened hulks of two Superforts still marred the parking ramp like ugly black boils. Even after five others had limped into the air that afternoon, four of the huge bombers still squatted in the deepening gloom awaiting parts.

Ross would have preferred to wait until later in the evening, but with the base blacked out, he needed what remained of the rapidly fading daylight. He cocked the airplane at a forty-five-degree angle to perform an engine runup and mag check. He could barely see Li-jen and Adkins crouched in a drainage ditch to his right.

The pair looked up from their work to give him a thumbs-up signal. Ross grinned and returned the gesture. The strange-looking gadget beside them could be the secret of success, he observed. Li-jen was as excited as a kid with his first BB gun; the Chinese love to invent things, Ross mused.

Adkins had shown initial signs of dismay when Ross described what he had in mind. "Captain, sir. We just got that thing. We need it in the worst way. The transport pilots bitch constantly that we're off by a hundred feet or so with our estimates of the cloud base. What if we break it?"

"It can make the difference in preventing what happened last night from happening again," Ross argued. "All we're doing is putting it on a flexible gun mount instead of shining it straight up."

Adkins capitulated. He stood by and watched an elated Li-jen attach his precious ceilingometer to a 20mm gun mount. Intended to be on a fixed base and shine straight up, allowing a theodolite to measure the height of the spot its narrow beam made on a cloud base, the device became a powerful searchlight capable of illuminating objects a thousand feet away. It was even shipped with its own miniature putt-putt generator. Ross threw the pair a final salute and applied power for takeoff.

He squirmed uncomfortably and reduced the airflow from the cockpit heater vent. The slightest trace of perspiration set his back on fire. He tried to ignore the pain as he searched the cloud tops ten thousand feet beneath his orbiting Mustang. The broken deck created a problem. Would his prey remain on top, or sneak in beneath the four-thousand-foot ceiling? Ross put himself in the Jap pilot's situation. I would stay on top and navigate by dead reckoning until I was thirty to forty miles out, then find a hole and make my final approach on the deck, he decided.

That was a gamble, he knew. If the Jap decided to stay below the broken clouds, he could hit and run before Ross could find him from this altitude. But, while Chennault's vaunted warning net was in shambles, three reporting stations still functioned with a degree of reliability. Evans sat in a parked P-51 ready to relay a sighting. The whole damn thing was a gamble, he conceded. Bed-Check Charlie—it had to be him—might decide to wait a few nights. No, the feeling was like a knife in Ross's gut. The guy couldn't resist coming back tonight to finish off the crippled bombers.

His headset came to life. "Shark from Codfish. Engine noise reported on bearing zero-eight-two, one hundred miles, at twenty-two-zero-four. Over." Ross recognized Evans's voice. It held a note of subdued excitement.

Ross keyed his mike to acknowledge and entered a shallow turn, peering intently at the cottony cloud tops below. The moon, just emerging from a pastel-hued haze layer, was of little help. He glanced at the instrument panel clock and made quick calculations. The raider couldn't be more than fifty miles east-northeast of the field by now. He resisted an urge to descend and intensified his eye-straining scrutiny.

There! The briefest of movements—framed by a cloud top one moment, then gone. Seconds crawled by. No doubt about it, an airplane was scooting west across the cloud deck. Ross's lips stretched into a feral snarl. He pushed the nose over, his gaze riveted on the tiny cross-shaped object below. Major Cipolla's words emerged from the past. "Hatred of the Japs, as people, can get you killed in combat, Ross." Fuck you, Major, he thought. This murdering bastard is going to pay.

The minuscule shape grew in size as Ross hurtled, power off, through twelve thousand feet—eleven thousand—nine thousand. He leveled and slowed to stay behind and slightly above his quarry. The urge to attack was strong. No, damnit, he admonished himself. If you miss, or if he spots you, he'll duck into those clouds and you'll never find him. Wait until he descends, *then* take up your position just west of the field, on the deck. If he repeats last night's pass, he'll reverse course to come in over the south end of the runway. That's when we'll catch him with his pants around his ankles.

Nakano Yusaki peered at his flight plan in the brightening moonlight. He estimated his position to be forty miles east of Hsinching. As he reduced power, the big radial's roar subsided to a burbling rumble. He adjusted the carburetor air control valve to reduce his exhaust flare to a minimum. A sizable hole in the broken cloud cover opened just to his left. He nosed over and let the darkened, silent Zero ghost downward.

He searched the faintly visible terrain below, seeking a landmark. The rising moon cast weird patterns, but other than isolated dots of light from open fires, the landscape was a dark, empty void. They've learned, Yusaki told himself with a grim smile. The blackout was near total. But not quite: Pinpricks of light grouped on the horizon revealed the old city of Chengtu. His heart leaped. His dead reckoning had been perfect. The airfield with its fat targets was less than five minutes distant.

Nerves taut, eyes glued to the horizon, he rolled to the predetermined heading and added full power. The engine responded with a gratifying growl; he felt the machine leap forward. By the time the runway's pale blur swam into view, the Zero was streaking toward its target at 400 MPH. He grasped the bomb release handle. Wait—wait—*now!* A barely perceptible lurch upward signaled that the bomb was away.

He counted at least four unmistakable shapes of the hated Superforts still on the ramp. They flashed out of view behind him, and he rolled left to circle back. The briefest flicker of movement off his right wing rang a small alarm bell in his brain. He ignored it and concentrated on clearing the terrain and rolling level directly on the runway's centerline.

Again, his timing was perfect. The parked B-29s loomed into view. His finger tightened on the cannon trigger. A vague feeling of unease caused him to hesitate. The antiaircraft gunners should have been alerted by his first pass. A rolling cloud of flame and smoke confirmed a hit with his two-hundred-kilogram bomb. Then, brilliant white light seared his eyeballs.

Blinded, temporarily confused, Yusaki sucked the stick into his gut. Searchlights! He reacted instinctively, throwing the stick all the way to the left. The Zero, its forward speed sharply diminished by the vertical turn, hung suspended in space, pinned by the ceilingometer's blue-white pencil of light—much like a butterfly pinned to its mounting.

The veteran Japanese pilot's last thoughts were not of having failed his emperor, but of Fukio's and his parents' grief-stricken faces. Then four streams of .50-caliber armor-piercing slugs, harmonized to converge at 250 yards, violently erased the scene. Ross had to pull up and sharply right to evade flying bits of the Zero . . . and Nakano Yusaki, Lieutenant, Japanese Imperial Navy.

Chapter Twenty-three

19 November 1944
Seattle

Janet sat without moving, transfixed by the Sunday paper spread before her on the breakfast table. Aunt Ruby seated herself opposite and advised, "That's the only cup of coffee you're going to get, and the last piece of buttered toast. If you let them get cold, that's the way you'll eat them, because they're too scarce to waste."

"Oh—uh, I'm sorry, Aunt Ruby." She reached for her coffee without removing her eyes from the paper.

"You look as if you'd seen a ghost, girl. Something in that paper that upset you? Bad war news?"

"Not the war," Janet replied. "This." She turned the front page so Aunt Ruby could read the headlines.

Her acerbic landlady peered nearsightedly and read aloud, "FEDERAL AGENTS ARREST NINE IN BLACK MARKET OPERATION—Ringleader shown here being led into federal courthouse for arraignment. Hmmmf," she sniffed. "About time they got some of them. If I can find enough food to put on the table, clothes to put on my back, and leave my car in the garage, well, so can everyone else. You upset 'cause you think you'll have to find another place to buy cigarets?"

"I—I think I know that man," Janet stammered.

Ruby peered closer. "Good-looking guy," she observed. "Who is he?"

"I don't just *think* I know him," Janet responded bitterly, "I *do* know him. His name is Duane Swoffard. I dated him."

"Not the one with that snazzy blue convertible. The one you was going after hot and heavy?"

"The same."

"Whooo boy!" Ruby exclaimed softly. "Good thing you found out about it in time. You *did* find out about it in time, didn't you?" she added with a shrewd look.

"Yes, thank heavens. I haven't seen him for months. We—we had a quarrel and broke up." Janet read further. "Why, that lying bastard!" she exclaimed. "Look at this. 'Swoffard, whose draft registration card identifies him as being classified 4-F, faces an additional charge of bribing a draft board member.'"

Aunt Ruby grunted. "Isn't he the smooth one. But I don't see why you're so flustered. You said you hadn't seen him for months."

"Aunt Ruby," Janet said, frowning, "this could mean *I'm* in trouble."

"How? Now don't tell me you were foolish enough to get mixed up in black-market dealings."

"Nothing like that. Right after I met him, they did a background check on me when I was moved to my new job—asked a whole bunch of questions. I had to give them names of all my close friends and associates. Duane told me I shouldn't include his name. He said he had government contracts, and someone might think he had inside information. What if they find out I was dating him—damnit, I even slept with him—and didn't tell the security people?"

Ruby unconsciously checked her impeccable, hennaed hairdo and cocked a birdlike eye at Janet. "I'd say you may have some tall explaining to do, girl," she replied.

"Shall I go to them first? Tell them I knew the man, but not well enough to list him as a friend?"

"Hard to say," Ruby mused. "Cops can be awful dunces sometimes." A smile twitched her lips. "But then, they can be bastards when they have something that may put another arrest on their record. I'm not going to advise you on this one. Odds are, it'll go unnoticed, but if it isn't, you may face charges. If you volunteer the information, you may lose your job, but that's all. It's your decision, my dear; your turn to roll the dice."

Roger Price greeted Janet with a broad smile. "Morning, Janet. Grace said you wanted to see me. Before we start, however, I want to congratulate you on that last research paper you did for Ernie Stephens.

He presented it to the army last week in Washington; everyone wanted a copy. He tells me you are not only picking up on engineering jargon, you're improving on it." He grinned. "That comparison of the XB-47 wing to a knitting needle—Ernie says he would never have thought of that, but it caught everyone's attention. A most graphic way of saying a *flexible* structure has more strength than a *rigid* one. The idea that the wing will have six feet of flex at the tip just scared the hell out of them until they read that. Ernie wants you assigned to his wing-design group full-time, and I've approved it. It means a promotion for you, by the way. Now, what can I do for you?"

Janet stared at her boss with unseeing eyes, her thoughts in turmoil. Her expression firmed. "I—I just wanted to ask you to say a few words at the bond rally next week, Mister Price. I'm on the program committee, you see."

"Glad to, Janet," Price responded affably. "Now you go talk to Banks; he'll take care of the paperwork on your transfer. Good luck."

Janet left Price's office, oblivious to her surroundings. She ignored Grace's raised eyebrows and walked blindly toward the elevator, thinking, I can't tell him. A promotion—I'm *not* going to blow it—I'll never have another chance like this. She felt her heart thumping and pressed a hand to her breast. The jade figurine rested there like an accusing, malignant growth. The elevator doors opened; she stared blankly at the curious faces, waiting for her to enter. Then she wheeled and walked swiftly, purposely back toward Roger Price's office.

The FBI man's ice blue eyes bored into Janet's tear-filmed ones. "Did you ever, at any time, discuss the nature of your work at Boeing with Swoffard?" he asked.

Janet returned the direct look without flinching. Her voice firm, she replied, "The fact that I was a riveter? Yes. That I was offered a promotion? Again, yes. But details of the XB-47 project? Never."

The granite-faced agent unconsciously tugged his left ear as he doodled interlocking circles and triangles on the yellow legal pad in front of him. Finally he said, "You made a wise decision to come forward, Mrs. Templeton. Otherwise, we would have been around to see you before too much longer."

He ignored Janet's startled look and continued. "You see, Swoffard is, shall we say, cooperating fully. In other words, he's singing like the proverbial canary. We have five agents following up the list of leads he gave us—people who collaborated with him. The man seems to place great value on his skin. *Your* name was on that list, I might add."

"He said I *collaborated?*" Janet gasped.

"Yes, but Mister Swoffard's veracity is somewhat suspect, I regret to say," her interrogator responded dryly. "I'd say that if you give me a sworn deposition, now, today, you won't be summoned to testify before the grand jury. They already have a list of witnesses that resembles a circus parade. The roster of coconspirators will read like a phone book."

"Grand jury? Coconspirators?" Janet's voice was barely audible.

"Yes, indeed. Your boyfriend was a *very* big fish. Now, I see no reason to withdraw your security clearance, and I gather from the endorsement your employers gave you that you have no reason to worry about your job. I can't resist adding, however, that you were a foolish young woman; you were lucky—no, I'll give you credit for being wise and patriotic—not to fall for his line."

"I do feel lucky, and, yes, foolish," Janet mumbled. "Imagine, me, called before a grand jury to explain my relationship with a black marketeer."

The FBI agent uttered a short, barking laugh. "He wasn't dealing in the black market, Mrs. Templeton; he's charged with espionage. Don't kid yourself into thinking that the customer for the information he hoped you'd provide was just another domestic aircraft manufacturer."

12 January 1945
Hsinching Airfield

Elliott Sprague shrugged deeper into the warm folds of his overcoat and watched General Wolfenbarger stride down the steps from his C-54. Despite the broad grin on the general's bulldog features, a premonition of disaster nagged at the XX Bomber Command's deputy commander. His emotions had been on a roller coaster since the message announcing Wolfenbarger's arrival landed on his desk. Promotion? A command? Maybe one of the wings being formed in the Pacific?

But the VHBs hadn't exactly distinguished themselves of late. Japan was just too damn far. The supply situation was better but far from adequate. Anyway, LeMay had curtly ordered a shift in targets—closer ones, without the big guns and fighters that ringed the Jap home islands. Even then, planes continued to break down and miss targets at a frustrating rate.

So . . . the expression on his visitor's face was cause for optimism, but where the hell was LeMay? If Sprague was to be reassigned as part of a routine shuffling of commanders, LeMay would normally be along to work out transition details. Plus, letting a senior-headquarters type out of your sight wasn't normal procedure for a field commander. Oh well, he thought, as he snapped to attention and saluted. He held the salute until Wolfenbarger returned it with a casual wave.

"Welcome to China, General," Sprague boomed, emitting plumes of vapor into the frigid air. He accepted the general's outstretched hand and added, "It's good to see that we poor slobs out here in the boonies aren't forgotten."

"No, Elliott, this east China operation has many aspects, but forgotten is certainly not one of them." Wolfenbarger's smile was still in place, but his tone had an ominous ring, Sprague thought.

"Well, you picked a good time, sir. We're launching a mission tomorrow morning that will set the yellow bastards back a few months. We're going to take out their airfields on Formosa. You'll have a firsthand look at what this airplane can do. Would you like to see the war room? I'll give you the general picture and we can talk there—the room is secure. Afterward, you'll have a chance to sample what a top Chinese chef can do to the rations we get."

"Not this time, Elliott." Wolfenbarger's tone was brisk. "This is just a quick in and out. I told the pilot to file for takeoff in one hour. Now, let's go to your war room, office, or wherever—anyplace to get out of this cold."

Inside the war room, Sprague motioned for Wolfenbarger to take the chair that Sprague usually occupied at the semicircular table facing the wall map. "You may want to keep your coat on for a while, General. Fuel for heat is rationed, I'm afraid. Is it too early for a drink?" he asked with only a trace of nervousness. "Scotch?"

"I'll pass, Elliott, but perhaps you'd best pour one for yourself. What I have to say isn't pleasant." Wolfenbarger ignored his host's advice and tossed his bulky overcoat onto the table.

Sprague was an old hand at the business of ass chewing. He knew how to take one as well as to administer one. First thing—you don't panic and start babbling. He took his time selecting a glass and pouring a generous measure of amber Scotch whiskey. He seated himself facing the bulky headquarters representative, sipped his drink, and forced a rueful, "Well, I get the impression I'm in the doghouse, sir. Whose toes have I stepped on now?"

"Not toes, Elliott." Wolfenbarger clipped the end from a cigar and lit it. Waiting until it was glowing satisfactorily, he continued, "Your own dork. You've stepped squarely on it."

"I'm afraid I don't understand, sir."

"Then I will enlighten you. Your little scheme to discredit Kenny Wolfe backfired. K.B. got wind of the fact that he was supposed to be a lush and blew his stack. Went to Arnold and demanded an investigation. As it turns out, you end up holding the baby."

"General Wolfenbarger!" Sprague's voice rang with righteous indignation. "I hope you don't think—"

"Save it, Elliott," the three-star snapped, cutting Sprague's protest in midsentence. "I don't *think* a damn thing. I *know*. Getting cozy with Madame Chiang wasn't the smartest thing you've ever done. You were playing out of your league there, m'boy."

"General, I've cut a few corners, maybe—hell, who hasn't? But K. B. Wolfe was not the man to send out here; all he wanted to do was 'wait 'til we get organized.' Between him and that dithering old woman, Stilwell, they would have had the crews too stiffened up with arthritis to fly a mission. Anything I did, including cozying up to that ice queen, Madame Chiang, as you put it, I did for my country. You would have done the same thing, and you know it. Damnit, you *have* done it."

Wolfenbarger puffed his cigar and regarded Sprague through a swirling cloud of blue smoke. "Maybe," he said briefly. "The difference is, *I* didn't get caught." He expelled a lengthy sigh. "You're a gambler, Elliott, and ruthless. That's one of the reasons I sent you out here; it was a time for bold thinking. You made a big mistake"—he waved off Sprague's attempt to respond—"not so much the Wolfe and Chiang deals, but you failed to recognize a no-win situation once you got into it. You took unacceptable risks. *That's* unacceptable.

"Okay, short and sweet. You're fired. My aide has orders reassigning you to Washington. You'll be my administrative assistant until the war is over. I suggest you plan on retirement then. In the meantime, I want your ass on the next Esso Express back to Kharagpur."

Sprague sat motionless, blood draining from his face. "I—I can't believe you're doing this to me, General. This fiasco was out of control when I got over here—you know that. It isn't *my* fault the VHBs can't do the job they were designed to do."

"Fault has nothing to do with it, Elliott." Wolfenbarger leaned back and contemplated the war room's thatched roof. "And don't feel like the Lone Ranger; other heads are rolling. Clay Bissel is on the way over to rearrange the China operation; Chennault will never serve under him. That's the price Vinegar Joe's lobby extracted for replacing him last October. If he went, Claire had to go as well. And all because a memo Stilwell wrote went astray. In it, he referred to the generalissimo as 'the peanut.' Chiang got hold of a copy and screamed to the president, who screamed at Marshall! That's what started the ball rolling.

"Curt LeMay will move the VHBs to the Pacific. Saipan is ready and within reasonable distance of Tokyo. So you see, Elliott, you're excess to the needs of the program—an embarrassing excess, I might add."

Sprague drained the last two fingers of his glass of straight Scotch. "A helluva way to hang up the gloves, General," he observed softly. "I gave the job everything I had; I earned my pay."

"You did that, Elliott. But you never learned that even the smartest fox on earth can't get away with raiding the henhouse forever."

Sprague didn't respond immediately. Finally he said, "I have only one favor to ask—something I believe I've earned. I want to lead tomorrow's mission—call it my swan song. I want Mort Sims to fly right seat; he's been my right-hand man during this assignment. Let us fly one more together—for old times' sake."

Wolfenbarger stubbed out his cigar, stood, and reached for his overcoat. "Okay, Elliott, one more. I'll okay it with Curt by radio from the plane. But I doubt that Mort Sims will want to fly right seat with you."

"Thanks, General. I'll take that piss-ant island off the map for you as a parting gesture. But what makes you think Mort won't go?"

"I also brought orders with me appointing Colonel Sims as your replacement; promotion to brigadier general is included. You see, Elliott, Sims is the one who blew the whistle on the K. B. Wolfe business."

3 March 1945
San Francisco, California

Janet crossed her legs and thumbed through a copy of *Life* magazine with unseeing eyes. International News Service's office was hardly opulent, to say the least. The waiting room was obviously not designed for that purpose. She sat in the only chair, a straight-backed, armless typing model parked alongside a two-by-four table with a cheap lamp, an overflowing ashtray, and a profusion of dog-eared magazines. She regarded with awe a gum-chewing blond maintaining a hundred-word-per-minute output on the big Underwood while carrying on an animated conversation via a cradled telephone.

Janet recrossed her legs, taking care to preserve the crease in her slacks. The selection of appropriate attire had been difficult. The light green slacks, with a faintly masculine white silk top, had been Aunt Ruby's recommendation as Janet was packing for the trip. "You're competing in a man's world, girl. They're going to be looking for someone who can sell news, not someone to sleep with. Well, not right away, perhaps. Anyway, if you got it, don't flaunt it, I always say—and you got it."

"Libby," a disembodied voice called from around an open doorway. The blond rolled despairing eyes at Janet and continued her conversation.

"Libby!"

Janet crossed to the door. "She's on the telephone, sir."

The lean, gaunt-faced man seated behind the office's cluttered desk glared at her from behind horn-rimmed glasses. "I know she's on the goddamn telephone. I want her *off* the goddamn telephone and in here. Now, who the hell are you?"

"Janet Templeton, sir. I have a two o'clock appointment to see Mister Henderson."

The blond appeared at Janet's elbow. "Did you want something?" she asked.

"Of course I wanted something," the shirt-sleeved man bellowed. "Did you think I was practicing voice lessons? Why didn't you tell me that my two o'clock appointment was already here?"

The girl frowned. "I planned to announce her seven minutes from now, at two o'clock," she said poutily.

Henderson rolled his eyes. "Come in, Mrs. Templeton. You," he added, fixing the blond with a glare, "can get back to work."

He waved vaguely toward Janet. "Clear yourself a chair and take the weight off." He grinned good-naturedly. "Don't let the way Libby and I talk throw you. She's a tyrant, insubordinate, and spoils me rotten. I couldn't get along without her. Now, I understand you want to become a news hound. Why?"

"I'm a widow, Mister Henderson. I have to earn a living. My job with Boeing Aircraft is being phased out. I've been told I have a talent for writing. Mister Osgood, my supervisor, suggested I talk with you—I believe he wrote to you on my behalf."

"Yes," Henderson said. He fumbled through a jumble of papers and emerged triumphantly with a single sheet of stationery. "Yes, he did that. Says that you have a knack for selecting words that make complex situations clear. Coming from Lawrence Osgood, that is a rare compliment. Larry and I were classmates; he may have told you."

"Yes."

"His statement intrigues me. It isn't often that someone grasps the kernel of newswriting. He says you have a degree. What was your major?"

"Art appreciation." Janet blushed slightly. "But I have a minor in English," she added hastily.

"No harm done—you just have less to unlearn. Now, here's the situation. I'll not pull any punches. If you get offended . . ."—he shrugged—"so be it. The war in Europe is all but over. The one in the Pacific is about to begin. The front office is looking ahead to that time. Our drafted employees are assured of getting their old jobs back. Preference will be given to hiring veterans in any event. We don't know what to expect in the way of applicants. INS doesn't presently have a woman journalist in the field. Those jobs have been in combat theaters. Are you beginning to get the picture? You'd be seen as a woman taking a needed job away from a veteran. Not that you'd start as a journalist anyway, but the door is going to be damn hard to break down—if that's what you have in mind."

"I started at Boeing driving rivets on the assembly line, Mister Henderson. I worked my way into the front office there. I can compete against men. And yes, that's exactly what I have in mind—a job in one of your overseas bureaus."

Henderson leaned back. His skull-like features broke into a grin. "You're a lot like Libby: not afraid to spit squarely in the devil's eye. Very well, I'll forward your application to the front office. Before I add my recommendation, I have a few more questions."

"Yes, sir."

"Your married name caught my attention. Do you know the senator Broderick Templeton?"

"He's my late husband's father."

"Have you asked *him* to help you find a new job?"

"No, sir."

"I see. So BT was your husband," he mused.

Janet threw Henderson a startled look. "Why—why yes. Did you know him?"

"Only indirectly. Do you know a Captain Ross Colyer?"

Janet gaped foolishly. "Mister Henderson, this is getting spooky. . . . Good heavens! *Henderson*—you're the one who wrote those articles from Benghazi. I saved them in a scrapbook. But you were with a newspaper then, weren't you?"

The lanky newsman laughed. "I'm glad *someone* appreciates my writing enough to save it for posterity. Yes, I was with the *New York Times* then. INS made me a better offer. Now, are you in touch with Ross? I lost track of him."

"Sort of. I can give you his APO address. He was in the CBI, I think."

"Do that. I assume you'll be seeing him when he finishes his tour?"

"I—I hope to. I'm working on a classified project I can't write to him about, but it's a super airplane I know he'll want to fly. Ross's world revolves around airplanes."

"The XB-47," Henderson observed casually.

"You know about it?" Janet gasped.

"Newsmen don't write everything they know about." Henderson's attitude turned brisk. "Okay. Ask Libby to give you a raw article off the wire. Rewrite it. I'll include it with my recommendation. Frankly, I'm basing my endorsement of your application on the fact that you *didn't* use your father-in-law as a recommendation."

25 May 1945
Iwo Jima

Ross wiped sweat from his forehead with an already saturated towel, then returned to his attempt to write a long-overdue letter. Outside his tent, a steady downpour turned the island's soggy, volcanic soil into black soup. It did nothing to dissuade the ever-present swarm of hungry insects, however. He had given up trying to identify them by species; the damn things all bit, stung, and clung like leeches.

Barely visible were the 41st Fighter Squadron's P-51s, huddled alongside the asphalt and pierced-steel-plank runway inherited from the Japanese. Mount Suribachi's bomb-pocked mass brooded in the background, as if still counting the dead that its conquest generated. Ross glanced at his watch. The lumbering B-29s would be lifting off Saipan about now. He didn't look forward to a takeoff and climb-out through this weather with a dozen of the sleek Mustangs strung behind him. They would go, however. The big birds, for all their vaunted defensive firepower, couldn't stave off the swarming Jap fighters desperately defending their homeland.

As if in response to his digressions, a poncho-draped runner entered without bothering to announce his presence. He thrust a waterproof envelope toward Ross. "Here's the frag order, Major. Rendezvous with the bombers at thirteen twenty-two. Standard load. You want me to alert ops?"

Ross opened the limp message form and scanned its contents. He scrawled his initials in a corner and handed it back. "Yeah," he told the dripping messenger. "Have Captain Deardorf compute a start-engines time and notify everyone on the alert roster." He returned to review what he'd written thus far.

Dear Colonel Wilson—and Doris, too,

Sorry I haven't written more often. I try, honest I do. I really look forward to your letters. Well, let's see what I can tell you. Censorship is getting quite loose, but I still can't tell you exactly where I am—just that it's within range of targets on the Jap mainland. We moved in here about six weeks ago. We can escort the bombers all the way to their targets from here and, of late, are carrying 2.75-inch air-to-ground rockets for strafing if the opportunity presents. That's a welcome change from flying circles at 30,000 feet.

I will tell you some of what I've been doing the past year, however, censorship notwithstanding. You knew, of course, I was in the CBI. It was an experience I don't care to repeat. I left any youthful idealism that remained back there in China. The place wasn't a theater of war, it was a political arena. Too many lives were lost and too much valuable equipment and money were expended without shortening the war by as much as one day, as best I could see. I was reunited with a girl I met at Kelly Field, and was very fond of—only to see her die.

That was my low point. If given the chance, I would have quit the army and come home then. It took General Chennault to put things back in perspective. He toured all the air bases in China on his farewell trip. He was a victim of the political process but didn't appear bitter.

I had a chance to visit with him and told him about my feelings. The effort that went into trying to bomb Japan with B-29s. They were totally ineffective and, because of their drain on the supply chain, we lost east China.

The general just nodded and said, "The Lord isn't the only one who moves in mysterious ways, Colyer. You and I are soldiers. We're prone to measure success by victories on the battlefield. It took the generalissimo to make me see that, despite the battles we've lost, we won a great but invisible victory. Japan has more than a million men and tons of equipment irrevocably committed here—men and equipment denied her for resisting the inevitable invasion. That factor, more so than any other, has sealed her fate.

"Was it planned that way? I doubt that we will ever know, for certain. Our reward is in knowing that we did our job—did it well."

I snapped out of my funk after that and went back to work. In case you didn't catch it on my return address, I made major in China and took over the squadron. It was a lucky break; as you know, all temporary promotions were frozen after V-E Day. After the '29s pulled out and moved to Saipan, my squadron was selected for reassignment here to fly escort. Much to everyone's joy, our war-weary B models were replaced with the new, bubble-canopied D's. What an airplane!

I'm an ace for the second time as well. I'm almost ashamed to tell you that number ten was an obsolete floatplane blundering along off the Jap coastline. I took some kidding, I'll tell you.

But now for the big news. Shortly after V-E Day, FEAF sent a briefing team to all the remote bases to spread the word on new personnel regs. I was told I have enough points for immediate return to CONUS and discharge.

Well—I was flabbergasted. Get out? A funny thing, I'd never given a thought to anything but flying. But with the war winding down (I wish to hell someone would tell the Japs that!), they say a bunch of reserve officers will be released from active duty—involuntarily in some cases.

Shit! I'd never paid much attention to who was reserve and who was regular, but I'm discovering there is a difference, a *big* difference. I figure I'll probably be out of a job after we finish off the Japs. Maybe before. Colonel Titus, our group CO, told me I was commanding a squadron under a wartime emergency clause—normally only regulars are selected for command.

I took a hop over to group headquarters and talked with him. He advised me to hang on to active duty as long as I can and to apply for a regular commission. A lot of regulars are being held past retirement for the duration of the war, and there are bound to be vacancies.

I made an application on the spot and saw the endorsement he put on it. I was embarrassed by the flowery things he said. He bucked it on to FEAF and swears they'll have even nicer things to say. So, that's how things stand. The best I can hope for is a permanent grade of first lieutenant, but I can live with that as long as they leave me in the cockpit.

Ross laid down the unfinished letter and checked his watch again. An hour to finish it and get it ready for the mail plane before suiting up. He grinned and resumed:

Doris: Has Janet called you? Now get that matchmaking gleam out of your eye. She and I had some good times when I was at Hickam. But what with the war breaking out and all, nothing came of it. Then she married BT. We've written each other a couple of times since I came over here. She's working with International News—for a friend of mine, as a matter of fact. Clayton Henderson, the reporter who was with us in Benghazi and who wrote those articles about the *Happy Hooker,* remember? Anyway, he wrote me and said that Janet was released by Boeing and his outfit hired her to be a reporter.

I told her to call you if she's ever in D.C. She's a friend, understand. I can't explain it, but while she's the best-looking, most personable gal I know, there'll always be BT's ghost between us, I guess. Well, about time to charge off into the blue again and save some democracy. Keep up the mail! I read everything I get until it falls apart.

All my love,
Ross

Chapter Twenty-four

1158 Hours, 25 May 1945
Iwo Jima

Ross sealed his letter to the Wilsons and tossed it into his OUT basket. He checked his watch. It was almost time to go to the mission briefing. He selected the least ripe of his khaki flight suits and, after dusting his crotch with a powder that was supposed to reduce the chronic rash they all had, he slipped into the suit's clammy folds. Looping the bag containing his cloth helmet, sun goggles, and oxygen mask over his arm, he donned a poncho and headed for ops.

He scanned the ready board while an assortment of weary, hollow-eyed young men straggled into the dripping canvas shelter. Lieutenant Evans groused, "Major, this is horseshit. Even the goddamn gulls are stood down today. If the good Lord intended man to fly in this weather, he'd have given us web feet—not that my toes haven't already started growing together."

Ross grinned. "Bitch, bitch, bitch, Evans. Count your blessings. You could have ended up in the navy—out there on some carrier, pissed off because your sheets weren't changed yesterday, no steak for a week, and nothing but girlie movies to watch."

"Perish the thought, Major." Evans spread his hands in mock horror. "What's the drill? Same-oh, same-oh?"

"Right. We won't know their drop altitude until the weather ship makes a winds-aloft check over the target. But we'll orbit at thirty thousand or thereabouts." He turned to face the remaining ten pilots.

"Now, for Christ's sake, try not to get lost on climb-out today. Briefed heading, briefed rate of climb, briefed airspeed, and we should all be over the same ocean when we break out on top. Tops are reported to be eighteen thousand."

A fuzzy-cheeked youngster asked, "What about landing back here?"

"Weatherman says four thousand broken, fifteen miles, Chuck. Enough ceiling for victory rolls."

Ross's forecast was greeted with a chorus of boos. "Those lying bastards," a voice called from the rear. "Everybody who believes that, stand on your head."

Lieutenant Evans, a broad smile on his freckled, cherubic face, promptly did a handstand, evoking hoots of laughter. Ross raised his hand for silence, then continued.

"If the bombers aren't under attack on the way out, we'll break off at the coast, one flight at a time, and rearrange the countryside a bit. Look for trains, truck convoys, and coastal shipping. No, I mean *no,* villages or other clearly civilian targets. Okay, I'm coming up on two-zero; stand by for a time hack."

Ross trotted to his water-beaded Mustang through rain that had slackened to a gentle mist. As always, he stopped short to admire the plane's sleek, speedy lines. The P-51D had a top speed of 437 MPH. The wing-mounted .50-caliber machine guns and pylons for either bombs or 2.75-inch folding-fin rockets provided almost as much destructive firepower as his 1941 version of the B-17.

He checked to ensure that the gunports were taped and that the dozen rockets were connected to their firing circuits, then clambered into the cockpit. His crew chief, MSgt. Henry Hankins, held a poncho above the opened canopy as Ross slipped into the waiting seat-pack chute and restraining straps, then plugged in the oxygen mask.

"Sure would like to stand 'er down long enough to do some proper maintenance, Major," he said in doleful tones. "Not that we have all of the spare parts I'd need. That canopy seal needs replacin', the oil cooler has a leak, an' them tires are downright threadbare."

Ross flipped the oxygen auto-mix to ON and took two quick inhalations. The gauge's little eye winked reassuringly. He removed the mask and grinned. "Hank, this bird is in top shape, and you know it. Get your red paint can handy. I have the distinct feeling you'll be able to put another meatball on her tonight."

"Now, Major. Don't you go overboosting that engine. Them pistons'll only take so much—compression on number four is already way down."

Ross gave the sergeant a derisive wave and slid the teardrop-shaped canopy closed. He scanned the cockpit and instrument panel. Armament switches, SAFE. Gunsight, ON and checked. Fuel tank selector, MAIN. He ran his before-starting-engines checklist with sure, practiced swiftness.

The Mustang's engine coughed to life after only one revolution; Hankins wouldn't have it otherwise. Its twelve unmuffled cylinders settled into a throaty rumble, as if impatient to be free of earth's tiresome surface environment. The instrument panel clock's second hand passed start-engines time. Ross grinned with pride as the squadron's other eleven ships simultaneously spat puffs of blue exhaust smoke. It was little things that made a good fighting outfit.

He signaled Hankins to pull the chocks and let the laden craft trundle onto the rain-puddled taxiway. The slipstream from the four spinning prop blades quickly cleared the forward windscreen of its beaded moisture. Leading his brood of sleek, aluminum-skinned birds of prey in a series of waddling S turns, Ross stopped short of the runway to allow his wingman to move into position off his left wing.

He tried whenever possible to put new pilots on his wing for their first sortie. Maybe he was wrong, but it seemed to him that the kids appreciated the "old man" taking a personal interest in them.

A steady green light from the crude platform perched atop four palm-log supports was the signal to shove the crouching Mustang's throttle to the stop. Picking up speed, he felt the wheels jitter across the uneven runway surface. A peek to his left showed his wingman in good position. The airspeed indicator labored past the 100 MPH mark. Then, with a final, disdainful kiss of wheels to runway, P-51 44785, call sign Red One, hurtled upward toward the dripping overcast.

The flight punched through cotton-topped clouds into sparkling sun. Ross donned his sunglasses and searched the bright blue void for his flock. He reduced power and entered a slow orbit. The gratifying sight of eleven converging silver shapes prompted a pleased nod.

Long hours of instrument training were finally paying off. Although leading his pilots into boiling thunderheads, forcing them to fly by instruments, had set off howls of protest, they soon accepted the wisdom of his actions. The entire squadron emerged on top this time within a two-mile radius.

Minutes later, loafing along at thirty thousand feet, he spotted the bombers. They were just entering a gradual climb to bombing altitude. Staying low after takeoff to burn off a few thousand pounds of fuel, and thus use less to reach operational altitude, they were apparently headed for a drop altitude in the twenties.

He frowned. It was one of those days when upper atmospheric conditions were perfect for contrails. Streamers of ice crystals, created by vortices behind wing- and prop tips, formed a glittering arrow, pointing directly to the bomber formation. The Japs won't even need to turn on their radar today, he thought.

Ross thumbed his throat mike. "Big Friends, this is your Little Friend Leader. We have you in sight. Over."

"Roger, Little Friend. Likewise. You're looking mighty good up there."

"The pleasure is ours. Give 'em hell."

Ross led his formation in a series of shallow S turns to maintain position above the heavily laden bombers, then he let his thoughts stray to more mundane affairs. It would be another hour before they would enter the Jap fighters' range.

The prospect of being forced out of the service nagged him. What would he do? Talk was rife among the young pilots of jobs with the airlines, going back to school, getting married. None of those options appealed to him. Would he get married? To whom? What would married life in a peacetime army be like? For that matter, what did a fighter pilot do without a war to fight?

He returned to reality with a guilty start as a terse, "Bandits, eleven o'clock, low," crackled in his headset. He should have been the first to spot them.

The same contrails marking the bombers' path betrayed their fighter cover as well. The wary Jap pilots circled well out of range, loathe to pit their dwindling inventory of planes and pilots against superior odds. But let one of the big B-29s lose an engine and drop out of formation, and they'd be on him like hungry sharks.

Ross watched the bombers enter angry black clouds of antiaircraft fire, lay their eggs, and race for safety. Back above the coastline, faintly disappointed that he hadn't gotten a chance to add another Zero to his record, he keyed the mike. "White Lead, this is Red Lead. I'm taking my flight down now. I'll rejoin after expending ordnance. You go next, then Blue Flight. Understood?"

"White Lead, roger."

"Blue Lead, roger."

Ross stood his ship on one wing, nosed over, and streaked for the shoreline thirty thousand feet below. He glanced at his new wingman.

The kid was hanging in tight—a good pilot, Ross noted with satisfaction. What was his name? Oh, yes, Harper. Well, he'd give Lieutenant Harper a look, close up, at the enemy. A hundred feet above lacy whitecaps, the four-ship formation thundered toward the shoreline. Ross counted only a scattered fishing fleet and a dozen terrified people on shore scampering for cover. No targets there. He turned to parallel the coastline. A railroad—he searched for movement ahead.

The radio crackled. "Red Leader, this is Red Three. Nine o'clock—looks to be an underground bunker of some sort. There's truck traffic."

"Roger, Three. I'll check it out. You go ahead. Rally over the bay in one-five minutes. Over."

Ross entered a 270-degree turn to the right with Harper still tucked in on his left wing. Rolling out, he saw the target—a mound of earth with huge double doors. Three vehicles sped out of sight, leaving plumes of dust.

"Rockets, Two," he called. "Spread of four—get in close." The double doors filled his windshield-mounted gunsight. Glancing down, he confirmed that the red ARMED light was on, made a final course correction, and fired. He saw the rocket tails, followed closely by his wingman's, streaking toward the target. He grinned to himself—bull's-eye! As the bunker disappeared beneath his nose, Ross rolled into a steep climbing turn.

The fighter's nose pitched straight up with startling swiftness; a shuddering jar flipped it nearly inverted. Fighting to regain control, a startled Ross saw bits of earth, wood, and metal fly past. What the hell—was he hit? The V-12 engine's throaty roar was reassuring. The ship answered to all stick movements. His wingman! A glance to the right failed to reveal Harper's ship.

About to attempt radio contact, Ross heard an excited shout in his headset. "Red Leader, Red Leader! Red Two, I've been hit."

Ross tightened his turn and searched beneath and behind, a sinking feeling in his gut. He took pride in never having lost a wingman. Then Ross saw the errant Mustang, in a shallow climbing turn. Thank God the kid had remembered to roll in slightly nose-up trim on his low-level pass. He looked closely; the entire canopy appeared to be missing. He keyed his mike.

"Okay, Red Two. I have you in sight. What is your condition? Over."

"It's my eyes! I can't see! Something hit my head and I'm bleeding—eyes are full of it. I'm blind!"

"All right, Red Two. I'm coming up from behind. Just take it slow and easy. Can you see any of your instruments?"

"No. I'm in a spiral—I'm—I'm going in!" The kid's voice sounded panicky. Ross saw the plane lurch into a steep turn and the nose pitch up.

"*Negative,* Red Two. Negative, do you hear me?" Ross's voice crackled with authority. "Listen to me; turn loose of the controls, understand? Turn loose of the stick. You have vertigo. Let the plane find its own attitude." He breathed easier as Red Two regained its former shallow turn.

"Now, is there a lot of pain?"

"N-no—not really. It's just this blood. I can feel it all over my face. It won't stop."

"It's okay, you're going to be okay," Ross said with calm reassurance he really didn't feel. His thoughts raced. "Hold your oxygen mask to your face and turn the auto-mix lever to a hundred percent," he continued. "We don't want you going into shock."

Ross sucked the fighter into a tighter turn, experience giving him an instinctive intercept angle. Suddenly he confronted a wall of red tracers. Damn! They'd apparently attacked a well-defended bunker. The gunners, now fully alert, were laying down a deadly pattern of .50-caliber and 20mm fire. He broke hard right and up.

Safely out of range, he took in the situation with a lightning-swift appraisal. Harper's shallow turn would bring him back over the waiting AA batteries. By the time Ross could go above and around the gun positions, Harper would be blown out of the sky. Only by flying directly through the curtain of defensive fire could he reach his injured wingman in time.

Without hesitation, Ross crammed on max continuous rated power and set up a shallow dive. Orange ping-pong balls whipped past. Clenching the stick-mounted trigger in a death grip, he let the .50 calibers lay down a path of annihilation. The airspeed indicator edged past the red line. Nearing its structural limits, the Mustang shuddered and bucked much the same as its namesake.

He shrieked above the dug-in weapons at less than a hundred feet of altitude and headed for Harper's floundering ship. Home free, he thought. In the act of expelling pent-up breath, his left foot lost all feeling. Simultaneously, the lower-left instrument panel disappeared in a shower of twisted metal and broken glass.

"Oh, shit," Ross muttered aloud. Some lucky bastard had scored with a deflection shot at extreme range. How bad was it? The engine's thunder never faltered. The sturdy fighter still answered crisply to the controls. Okay, just some of the less-essential instruments. Then he felt a warm wetness in his left boot. He glanced down. It was dark down there, but he glimpsed blood on the rudder pedal. The numbness in his foot became lancing pain.

The sight of Harper's ship filling his windshield jolted Ross to awareness of the task he faced. He hauled the throttle to full idle and threw the plane into a flat, skidding turn. Pressure on the left rudder almost made him yelp with pain. As he drew alongside the erratically flying Red Two, he gulped and pressed his mike switch.

"Okay, Red Two, you're going to feel a little bump. That'll be me lifting your right wing with my left one. Stay off the controls. We're coming up on a heading for home. I just want to get your wings level."

"Oh—okay" was the tremulous response.

Ross eased his own ship closer and closer. "Red Three, what's your position?" he called.

"'Bout twenty miles north, Lead. You got problems?"

"Right. Red Two was hit with debris—must've been an ammo dump. He can't see. Get back here. We're at a little over two thousand on a heading of one-four-oh."

"Roger, Red Lead. Be there in about three to four minutes. Changing course now. Over."

Ross returned to Lieutenant Harper's crisis. "How're you coming, ol' buddy?" he asked. "That bleeding under control yet?"

"I—I don't think it's as bad—maybe. I still can't see; everything's just a red blur."

"That's great," Ross forced a cheery note to his voice. "Means there isn't any serious eye injury, at least. Here's what I want you to do. Pull the throttle back about an inch. That'll give you a slow cruise speed. That's it. Now ease the prop control back. You can tell by the sound when you're in minimum cruise RPM.

"Great, you're doing fine," Ross added as he observed Red Two's speed diminishing. He found it increasingly hard to concentrate. Any movement of his left foot sent electric-like shocks up his leg. "Okay, your nose is dropping now. Give her a touch of up-elevator trim—just a hair. Don't try using the stick, just the trim button. Hey, that's great. We've got you pretty much straight and level now. We'll have you back home before you know it."

Another voice cut in. "Red Lead, Red Three and Four in position above and to your left. What's the plan?"

"Well," Ross said, forming his words carefully, "Three, you take up position on Two's left wing. He can maintain an even pitch attitude with trim. We'll keep his wings level by tapping the underside of his with our own. Understand?"

"Roger, can do. Hey, Red Leader, you got battle damage! Just ahead of your left wing root. Did you know?"

"I know," Ross replied laconically. "Red Four, you take over the lead—do our navigating."

"Wilco."

"White Lead, Blue Lead, do you copy?"

"Roger, Red Leader. We've been monitoring the situation. Over."

"Okay," Ross said. "White Lead, firewall it and get back within VHF range of the base. Tell them to get in touch with the army and get some equipment down to North Beach—an amphib if they have one. They're going to have some work to do very shortly. Blue Lead, you drop back and cover us. Over."

"Blue Lead, wilco."

"White Lead, wilco. What shall I tell 'em to expect? You gonna have him belly-in on the sand, ditch, bail out, or what?"

Ross hesitated. "Uh—those are all possibilities. We'll decide that when we get there. Over."

Harper's voice was weak, and a slight quaver betrayed his distress. "I don't think I can do it. I can't see a thing. I'm not bleeding as much, but my eyes are swollen shut."

"Just hang in there, Two. We'll get you down in one piece. Lean back and enjoy the ride." Ross ignored Lieutenant Evans's negative headshakes; he had forgotten that the young redhead was flying Red Three.

A tension-laden hour passed before the humpbacked pile of black volcanic deposits that was Iwo Jima loomed in the distance. Ross drew a deep breath and shook his head violently, attempting to clear it. Damnit, ignore the foot, he scolded himself, it's no more than a scratch. You're coming up on the tricky part; keep your head clear. Then it was decision time. "How're you feeling, Harper?" he asked casually.

"Not good, Lead. It's starting to hurt. I still can't see shit."

"I understand." Ross's own voice sounded fuzzy and strained—even he could tell. "White Lead, do you copy?"

"Roger, Red Leader. I'm orbiting the island. Listen, Skipper, you sound kinda funny. Are you sure you're okay? I can come down and take over for you."

"Negative."

"Okay. The army has equipment standing by. Any instructions you want me to relay? Over."

"Not just yet. Stand by." Ross bit his lip. This was it. The odds of Harper making a successful gear-up landing on the beach or ditching offshore were remote.

"Harper." His voice became crisp. "Here's what we're going to do. We're coming up on the island at about two thousand feet. I'm going to have you start slowing down. When we get over North Beach, I'm going to tell you when to bail out. You'll have plenty of time to pull the rip cord and for your oscillations to dampen. The army is waiting for you and will pick you up immediately."

"Bail out?" Harper's voice was shrill. "Major, I can't do that."

"It's the only way, guy. We can't keep your wings level all the way to touchdown. If you drop one, you'll cartwheel, and that'd be all she wrote."

"But, sir—"

"Island's coming up," Ross said, cutting Harper off. "Pull off about an inch of throttle, get a few degrees of flaps down, and hit your up-elevator trim a couple of times. Come on, now. Time's getting short." Ross kept up a steady flow of instructions, giving the terrified pilot no time to refuse.

He watched the chute billow—God, what must be going through the kid's mind? He clenched his jaws as the khaki-colored bundle impacted with a visible spurt of black sand. OD-clad figures rushed to the scene. Ross released pent-up tension with a wild yell as he saw them help Harper to a standing position. He thumbed his transmit button. "Let's go home, Red Three. The party's over."

Chapter Twenty-five

7 July 1945
Washington, D.C.

Lieutenant Colonel Ted Wilson reread Ross's letter. He removed his reading glasses and pinched his lower lip, deep in thought. Laying aside the handwritten missive, Wilson retrieved a buff-colored eight-by-ten-inch envelope with Janet Templeton's return address in the upper left-hand corner. He extracted the contents, a handwritten note on light blue stationery and a clipping from the Justin Falls *Tribune.* The note read:

> Dear Colonel Wilson,
> I ran across the enclosed in the daily wire releases and thought you might find it interesting. Knowing Ross, I'm sure you'd never hear it from him.
> Janet

A two-column spread of newsprint was attached.

> LOCAL BOY EARNS NATION'S SECOND HIGHEST VALOR AWARD
> Major Ross Colyer, a 1935 graduate of Justin Falls High School, has been awarded the Army's Distinguished Service Cross for displaying exceptional courage in air combat.

> Acording to the citation, "While leading his squadron of P-51 fighter planes in an attack against a heavily defended target, Major Colyer's wingman suffered incapacitating injuries. To reach the disabled pilot and plane, Major Colyer was forced to fly deliberately through heavy ground fire. He received a painful wound in the process, but nevertheless proceeded to guide his wounded wingman back to safety. . . ."

The article concluded with: "Major Colyer suffered several broken small bones in his foot and is presently convalescing. Second Lieutenant Douglas Harper, Colyer's injured wingman, is expected to make a full recovery."

Wilson reached for the phone and dialed a three-digit number with rapid, angry movements.

"Duke?" he barked. "How about a cup of coffee over in the canteen? I'll buy."

Once he was seated opposite the saturnine light colonel from personnel actions, Wilson didn't waste time. "Duke, who's handling applications for regular commissions?"

"You know damn well I am," his companion drawled.

Wilson grunted. "I thought so. What's the picture?"

"The competition is going to be stiff. I'd say about one in a hundred will be approved."

"Yeah. How about a guy who was awarded a Silver Star and Purple Heart at Pearl Harbor, got a couple DFCs and a bunch of Air Medals during two combat tours, and was a fighter squadron commander even *before* this happened?" Wilson tossed the folded newspaper clipping on the table. "He's a double ace, by the way."

Duke scanned the article and whistled softly. "Well, he'll for damn sure make the finals, I'd say. Someone you know?"

"Just the guy who saved my life after I had a heart attack in a Stearman trainer back in '42."

"I see. Ted, you know the game. Do either of you have some heavy artillery to bring up?"

"That's the problem. The big guns are all on the other side."

"How's that?"

"I got a look at his 201 file about a year ago. It had a political-interest flag on it then. I want to know if it's still there."

"He has a rabbi?" Duke raised his eyebrows.

"Just the opposite. He got himself crossways with no less than the chairman of the Military Affairs Committee—Senator Broderick Templeton."

Duke pursed his lips and shook his head slowly. "Your man sure knows how to pick 'em. Okay, you know the setup. If that PI flag is still there, it's standard procedure for us to touch base with legislative liaison. Plus, naturally, the appointments have to be confirmed by the Senate."

Wilson slammed the table. "Damnit, Duke. This kid has what it takes to go all the way. How can we let some damn politician rob the army of a potential chief of staff?"

Duke shrugged and avoided meeting Wilson's outraged glare. "I feel for you—your friend, too. But I hope you aren't thinking, even in your wildest dreams, of asking me to do what I think you're thinking of asking. I have to level with you; if that flag is still there, and a high-horsepower type like Templeton is opposed, the poor bastard is sucking wind. I'll check it out, though, and get back with you. Okay?"

"Yeah. Do that if you will, Duke." Wilson's voice was suddenly dejected. "Do that. But I have a sinking feeling we both know what the answer's going to be. You know, my son, Kyle, is over at VMI. I'd always assumed he would make the army his career. Sometimes I wonder." He tossed some change on the table and plodded toward the door.

15 August 1945
Iwo Jima

Lieutenant Evans leaped atop one of the mess tent's trestle tables. Placing two fingers in the corners of his mouth, he loosed a piercing whistle. The hubbub of voices lessened, but only slightly. "All right, you guys, pack it in, d'you hear? *At ease,* damnit!" He regarded the sea of suddenly silent faces. "The major says to listen up. The president is getting ready to make an announcement on the radio."

Ross toyed with his cup of coffee and listened to the squeals and squawks produced by a shortwave receiver mounted above the mess line. He'd assembled the entire squadron at the group commander's order. All troops were to hear President Truman's broadcast. He was certain he knew the subject—that god-awful big bomb dropped on

Hiroshima. It was mind-boggling. An entire city had reportedly been wiped off the face of the earth by a single bomb.

He heard a distorted voice announce, "Ladies and gentlemen, at a just-completed news conference, President Truman released the following statement:

> I have received this afternoon a message from the Japanese government in reply to the message forwarded to that government by the secretary of state on August eleven. I deem this reply a full acceptance of the Potsdam declaration, which specifies the unconditional surrender of Japan. In the reply there is no qualification. Arrangements are now being made for the formal signing of surrender terms at the earliest possible moment. General Douglas MacArthur has been appointed Supreme Allied Commander to receive the Japanese surrender. Great Britain, Russia, and China will be represented by high-ranking officers. Meantime the Allied armed forces have been ordered to suspend offensive action. The proclamation of V-J Day must wait upon the formal signing of the surrender terms by Japan.

A stunned silence followed the excited announcer's statement. It lasted all of thirty seconds. Ross, his thoughts churning with the implications of what he'd just heard, sat slack jawed. Behind him, pandemonium erupted. "The war's over! We're going home! Hear that guys, it's all over—wow!" It was soon impossible to hear even what the person sitting next to him was screaming.

Ross supposed he should try to restore some measure of order; a commanding officer should have some sage words on such an occasion. A slow grin emerged. Piss on it. Tension had been building ever since "The Bomb" was dropped last week. All missions had been scrubbed. Stand down, the frag order read every morning. Let 'er blow, he told himself.

A grinning master sergeant leaned to shout in his ear, "Request permission to break out the beer, sir."

Ross stood and said, "I'll come help you."

Outside, men milled in small groups, slapping each other on the back, saying things like, "We made it—by God, Clyde, we made it." "How soon do you think we'll get outta here?" "Oh Susie, get yourself rested up. You ain't gonna get any sleep for a week." Ross collected a can of warm, foaming Pabst Blue Ribbon and joined a chattering group of pilots. Lieutenant Evans raised his beer in a toast. "Here's to the best damn CO in the whole Air Corps, guys."

Ross reluctantly faced up to what he knew to be his responsibility. "Evans, would you collect the flight commanders and come to my tent? Fun's fun, but we have to keep some kind of lid on it."

A short time later, seated on his cot, Ross told a circle of foolishly grinning faces, "I don't want to sound like a wet blanket, guys, but a few of us will have to forgo celebrating for a while. I want the airplanes secured before some beered-up pilot decides we need a buzz job. Post a guard at supply and on the flight line. Someone is going to get the idea to collect some souvenirs pretty soon. And ammo—for Christ's sake, don't let a bunch of drunks get their hands on anything that will go bang. That goes for sidearms as well. . . ."

The clutch of somewhat disgruntled officers departed to make half-hearted efforts to prevent chaos. Ross discovered that his beer can was empty and debated the wisdom of going after another. The supply was bound to be exhausted by dark. Instead, he crushed the empty can in one hand and reached for the letter.

Already crumpled from rereading and being formed into a ball, it bore Ted Wilson's return address.

Dear Ross,

I'd rather take a beating than to have to write this letter, but I thought you'd rather hear it from me first. Your application for a regular commission was disapproved. I did everything I could. . . .

Ross skimmed the remainder.

. . . the fact you didn't finish college . . . the forecast surplus of pilots . . . peacetime manning standards are all guesswork. We both know what happened, Ross, and it makes me want to throw up. . . . Doris sends her love. . . . Whatever you do, come see us after you get back to the States.

Lieutenant Evans stuck his head inside the tent. He wore a broad smile and held a paper-wrapped, cylindrical object in one hand. "Canadian Club, Major. Genuine prewar, skillfully smuggled past hundreds of grasping, greedy hands and worth its weight in platinum. I can't think of anyone else I'd rather drink it with."

Ross folded the letter carefully and returned it to its envelope. "Lieutenant Evans," he said, bowing with exaggerated courtesy, "I welcome you to this humble house. I feel unworthy of the gift you bear. Cleanse thy hands, and we will perform that solemn Colyer tribal ritual passed on by my forefathers known as 'Breaking the Fucking Seal.'"

14 September 1945
Kansas City, Missouri

The smooth-shaven, well-barbered man regarded Ross from behind a sign reading: GEORGE SMITHERS—ASSISTANT DIRECTOR, PERSONNEL. He smiled to show even white teeth. "A most impressive résumé, Mister Colyer. You certainly have a distinguished flying record. And, of course, TWA has expansion plans requiring more pilots. But for the immediate future, we aren't accepting applications for flight crews from anyone over twenty-seven years old."

16 September 1945
Minneapolis, Minnesota

"My, but you have an impressive war record, Mister Colyer." The sleekly coifed, middle-aged woman smiled her most winsome smile. "And, of course, Gibson and Appendorp is committed to giving first priority to hiring our boys coming home from the war. Your transcript shows you were pursuing courses fitted to our engineering needs, but, without a degree, I'm sorry. There was a vacancy in our accounting department you qualify for, but we just filled it with a young man who was fortunate enough to spend his entire service in the Army Finance Center, working with the new EDVAC computer system."

18 September 1945
Detroit, Michigan

"Sure, the auto makers are scrambling to convert back to car making, Colyer, but without a degree in engineering, they can't use you. The Veterans' Placement Service has a foot in the door of every major employer in Detroit, and I have a list of job openings you wouldn't believe. But, I gotta level with you, they're not going to hire you. Know why?"

"I can't wait to hear," Ross replied bitterly.

"You're overqualified. Look, you've been a big man in the army. You've been in charge of expensive equipment, responsible for a hundred or so GIs. So you get a job on an assembly line. What happens? You get bored. The company spends six months training you, then you walk off the job. It happens, and the companies know it. You want my advice?" the shrewd, sharp-eyed man asked. Without waiting for Ross's response, he went on, "Go back to college under this GI Bill thing and finish your engineering degree. Come back then, and I'll get you any one of a half-dozen good jobs."

Ross closed the door to the telephone booth, decreasing only slightly the babble of voices filling the vaulted train station. He thumbed coins into the appropriate slots and heard the bored operator say, "You may go ahead, sir."

"Mrs. Lasher? Mrs. Edwin Lasher?"

"Yes."

"Mrs. Lasher, my name is Ross Colyer. I was stationed in China with your daughter, Ruth."

"Yes."

"She told me I could always locate her through you. Did she mention me in her letters?"

"Y-yes."

"Did she tell you we—we were fond of each other?"

"Ruth told me a great deal about you, Mister Colyer. She said you planned to marry after the war."

"Good, I wasn't sure. I would like to talk to you, Mrs. Lasher. May I come visit you and Ruth's father?"

"I don't believe that would be advisable."

"I—I beg your pardon?" Ross stammered. "Ruth was a very brave woman. I was there when she died, trying to save others. I thought perhaps you would like to know more—"

"I had a long letter from her commanding officer," the woman interrupted. "He sent some kind of medal along with it. I threw them both away."

"Why, Mrs. Lasher? I'm afraid I don't understand."

"You say Ruth was a brave woman; she was also a very foolish one. She lost one husband to this war, a fine man. She told me about the doctor she was seeing there in China, another fine man. Then you came back into her life. She followed you to a dangerous place, then died there. I hate this war, Mister Colyer, and what it has done to my family. I hate everyone connected with it. Now, I don't care to discuss the matter further. Good day, Mister Colyer."

Ross stared at the mute transmitter until the operator came on the line. "Your three minutes are up, sir. Deposit seventy cents, please." He hung up without responding.

1 October 1945
Detroit

Big Mike Flaherty hooked his thumbs in the belt straining to contain his forty-four-inch beer gut and smiled happily around the stub of a cigar. Ross stood beside the balding, pink-scalped Irishman and grinned wryly at the newly completed sign across the street. VETERANS' BAR AND GRILL now covered MIKE'S IRISH BAR AND GRILL.

"Got to keep up with the times, boy-o. With a genuine war hero tending the bar, we'll draw every ex-GI in South Detroit. They'll be flocking to the auto assembly plants, you know. You can work up a good trade of regulars before your classes start over at Ann Arbor next January, then continue part-time as your classes let you. Forty-a-week and tips to start—then we'll work out something good for you on weekends. Sound okay?"

"Yeah, Mike. I really appreciate your taking me on. The GI Bill will take care of my expenses at the university, but it won't leave much. I don't have a car yet, for one thing."

"Well, we'll take care of that in short order; you're in the car capital of the world, boy-o. Now, c'mon inside and let Mike buy you the first beer served in The Vets' Bar."

Ross drew the line at framing his medals and displaying them behind the bar, but the shrewd Irishman was right about the clientele. Men, still with short haircuts and the unsettled look of those recently thrust back into civilian life, soon stood in line to be served by a fellow veteran.

Mike showed his new bartender how to wink and seemingly add an extra measure to his favored customers' drinks. Shortchanging was strictly taboo, but it wasn't necessary. Ross was a good listener; the conversation and the booze flowed—and Big Mike beamed.

On a crisp, sun-drenched Monday morning, Mike showed up grinning like a schoolboy with a new girlfriend. "Come out back, Ross, I got something to show you," he bubbled. Following the bouncy Irishman into the alley, Ross confronted a dark red 1941 Ford convertible. "Twenty thousand on the clock, actual," Mike boasted. "Prewar tires, and spent every night in the garage. I still got a few connections in the car business. It's a steal. I already paid for it. You can pay me back out of tips, the way business is. What d'ya think, boy-o?"

Ross felt a sudden chill course down his spine. He blinked and shook his head. He could almost see Ruth lounging behind the wheel, waving, with that shy smile on her face.

"I—I—well, damn, Mike, I'm overwhelmed. You didn't have to do this."

His boss slapped his shoulder. "I know I didn't, Ross. But I like you. You're a hard worker and know how to handle customers. Hell, don't put the idea of a partnership out of your head. Someday, who knows?"

Ross gulped. "Mike, I don't know how to tell you this, but I like you, so I gotta level with you. You see, for personal reasons I don't want to talk about, I couldn't bring myself to drive this car. If you're going to be out of pocket, well, I'll make it good. But, please understand, I have to say no."

Mike's face clouded. "If that's the way you feel about it, well, okay. Forget it. Don't worry about the money. Hell, I can make a clear five hundred on it this afternoon. I just wanted to do something nice for you."

Ross watched the rotund figure stomp back inside. He gave the car a long last look. Damnit, he thought, after all I went through to put Ruth out of my mind. He shook his head as if to clear it, then followed his angry boss inside.

A week later, during a hectic Saturday night, a familiar voice made Ross look up from mixing a tray of drinks. "Ross Colyer, my God, I don't believe it."

Ross recognized the impish face at once. "Weary Willy Wilkinson," he shouted. "You old bastard, someone told me you stayed over there in Libya and went into the second-hand goat business."

"Probably should have," the former B-24 pilot replied. "God, it's good to see you again. Last time I saw you, you had a pair of one-oh-nines on your ass, pieces of the city of Ploesti hanging onto your bomb-bay doors, and one engine on fire."

"Not to mention a crazy general on the flight deck," Ross added soberly. "Look, your drinks are on me. Stick around until closing, will you? We'll go out for breakfast and catch up."

* * *

The all-night diner was nearly empty when Ross added another cigaret butt to the already overflowing ashtray. "That's the whole nine yards, Willy. Bartender in a crummy joint—looking forward to being a has-been student with a bunch of kids who'll probably want to help me up the steps."

"What a rotten break." Wilkinson paused to sip his coffee. "The old fart going to be a senator forever?"

Ross barked a short laugh. "Not if he gets elected president. I'm serious. Colonel Wilson told me it's in the cards. Now, tell me more about this new Boeing—Stratocruiser, you're calling it?"

"Yeah." Wilkinson's face lit up. "The airlines are shopping like crazy for big airplanes. Douglas is using the old C-54 as a prototype for a DC-6. Bigger and faster, you know. Lockheed is stretching the Constellation they developed for TWA just before the war, but Boeing seems to me to have an edge. They had those four pressurized passenger versions of the B-17 they built for Howard Hughes before the war to work with. The mock-up I saw in Seattle is mind-boggling. Two decks—carries sixty to seventy passengers at twenty-five, even thirty thousand feet at more than three hundred miles an hour."

"And you're actually going to fly one?" Ross's voice was filled with envy.

"That's what they tell me. Pan American is already mapping overseas routes like crazy. I'm in their four-engine school and will be one of the first copilots based in Miami. Ross, the flying business is going to be the biggest thing in this country. Hell, just think of the lightplane business. Everybody is going to have one. But, the big item is going to be jet engines."

"How so? I heard that they've been playing around with the idea out at Edwards. They supposedly go like hell but can carry only enough fuel for short hops. The Germans had a few right at the end of the war—the Me 262, remember?"

"Yeah. A pair of them shot down six out of a thirty-six-plane group of B-17s in less than fifteen minutes," Wilkinson replied. "Even your precious Mustangs couldn't touch them. Anyway, when I was in Seattle, I ran across your old copilot, Rex Compton—the one who got shot in the leg on that fucked-up mission in England."

"Yeah, I remember him. He transferred to P-47s."

"Well, he stayed on active duty. He's at Edwards now—doing flight tests. A lot of the stuff is still classified, but what he told me is wild.

They have a new fighter, the Lockheed P-80. The thing would be in production now if the war hadn't ended. The sonofabitch will do better than four hundred at forty thousand feet—how much better, he couldn't tell me. It has an hour and a half of flight time and plans call for four hours."

Ross formed a skeptical grin but remained silent.

Wilkinson leaned forward, his eyes gleaming. "Ross, before you know it, they're going to hang that engine on commercial airliners. When they do, hold on—you'll be able to go anyplace in the United States nonstop—at five hundred miles an hour. You simply *have* to get back to flying—get in on the excitement."

Dawn was starting to streak the city's eastern skyline when Ross trudged up the back stairs of his boardinghouse. He scooped up a letter that had been shoved beneath his door and entered the shabby room, still smelling of the corned beef and cabbage that Mrs. Rafferty had served her boarders for supper. He tossed the envelope onto the rickety dresser without interest.

Not bothering to turn on the light, Ross sloshed a water glass half full of cheap bourbon and diluted it only slightly with warm tap water. He carried his drink onto a second-story porch gracing the aging Victorian house. Ignoring the fall morning's chill, he slumped into a creaking metal glider. Preoccupied with Wilkinson's words, he sipped raw whiskey and watched the sun emerge through a layer of haze and smoke.

Then he remembered the letter and reentered the room to get it. He read the return address and searched his memory for a matching face. Alex Taylor. Oh, yeah. His buddy-pilot in the instructors' school at Kelly. He ripped open the envelope, extracted a single sheet of notepaper, and scanned it quickly. He reread the page of scrawled handwriting, sat down, and read it again even more slowly.

Dear Ross,

Had a helluva time running you down. Finally called Justin Falls (I remembered you said it was your hometown) and talked with your Aunt Bea. Anyway, the reason I'm writing is I'm thinking of starting my own airline. I can't swing it by myself, even with a GI loan. So, I'm looking for a partner. I have a line on two war-surplus C-47s and a Norseman here in

Kansas City. I've looked at them, and they're low time and in perfect condition. I figure to operate passenger and cargo charters. The field is wide open here.

I don't know what you're doing, but I remember that you're probably the best pilot I ever flew with. I'd sure like to have you. If you're interested and can come up with about five grand, get in touch.

Sincerely,
Alex

Ross took a long pull from his drink and stared into the murky dawn. Early traffic began to disturb the Sunday morning silence. The bonds. Pop had left them for his college. He'd vowed to cash them only in an emergency. They were still in the safe-deposit box in Justin Falls.

He glanced at his watch. Damn; it would be an hour earlier in Kansas City. Oh, well. If I don't do it now, I may change my mind, he thought. He finished his drink in one swallow, grimaced, and went inside. Fishing a handful of quarters from his tips jar, he headed downstairs to the pay phone that Mrs. Rafferty had installed in the old house's entry hall.

The sound of a departing airliner penetrated the hallway. The throaty roar of its engines sent a shiver of anticipation through him. Four engines, his practiced ear told him—R-2800s—a big one. He grinned into the tiny room's dimly lit interior. "Kansas City, operator. Plaza four-three-eight-three-five."

Chapter Twenty-six

29 November 1945
Kansas City

Ross hunched deeper into his leather flight jacket—inadequate protection against the raw, late autumn night—and let his shoulders slump in resigned dejection. Rosy light cast by the raging fire etched deep lines in his somber features, making him look older than his twenty-eight years. He winced as the hangar's corrugated steel roof collapsed, enveloping the parked DC-3 transport in a shower of blazing debris. What a helluva way for the gallant plane to go, he thought. She survived two years flying combat as an army C-47, only to meet an ignominious end as a civilian aircraft.

Heat shattered the window of a small office tucked into one corner of the burning building; the neatly lettered sign reading ALLIED AIR, INC. disappeared in a hail of broken glass.

A bitter chuckle emerged from Ross's lips. He turned to the stocky, balding man beside him. "That pretty well sums things up, wouldn't you say, Alex? Allied Air just went down in flames."

Alex Taylor, his darkly tanned, square-jawed features matching Ross's doleful expression, spat. "It's a bitch, all right, but we've got insurance. It's not like it was a total loss. We still have the other DC-3 and the Norseman. We're still in business."

The arrival of a yellow slicker–clad fireman cut off Ross's response. The man removed a helmet that identified him as an assistant chief. Between shouted orders over the background of roaring pumper engines, he informed them, "She's a total loss, fellows. It'll be daylight 'fore we can get 'er cooled down and get in there, but I wouldn't count on salvaging anything."

"Any idea how it started?" Ross asked.

"Not for sure. The fire was out of control when we got here. Seemed to originate in the northwest corner, though, where the electrical service panel is. Looked like there were some drums of oil and such that blew and scattered fire all over."

"Where was the fucking watchman?" Alex raged. "What the hell do we pay him for?"

"He's the one who turned in the alarm," the fireman replied. He hesitated. "He maybe was calling from that all-night diner across the street."

"I'll just bet he was," Alex snapped. "Lazy sonofabitch was over there where it was cozy warm drinking coffee while our business turns into toast. Wait until I get my hands on him."

"Well," the fireman responded phlegmatically, "if he'd have been inside when she blew, there wouldn't have been anything left for you to get your hands on. Now, I gotta get back over. There'll be an inspector 'round first thing in the morning. We don't think there was anyone trapped in there, but we'll have to sift through everything, determine the origin, and such. I'm sure sorry for you. Guess you had good insurance, though."

"Yeah," Ross answered. "The outfit we lease from carries liability insurance for anything that's in the hangar for maintenance. Well, thanks for trying. Tell all your men that we appreciate their efforts." He turned to Alex. "Well, partner, what say we go across to that diner, have some coffee ourselves, and figure out what to do next."

Ross sank into a booth and regarded Alex with a wry grin. "A bad day at Black Rock, huh? I could sure use a stiff drink just now, but I guess we'll have to settle for caffeine. Any ideas about where to start?"

The still grim-faced Alex waited until the waitress took their orders. "You mean after I shoot that night watchman? Well, I guess the first order of business is to figure a way to deliver that four thousand pounds of priority repair parts to Dallas for Ralston Mills. Pete and Andy won't be back with Six-ninety-three in time to make our deadline."

"Yeah." Ross added sugar to his just-arrived coffee. "That contract has a penalty clause, too. Damn! Of all times for me to go farting off to Washington. It was going to be close for me to make the run to Dallas and get back in time to catch that TWA flight. If we can't find something to lease on short notice by tomorrow—hell, this morning—we'll have to ship it by commercial air."

Alex whistled softly. "That'll mean a loss for the entire contract. Can't you get out of that trip? I mean, this is an emergency."

"I doubt it. I talked with Colonel Wilson when the army sent me the orders. He was my primary CO, and he's a close friend. The colonel is assigned to personnel at army headquarters and knows about the hearing. The army can legally order me from inactive reserve to temporary active duty to testify—and they did."

"I still don't know why they're bringing up that Ploesti raid after all this time," Alex grumbled. "From what you've told me, it was no more screwed up than a dozen or so other missions."

"It's that asshole Senator Templeton. He's the one who blocked my application for a commission in the regular army. If he hadn't, I'd still be flying army airplanes."

Alex lit a cigaret and squinted at Ross through the smoke. "You didn't tell me *that*."

"Yeah, well, it's history," Ross said wearily. "Now, back to our problem. Assuming we can't lease an airplane, why don't you go to the bank and ask for an extension to our loan. This business of relocating, replacing that airplane, and meeting overhead is going to get expensive. Getting an insurance settlement and collecting from Ralston will take God knows how long. In the meantime I'll work on a way to ship those parts and start talking to the insurance people."

Alex stirred his coffee, a dark scowl on his face. "If it's all the same to you, I'd rather *you* went to the bank," he muttered.

Ross shrugged. "No problem. You have something against banks?"

"Not banks, as such. It's just I don't like doing business with that fat slob Katzenbaum."

"Oh, shit, Alex." Ross snorted and his voice took on an irritated edge. "The guy has bent over backward to help us. Oh, well, it doesn't matter to me. I'll see you later. I'm going home and try to get back to sleep. We have a busy day ahead." He tossed some coins onto the table, and the dispirited pair trudged toward the door.

6 December 1945
Washington, D.C.

Ross regarded swirling snowflakes, the size of white cornflakes, with a grimace of disgust. He supposed some folks might ooh and ahh, and spout drivel about how beautiful they were. Watching them dance in the glow of streetlights, turned on early this gloomy winter evening, prompted a glum, "We'll never in hell catch a cab in this mess."

Janet tied a scarf over her mahogany-hued hair, then tucked a gloved hand beneath Ross's elbow. "Rush-hour traffic during a snowstorm," she murmured. "It doesn't look as if we'd go anyplace if we found one. That string of cars isn't moving."

The pair stood beneath the theater's protective marquee as Ross pondered their next move. He noticed a fur-coated matron, scurrying along with loot from an afternoon of Christmas shopping, give them an envious glance in passing. "What a handsome couple," he heard her mutter to the sour-faced man trudging at her side.

Ross glanced at Janet, slender and fashionably attired, and agreed that any man would be proud to have her on his arm. The woman must be thinking that he and Janet had spent a romantic afternoon at a matinee—*Road to Morocco,* the billboard proclaimed. Perhaps she was recalling a time when . . . before . . . Oh, well. He grinned as the woman passed from the little, brightly lighted, snow-free island back into the gathering dusk.

"Well," Ross finally announced with a rueful grin, "I guess the question I posed at lunch, 'My place or yours?' becomes sort of academic."

Janet arched her eyebrows. "Mother *insisted* that I ask you to have dinner with us."

"Great. Would you have me invoke my supernatural powers and produce a miniature sleigh and eight tiny reindeer?" Ross quipped. "Look, I'm staying at the Willard. It's only six or eight blocks from here. We can walk it in no time. We'll have a drink, dinner, then finish bringing each other up to date."

Janet's expression changed to one of indignant astonishment. "Good God," she blurted. "Don't tell me you're still obsessed with walking. Why you didn't join the infantry, I'll never know. The answer is no, Ross Colyer. Look at these heels; look at that snow. The *only* walking I will consider is back inside to sit through the next performance.

And Santa will leave you a bundle of switches and a lump of coal for making fun of me."

Ross's laughter caused heads to turn. "Okay, pantywaist, here's plan B. There's a friendly-looking bar across the street. If you can make it that far, we'll have that drink, wait for the traffic to clear up, go to the Willard—where I have a table reserved—and resume our reminiscing. Okay?"

"You seem to have me in your power, you fiend," Janet said dryly. "Lead the way."

The pair emerged from the storm into a crowded, overheated barroom, redolent with the smell of wet wool, spilled beer, and cigaret smoke. A lumpy, gum-chewing waitress greeted them as they shook snow from their coats. "Hi. If you don't mind a table by the kitchen, a couple back there is just leaving."

"Deal," Ross answered promptly. "Any port in a storm, you know." He and Janet trailed in the waitress's wake as she elbowed her way through the press of chattering patrons. He ordered martinis, then asked Janet, "Well, did you enjoy the rerun?"

Janet considered the question. "Somehow, it didn't seem as funny as it did four years ago," she replied.

Ross sobered. "Yeah, that could apply to a lot of things. Four years of war will do that. The Morocco I know doesn't much resemble the one that Hope chased Dotty through. So much for a nostalgic trip into the past."

"Yes, a lot has changed since those days at Hickam before the war," Janet observed as their drinks arrived. She took hers and raised her glass. "Well, hail to the conquering hero—Ross Colyer, Major, United States Air Corps, holder of the Distinguished Service Cross, Silver Star, Distinguished Flying Cross with cluster, Purple Heart, and other assorted decorations."

"I'm hardly that," Ross replied, frowning. "Make it a has-been Air Corps pilot, add 'Inactive Reserve' to that major bit, and end up with 'screwed by a corrupt politician,' and I'll drink to it."

The twinkle in Janet's gray-green eyes faded. Her voice soft, she asked, "Are you terribly bitter?"

"Well—yeah, damnit. I was a good pilot—a good officer. I did my job, and did it well. To have my application for a regular commission turned down because of that miserable excuse for a senator . . . Yeah, Janet, I'm bitter. I never liked his son. I didn't like him at Hickam even before he married you, but I sure as hell wasn't responsible for him getting himself killed." Ross drained his martini glass and signaled for another.

Janet made little rings of moisture with her glass, seemingly talking to it instead of Ross. "BT left his mark on both of us, didn't he?" she asked, then added abruptly, "Why didn't you see me when you were here in '43 Ross? Why didn't you answer my letter? You see, I don't know exactly what went on over there—in Turkey."

Ross chewed his lower lip as he framed his reply. "I should have, I know. I apologize. But I knew you wanted answers about BT's death, and I didn't have any—at least not ones I could have given you then. The whole incident was still classified, remember?"

"And now?"

"Are you sure you want to know? BT was awarded a Distinguished Flying Cross for his part in the Ploesti raid. It was a bad time for everyone; we all did things we aren't proud of. Why not leave it at that?"

"I already know most of it. Doris Wilson told me," Janet said absently.

"*Doris Wilson?*" said Ross, astonished by the mention of the name. "I can't believe Colonel Ted would blab classified military information—even to his wife."

Janet smiled. "He didn't. Doris is quite a gal. She gets her news through the officers' wives club. It's high grade. She also gave me some of the best advice I've ever had. I love her."

"What kind of advice?"

Janet arched her eyebrows. "Now that, Major Colyer, is information with a higher classification than you have clearance to hear."

Ross chuckled. "I can believe it. She keeps the colonel in a state of chronic, confused astonishment. I owe a lot to both of them. He saved me from another assignment under General Sprague."

"That bastard," Janet spat.

"Oh, he was that," Ross agreed.

"*Was?*"

"Yeah. I ran into him again in China—still manipulating, still hot after that second star. He got in over his head, though. When it came to political intrigue, that crew in the CBI could give lessons to even Senator Templeton. But, you know, I have to admire the ornery old cuss. Sprague was a schemer—egotistical, arrogant, ruthless, but, by God, he was always in the lead airplane. A coward he wasn't. It got him killed."

"General Sprague? Killed? I didn't know."

"They didn't publicize general officers getting killed. He led a raid on the airfields on Formosa. His ship had an engine fire coming home. The explosion took off about half the right wing. He ordered the rest of the crew, including his copilot, to bail out. He refused. He's supposed to have told the copilot that he was damned if he was going to give up. He tried to set 'er down in a dry riverbed. . . ."

"And he didn't make it," Janet finished.

"Nope. I'm sort of surprised, actually. He was a good pilot; he must have known his chances were something like zero to none." Ross glanced at his watch. "Hey, I reserved a table for seven o'clock. We'd best call a cab, and get under way, if I'm going to feed you tonight."

"If the traffic is cleared out, we can still have dinner at Mother's," Janet murmured.

Ross gave her a level look. "This is my last night in town. I love your parents dearly, but somehow I can't get excited about dinner with your mother."

Janet returned his gaze with a brief glance. "I'll phone her while you get a cab."

Janet studied the dessert list while Ross ordered after-dinner drinks. She told the waiter she wanted cheesecake, then turned to Ross. "I still can't get used to unrationed steak and rich desserts. Excuse me if I make a pig of myself."

"I know what you mean," Ross agreed. "Now, about this new job you mentioned."

Janet's eyes sparkled. "I'm simply thrilled with the opportunity. It's with the *Chicago Tribune*—on the overseas desk. Your old reporter friend, Clayton Henderson, finagled it for me. I could have stayed at INS in San Francisco, but with the war over, most of their overseas posts are being closed. I was in a dead-end office job. I'll stay here with my parents until after Christmas and report to Chicago on January second.

"Actually, I couldn't wait to tell you, in private, about the project I was working on with Boeing—just before I went to INS. It's a four-engine jet bomber, Ross. Unbelievable. It was—still is, I suppose—highly classified, but I thought you'd like to apply for an assignment to fly it. That was before I found out that you'd been released from active duty. Now, I want to hear more about your airline."

"You're right, I'd give my right arm to fly one. I met a guy I flew with in Africa who told me a bit about the new jet-powered planes. But"—he shrugged—"I guess I can forget that idea.

"About my 'airline'; that's a somewhat grandiose label. Our fleet of two surplus DC-3s and a beat-up Norseman was reduced by one last week. The hangar burned up with one of the '3s inside."

"Oh, how awful!" Janet exclaimed. "What will you do?"

"It's a setback, of course," Ross replied. "It's not catastrophic—the plane was insured—but insurance won't cover all the expenses, loss of business, and such. My partner, a guy I met at Kelly during an instructor's school, is getting things moving again while I'm here.

"It'll be a tight year. But we're getting some good contracts, and best of all, I'm flying again. It's not as exciting as combat, but it beats what I was doing: tending bar and trying to finish my degree. Like I told you at lunch, I'll make more money from my travel voucher coming here at army expense to testify at the hearing than any hourly wage we average. Are you going back to the hearing?"

Janet shook her head. "No, I don't know why my father-in-law insisted on one. His son is dead; Ploesti is a closed issue. General Woods is just going through the motions. I wonder, though, why they didn't call you to testify after bringing you all the way from Kansas City."

"I really don't know," said Ross. "The recorder read my deposition and said he couldn't see that I had anything new to offer."

Ross made a pretense of scowling at the hushed, ornately paneled dining room, half filled with discreetly reserved patrons. "Anyway," he added with a smile, "all this noise and loud, boisterous talk is getting on my nerves. I propose we retire to my room, open a bottle of Old Grand-dad I have stashed there, and enjoy some peace and quiet."

Janet concentrated on scooping up the last of her cheesecake with her fork. Without looking up, she said, "We both knew it was coming down to this, I guess."

"I believe we did," Ross said softly. "You can still say no."

Janet sighed. Her gaze, when she looked up, was as shy as a teenager's on her first date. "God knows I've fantasized this moment often enough," she answered simply. "Shall we go?"

Janet paced around the elegantly appointed room, examining its antebellum furnishings, while Ross mixed drinks. "I've heard that presidents slept in this hotel," she observed idly. "I wonder if any of them used this room?"

Ross chuckled as he crossed to where Janet stood by a brocade-draped window and handed her a moisture-beaded glass. "Are you afraid, perhaps, that the ghost of President Harding is watching over your shoulder?" he teased.

Janet touched her glass softly against Ross's, looked deep into his eyes, and murmured, "Not if he keeps his clammy hands to himself."